THE
STAKES

THE
STAKES
BEN
SANDERS

MINOTAUR BOOKS
À THOMAS DUNNE BOOK
NEW YORK

A THOMAS DUNNE BOOK FOR MINOTAUR BOOKS.
An imprint of St. Martin's Publishing Group.

THE STAKES. Copyright © 2018 by Ben Sanders. All rights reserved. Printed in the United States of America. For information, address St. Martin's Press, 175 Fifth Avenue, New York, N.Y. 10010.

www.thomasdunnebooks.com
www.stmartins.com

Designed by Omar Chapa

The Library of Congress Cataloging-in-Publication Data is available upon request.

ISBN 978-1-250-14011-1 (hardcover)
ISBN 978-1-250-14012-8 (ebook)

Our books may be purchased in bulk for promotional, educational, or business use. Please contact your local bookseller or the Macmillan Corporate and Premium Sales Department at 1-800-221-7945, extension 5442, or by email at MacmillanSpecialMarkets@macmillan.com.

First Edition: March 2018

10 9 8 7 6 5 4 3 2 1

For Dan Myers

THE
STAKES

PROLOGUE

LOS ANGELES, CA

Nina Stone

They were quite the pair, the fat man and the killer Bobby Deen. Nina said to him when they put her in the car, "How're you spelling Deen—like the movie star, or the porn star?" Like she was trying to connect, steer them down a road where she wouldn't end up dead. But the man just gave her a look and said, "Double 'e.'"

He only had a few expressions in his repertoire, but she figured that was the idea: the one look did a lot of work. He'd give you the line and those eyes, and you'd know it wasn't going any further. He was dressed sharp as always, wearing his tan hat that wasn't quite a Stetson—too flat and narrow—the brim low across his eyes but never quite hiding them. He had on a black suit today, and even seventy-degree L.A. couldn't draw a sweat. The fat man was dripping for two though, funking up the Chrysler as they turned off Washington Boulevard into Marina del Rey, a thicket of masts on their right, apartment buildings farther off, on the other side of the water. She and Bobby were in back, the fat man alone up front and driving with one hand, tapping a beat on the wheel with a finger that had three gold rings and an extra knuckle. He leaned across the passenger seat to see something across the marina, clucked his tongue as he pointed.

"Yeah, Bobby, that's the place." He came upright again, lifted his head to find Bobby Deen's eyes in the mirror.

Bobby said, "Oh yeah." Courteous, but not making it a question.

The fat man said, "We took a guy in that place on the end, top floor, had a mess by the end of it, get halfway through the cleaning and the plumbing backs up—I mean like, the shower's full of goo, and it just *would not* go down." He laughed—lots of fluid, a pack-a-day acoustic. "And of course there's like a Realtor or buyers or whatever coming the next day, so there we are out at three A.M. trying to buy a sucker thing. A plunger."

Bobby Deen said, "Mmm." Not getting anything out of it. He was Hispanic, but he wasn't the gangbanger type of thug. He had tattoos showing at his collar and at his wrist when he checked the time, but they were too well done to be prison ink. He looked like a well-turned-out cartel guy, if there was such a thing.

The fat man watched him in the mirror a moment longer, maybe wanting a smile or a new expression out of Bobby Deen, but he gave it up and just grinned at the road, shrugging as he said, "You gotta be there, I guess. I don't know. It was something. Place wouldn't sell, either. We still got it."

Nina said, "So why don't you keep me there, instead of dumping me at sea?"

The fat man said, "Yeah, that's a good idea. You promise not to stand on the balcony and shout for help?"

Bobby Deen smiled at that one. The fat man saw it in the mirror and seemed to take it as high acclaim: cracked up with a fake laugh, like trying to cash in on his comedy gold. He faded off into wry chuckles and said, "I'll just lock you in the kitchen, call ahead so you've got time to bake me something."

Nina said, "I'd probably just start you on salads."

The boat had easy access. The road was on the edge of the marina, and there were little gated jetties off the sidewalk where the yachts were moored. No one out here today though, on a Wednesday afternoon. The fat man counted gate numbers, saying them on his breath as they crawled along, and he stopped them at the curb just before the road went off to the left, away from the marina. He leaned across to open the glove compartment, wheezing as he stretched, the wind coming out of him like sitting on a broken air mattress.

Nina looked at Bobby again, and somehow he had his switch-blade out. He held it underhand with his elbow cocked, and when the blade sprang the point appeared just below her eye.

He said, "Hands."

She said, "You could cut me up in the apartment. I wouldn't be too hard on the pipes."

The fat man was tuned out, reading off a sheet of printed instruc-tions: "If your access system is the Trident Three-Fifty Prestige—yeah, yeah, yeah—here we are, *hold the Trident access card* to the reader window and wait until the permission light is green. I fucking did that last time, I don't know why they just tell you the exact same thing."

Bobby Deen wasn't listening, still looking at Nina from under the edge of his hat. He said, "There's no mess this way. Hands."

She held up her hands and without glancing down he slipped the blade between her pressed wrists, jerked slightly, and sliced the plas-tic cuffs like they were twine. Bobby kept his eyes on her as he picked up the scrap of plastic and slipped it in his coat.

He said, "Once the gate's open, you're going to get out and walk down the ramp to the boat."

He'd nailed the art of talking quietly enough, you could hear the threat between the lines. What would happen if you didn't do as he said.

The fat man was out of the car now, all two hundred seventy pounds of him rounding the hood, and as Bobby Deen got out and joined him on the sidewalk, she saw that funny contrast again: Bobby all squared away, and the fat man looking like he'd just run a brisk mile—breathing hard, aviators askew, wet hair sticking up where he'd palmed it back. His shirt was open three buttons, and the cross on the gold chain he wore was hidden in a thatch of chest hair.

Nina's door was locked on the inside, and Bobby came around and let her out. The masts were pinging from the ropes moving in the breeze, and there was a salty odor coming off the water—a nice cleanser after the stale heat of the car.

The fat man was waving the card at the reader, not having any luck. He was giving the thing a piece of his mind, too, swearing at it with language that'd make his gums bleed if he kept it up.

Bobby shut the car door with a careful knuckle and said, "Hold it still, might be better." Looking at Nina as he said it, and not seeming impatient. Happy to stand here on the sidewalk in the sun.

"Yeah, I tried it every goddamned way. Ah, here we go." Something beeped, and the gate clanged as the lock disengaged, and the fat man shoved through.

Bobby said, "You didn't lock the car."

"Oh shit. Yeah." The fat man turned midway on the ramp and locked the Chrysler with the remote, grinned at Nina now approaching.

She stopped in front of him, shaded her eyes as she looked across the water. "Where's this apartment, exactly?"

The fat man said, "It's on Shut Your Mouth Avenue." Looking past her to Bobby as he said it, and the lack of fake laughs told her Bobby hadn't smiled this time.

She waited a moment, forming the line, and then said, "If I'm going to be sleeping with the fishes, it'd be nice to sleep with one of you two first."

Bobby would be her preference, if it came to it, but she wanted the fat man to think it was an equal-opportunity offer.

It went quiet.

This was the first time she'd suggested something and the fat man hadn't laughed it off. He turned and glanced at the apartments across the water and then looked back at her, still not saying anything and still not moving on the ramp. She knew he was taking this idea seriously, or he would have said something by now. Bobby must have reached the same conclusion, because when the fat man finally opened his mouth, Bobby got in first:

"Lenny. Get on the boat."

"Bobby, chill." The fat man raised his shoulders, spread his arms. "It's my job."

"And the job's a boat ride, so that's what we're doing."

The fat man didn't answer, just gave a half-smile and vented disbelief in a whisper as he looked across the water. Then he shrugged like he could take it or leave it, and started down the ramp again.

Bobby said, "You too."

His voice right in her ear. She turned and looked at him, his expression neutral, eyes on the boat and the task at hand.

Nina said, "And what's your price?" She looked him up and down. "Maybe a Brooks Brothers voucher?"

He gave a long blink, but that was the only sign that maybe his patience was running out. He said, "Get on the boat."

Ten minutes later they were heading west on calm water, their wake in a long, wide swath behind them and L.A. disappearing in the east like it was being lowered on a slow platform. The fat man was at the helm, shirt off and a life vest buckled on over his folds, glasses dewy with bow spray. The sea was flat enough the nose was holding even, just a gentle rise and fall as they clapped along through a light ripple. They had Nina in the little cabin up front, hands and wrists bound with plastic ties, but she could see through the open door to the stern: Bobby Deen with a finger to his hat and dressed up like Death's right-hand man, paying his respects to the fading city. She wondered what people would think if they saw them heading out, this thirty-foot launch with a 5XL thug at the wheel and Bobby Deen standing at the back like a figurehead stuck on at the wrong end.

After twenty minutes Bobby turned and shouted, "How far we going?"

The fat man eased back the throttle, and Nina felt the nose level out as they lost speed, the motor dropping from roar to deep burble.

The fat man said, "Far as we like. Want her dead, anything'll do. Want her gone for good"—he shrugged—"normally go out past Catalina, even then we've had stuff wash up. She'd be news though, dead lady in Dolce Armana or whatever. Unless she's shark food—that'd be funny." He tugged a strap on his vest, getting it even tighter. "Depends on the current too, might take her all the way to Mexico, show up at Tijuana." He smiled, pulled his chin back as he made his voice high and strained: "And den señor, you don' know what happen, unteel Mehico police, dey call da fam'lee. Tell da mozzer all bout it, eh?"

He cracked himself up saying that, and Bobby Deen smiled again too, fixing a cuff button as he looked across the water, not seeming bothered by the cradling of the deck.

The fat man pointed at him and clicked his fingers. "Hey, yeah, see: that's twice now. You got a sense of humor."

Bobby Deen regarded him pleasantly, hands at his sides. "Who says I don't?"

The fat man shrugged. "I don't know. Someone was saying you're like special relativity, you heard that one?"

Bobby shook his head.

The fat man said, "You know how like, speed of light's always the same, doesn't matter where you see it from?"

Bobby said, "So I'm told."

The fat man grinned, coming to the punch line, folded his arms on his life vest as he said, "Same with you, any way you look at Bobby Deen, he's always looking back from under his hat." He clapped his hands and rocked his weight from foot to foot, and the whole boat joined in.

Bobby said, "I'll remember that one," and looked out over the water again, two shades of blue all around, the sky and ocean and the three of them in the center of it. He said, "Let's put some blood in the water."

"Nah, we'll take it out a little farther."

Nina said, "Don't you want to rape me first?"

The fat man glanced at her and nudged his shades, a look on his face like the candy shop had talked at him through the glass. He glanced over at Bobby Deen as if waiting for permission.

Bobby said, "Close the door. I don't care."

The fat man leaned on the gunwale and then came upright again as the whole vessel yawed. He ran both hands through his hair and blew his breath out, getting flushed with just the thought of it. He said,

"Yeah . . . but why'd she say it? She wants me in close so she can have the gun."

"Or stab you with the keys."

"They're in the locker."

"All right. So give me the gun."

The fat man said, "You want a turn too?"

Bobby Deen shook his head. "No, I do not. And whatever you're doing, do it fast."

The fat man sucked air through his teeth, looked at the sky. "Yeah. Be good to get out of the sun, anyway. I didn't put lotion on."

He grinned and arched back to reach the revolver in his belt, and then passed it to Bobby. It was a little snub-nosed revolver, which Nina knew was a Smith & Wesson 500. The fat man started loosening the straps on his life vest and Bobby checked the load, opening the cylinder to see five .50-caliber rounds looking back.

The fat man was getting breathless, the rush kicking in too soon. He licked his lips and said, "You can do it with concrete too—make a big lump, forty, fifty pounds, cast a handcuff in, best anchor you ever seen." Trying to seem offhand, bring his heart rate down so he'd be slower coming to the boil.

Bobby didn't answer. He was out at the stern again, on the little swim platform that hid the propellers, the gun in his right hand hanging at his leg. He said, "Think you were right about the sharks. We should move farther out."

"You got a fin or something?"

"I don't know. Something just crested briefly. There you go."

Bobby pointed with his free hand at something off at their eight o'clock, tracked it around the back of them, to seven, six—

The fat man came out onto the stern too, the boat sitting low and wallowing as he went out to the starboard corner, two hands in a visor at his brow and water lapping at his ankles. "How far out?"

"Hundred yards or so, he's going pretty wide. Look, you can see him coming around."

He kept his hand up, the finger sweeping through five, four, the fat man following but not seeing it yet, and at the three-o'clock mark Bobby Deen brought the pistol up and put a .50 Magnum through the back of the guy's head.

The body made a slow, forward topple and landed with a hard splash, the foam going pink while the sound of the shot was still rolling out across the water.

Bobby stood there watching the body submerge, a finger to his hat brim and the smoking gun back at his side. He said, "What part of 'Keep quiet and I'll handle it' did you not understand?"

Nina said, "I didn't know if you were going to save me or help throw me over the side."

"I would've just shot you and stayed on dry land."

"Yeah, thanks. If we went to the apartment, you could've made him look like suicide. Now we have to hope the sharks eat his head."

Bobby didn't answer.

Nina said, "You mind if I drive?"

ONE

Miles Keller

He didn't like working close to home. There was a chance of being recognized. Even in a town of eight million people, overlaps happen in ways you never guess. That'd liven things up: roll in on a job, and someone knows your voice, remembers *exactly* where they met you. He made exceptions, though, when payoffs warranted, and tonight would be worth it: visit a lawyer, and pick up two hundred grand for the effort.

But big money often meant big risk, so with the take being six figures, he'd felt backup was justified. His man tonight was Walter Stokes, thirty-six years old, already on his first strike after doing time upstate for robbery. Miles thought that was ballsy, signing on for a felony given his record, but then again, this being an aggravated offense, a clean slate wouldn't be much help if he got caught. Balls notwithstanding, Stokes hadn't been his first choice: the backup referrals came through Wynn Stanton—Miles's talent agent, as he called himself—and Wynn had recommended a Special Forces guy who'd done good work on two prior jobs. So that had been that, until the Special Forces man got redeployed on some government-sanctioned abduction job, and Miles had to go with Stokes as a consolation prize. He took it as a sign: if it was okay to rendition terror suspects, it was okay to rob bent lawyers.

Which was how he and Stokes came to be parked on a street up in Kings Point, New York, at ten P.M. on a Saturday in October. It was an affluent-looking street, tidy New England clapboard fronted by thick lawn, trees lining the verge. The lawyer's place was two hundred yards away, on the other side of a T-intersection. His name was Lane Covey. He was the go-between on an assassination designed to look like B-and-E gone wrong. The hit fee was a very sweet two hundred cold, and it was coming tonight. Miles's plan: wait for the delivery, and then go in and take the cash.

All Stokes had to do was carry a gun, but the man seemed determined to prove he was someone to worry about. He'd been fidgety when Miles picked him up in the stolen Subaru, eyes wide like he'd just heard good news, and you had to wonder how many lines he'd sniffed to blow the rust out. Now here he was, thirty minutes from go time, and he wanted to smoke some grass, too.

Miles let him roll the joint and stick it in his mouth before he said, "Not on my job, you're not."

Stokes glanced across at him. He was one of those pitch-black black guys, a streetlight up ahead putting a rind of glow on the edge of his shaved skull. He said, "Helps me come down easier." He traced a shallow slope with his hand, like graphing the tail end of his high.

Miles hooked his gloved thumbs in the bottom of the steering wheel. He said, "You don't go up, you don't need to come down, so if you'd stayed clean, you'd be fine."

Stokes held the joint in two fingers, the tip tracing little circles, like he was coming up with something nuanced. He said, "Yeah. But this is like one of those what-do-you-call-it. Sunk costs." He leaned in a fraction, like it would help the argument: "Like, I can't *unsniff* the coke, so I gotta intervene."

Miles thought about that, watching the lawyer's place. It was two-story, rectangular in plan, a garage on the left and a portico midway down. He'd used the county's architectural drawings to memorize the internal layout. Right now, there was a black Range Rover Sport parked out front, which he knew was the property of a Mr. Edward Rhys, an associate at a security firm called Hayman Coates. As far as Miles could tell, there were only three of them in the house: Covey, Rhys, and Covey's wife, Marilyn. Marilyn had actually proved herself quite useful. The Division of Corporations listed her as a director at an accounting firm based in Queens. Miles had visited last week, broken into her car, and used an RF detector to tell him the frequency of her garage-door opener. One of Wynn's guys had programmed another unit to the required signal, and now, in theory, Miles had keyless entry to the house.

He said, "Walter?"

"Mm-hm?"

"My experience, the answer to the problem is never 'more drugs.'"

Stokes didn't answer.

Miles said, "Great way to get noticed, too, lighting a match in a dark car."

Stokes said, "They gonna see my teeth anyway," and grinned to prove it, a faint gleam in the dark. But he put the joint away in his little joint pouch, whatever it was, and said, "Funny, you're not really what I pictured."

Miles didn't answer, waited to hear what he was supposed to look like.

Stokes said, "Wynn told me you're Mr. Meticulous, so I thought you'd be like, three back and sides and a clenched jaw."

Miles said, "I got a clenched jaw, you just can't see it with the beard."

Stokes liked that. He laughed and said, "Yeah. You're all right, man."

Miles said, "That's good."

They'd been quiet the first twenty minutes, but now Stokes was warming up. He said, "You do this much?"

Miles said, "Every now and then."

Stokes said, "I figured you must be like a pro or something, Wynn kind of said all the intel came through you, which was different. I mean, he normally coordinates, so sorta made me wonder what your background is . . ."

Miles said, "I'm a pro, but I'm not a regular, put it that way."

Stokes turned his lip out and nodded. "That's cool." He smiled again. "Maybe the next guy wants to inhale a bit of the Mary Jane, you could let him know it's off limits before he rolls the whole thing, know'm saying?"

Miles said, "Yeah. But my way was more memorable, right? Next time you want to light up on a job, you might have second thoughts."

Stokes laughed again. "You lucky I'm not having second thoughts now." He went quiet a moment and then said, "You know what I did before this?"

Miles did, but he shook his head anyway.

Stokes said, "I was with the cops, up in New Paltz? We used to go along to B-and-Es, not that often we actually solved one, you know? Hardly ever. So after a while, I just thought, Fuck it, I'm on the wrong side of the line."

"You're on the right side of it tonight."

"Yeah? How's that?"

Miles didn't answer.

Stokes said, "I had this long-term goal when I was PD, I was gonna be Secret Service one day, guard the White House? Went down to D.C. this one time, see them in action, and get this: they make them go round on bicycles. Like, ballistics gear and assault rifles and shit, and they're on a bike with pedals."

"So you canned that idea."

"Yeah, well, like. It'd piss you off, join the Secret Service thinking you're gonna be the king of cool, and then they make you ride a fucking bicycle."

Miles didn't answer. He could see headlights on the cross street, coming up to Covey's place.

Stokes said, "Mm, Audi. I had a spare hundred grand, I'd have me a bit of that. This isn't actually the real rich area, you know? Gotta head about ten minutes that way"—he hiked a thumb—"gets *real* nice. Like, offshore trusts, butlers called Jenkins and shit."

The car was a sedan, maybe an A8 model, Miles thought. It turned in to the lawyer's driveway and idled for a moment, headlights bright as a UFO landing. Then the door rose and the car eased inside, into the vacant space beside Covey's black Lexus.

Stokes said, "Where's Mrs. Lawyer's car?"

"Must've moved it."

Stokes said, "What you listening to?"

Miles had a speaker bud in one ear, wired through his collar to the iPod in his pocket. He said, "Audiobook. *The Luminaries*. Eleanor Catton."

"You keep it playing while you're on the job?"

Miles said, "Depends on the job."

"Dude I know, he's a PI? Does that on stakeouts, listens to audiobooks on YouTube. Reckons he's got through all of David Foster Wallace, just sitting in his car, waiting for shit to happen."

The house's ground-floor lights were on, but the blinds were down. Miles checked his pockets. He had the iPod, his hacked garage-door opener, and a slim fold of cash clipped to his hotel keycard. The Sig was on his belt, and he had a backup clip and lockpicks in his coat. He reached behind him to the backseat and felt around for his ski mask and tugged it on.

Stokes said, "That's not bad, what is that?"

"Merino wool."

"Yeah, I like it. Looks real light."

Miles tugged the speaker from his ear and let it dangle at his collar, reached in his pocket to pause the iPod. The garage door was coming up now, a red tinge inside from the Audi's brake lights. The drop was done, and now they were getting out of there.

Stokes said, "They don't mess around, do they?"

Miles said, "You got a gun?"

Stokes patted his right hip. "Colt .45. America's finest."

"You know how to drive a car?"

Stokes scoffed. "Yeah, that's the one thing I just never got around to learning."

Miles looked at him, waiting.

Stokes said, "Yeah, Christ, I know how to drive a car."

"Good. When you see me come out of the house, come on over and pick me up."

"What, you going in solo?"

"I am now."

"Yeah? Why's that? 'Cause you found out I'm black?"

Miles said, "No, 'cause I found out you're high. You're lucky I trust you enough to take the wheel."

"Yeah, whatever, I don't give a shit." He nodded at the house "What about the Range Rover guy?"

"I'll be okay."

"You give it thirty minutes, he might be gone."

"Yeah, or I give it thirty minutes, and someone else'll show up for their cut."

The cabin light was off, so there was no giveaway glow as he opened his door. It was a cold evening, and it smelled like squared-away suburbia: cut grass, and a hint of fresh paint from somewhere. The only traffic noise was from the disappearing Audi, a smooth V-8 howl fading off into the night. He drew the Sig from its holster and walked up the street in the middle of the lane with the pistol in one hand and his garage-door opener in the other.

There was a light on upstairs at Covey's now, and Miles figured that was where the money was headed—probably to a safe in the walk-in closet in the master bedroom. He reached the curb and pressed the button on his pirated remote, and the motor kicked in with its dull hum. He walked down past the garage and made a right, headed along the rear of the house. There was a swimming pool lit arctic blue by underwater lights, and a patio area with an outdoor grill.

A pair of French doors accessed the kitchen. Miles liked the décor: blond timber floors, and polished concrete countertops. By the sink were two used plates and some cutlery, and a baking dish crusted with what might've been lasagna. He held the pistol under his arm and took the torsion wrench and the half-diamond pick from their loops in his inner coat pocket.

The French doors had a Schlage deadbolt, too high-end to be rake-picked. He had to set each pin in turn. He worked back to front, the plastic earbuds at his collar swinging and tapping with each small motion.

Time obeys a different scale for break-ins, so slow it's like each second is drawn out through the barrel of the lock. He had that impression every time. You have to open the door to regain normal speed.

It took him ninety seconds.

The last pin finally sat up on the shear line, and the barrel made its solid click and turn. He nudged the door back quietly and saw the night reflections pan across the glass. He put away his tools and held the gun in both hands. He could smell the lasagna now, and hear a television off to his left, in the main living room.

He closed the door behind him and turned right through the kitchen, headed along the corridor toward the garage. No photographs on the walls, but there was artwork that seemed to have a Catskill theme: moody oil paintings of pine-covered hills, a tableau of two kids kneeling by a forest stream. He could hear the garage-door motor again, a quiet, meditative hum, and then a faint boom preceding the quiet.

He made a left just before the garage, and went into the guest living room. It was a comfortable-looking space: A full-height bookcase in dark timber against one wall, with an alcove for the television—currently set to CNN. A sofa opposite the TV, with a coffee table between them, and a straight-back chair by the door. Two leather recliners on either side of the window that faced the front yard.

Miles took the chair by the door, sat with an ankle across his knee, and the pistol raised in one hand. He knew it would give the right impression. No one wants a cool intruder. If you make yourself at home, it always unsettles them. They've lost their sense of possession and control.

He could hear footsteps in the garage, cautious and measured, Eddie Rhys no doubt giving the place a once-over. Miles kept the gun raised, the sights chest-high on the oblique slice of doorway. Footsteps again, a brisk rhythm as the guy crossed the garage.

Miles let his breath out, watched the muzzle move slightly with his heartbeat. A tiny waver on a slow rhythm. He heard the snap of the light switch, and then softer footsteps on the carpeted hallway. He tracked the guy with the gun as he entered the room, and it wasn't until Rhys was seated on the sofa that he noticed Miles in the corner: the quiet visitor with his black suit and black mask and black gun.

To the man's credit, he hid his shock well: just a quick jolt like he'd touched something hot, and then he closed his eyes and let his breath out his nose.

Miles said, "You security?"

The guy didn't answer. He had the short-back-and-sides look that Stokes was obviously fond of.

Miles took silence to mean yes. He said, "Nice job."

"What do you want?"

Miles heard faint laughter at the other end of the house, and then glasses clinking. He said, "Just the money."

"There isn't any."

"So what are you doing here? Just a sleepover?"

Rhys didn't answer.

Miles said, "They give you some lasagna?"

Rhys didn't answer. He was a thickset man in his forties, probably ex-military or police, probably thinking retirement was meant to be easier than this.

Miles said, "Nice you get your own living room. Spread your arms along the back of the chair for me, tuck your hands down the cushions."

Rhys complied. He had a big wingspan. Miles saw a pistol in a holster on his right hip. He said, "Covey's just the middleman. So when's the pickup?"

He saw the guy glance away and then back, some kind of calculation going on. Rhys said, "Any minute."

Miles doubted that. The drop was only ten minutes ago, and Covey wouldn't want an overlap. But he said, "All right. We better make it fast. Tell the criminal attorney his TV's on the fritz."

Rhys looked at him and drew a breath and called, "Hey, Lane? The picture in here's gone all splotchy."

Miles nodded. "Nice. I like that." He tilted his head to listen and said, "Try again. It's a big house."

Rhys drew another breath and shouted, "Hey, Lane? Can you take a look at this?"

Silence for a few seconds, but then he heard feet in the hallway, and then Lane Covey was in the room. Seeing a masked visitor gave him a shock—the same little jump Rhys had done—but he recovered fast. He looked down at Miles with disdain and said, "The fuck is this?"

Not impressed, and not intimidated, either. He was a tall man in his midsixties, longish gray hair and features that were starting to age, eyes going dark and hollow under his brow. He had some spine though, and he smiled lopsidedly, trying to seem bored as he said, "This is the wrong fucking jackpot to be ripping off, pal."

Putting some Boston into an accent that had been plainer a moment ago, wanting to sound like he meant it: wrong fucken jackpawt.

Miles said, "Well, at least we know there's a jackpot."

No one answered.

Miles said, "Let's get Mrs. Covey in here too, shall we? Don't startle her."

Lane Covey smiled, like this was a game he'd go along with for now. Then he closed his eyes and turned his head to the door and called, "Sweetheart. Can you give me a hand with this, please?"

Miles said, "That's a good way to put it."

They all listened to her footsteps in the hall, and then Marilyn Covey was in the doorway. She was a similar age to her husband, but kind of prim and regal, Miles thought, the way she stood with her heels together and her wineglass in both hands, looking at him down her nose.

She said, "Oh."

Miles said, "Don't worry. I've just come for your loot."

Marilyn Covey took a sip of wine and said, "You've come to the wrong house."

"Your husband just told me there's a jackpot."

Marilyn looked over at Lane and then back to Miles. Their composure was interesting. He'd anticipated more tension. Maybe they were used to people showing up with guns. He put his elbow on the armrest and tilted his head to keep his eye line on the pistol sights. He said, "I'd thought you'd be more grateful. I could've come in here and shot all three of you."

Marilyn Covey lifted an eyebrow and said, "But then how would you find the money?"

Miles said, "It's in the safe in your walk-in closet upstairs."

Marilyn held his gaze, but her husband ran a hand through his hair.

Miles said, "Look. Let's get past the bit where you pretend there's nothing for me to take. I know the drop just now was payment for the murder of a man named Carl Tobin. I know the Russian mafia was contracted for the hit, and I know the attorney here was the middleman. So you can bring me the money now, or tomorrow NYPD will come asking for it. I think my way's easier. Police at your door, kind of unseemly in this zip code."

No one moved.

Miles looked at Marilyn and said, "I was interested to see your reaction. Wasn't sure if you were in on everything, or if it'd come as a bit of a shock. So it's nice to know that you're part of it. If I have to shoot you."

She watched him over her glass as she had another sip of wine, and Miles looked back at Lane Covey to see him smiling now.

The lawyer said, "So now what? We all going upstairs to get the cash?"

He seemed trapped with this notion that things would end in his favor. Miles decided this wasn't their first experience of pistol diplomacy. He said, "Lane, if I pull the trigger, your neighbors are going to call the police. You probably know more about it than me, but from what I understand, gunshot noise counts as probable cause, which means the cops can come in without a warrant. And I don't think you want cops in your house, do you?"

No one answered. Marilyn Covey looked at the television—Wolf Blitzer, and a BREAKING NEWS banner—and he saw a muscle tighten in her jaw.

Miles said, "I can walk away and never think about any of this again. But I don't think you're in the same position. So you should bear that in mind. You've got more to lose than I do. You keep saying that under your breath, everyone'll be fine."

He had their attention now, and the disdain seemed to be fading. They seemed to realize he was taking this seriously, that he wasn't just some guy in an outfit.

Miles said, "Mr. Rhys, use your left hand, take your phone out of your pocket for me."

"It's in my right pocket."

Miles said, "I'm sure you'll cope. Make sure you don't touch that gun, though."

The three of them watched while Rhys reached across himself awkwardly and removed an iPhone from his trouser pocket.

Miles said, "Throw it here."

Rhys lobbed it underhand, and Miles caught it without shifting his gaze from the gunsights. He waited for Rhys to slip his hand down behind the cushion again.

Miles said, "What's your code?"

"There isn't one. You just swipe."

Miles did as directed, and then navigated to the address book. He found Marilyn Covey under "C," and pushed the icon for a video call. Silence—she didn't have it on her. He scrolled down farther and found Oswald Lane Covey, and tried that number. Covey's trouser pocket started singing. He glanced down as if baffled by the sound.

Miles said, "It's for you, Lane."

Covey took the phone from his pocket, flipped it on one axis and then another to get it upright, and then the screen in Miles's hand showed a low-angle shot up Covey's arm to a disapproving face.

Miles said, "Power of technology. This is going to be easy."

No one answered, but he saw the digital Covey glance right, over to the window, and Miles looked up in time to see long blades of head-light glow panning through the blinds, and then he heard the sound of a car pull up outside. Rhys hadn't lied after all: this must be the pickup.

Covey smiled down at him. "How's your multitasking?"

Meaning four- or five-on-one might be a handful.

Miles said, "We'll find out. If it gets too much, I'll just have to shoot someone." He said to Edward Rhys, "Use your left hand again and take the holster off your belt. And I mean the whole thing." He heard a car door slam. "You touch the gun, I'm going to put a bullet in you."

Rhys complied, right hand raised palm-out like it might fend off lead. He lifted the holster off his belt and leaned forward and placed it in front of him on the coffee table.

Miles said, "Well done." He kept his aim on Rhys and looked over at Lane Covey. "Give Marilyn the phone."

The doorbell rang.

The three of them looked toward the noise, and then Lane looked over at his wife—a silent question—like trying to decide if there was an exit coming up.

Miles said, "Just look at me. I'm the one who decides who gets shot." He nodded at Lane and said, "Give Marilyn the phone."

The picture on his handheld screen blurred and then gained clarity as the lawyer passed the phone to his wife.

Miles said, "Hold it out in front of you."

Marilyn complied, the phone at arm's length like some kind of Geiger counter. On the screen in his hand, Miles saw an image of himself, sitting there masked in his armchair with the gun, and his elbow propped on the rest.

He kept his tone conversational: "All right. Mr. Rhys, in a moment you're going to answer the door and bring our guest in here. Marilyn, you're going to collect my two hundred grand. If either of you can't manage, then I'm going to have to take it out on Mr. Covey."

Marilyn Covey said, "Fuck you, you little shit."

It wasn't a royal turn of phrase, but she gave it a noble edge somehow, lifting her chin as she spoke, like he was violating hallowed privilege.

Miles said, "You can go now, Marilyn. Keep the phone out in front of you."

She just watched him.

Miles said to her, "I've weighed this all up very carefully, and if I have to shoot the crooked wife of a crooked lawyer and walk away without my payoff, so be it. But there're two sides to all this, and yours is the fatal one."

She turned away then, but she was smiling to save face, letting him know this was far from the end of the matter. He watched on the little screen as she walked along the corridor, and then made a left and started up the stairs.

The doorbell rang again, and someone knocked this time, too. Miles pointed the gun at Covey and held the phone up close to the pistol. He said, "Mr. Rhys, you can go to the front door, but don't open it until I tell you to."

Rhys got up and crossed the room, and Covey ran his hands through his hair. He didn't seem so bored and unimpressed now.

Miles waited until Rhys was along the hallway, and said, "What's your liquidity right now?"

"My liquidity?"

Miles watched Marilyn's progress in the upstairs hallway, and said, "Yeah. How much have you got in the bank?"

"What's that got to do with anything?"

The doorbell rang again, a double push to convey impatience.

Miles said, "Well, if the money goes missing in your custody, common sense implies you're liable. So it's a question of whether or not you can pay."

Covey said, "Jesus Christ, fuck you. I'm going to be out a hundred and eighty grand."

Miles raised his voice slightly and said, "Mr. Rhys, you can open the door." Then to Covey: "Twenty K's not a bad fee. So what's your liquidity like?"

"Fuck you, I got debts."

"Which is why you bought into this circus, right?"

Covey didn't answer.

Miles's screen showed a large document safe, door open, a leather duffel inside, standing upright. Stacked cash on a shelf above, and Marilyn's hand raking up a bundle, the close-range lens giving her a giant's fist. In the entry hall he heard Edward Rhys saying, "Follow me."

Miles kept the phone up by the gun and shifted the sights to the narrow slice of door, and a second later Edward Rhys stepped in, followed by a bald man in his early forties. The guy was wearing a bright-red Adidas tracksuit, the top unzipped over a white T-shirt.

He saw Miles, but didn't break step as he entered. He gestured at him as if tossing out the dregs in a glass and said, "What's this?"

Miles said, "Everyone's been very composed so far."

The tracksuit man walked over to the window and claimed an armchair, sat leaning forward with his elbows on his knees. His mouth curled up on one side as he said, "You trying to set a record or something? Dumbest goddamned hijacking anyone ever heard of."

He sounded Russian. Miles said, "Are you Russian?"

The guy smiled. "Are you a moron? Do you know who you're ripping off?"

Miles didn't answer, watched on his phone as Marilyn Covey descended the stairs, and a few seconds later she was back in the room with the leather duffel from the safe. She dropped it on the floor at Miles's feet. The label said Gucci.

Miles put the phone down and said, "They could've just used a Costco bag, saved another few thousand."

The tracksuit man said, "We'll see if you're still Mr. Funny Guy when we find you."

Miles said, "I don't think you'll find me."

The tracksuit man seemed to be enjoying himself, not too bothered by the fact he'd be leaving with less money than he should be. Or maybe it wasn't his money. He said, "There's only a few people who could put this together. So we'll catch up eventually."

Miles leaned forward and tugged the duffel's zipper open, saw bundled hundreds in ten-thousand-dollar bands. He thumbed a random stack in case it was bulked with ones or paper, but it looked legitimate. He took out four bands—forty grand—and lobbed them gently underhand onto the coffee table. The stack slid apart on impact and ended in a vague grouping.

The tracksuit man said, "What's this?"

Miles said, "Insurance."

"Yeah? For what?"

Miles said, "Mr. Covey owes you a hundred and eighty K, so we'll call that a down payment. I don't want him murdered before he can get the rest of it together."

Tracksuit man's smile grew, showing teeth. He said, "What are you, the gentleman thief?"

"Yeah. I guess so."

The man leaned back, put a white Adidas sneaker up on the opposite chair, rocked the knee from side to side as he looked at Miles, thinking something over. He said, "Well, I can be a gentleman, too. You want to leave the bag on the floor, we don't have to take this any further. You walk away, we can forget the whole thing. Otherwise." He made a gun with his fingers, pursed his lips, and kissed the sound of a shot.

Miles said, "Everybody does that." He stood up. "I need your car keys."

He told Stokes to take backstreets for the getaway: Great Neck Gardens to Kensington and then down through Thomaston. Stokes kept it slow, thirty miles an hour through the quiet suburbs while Miles checked the cash, thumbing each band for cutouts or a GPS unit. But the money was clean: a hundred and sixty grand in nonsequential used bills, and no antitheft measures. He transferred it all to a briefcase he'd brought with him, and then dropped the duffel out his window as they went past a golf club. He figured it wouldn't be too incongruous. Golfers would've seen Gucci before.

A minute later they joined the Long Island Expressway, and he finally felt himself relax, the stream of westbound traffic turning them anonymous. Stokes stayed quiet another mile, watching his mirrors as he drove, and then said, "Who was the dude in the tracksuit? He had some flair."

His voice sounded tight, like he hadn't quite worked off all the nerves.

Miles glanced across at him, Stokes driving with one hand and the other in his lap, the .45 nestled cross-draw in his belt.

Miles said, "I don't know. He was colorful though, wasn't he?"

Stokes was silent another minute, finger tapping the wheel like he was counting the yards. Eventually he said, "Maybe like, in the mother country, it's a strict dress code, and then they come here and it's way more chilled. Let them wear Adidas."

"Yeah. And drive convertibles." He jiggled his confiscated keys. It was a nice collection: Covey's Lexus, Rhys's Range Rover, the tracksuit man's Bentley coupe. He said, "If we had a buyer set up, could've taken a car too, made a bit extra." He clucked his tongue. "Bentley and the Lexus together, might've been another three hundred K."

Stokes smiled, ran a hand around his jaw as he watched the road, but he didn't answer.

Miles put a speaker bud in one ear, but didn't hit play on the iPod. He said, "I don't think it's worth turning back, though."

He placed the briefcase on the floor and rested it against the door, turned slightly in his seat so he had a shoulder to the window. Stokes watched the road, still massaging his jaw as he drove, like trying to warm it up for small talk.

Miles said, "If you take the next exit, you can let me off in Fresh Meadows. I'll get a cab." He dropped the Range Rover and Bentley keys in the footwell.

Stokes glanced at him. "We can go all the way to Manhattan, if that's easier?"

"No, this is fine. Next exit."

Stokes changed lanes and got off at Utopia Parkway, hung a right at the bottom of the ramp. It was almost midnight, not much traffic on the through-road.

Miles said, "Anywhere's fine."

"I'll go around the block."

He went right again, onto a quiet suburban street, tidy brick town houses on both sides, minivans in the driveways. Miles made a show of glancing around, no pedestrians out at this hour, and said, "I guess if you want to roll me, now would be the time."

He knew he'd called it right: Stokes's first reaction was to dab the brake, like he'd been caught off-guard and his driver's instinct kicked in, telling him to slow down. After that, the panic seemed to hit, and he clawed for the gun.

Miles let him do it: watched him draw the Colt right-handed and then start to line it up, the frame held sideways and the barrel rising, coming for his head. Miles waited until the pistol was up at eye level, Stokes's thumb on the hammer, and then he ripped the handbrake. The car stopped like it had hit a wall. The pair of them jerked against their seat belts, and Stokes's arm and the gun at the end of it received the same forward jolt, swinging out like a horizontal pendulum, and so for a long clumsy moment the gun's aim was not on Miles's head but on the window beside him. Miles caught the pistol with his right hand and rammed the Audi's ignition key into the underside of Stokes's wrist. Stokes swore and lost his grip as he yanked his arm back, and Miles stripped the gun from his loose fingers and then leaned against his door. He held the Colt two-handed at his hip, aiming at Stokes as the man sat cradling his injured arm and sucking air through his teeth.

Miles watched him for a few seconds, didn't speak until he felt his pulse level out. He said, "If you hadn't done that you could've walked away with ten grand, be the highest-paid chauffeur in America."

"Could've walked away with more, though. Even better."

Miles checked both ways along the street and then dropped the handbrake. The car crawled forward. Miles said, "Pull over. Can't sit here all night."

Stokes took them to the curb, steering with his good hand, the injured arm lying palm-up in his lap.

Miles said, "You'll have a bruise, but you'll survive." He put his back to the window and a foot on the transmission and said, "Most guys if they're talkers, they're quiet on the buildup, and then you can't shut them up afterwards. But you were the other way around. Made me think your job hadn't actually started yet. So that was a good guess, wasn't it?"

Stokes didn't answer.

Miles said, "Next time you pull this kind of thing, make sure you're nice and chatty. And you swapped your gun over, too. Had it on your hip before."

Stokes looked at him and said, "Any chance I'm getting it back?" He didn't seem too concerned about his botched double cross. Maybe he thought it was just business—win some and lose some.

Miles said, "Turn the lights off, or we're going to look mighty obvious, aren't we?"

Stokes killed the power. The lights died, and the pair of them turned to silhouettes.

Miles waited for the keys to stop tinkling, and said, "Stanton told you I know what I'm doing, but you had a go anyway. So what's made you so desperate you'd take the chance?"

Stokes didn't answer.

Miles said, "This is what they call shitting in your own nest. You won't be getting any more work out of Stanton. In fact, I'd change your number. And your locks."

"Thanks for the advice."

"Sure. So how much debt have you got that you'd take this kind of risk? Or are you just a spur-of-the-moment dumbass?"

Stokes started to say something and then changed tack. He said, "Look." He pinched the bridge of his nose and looked out his window, tidy dark suburbia with nothing stirring. He said, "I got a wife, man."

"You don't need to tug my heartstrings. I'm not going to shoot you."

Stokes didn't answer.

Miles said, "You know, I'm pretty comfortable with the ethics of everything tonight. Don't know about you, I won't lose much sleep, taking murder profit off a bent lawyer. But I didn't think I'd have to deal with you, trying to serve up moral dilemmas."

Stokes tipped his head back on the rest and smiled. "Don't know about moral dilemmas. I just wanted your money."

"Well, whatever. Just be thankful the loudest voice in my head is saying don't shoot."

Stokes didn't answer.

Miles said, "What's your wife think you're doing, when you head out on these little adventures?"

Stokes laughed through his nose, palmed his shaved skull. "Thinks I'm having an affair."

"Perfect."

"Yeah, well. She asks am I seeing someone, I tell her no with a clear conscience."

Miles said, "You're a genius. What's your debt?"

Stokes let his breath out through his teeth, took a moment to answer. He said, "Eighteen K."

Miles said, "Gambling or drugs?"

The silhouette of Stokes's head rocked back and forth. He said, "Bit of this, bit of that. You know how it is."

"No, not really."

Stokes didn't answer.

Miles said, "Big risk for a small debt."

Stokes shrugged. "Big risk, big payoff. You got a hundred sixty grand there."

Miles didn't answer. He knew he should walk away from it right now, but that was just setting himself up for a long spell of feeling like shit: lying awake thinking he should've put Stokes in the black, or wondering how the wife was doing, or whether there were kids in the picture yet. People he'd never meet, but he'd still chew on whether he was culpable for any debt-related strife they might face. Problem was, right now, he could pay Stokes nothing and feel fine about it for the next thirty minutes, but once hindsight was up and running, there'd be no reprieve. He'd second-guess himself into insomnia.

He said, "Jesus Christ," and popped the lid on the briefcase. He took out two bands—twenty thousand dollars—and tossed them in Stokes's lap. He snapped the briefcase closed and said, "How's that for irony: pull a gun on me, and double your take."

Stokes didn't answer. Miles wondered how he saw it: twenty thousand up from zero, or a hundred and forty down from one-sixty. He didn't have time to delve into his philosophy though, whether he was a glass-half-full or half-empty sort of guy.

He said, "Don't be too cut up about it: you could be dead."

He racked the slide on the gun and tipped the chambered round in his lap, dropped the magazine and thumbed out the bullets one at a time.

He said, "You can have the gun back, but I need to keep the car."

He clicked the pistol back together and tossed it in Stokes's lap. "You can get out now."

It was only a ten-minute drive down Midland Parkway to Jamaica. Prosperity faded as he went south: brick to clapboard, lawn to dirt, hedge to chain link. He parked on 179th Place, only a hundred yards past the subway station, left the car with its door open and the key lying on the seat. It was a 2008 Subaru Legacy: black paint, cream leather interior, smoked rear windows. He hoped a car thief would see its merits.

He walked back to the station and dropped the confiscated keys and Stokes's bullets in a trashcan, and then caught an F train all the way west to Manhattan—Lexington and Sixty-third. He transferred to a downtown 6 train and got off at Fourteenth, caught a cab up to Herald Square, dropped his mask in a trash can, and then rode a Q train all the way back down to Canal. If anyone had tracked him through all that, they deserved to find him.

His hotel was the Tribeca Gardens, an upmarket high-rise place that seemed a strange addition in this area, the south side of Canal mostly cheap gift shops and stores done up in neon, groups of guys lining the sidewalk, pushing homemade CDs on anyone with an empty hand. It was like Times Square, with a smaller headcount and more grime. He went into the hotel and nodded to the deskman on the way past, used one of the lobby phones to call Wynn Stanton.

"Hey, it's me."

Stanton said, "Detective. How you doing?"

TWO

Miles Keller

Miles said, "I don't think you can call me that while I'm suspended."

Stanton said, "Yeah, tell you what: I'll call you Detective, you call me Counselor, we'll just keep it between us. How'd it go?"

Miles said, "It had a happy ending." Other than Stokes, of course, but he could bring that up later. He said, "I need to square it tonight, though." Meaning he wanted Stanton's fee off his hands.

Stanton answered with a sigh that crackled the line, working hard to sound inconvenienced. "Yeah, all right. Where you calling from?"

"The hotel. Canal Street."

"Shit, why you still down there?"

Miles said, "You got time or not? I want to draw a line under this."

He held the phone with his shoulder, leaned against the edge of the booth so he could watch the bar area at the back of the lobby. There were two guys his age, and a woman slightly younger, late thirties maybe. It was a nice composition: the three of them side by side on stools, holding wineglasses by the stem as they flicked through text on their phones, the wall beyond just shelves of liquor and the light a honeyed amber.

Stanton said, "I'm on another job right now. Hang on—Kenny, Jesus, you don't need to slow down on a yellow. Less it's red, you give it gas the whole way." Then to Miles: "Can you make it up to Fourteenth Street? I'm seeing a guy afterward."

He didn't want to be walking around Manhattan with six figures in a briefcase, but he didn't want to say that to Stanton on the phone. He said, "You come down here, that'd be ideal." Dropping his voice on the last word to get the point across, but Stanton wasn't having it.

"No, what'd be ideal, we do this in a couple days when I got time."

"Thanks for being so understanding."

"Yeah, maybe this is news, I actually got more than one client. You know the Coffee Shop? Up at Union Square?"

"Yeah."

"See you there in forty minutes. I think I got more work for you, too."

Miles said, "I don't want more work."

He scanned his access card in the elevator and rode up to his room. He'd been here three weeks now, and he couldn't wait to leave. He hated the austerity, coming home to a space devoid of character. All he had was his luggage and a photo from his honeymoon—he and Caitlyn in Hawaii. He figured he could go another week maybe, and then he'd have to hang a picture, or hang himself.

The gloves he'd worn at the Coveys' were leather, and therefore safe enough to keep: they had a smooth finish, nonadhesive, and wouldn't have caught any stray fibers. But the suit and shoes would have to go. Hard as it was to part with polished loafers and a nice two-button from Hugo Boss, they could have picked up hair, soil from the yard, all kinds of forensic giveaways he couldn't afford.

He folded the suit and put it in a duffel bag he'd bought earlier—a cheap tourist item with a low-res impression of the Statue of Liberty stitched on one side. He dressed again in jeans and his trench coat, hit play on his iPod, and left the room heading for the elevator: briefcase full of cash in one hand, bag of mothballed heist gear in the other.

•   •   •

He walked a block up Broadway, and donated the duffel to a homeless man sitting outside American Apparel. Back at Canal Street, he caught a 6 train uptown and got off at Fourteenth, followed the exit crowd to the upper level. Even at night the station was armpit-hot, the smell somewhere between train fumes and trash, and tonight the iron squeals had competition: sax music from a dwarf in a wheelchair, the guy hunched forward red-faced as he cradled his instrument, blasting out a jazzy tune Miles didn't know. He came out into Union Square and a late-night crowd that seemed silent by comparison: an army of mimes composed of tourists and kids walking hand-in-hand. He walked across to Union Square West and went into the Coffee Shop, on the corner of Sixteenth. Wynn Stanton was already there, sitting by himself in the corner booth just past the waitress station. He raised a hand in what looked more like sad farewell than greeting. Miles went over and put the briefcase on the seat and slid in behind it, saw his motion in duplicate in the lenses of Stanton's aviators. He had a grilled cheese sandwich and a coffee.

Miles said, "Midnight snack?"

Stanton shook his head and chewed patiently. The aviators bounced in a small amplitude. "This is lunch." He made a C shape with his thumb and first finger, waggled them back and forth. "Flipped my day around. Everyone I deal with's a nighthawk, so I'm giving it a try." He wiped his mouth. "How was Kings Point?"

Miles shrugged. "Tidy."

Stanton aimed a finger at him. "We should go back sometime: they got a new restaurant at the golf club there—public as well. Me and Ken checked it out when we were running the prep. Had this miso eggplant thing with this kind of paste on the side . . ." He shook his head, eyes closed, like trying to channel the taste through his cheese sandwich. "Shit it was nice. Ken had this snapper, came out under one of those big domes, real slick."

Miles just smiled, wanting a quick segue into shoptalk. Stanton leaned back and drank some coffee. He was from Venice Beach originally, a surfer and marijuana enthusiast who had a late-twenties epiphany, or so he said, and decided to put himself through law school. Miles didn't think the legal education had ever been used for legal ends, but for this kind of work, deceit was a virtue. These days, he wasn't an attorney so much as a talent agent—that was Stanton's description, anyway. He called himself The Man Who Makes Shit Happen. If you brought him talent—a driver, a safe man—he'd find them a project. And if you brought him a project, he'd find you the talent to get it done.

He wore Hawaiian shirts most of the time—maybe an homage to the coast life—but the surfing was forty years behind him now, and it was obvious: his autumn physique was dangle and bone.

Miles said, "You might have to take Stokes off your books."

"Oh yeah?"

Miles told him what happened.

Stanton said, "Oh, Christ." He looked down at his sandwich, a fat weld of cheese sealing the edge, looked up at Miles from under his brow. "You cleaned up okay though?"

Miles shrugged. "There was nothing to clean up. We went our separate ways with no injuries."

"So what was his deal?"

"Debts, apparently."

"You should've just drilled him."

Miles didn't answer.

Stanton chomped deep and said thickly, "So what, you just let him walk?"

Miles nodded. "Gave him twenty grand, said see you later."

Stanton's head came forward maybe three inches, a quick shunt. "What, he needed bus money or something?"

Miles didn't answer. He could've said he had a nose for honesty, and that Stokes seemed to ring true, and that he didn't want to be liable if the man hit bad luck farther up the road. But he didn't think Stanton would understand that. Stanton's law was dog-eat-dog. So he just said, "It was nothing in the scheme of things."

Stanton had a contemplative chew. He nudged his glasses. "Yeah, but you can say that about anything. Everything's nothing in the scheme of things, you break it down small enough." He wiped his mouth with his wrist, leaned forward with his mouth ajar, still casual as he said, "I can send him a visitor, no big deal."

Miles shook his head. "I don't want him clipped. I just don't want you sending him more work."

Stanton grinned. "Well, you gave him twenty grand, imagine he's set for a little while."

"I saw it as a preventative measure."

"Yeah, nice. Should go back down the subway, give all the homeless guys twenty grand, fix them right up, I'm sure."

A waitress came by. Miles ordered a cappuccino. He waited for her to move on and said, "I don't think I'm going to get my job back. I think Force Investigation will push charges."

Admissions were meant to be cathartic, but it didn't feel good, saying that. It had already done the rounds in his daydreams, but it was a new frontier when you formed the words aloud.

Stanton watched him flatly from behind his lenses and said, "Someone tell you that, or you going off a hunch?"

Miles laid his palms on the table, looked down at hand and mirror-hand. He said, "You know you wake up in the dark at two A.M., and you just know something for a fact?"

Stanton nodded. "Yeah. That's called a hunch." He looked past Miles to the waitress station. "You ever notice all the girls in here, they're like an eight or nine out of ten, minimum?"

Miles clicked his fingers. Stanton looked toward the noise and then looked him in the eye.

Miles said, "If I get a murder charge, I got two options: I either blow the money on attorneys, or I blow the money on a getaway."

"Getaways are cheap. It's the new life that can get pricey. How much you got right now?"

"Including this"—he tapped a finger on the briefcase—"four hundred, maybe."

"It's workable. Wouldn't call it a shitload, though, would you?"

Miles shrugged. "Depends where I go. Probably get a place in shits-ville for a hundred grand, have three hundred K walking-around money."

Stanton finished off his sandwich, pushed the plate to one side. "Where's the rest of it?"

"In the safe in the hotel room."

"Holy shit. I thought you were a pro."

"I am. Part of being a pro, you know what's a risk and what isn't."

"Yeah, well." Stanton watched a waitress as he formulated. "I think staying in the same hotel for weeks on end, keeping all your cash under the bed, that's setting yourself up for disappointment. That'd be my lawyerly advice, anyway."

Miles said, "Lucky you're disbarred, then."

Stanton looked at him a moment, sucking something off a molar, bottom jaw pushed to one side. He said, "Well here's option three: you hang around, I feed you a couple more jobs, you make a few hundred K." He spread his hands, like underlining the ease of getting rich. "Then if the DA lays charges, you can reassess."

Miles didn't answer.

Stanton turned slightly to observe the arrival of Miles's coffee. He waited for the waitress to move on and then said, "And if you have to split, you got a bit more up your sleeve. Look, Christ, there's nothing to worry about." He leaned forward again. His nose bore capillaries so intricate they'd be a marvel if they were there on purpose. He said, "We got a guy on contract we talk with, used to be Force Investigation, out at LAPD? He read your file, emailed us back yesterday, all he said was, 'Keller should walk.'"

"Right. And does that mean they won't press charges, or does it mean I won't get an indictment when it goes to a grand jury?"

"I don't know. Look, cops shoot people all the time, no one charges them."

"Depends what color they are."

"Yeah, you should've shot a black guy, this'd be all wrapped up."

Miles spooned fluffy milk off his coffee. He said, "Thing about splitting, it only works if it's preemptive. Kinda late if they're knocking at your door with cuffs and a warrant."

"I'm running out of ways to say you did nothing wrong."

Miles shrugged. "You can't trust big institutions to have any kind of moral insight."

Stanton watched him take a drink and then said, "So what do you want to do?" Saying it slow enough to make it cautionary.

Miles said, "I'm not staying put for a trial. I want to be able to run and not have to lug a bag full of cash around with me."

Stanton nodded slowly. "What's your time frame?"

"For leaving? I don't know. Soon. Eventually."

"Yeah, see, that makes me worry. If you said Tuesday, or two weeks from tomorrow, that'd be all right. But when it's open-ended it makes me think you got something else going on."

Miles shrugged.

Stanton said, "You wanted to leave, you could be gone tonight. So who you hanging round for?"

Miles said, "Tell me what my options are. How do you bank four-hundred-odd grand?"

Stanton blew cheese breath out his teeth. "We can send it offshore. Probably the safest."

Miles waited.

Stanton said, "We got a partner firm down in New Zealand. Basically what they do, they set up a trust, and then they open a limited liability company *owned* by the trust. Or something like that. It's pretty straightforward—their tax reporting is shit, so they don't have to tell their IRS who benefits. But basically the end result is an offshore base for funds, with you as the secret owner."

"Nice."

"The law firm knows your name, but no one else does. They have to disclose upon request, but they never get requests."

"What's the setup cost?"

"Twenty percent."

"Jesus. All right."

Stanton said, "I told you I got other jobs."

Miles didn't answer.

Stanton said, "Had a call for you, too: lady from the *Post*. First time, I tell her—plain English, right—no fucking comment. Second time she calls up, I was just—bam, straight down." He made a phone from a cocked thumb and pinkie, mimed a big hang-up.

Miles said, "That'll teach her."

"Yeah. Didn't try a third time. One-nil, Stanton."

"How'd she even get my name?"

Stanton shrugged. "Someone at FID probably put it out, picked up a sweet fee." He sat back, rubbed his hands as he looked at the window, slits of night-light showing in the metal blind. He said, "Look, I'm serious, you wait around a little longer"—he spread his hands to imply freedom of choice, scale of possibility—"we can set you up with something else, make another hundred grand, two hundred maybe. You'd be thanking yourself later."

Miles swirled his coffee. He liked to bring the liquid all the way to the lip without it cresting, let it back down nice and gentle. He said, "In the movies when they bring the main guy in to do one last job, shit always hits the fan."

Stanton said, "How you know you're the main guy?"

Miles didn't answer.

Stanton said, "Even if he says no at first, they always wear him down, make him an offer he can't refuse."

Miles shook his head. "I'm pulling the pin. Or the rip cord. However it is people get out and do something else with their life."

Stanton looked at him quietly and then leaned back, as if seeking a more comprehensive picture. Miles sensed that a mildly interesting observation was on the way. He waited. Eventually Stanton said, "Never actually thought I'd have you as a client."

Miles said, "Yeah? Why's that?"

Stanton shrugged, gave a half-smile that pushed up one sunglass lens. "You were supposed to be the good one."

Miles said, "I'm morally immaculate."

The smile grew and showed teeth. "Yeah. Everyone thinks they're Robin Hood. Then they realize scruples cost too much."

Miles didn't answer.

Stanton looked at him over the sunglasses, trying to show him this was serious now. His bloodshot eyes wavered slightly, a tremor in the focus. He said, "If you won't let me book you another job, you got no reason to hang around."

Miles didn't answer.

"So what're you hanging around for?"

Miles drained his coffee and placed the spoon in the mug. He stood up and said, "Can you drop me at the hotel?"

Stanton called his driver and told him they needed a ride down to Canal Street. Kenny picked them up outside a minute later, the car humming with the force of its stereo. A nightclub-volume blast of Korean pop greeted Miles as he opened his door.

Stanton said, "Phwoah, turn it down, boy. I worry about your ears."

Kenny obliged, dropped the music to a safer level. They got across Union Square and went south on Broadway. Stanton sat in back with Miles and made himself at home, took a pre-rolled joint from a compartment in the center console and lit it with a match. Miles thought maybe he shouldn't have been so hard on Stokes. He wasn't about to give Stanton a speech about quitting the drugs. He listened to him make a call on his cell. "Yeah, it's me. I'm just going downtown for something else, but I'll be with you in thirty minutes." There was a sense of exhibition to it, the way he talked at high volume, the joint wagging in his mouth and his nose leaking pot smoke.

He clicked off and said, "Kenny, you just gotta be careful we don't run a stoplight or something. I don't want to get pulled over and caught with a joint. And what've you done to your hair?"

The hair in question was bright red—quite a striking look on a thirty-one-year-old Korean man. Kenny said, "I dyed it, like Chanyeol. You know Chanyeol?"

Stanton shook his head. "Nope. I don't know Chanyeol."

"Rapper in a band called EXO. He's the man."

Stanton sucked his joint delicately, eyes narrowed. He said, "I doubt that."

As far as Miles could tell, Wynn Stanton thought that Wynn Stanton was the man, and he was reluctant to share the honor.

Kenny said, "Why? You don't like K-pop?"

Stanton didn't answer, sat listening to the music with one finger raised, as if poised to pass judgment. The song reached peak momentum, hyperspeed Korean backed by digital bass, and then it all went silent to let another voice say in English: "smash your limit." That single admonition, and then the lyrics and the disco beat were back at full tempo.

Stanton said, "Yeah, right there: that's my problem with it." He aimed forward with the raised finger, like he'd skewered the offending line. "If they just stuck to Korean, that'd be fine. But I don't like picking up random phrases that make zero sense—feel like I'm getting dementia or something." He puffed his joint. "I'm too young for that shit."

He looked across at Miles, wanting corroboration, but Miles kept his eyes on the street. Storefronts going past, window after lit window, a reeled backdrop for the sidewalk crowds glimpsed in silhouette. Even the backseat view was too broad a focus, too much data. A few blocks down Broadway showed him countless lives. You just had to accept you didn't know what was going on.

He looked across at Stanton blowing smoke out the gap in his window and said, "Who was it who called from the *Post*?"

Stanton clicked his fingers. "Umm. Nina Stone."

Miles said, "Huh. I know her." Stanton glanced across at him, and Miles said, "She's not a journalist, she's a bank robber."

THREE

NEW YORK, NY

Miles Keller

Stanton said, "Hang on, wait. Ken, give that stuff a rest, will you?"

Kenny killed the music, but Stanton's joint had gone out. He fumbled his matches and got one lit, but that was only half the struggle, potholes on Broadway making the car yaw, the flame and the joint tip in close orbit but resisting unity. They hit a smooth stretch and Stanton found alignment, drew deep and got the joint tip glowing just as Kenny changed lanes. The flame lost contact on the swerve but the deed was done, and Stanton shook the match out as he leaned back and blew smoke out his teeth. The cabin smelled sweet with marijuana.

He said, "How'd you know that?"

Miles said, "Met her on a case. While ago now, five years or so." Five years to the month actually, but he knew precision wouldn't serve him well. No point raising questions about why he knew the date.

Stanton grinned at him. "Back in the innocent days, when you didn't know robbery's the fun part of robbery detective."

"I don't do it for entertainment."

"Oh, yup, I forgot: restoring karmic balance." Stanton blew a smoke ring. "So she was a suspect, then?"

Miles nodded. "Looked at her for a heist."

"Did she do it?"

Miles shrugged. "Maybe." He watched some of the Broadway view, pedestrians just still-frames at this speed. He said, "It was a cool job and she was a cool lady. It was this banking executive or something—he'd had some people over one night, they got him drunk, shot him up with sodium pentothal he figured, asked him what his safe code was. And because he was full of truth serum he came right out with it, and they walked away with about a million bucks."

"Nice."

"We didn't have enough on Nina, so she walked."

Stanton puffed and watched the night roll by. "You said she's a bank robber. I don't think it counts, if you just rob the boss over dinner."

Miles said, "I think bank jobs were her main occupation." He paused, looking back through the years, and said, "I brought her in for an interview this one time, asked her straight up whether she'd drugged and robbed anyone before. You know, wanting to see how she'd play it, and she just told me she was used to going in the front door, point- ing a gun at the teller. I thought that was pretty good."

"So why's she calling up, five years later or whatever it is?"

"I don't know. Maybe she wants to cop to it."

He doubted it though. Meeting her at the time, he got the impres- sion that she knew her own mind, and that there wasn't a lot of guilt in there.

He said, "Probably got bailed out during the GFC, and now he's back on seven or eight figures."

"Who?"

"The bank guy she robbed."

Stanton said, "Yeah, but he might've worked hard for it all."

"I doubt it."

Stanton did his little half-smile again, looking superior. "You don't know what's on his scorecard, might've had something buried way back, made him deserve a shitload of loot. Might be good deeds you're not privy to."

Miles said, "You see the bright and shining goodness in everyone, or you just playing devil's advocate?"

Stanton grinned around his joint. "Yeah, I work for the devil."

They crossed Houston Street, into SoHo now and through the sheer and narrow corridor of grand facades. Stanton said, "How'd she even know to call me?"

Miles had been chewing on that one himself. He said, "Probably tried NYPD first, and they referred her on. Might've been something good too, if she called you twice."

"She sounded hot. You know how some girls just have that phone voice?"

Miles didn't answer.

Stanton puffed away for a few blocks and said, "Ken, your joint rolling's come a long way. I'm liking this one a lot."

"It's good weed, too."

"Yeah, you're right. It is good weed."

They reached Canal Street and made the right turn. Miles leaned forward over the console for a better view: shops lit up in every shade of fever dream, hipster-looking kids in threes and fours, no doubt headed for some eardrum-busting rave, the same group of guys outside the gift shop on the south side, not quite ready to call it a night. He saw cabs over by the hotel, a black Chevy Tahoe at the curb toward West Broadway. He turned to look out the rear window, saw another Tahoe back by Lafayette Street.

Stanton saw him looking and said, "Chill, they're just cabs. Or what's that thing called? Uber, or whatever."

"No they're not. Pull over."

Kenny said, "Where, here?"

"Yeah, anywhere. Pull over."

Stanton said, "Ah, Jeez, come on," but Kenny pulled over.

Miles said, "There's only one hotel between Lafayette and West Broadway, and they're nowhere near it. So they're not cabs."

Stanton looked like he might argue, but then he stubbed out his joint in the ashtray on his door. "Might not be for you." He looked out his back window. "And don't tell me how like, you wake up in the dark at two A.M. and you just know. They're just cars sitting there."

Maybe he was right. Then again, he would've bet ten-thousand-to-one he was the only man on the street with his name on a hit list. Maybe the Coveys had found out who he was, and sent someone. Or maybe the guy in the red tracksuit was well connected. But it could be anyone. He'd been running heists for years now, which was just another way of saying he had no shortage of people wanting payback.

Stanton was still twisted around, looking out the rear window. He said, "It can't be from that Covey thing, it's too soon. Probably to do with your what-do-you-call-it." He made inverted commas with raised fingers. " 'Officer-involved shooting.' "

Miles said, "Just wait here a second, I need to think it over."

He had a hundred and forty thousand dollars in the briefcase. He could keep going and never come back, forget about his hotel stash. But two hundred fifty grand was a lot to sacrifice for what was so far just a bad vibe.

He said, "Let me out by the entrance, and I'll see if I get a follower."

Stanton said, "Atta boy. They're just corporate cabs or something."

Kenny moved away from the curb and merged with thin traffic. Miles unclipped his briefcase, smelled used cash as he raised the lid. Those bills would have seen it all: everything from Walmart to mounds of coke. If only money talked. You'd have a record from the gutter to the heavens. He took out twenty grand and dropped the bands on the seat beside him.

Stanton picked them up—a wad in each hand—and fanned himself with the cash, eyes closed and face serene. "You know how to make a man happy."

Kenny made a U-turn just before West Broadway and pulled up outside the hotel. Miles clicked the briefcase shut and said, "You want to do me a favor?"

Stanton said, "Yeah, why stop now?"

"Pull over somewhere, give me a call if anyone follows me in."

"How long we gotta wait until it counts as a favor?"

"If you sleep easy, you know you've done it right."

Miles climbed out, and got a smile and a nod from the concierge who held the lobby door for him, and when he glanced back, Stanton's car was already pulling away into traffic with a long, slick note of ground water.

Inside, there was a guy behind the desk, and a family of four who appeared to be checking out, given the nearby colony of luggage. The bar at the back of the lobby was closed, but there was a little business center in the middle of the floor, with a few computers and a printer set up on a long table, corralled vaguely by potted plants. He took a seat at a screen and opened an internet browser. The deskman was too friendly, laying on the charm extra thick with the mother, maybe polishing his moves. The dad had that thin, empty smile that signaled dangerously low patience. Miles brought up nytimes.com, scrolled aimlessly while he watched the lobby doors. No one entered. The deskman wrapped up his schmoozing. The family of four departed in size order: Dad toting duffels, Mom with her sheaves of map, the sullen and pear-shaped teenaged boy and girl.

The man at the desk made a brief call and then paced slowly, hands behind his back. Miles clicked random links. He scrolled and watched the street. He gave it up after twenty minutes and headed for his room.

He had an elevator to himself, quiet violin music and a measured ding as the sign above the door counted floors. His room was on fifteen, which in real terms meant fourteen, given the absence of a thirteenth floor—at least as far as the labels were concerned. Miles thought the best way to thwart bad luck would be to keep the numbers honest and just leave the thirteenth floor unoccupied. Surely false accounting was just tempting fate even further.

His room was at the end of a corridor behind two blind turns, and he decided if he heard the phone ringing he'd just turn around and head straight back down. But nothing like that awaited him: just silence, and Nina Stone leaning against his door.

Part of him wondered if she was here to take him out, but this seemed like a strange way to go about it, unarmed and looking pleased to see him.

She said, "I saw you yesterday. I was in a cab, you were walking down Canal Street, and I thought: I know who that is."

Like he'd lived next door when they were kids or something, not investigated her for robbery. He realized too, he might have to revise his odds: maybe he wasn't the only one with people after him. His one-in-ten-thousand estimate could be wrong, by the dark light of Nina.

Miles said, "You know anything about those two black SUVs out front?"

She smiled slightly, looking vindicated, like she knew he'd ask. "They're not here for you, if that's what you're thinking. But we can talk about them if you like."

She must've been thirty-five now, but she hadn't lost any magnetism. He remembered interviewing her, trying to catch her off-guard with that question on past crimes, and she'd come straight back with her line about pointing guns at bank tellers. Facetious enough to make it inadmissible, but at the same time he knew she was giving him the truth, in a certain shaded way. He'd been hooked by that one phrase, wanted to know everything about her, this woman who'd showed up for a police interview about a felony, and didn't even bring a lawyer.

She said, "Five years is a nice round number. Almost feels like it's meant to be."

It was a lure framed as small talk. She wanted a question in return. She wanted him to ask what she was doing here, context and coincidence and all the breathless wonderment of how she found him. An hour ago with Stanton, he'd said farewell to risk, and nothing would have made him take another job. But faced with Nina Stone, he felt that earlier conviction fading, the old feeling of intrigue tugging at him. In an almost out-of-body way, he could see his mind-set changing: Forget caution—let's see what the lady has to say.

He turned and checked along the corridor, but it was just the two of them. He wondered what he'd be doing now if he hadn't found her waiting. Maybe he'd be on the phone to Stanton, asking for her number.

Or maybe it was just her being here that made him want to know more. It could all be simple and male: a pretty woman outside his room, and he couldn't tell her no. But whatever, even with part of him knowing this was how bad endings started, he took out his keycard and said, "Let's sit down."

FOUR

Miles Keller

The room was the shoebox standard: a double bed, with a desk and television opposite, and an armchair in one corner by the window. Miles let Nina go ahead of him, and she walked in with enough disinterest that he wondered if she'd been here before. She cut a nice figure though, in her jeans and denim jacket, shoulder-length hair that showed off the bounce in her walk. She was tall, too—six foot, maybe six-one—and built like a pro tennis player: that lean perfection, still intact five years on. He liked how she carried herself as well: confident, knowing she looked good, but not flaunting it too hard. He remembered back when he interviewed her, how she'd showed up in a cream sleeveless dress and carrying a little clutch that matched. He remembered trying out a few headlines: THEFT OF A MILLION DOLLARS BY WOMAN WHO LOOKS A MILLION DOLLARS. It needed some work, but she'd definitely turned heads in the corridor.

He'd pictured her every now and then over the years, and she was always in black for some reason—black, but with a moneyed California vibe: wide-brimmed hats and big shades, clicking along in heels, a cigarette in one of those long filters. Five years ago, she'd told him she was in New York on vacation, that the bank man she'd supposedly robbed was a friend of her husband's, but she sure as hell hadn't drugged him and gone off with his money. She said her husband owned a film studio in L.A., and that the allegations against her would make a good movie—they seemed to like stories that shared zero ground with reality.

She claimed the armchair, and he took the seat at the desk, spun it around to face her. It would block her view of the honeymoon photo on the desk behind him. He said, "Were you standing out there all night, or do you just have good timing?"

She smiled. "The deskman was a sweetheart, said he'd give me a call when you came in. Scored himself double points actually—I was out the first time he tried."

"He must've been a sweetheart if he told you my room number."

She put an elbow on the rest and propped her temple with a finger. Her hair leaned out to find the vertical. "He didn't mean to. I just went down this morning and asked him to call your room, watched him type the number in. They had me up on twenty at first, so I said we were colleagues, and they moved me down here." She nodded at the entrance. "I'm three doors along."

Miles laid the briefcase on the bed and put his feet up next to it. "So is this a little catch-up, or work-related?"

She drew a long breath without looking away. "I wasn't quite sure at first."

He said, "Well. Do you need a police detective or not?"

"I don't know. But they have more than one use, presumably."

That was pretty good. He let that sit between them for a moment, and in the lull, reality began to show itself: the fact he'd let her in on some emotional whim because she'd piqued his interest five years ago, and now here he was, a hundred twenty grand in the case on the bed, another two-fifty-odd in the safe, and a stranger seated opposite.

Miles said, "How can I help you?"

Nina nodded again, aiming at the window this time. She said, "I saw you walking around in your suit with your briefcase, thought maybe you were on some shady law-enforcement job. But then I called your old number at NYPD, and all they did was refer me on to whoever it was. Stanton and Co. Which I thought was strange. But then I did some Googling, saw your name on a cop-hate forum, said you shot and killed a guy last month. And I thought, well, maybe that's standard practice, putting me through to your rep." Offhand, but not too breezy, nothing accusatory in her tone.

Miles said, "There were extenuating circumstances."

"Such as?"

"The man was a hit man. And he had a woman captive." That wasn't quite true—it was a break-in, not an abduction. But for some reason, he wanted Nina on his side.

She said, "Well, maybe it's a good thing that you shot him." Like this was all pretty routine.

Miles said, "That's what everyone's trying to decide."

She let the shooting have a quiet moment, and then said, "The deskman told me you've been here a few weeks." She looked around, the little room devoid of homeyness, unless his luggage counted as a personal touch. "Made me wonder if you're on the brink of cutting ties."

He'd caught a slight pause midsentence, like she was going to call it "running," and then changed her mind, went for the euphemism.

She said, "So can I make a guess, see how close I am?"

Miles shrugged. "Guess away."

She was biting her lip lightly, like she was putting things together, but he knew her conclusions would be locked in by now.

She said, "I think you've gone from detective, to detective-with-a-question-mark, and now you're getting ready to run."

Run. There we are: she'd just wanted to land it with the right punch.

Miles didn't answer, waited for her to get to whatever she was building up to.

She glanced around again and said, "Bit of a squeeze too, if you brought the wife. So is it married-with-a-question-mark, or just plain divorced now?"

He knew his face didn't change, but she read something anyway: "Sorry. Too close to the bone."

Miles said, "I'm considering my options."

Nina shifted in her seat, looking at him from a new angle. "Well, see what you think about this option: I'm here on business, and I thought you might be interested. If you want in, I'll pay you half a million dollars."

He wished he'd booked a bigger room, an executive suite maybe with the bedroom separate from the living area, so he didn't have to use the mattress as a footstool. He could picture himself walking to a side table, pouring a couple of drinks, a finger of something Scottish on ice. The way he'd do it, he'd hold the tumbler overhand as he passed it to her, and then they'd share the sofa while she told him what was worth five hundred grand. He could do it here, but he wouldn't seem quite as smooth, using the minibar under the desk.

He said, "You proposing legal employment, or will I have to feel guilty about it?" Keeping his voice flat, trying to match her tone.

Nina said, "Don't you feel guilty already?" No smile, but there was a light in her eye that made the question playful. He wondered what she meant: guilty because he'd let her in the room, or guilty due to prior actions.

He said, "I try to avoid extra, if I can."

She said, "Not many jobs pay half a million dollars and keep you out of trouble."

Getting closer to the truth, but he sensed reluctance. It was quite a risky endeavor, proposing lawbreaking to a police detective.

He said, "You want a drink?"

He thought alcohol might make her more forthcoming, but she said, "I'll have a water, if there's one going."

The Nina in his mind wouldn't do that—he saw her as a stiff-drink lady, a cocktail to go with the cigarette. He got up and knelt beneath the desk and opened the little fridge. There were two cardboard cartons printed with redundant hipster talk: THIS IS A CARTON OF WATER THAT COSTS $1.80 AND IS INTENDED FOR HUMANS BUT—

He didn't bother with the rest of it. He said, "You need a glass?"

"No, I'll manage."

He passed her the carton and took a bottle of Corona from the lower shelf and popped the cap with the little frosted opener they'd left for him. He sat down again, and the fridge door swung closed with a polite clap, a nice touch, he thought, as if to say: Done.

Nina leaned forward, carton at arm's length. "Cheers."

He touched it with his bottle, and she watched him as she took a drink, one eye staying with him as her head tipped back, throat working gently.

Miles said, "Robbed anyone else lately?"

She dabbed her lips with the back of her hand and shook her head. She had tidy little features all carefully balanced. "No. Not in a little while."

He couldn't tell if she was serious or not. She had a way of pitching her voice, just light enough that he heard more brevity than honesty.

Miles said, "Shall we small talk about what we've been up to for the last few years, or are we discussing business now?"

She laughed, and with her head back he saw that nice horseshoe of upper teeth. She said, "My last few years have been pretty ordinary." He didn't know how to parse that: she'd seemed to think being investigated for robbery was pretty ordinary, as well.

Nina said, "The last two weeks were interesting though." She took a moment, and he saw her swallow, as if making sure she could talk with no emotion. "I weighed up my life and decided it's time for a change." A little smile as she said it, signaling the understatement. "But let's not dwell on the woe-is-me bullshit. I don't want to talk about it."

Miles said, "My last few weeks have been interesting, too."

"You shot a guy and lost your wife?"

No, Caitlyn had left six years ago. She'd married an NRA lobbyist with too much money, and they lived up in Kings Point now—not far from the Covey place, actually. Miles had heard the new man's voice a few times: a stern "fuck off" down the phone whenever he called. He'd been by the house once but didn't even make it to the door, intercepted on the driveway by the new husband and his new .357.

Miles said, "Well. I shot a guy."

She said, "Did it happen kind of like TV, where you square off, and he had a look in his eye like he knew he was going for a gun, made a grab for it even when you told him not to?"

Miles said, "I didn't really look in his eyes."

"Shoot and ask questions later?"

He said, "What do I have to do to get paid?"

She said, "You worried I'm going to ask you to break the law?"

Closer still, but she hadn't come right out with it. He had some Corona to give himself time. "I need to know what I'm getting into."

She angled the carton so she could read the dumb shit written on the side. She scanned it idly, still reading as she said, "My husband operates a business with a co-owner. The co-owner's selling out. I'm negotiating the exit with a New York buyer."

"What's the business?"

"Various things. All illegal, of course."

Getting close to trouble now, but she wasn't quite across the line. She had another drink and held it for a moment, working through something in her own time.

She swallowed and said, "His holdings are significant, so the buyout's nearing ten million. In theory, the people I'm talking to have enough cash on hand to pick up whatever's being sold. If you follow."

He could guess what the plan was, but he wanted to hear her say it. She had that playful look in her eye again, and he thought maybe this was it, but she said, "What's in the briefcase?"

He didn't answer.

Nina said, "I'm parting with delicate information. I'd be more comfortable if I knew what you were carrying."

He guessed that she knew already—or at least knew he wanted to keep it private. No point asking if she didn't expect a big admission, something in exchange for her proposal. Which brought them to another door, figuratively speaking, and it was a bigger decision than just letting her in the room. There was a difference between letting her in for a drink, and letting her see his lifestyle.

Although the stakes were different, now she had half a million dollars in play—the reward side of the ledger was looking even brighter. In some ways, the risks didn't even matter. Five hundred grand plus the Nina je ne sais quoi made decisions much easier:

He said, "The briefcase is full of money."

She waited, like she was expecting more, and then said, "Are we going to talk figures?"

Miles shrugged and said, "It's six figures."

She drank some hipster water and nodded to herself, like his confession was matching with her guesswork, and she knew the whole story. She said, "I'll come by tomorrow night. If you're still interested, I'll take you to see the money."

"You still haven't told me what I have to do."

She shrugged. "You haven't told me no, so I imagine you'll do as you're asked."

"Up to a point. But if you give me the lowdown now, I can tell you if it's within my risk threshold, and then we won't waste time."

She didn't answer.

Miles said, "There's a bar downstairs. Maybe a real drink will help you part with the details."

"I think the bar's closed."

"This is New York City. I'm sure we'd find something."

"Probably." She raised one eyebrow a touch. "But then what happens?"

Miles said, "Well. I guess we'd share a cab."

"And then you'd drop me at my room, like a gentleman."

"I guess so. Though you don't strike me as a gentleman."

Nina laughed and looked away. "I think this'll do for now."

For now. He wondered if she'd given those last two words slight emphasis, or if wishful thinking warped his hearing.

He nodded and said, "Yeah. Getting into taxis together might be a bit much at this stage."

She was still smiling as she placed the carton on the floor beside her.

Miles said, "You going to take me to a meeting so I can rip someone off?"

She drew a long breath as she rose from the chair. "Well. It's your call. You can decide what's in your purview as a cop."

That was a tidy way to handle things: if he sold her out and arrested her, she could just claim she was giving him a tip-off, that robbery was never her intention. Although the five hundred grand would be harder to explain.

She said, "I like the new look, by the way. Are you trying to blend in with your clientele?"

Meaning the long hair and the beard.

Miles said, "I transferred to narcotics for a while, so it was part of the costume."

Nina said, "Do people tell you more if you look like a yeti?"

"Yeah, sometimes. Do I still get my five hundred grand if I just come with you and arrest everyone?"

She was crossing the room, paused as she reached his chair and looked down at him, like giving genuine thought to the matter. She said, "We might have to renegotiate."

They were veering away from how he'd seen things going a moment ago. Drinks at a bar, the cab together, maybe into bed if he was very lucky. But the real Nina wasn't on that wavelength just yet. She had the front door open.

He said, "And what are you going to do in the meantime?"

She turned back to him with the door half-open. "Probably the same as you: wonder whether I'm making the right decision."

She was still watching him as the door closed.

FIVE

LOS ANGELES, CA

Bobby Deen

Ever since the thing on the boat with the fat man, he couldn't get the woman out of his head. He'd see girls on the street that had her hair or her walk, accidental mimics that always made him double-take, and then put him back on the launch. Girls' voices too: he'd catch some turn of phrase, or a laugh, maybe hear someone say his name—Robbie misheard as Bobby, that kind of thing—and it was like she was right there with him.

All of that was fine, having her slip in at the edges of his thoughts, but he was finding now that the Daydream Nina was getting bolder, starting to show up front-and-center. Even at the funeral this morning, everyone either somber or in tears, he couldn't help but skew things slightly in his mind, wonder what would happen if the funeral was for her: Nina's face on those little program booklets, no Photoshop required. And how would the eulogies go? Did people actually know her, or would they just show up and sit there mute, everyone speculating?

She was with him again now as he was driving, heading up through the Bird Streets with Sunset behind him. There she was at the helm of the launch, plastic cuff still hanging from one wrist and her hair blowing straight back in the headwind. She'd stood out at the stern with him and watched the fat man submerge, the corpse hovering two feet under like some slack-jawed ghost, but if she had any thoughts on the matter she didn't share them.

The fat man's name was Lenny Burke, and he was still missing. He'd been muscle—or, as Lenny himself sometimes put it: mostly fat—for the Garcia crime family. Bobby had worked with him on and off over the years, so he knew him a little. It wasn't that he'd always aspired to shoot him, but when it came down to Lenny or Nina, it was pretty clear which way the scales leaned. But that was the funny thing as well: he never even had to weigh it up. There was only ever one option.

He hadn't even known she was in trouble until two days before the thing on the launch. He kept calling it that—"the thing on the launch," or "the thing on the boat"—instead of "the day I shot Lenny." If it really didn't bother him, he'd call it what it was. Anyway, Charles Stone called Bobby up and told him the situation: the Garcias had bought out a couple places in the Valley that still owed Charles money—circa two hundred K, so not exactly small change. The catch of course was that the Garcias weren't honoring the loan. Charles had sent Nina in to negotiate a buyout, and then heard nothing for twenty-four hours. He managed to keep it together on the phone though, and he was pretty succinct: "Kill them all if you like, I just want my wife back."

Bobby said he could do it.

He'd never worked for the Garcias—his cousin Jack had handled their shit. But with Jack dead now, he figured Lenny Burke would be running their cleanups.

He called Lenny and asked if he had any work on.

Lenny said, "Matter of fact, I do." Something about his tone, Bobby pictured him with his feet up on a desk, swinging back and forth in a swivel chair. Lenny said the Garcias had him on retainer, and that he had a cleanup job tomorrow that might be a two-man task. Bobby dropped by the next day, and sure enough, Nina Stone was the job. He'd met her a few times, but she didn't show it. She had a World

Series poker face, and it never slipped. He wondered if she'd had a plan of her own, given how long she went without looking rattled. Maybe she assumed he was in Lenny's corner. Maybe she'd been lining up a double hit.

Looking at it now though, it surprised him, how easily he'd committed to killing Lenny. Not that he regretted it, but clearly he was risking fatal penalties, stepping in on a Garcia job and smoking one of their guys. He could live with the risk, but he'd never thought about it at the time. As if everything was blurry beyond that tense little sphere: the three of them, out on open water.

He went up North Doheny and took a left at the top of the hill, heading for Charles's place. He could've told him the time didn't suit, almost ten P.M. on the day of cousin Jack's funeral. But a visit to Charles might mean a visit to Nina too, and that was the kind of possibility that canceled inconvenience. And here was the other funny thing: it was only since the day on the boat that she'd been on his mind. It was like the danger had brought it on, like they'd shared a tight situation, and now part of her was stuck to him. He didn't have another way to explain it.

He slowed just before the gate and pulled his hat on, tilted it just right so he wouldn't have to fuss with it getting out of the car. He was in a red Camaro Charles had hooked him up with—Frank Garcia himself had called to tell Bobby he was a dead man, so a change of ride seemed like a good idea. Frank actually seemed more pissed off about the boat, which was AWOL along with Lenny, but the thing that stuck in Bobby's mind was Frank's sign-off: "Tell Charles I was doing him a favor by getting rid of the girl. All she wanted was a side deal for herself, so you pass that on, see how happy he is to have her back. If he can't live with it, say he can just return to sender: we'll handle it right second time around."

He never passed that on, and he wondered if Frank had delivered the message himself.

Maybe that's what this was about.

He pulled up at the gate, and through the bars he could see the fountain in the middle of the turning circle, and behind it the house in its shallow curve, looking back down the canyon toward Sunset. Charles had another place up by Coldwater Canyon, on the north side of Mulholland. That place had better views, but this was the better zip code. The old man liked the prestige of the Bird Streets. He liked telling people he was in the same hood as DiCaprio.

Bobby lowered his window and pressed the intercom. "Hey. It's me."

The gate hummed and began to open. All the times he'd been here, he never had an answer when he pushed the button. He rolled through and parked on the far side of the fountain, and then got out and locked the car. It was quiet up here. No traffic noise, the night cool with a trace of pine. That was the tough thing about L.A.: you had to be rich to live in the clean air.

There was a light on in the foyer, shadows moving in the strip of frosted glass by the front door. He felt a little jolt, thinking it was Nina. He tried to dream up something clever, greet her with a pithy observation, but he was still stringing words together when the door opened. It wasn't her anyway. It was Charles's security chief, decked out tonight in full ballistic gear and an AR-15. He was Serbian or something, according to Charles, and he seemed to communicate solely by nodding. He nodded at Bobby as he stepped in, and then nodded to his right, meaning the boss man was in the living room, apparently.

Bobby gave him a nod in return and headed down the corridor as directed, and there was Charles incoming, the old boy hunched forward in his wheelchair for speed. Seventy-one years old with osteoporosis, but you wouldn't call him an invalid.

He coasted a few feet and said, "Thanks for coming up."

"It's all good."

"And sorry about your cousin, that's real shitty. I forgot you had the funeral this morning."

Bobby doubted that, but it came close to a genuine apology, and close was about as good as you got from Charles. He said, "It's fine."

The old boy pulled a neat one-eighty. There was a lump in his pocket Bobby knew was a Ruger .22. He packed heat, even at home. He said, "You heard any more on it?"

Bobby laid out the basics: Cousin Jack flew to New York to kill an NYPD informant. The informant knew about the contract, and snitched to a robbery cop called Miles Keller. Keller lay in wait and clipped Jack on the job.

Charles said, "Well, his name's out, so he can't have long."

Well, that was all up to Bobby, really. The Garcias wouldn't try anything. It wasn't their fault Jack fucked up, and revenge hits brought massive heat—especially if you took out a cop. The best tactic was to wait a year and then do it. Not that he was anxious to get it done—he didn't know Jack well enough to care—but honor was a different issue. Jack was family, and you had to be able to look in the mirror and say you'd done your best to balance the score. So he had Miles Keller on the black list in his head, awaiting action. The Garcias had got him the intel—a photo and the name. Detective Miles Keller, NYPD. He didn't have a firm plan yet, but that had its benefits in a way. He liked turning scenes over in his head: Keller coming out of some cop bar—the last patron at three A.M.—Bobby following him somewhere dark and then giving him the bullet. The setup needed work, though. Couldn't have Keller so drunk he didn't know what was happening, didn't know it was vengeance for Jack. There was no point to it, unless they died wishing they'd done things different.

He followed Charles to the end of the corridor and into the living room. Full-height windows faced down the canyon, the black hillsides studded randomly with the lights of other houses.

Charles said, "Never thought I'd have a problem, being cooped up in here. You know, watch DVDs, eat fast food all day. But it's shit, I tell you—doesn't matter how big the place is, you still go stir-crazy. Done so many laps I've got a squeaky wheel. Got the chair guy coming tomorrow."

There was a swimming pool out of sight on the slope below them, but the water made reflections on the ceiling—a shifting blue-vein pattern that blipped his Nina radar. He stood at the glass in case she was down there—nada.

Charles misread it as caution: "Yeah, don't worry, I got another guy down in the trees. I'm not taking any chances after the other week. They told me stay away from the windows, but you can't in this place, it's a fishbowl."

Bobby didn't answer. There were old film posters on the wall opposite the window, nineties moneymakers from Stone Studios' heyday: *Bloodhunter, Bloodhunter 2, Bloodhunter: Vengeance.* There was a TV in the corner playing some sci-fi show, and a guy of about thirty asleep on a sofa under a blanket.

Charles saw him looking and said, "Yeah, he's all good. Big day on the spirits, now he's sleeping it off."

The curve of the house meant he could see into other windows. A shadow moved, and his Nina radar blipped. False alarm—just a security man.

Bobby said, "How long you going to keep these guys here?"

"I don't know. Forever, if I have to. Probably get used to it, I guess."

Forever—Jesus. Bobby wouldn't last that long.

He had his seventy-year-old mother in lockdown in his Culver City apartment. He was sick of it already. His mom thought he was a producer for Stone Studios. She'd ridden that lie so long the truth would probably kill her. She still looked for him in the fine print on posters. She'd never found his name, but it didn't stop her telling people about his projects, films he'd never even heard of. He'd never confess he was a debt collector turned hit man.

Charles said, "You need a drink?" He wheeled to the island counter, a glossy slab of marble like something pillaged out of Rome. "I got a ton of whiskey, beer as well if you want."

The Nina radar blipped. There: a framed headshot on the counter.

Bobby said, "No, I'm good."

"You sure?"

"Yeah. I had a few already."

Charles wheeled over and joined him at the window. He didn't look so good close up: gray bristles and a couple of shaving nicks that had scabbed over, bags under his eyes and a lot of dangle around his jaw, like his face was trying to drip right off the bone. He wondered what Nina saw, what she felt when she heard the wheelchair inbound. Which way she rolled over in the bed.

Charles said, "I got something I need tidied up again. Figure you're my man, given the Garcia thing." He sucked a breath, and his voice went tight: "Oh shit, hang on." He made a fist and pressed it to his chest, leaned forward slowly in his chair. "Goddamn arrhythmia."

His other hand grabbed the Ruger. He always went for the gun when his ticker played up. He coughed and straightened. "Shit. There we go." He dug a pill container from his other pocket.

"You okay?"

"Yeah, it just takes off every so often. Have to ride it out a few seconds."

Bobby said, "Where's Nina?"

Charles knocked a pill back, eyes shut. He said, "That's the issue. I'm worried it's like the other day."

Not too worried, or he'd have come straight out with it. Bobby waited. The kid on the sofa stirred.

Charles said, "The Garcia thing obviously shook her up, she wanted some time out . . ."

"Sure."

"I sent her to the New York place, let her chill for a while. Therapeutic spending, and all that shit."

Bobby saw it now: Nina off on holiday, and then radio silence. It's a repeat of last time—

Charles said, "It's a repeat of last time. There's no fucking word from her."

He wondered if the old boy had his suspicions, whether Frank

Garcia passed on the message. Nina cutting side deals, out to make a buck of her own. He didn't seem panicked though.

Bobby said, "Where is she exactly?"

"The Manhattan place, in theory. But here's the thing: I got cameras in there, but I've got no feed. Everything's just coming in black."

Bobby wondered if the vacation was a hard sell, packing her off to New York, postabduction. The kid on the couch slurred "no, no, no" in his sleep.

Charles hiked a thumb at him. "You know that show *Hooked*? About the college professor, dreams up scams?"

Bobby shook his head.

"Well, anyway, he wrote it. Had a breakdown last week, working on this novel, can't get past chapter three. I said to him, well, you know, what's the issue, you just type something. He goes: none of the characters are talking." He shrugged. "I don't know. He tells me all the time they don't say anything, but then all he does is watch TV all day. I said to him, You won't make anyone talk unless you actually sit there and try and make them say something. You know?"

Bobby nodded. He wanted to bring things back to Nina, but he couldn't force it. He could see lights way off down the canyon, cars on a boulevard maybe. He figured traffic was the pure essence of L.A.: everyone came here because they were trying to make it, trying to get somewhere else.

He said, "You want me to bring her back?" As if he could take it or leave it, even with the Nina radar full volume, all his dials screaming Take the Fucking Job.

Charles said, "I don't know what's gone on, whether she needs bringing back, or what." His tone still down at blasé. Maybe it was drugs.

He said, "It's just one more thing I gotta worry about, you know? I've got this Garcia bullshit to handle, and then the buyout as well."

The buyout: Charles's business partner was selling his share.

Charles wanted to bring in clean money, turn the business honest. He'd started the studio with mob cash, but now lawbreaking didn't hold the same appeal. Bobby figured Charles wanted stress-free retirement.

The old man popped another pill. He cracked it between his molars and said, "I don't know whether she just wants no phone for a while, or whether someone's followed her up there. I'll email you some stuff." He nodded at the entry. "These guys got ears that go round corners."

Bobby said, "When did you last hear from her?"

"Two days ago."

Bobby didn't answer. He wanted a copy of the photo on the counter. But he knew he could tip this in his favor—

He said, "The Garcias have a contract out on me. I can't risk a job unless it's going to set me up for a while." His voice almost caught in his throat, the risk of missing out, losing another brush with Nina.

Charles took his time, and Bobby knew he was on the cusp of telling him Too Bad.

Four seconds.

Five.

Charles said, "Two-fifty. But for that, you fucking tidy up anything, on your own."

Bobby kept his eyes on the view, all those vast offerings out there in the dark, and he said, "Three." Knowing he was right out on the razor's edge now.

Charles rolled in close, shin-strike range. "Two-eighty. And that's my absolute ceiling. Even two-five's extortion."

Bobby said, "Fine, two-eighty," and felt his blood pressure nosedive.

He took his phone from his pocket as he turned from the window, stepped in close by the Nina photo on the counter. She'd been touched up slightly—stunning, coaxed to flawless. He snapped a picture. The flash leapt off the marble.

Charles saw him do it, but didn't ask. He said, "You fly out tomorrow morning. I've got you booked at five A.M. out of Burbank."

So the old boy *knew* he'd do it.

Charles said, "And it's a hundred percent on delivery—I'm not doing anything up front on those sort of numbers."

Tight bastard.

Bobby snapped another picture, HDR this time. He wanted to blow it up double size. Charles threw back another pill, and the kid on the sofa mumbled "no, no, no" as Bobby headed out.

SIX

Miles Keller

His room had no view—nothing to see other than the brick wall of the adjacent high-rise. There were still some windows lit, and now and then a human silhouette would pause, as if people could see him looking back.

It was far from perfect, this Nina situation, the main problem being that it was only with her out of sight that his logic started working. She seemed to cause a block on basic observation, inhibit the safety reflex that was finally yelling: big money means big risk. For half a million dollars, he was probably facing death or prison if things went south, but he didn't even know his obligations. How did she even do that: tell him nothing but the payoff, and still pique his interest?

Five hundred K and Nina. Maybe that could buy anything.

He'd walked away from bigger money on nothing more than a bad feeling, because he didn't like the guys involved, or some minor blemish on a résumé told him the risk wasn't worth it. His rule was to work with contacts of his own, or people Stanton vetted. By those standards, Nina was a bad idea. But every worry that arose had an image as a counterpoint—fatality was abstract, maybe a long way up the road, whereas Nina was right-now and real: Nina walking in the room, Nina with that bounce in her hair, Nina with her head back, laughing.

He opened his valise and took out an old business card. He'd had to surrender his badge, but there was no return policy on stationery. He stepped outside into the corridor and let the door tick gently shut behind him.

It was empty and quiet: just the dull sound of the elevators—the building's stomach-rumble. He walked three doors down, and stood outside Nina's room.

There was a soft edge of yellow light along the bottom of her door. He could go in, take up the conversation where they'd left off. See where they ended up, second time around. He raised a hand to knock, but caught himself an inch short, a sudden gut instinct saying:

Don't.

His knuckles hovered at the panel.

If he couldn't even knock, why take this any further?

He saw the light interrupted, a shadow and its twin, feet crossing the doorway. The light died, and he heard the faint click of the switch. She was standing there in the dark on the other side of the door. He pictured her with wet hair, maybe in a white hotel robe. Nothing wrong with that image, and not a bad starting point if he entered. She'd probably leave the light off, greet him with something wry and half-amused, maybe a question. He couldn't hear the words, but he could hear the rhythm of it, and she'd call him Detective: Something, something, something, Detective? Playful and rhetorical.

But he still couldn't knock.

He lowered his hand. Her door number showed a brass reflection, a skewed analogy of motion. He walked away quietly and pushed 1 on the elevator panel, rode down to the lobby with the same tune he'd had coming up.

The staff hadn't changed yet—still the same two guys he'd seen when Stanton dropped him off. The concierge was pacing in slow motion just outside the door, looking at his clasped hands like he was on the brink of some profound announcement. The deskman glanced up as Miles approached.

"Hello, sir."

Miles said, "Hi. I have a couple of colleagues booked on my floor. I just need to check if it's Nina Stone in fifteen-oh-three."

He knew immediately that she'd checked in as someone else. The guy didn't recognize the name. He looked at his computer and frowned and clicked and scrolled.

"No . . . we've got a Joan Ryder in fifteen-oh-three."

Miles put his business card on the desk, slid it forward with an index finger. The guy's eyes dropped to it for a long moment and then he raised them again, knowing an instruction was coming.

Miles said, "I need to see the ID she checked in with."

The guy sucked air through his teeth as he looked away. "Yeah, man, I don't know . . ."

Miles said, "What happened to 'sir'?"

The guy made a little shape with his mouth, trying to broach something delicate. He said, "Look . . ."

Miles waited.

The guy said, "That's not a badge or a warrant, is it?"

Miles said, "She told you herself, we're colleagues. So we know each other, and you can show me what you have on file. Or, if we don't know each other, why'd you tell her I was in the building?"

The guy didn't answer.

Miles hadn't moved yet, still standing there with his finger on the card like it needed anchorage. He said, "You called her thirty minutes ago, told her I'd showed up. Which is fine if we know each other. Serious breach of my privacy if we don't. I'm sure management would agree."

The guy looked out at the concierge, still pacing. He said, "Look, I gotta get approval."

Miles shook his head. "No you don't. You didn't need approval to tell her I was in the building, you don't need approval to show me her ID."

The guy wasn't sold on it, but Miles could tell he was almost there. He said, "It's easy. Either I make a complaint that includes your name, or we can tidy this up right now and go our separate, happy ways."

A minute later he was in the elevator, a folded sheet of paper in his hand. Back in his room, he sat down in the armchair—Nina's armchair —her perfume in the air, her water carton on the floor beside him, still covered in a light sweat. His printout from the desk showed the New York State driver's license and Visa she'd checked in with, both in the name Joan Ryder. It was definitely her face in the photo, and the date of birth was about right. The license was seven years old, only ten months from expiry. He wondered if it was fake, or if she had more of a story.

He picked up the bedside phone and dialed his NYPD partner, Pam Blake. He figured she'd still be up. Either she worked overtime, or she worked on her retirement scheme, a script for a TV show about a one-legged ex-cop she'd told Miles was destined for HBO.

She said, "Shit, you're still in that hotel." Seeing the caller ID.

He pulled the console across to his lap. "How did you know it's me, and not someone else, happens to be staying here? Call up hoping for a soothing voice, get greeted with obscenities."

"Yeah, well. They call me up at one A.M., they deserve it."

Miles said, "Thought you'd be burning the candle at both ends."

"Yeah, I was. Just got home."

"From what?"

"From surveillance you could've helped me with if you'd stayed in FID's good books, stopped shooting people."

Oh God. He didn't want to run through this.

She said, "Where've you been, man? Why you living in hotels?"

He gave himself a moment, looking for the way through. He said, "Because I'm facing difficult circumstances."

Quiet on the line, and he knew he was stuck in the weeds now. He pinched the bridge of his nose.

She said, "Can you just tell me one thing?"

"Depends on the thing."

"I keep hearing shit . . ."At least she was struggling to say it. "Like, that your shooting wasn't clean—"

"Oh Christ. Who's saying that?"

"I don't know. I've just heard it. Look, I just . . ."

He waited.

"I heard they pulled bits of paper out of the guy's wound, but they couldn't tell where it had come from. Like he had paper in his pocket or something . . ."

He was still pinching the bridge of his nose, and he closed his eyes, too.

She said, "Look, however it went down, I don't care, I honestly don't give a shit. But you can tell me about it. People say you were waiting for him . . ."

Miles sighed, looked at the window and then looked around his bare hotel room. He said, "I got a call, totally out of the blue, this old CI I used to run, woman named Lucy Gates. Had her for a while when I was with the narcs, down at Brooklyn South . . ."

Even with all he'd been through with Force Investigation, writing up the report in the most cautious language, he still wasn't sure how to put it to her. He decided to go with the moral summary, give her the right spin on everything.

He said, "Way I see it, it's kind of like splitting hairs, whether I lay in wait or I didn't. This guy, he flew all the way from L.A. to kill her. That's a six-hour flight, plus a solid drive for him to actually think it through. You know: whether shooting someone's a good idea. But he didn't. So why does it matter who was there first: me or him?"

Pam didn't answer.

Miles said, "Anyway, that's me. How's things with you?"

He normally steered clear of that question. She had a husband with debts and bowel cancer. Miles had given her ten grand toward one or the other. She thought it was honest profit, but he'd taken the money from a crime scene in Astoria, and then swapped it for chips at Caesars in Atlantic City. He spent a couple hours at the slot machines to give the right impression, and then banked the remaining ninety-eight hundred dollars as clean gambling profit.

He heard a light click on at her end. She said, "I'm doing okay." Drawing it out slow, reluctant to come away from his story. "Gonna call the show *Moonlight*. 'Cause of the whole nighttime thing, but also the guy's working unofficially, you know? Like, moonlighting."

"Nice." He held his printout by the fold and waved it up and down, bird wings in slow-mo.

She said, "Main dude's a real lazy-ass, doesn't give a fuck, but now he's finding because of the amputation, can't be a cop anymore, he's actually got his passion back, being real diligent. Kinda cool."

"Yeah, nice."

She said, "So what do you want?"

He held his paper still, looked at the Visa and DL copies. He wanted her to run the details, check out this Joan Ryder moniker. But he couldn't pull her into it. What if they had something on file—Joan Ryder, wanted for grand theft? He'd have to admit how he came by the name, and then say good-bye to half a million bucks and a sweet retirement. He shouldn't have picked up the phone. It was a common theme with Nina business: you do the thing, and then wish you hadn't, wish you'd thought about it more.

He said, "Just wanted to see how you're doing."

She coughed soggily and said, "And you like the sound of my voice, right?"

"Yeah, that too."

"What do you want, Keller?"

"I told you what I want."

"What's on the piece of paper you're holding?"

Idiot. She'd heard the flapping.

Miles said, "Nothing. It's hotel stationery."

"Your voice sounds different when you lie."

"I didn't want to admit to my paper-dart hobby."

She said, "Makes you seem more suspicious, you don't even tell me what you want."

Miles figured that was still no reason for total honesty. He said, "I'll see you, Pam."

SEVEN

Bobby Deen

Here was his problem. He got swept up in The Life before he could assess the cost of it.

The Life:

Charles described it as the B-list. You hang out with bagmen, bent cops, blackmailers, B-and-E artists, bone breakers, numerous bastards. He said Bobby would be the perfect fit.

They'd met in '97. Bobby had scored work on *Bloodhunter* as an extra. He was a nuke-frazzled cabdriver, briefly visible as the steroid-pumped hero who checks out a wrecked L.A. The scene got cut, but it let him cross paths with Charles Stone. He saw him on set at the Fox lot, and then again two days later, getting into his car by the Stone Studios office. Bobby knew he hated walk-ups, but he went and spoke to him anyway. He'd planned on small talk, but it didn't transpire: he just stood in front of the guy and asked for more work.

In those days, Charles was pre-Nina and pre-rehab. He checked Bobby out carefully, a head-to-toe scan, put a hand on his shoulder and told him he was loaded on whiskey and coke. If Bobby wanted a job, he could drive him home.

Why not? A quick hundred bucks, and he got to drive a Mercedes. Charles was still in the Mulholland place back then, and when they pulled up he said another DUI would really screw him—if Bobby wanted to play chauffeur again, there was a guesthouse out back. Be ready at nine thirty tomorrow. Bobby said that sounded fine. He'd been unsure what Charles meant by "whiskey and coke"—whether he preferred the soda or the powder.

That was all clarified in due course, as the guesthouse had a view across the pool to the main living room, and for two hours he could see through the French doors as Charles downed Johnnie Walker with a half-dozen lines on the side.

There was plenty more driving—chauffeur work, and then courier duty, too. Charles's drug habit was an economy in black duffels. He'd load up a bag of cash, and Bobby would take it down to a guy in the Valley, swap it for a load of coke. It wasn't until he'd made the trip three or four times that he realized he'd go to prison if he was pulled over. He stopped by Charles's office on the Fox lot and told him his payments should reflect his risk. Charles was bloodshot, half-lidded, slack-jawed. Common symptoms, and they could've meant last night was huge, or this morning was heavier than usual. Charles rubbed his gum with a finger and said, "How far do you want to take that principle?"

Bobby didn't answer. He didn't know what he meant.

Charles said, "I got as much risk as you want. And there's plenty of reward, too. You just got to tell me when you want out."

So there was the issue: he never said stop. And when you're on forty grand a month, there's a big incentive to not think too carefully. Or at least keep any moralism on hold.

He paid cash for his car, the subpenthouse apartment in Century City, his wedding to Connie five years ago. She was an actress, and he'd seen her at Charles's parties and around the studio a few times—even in crowds she could catch his eye—but it took him two months before he finally asked her to dinner.

They went to Spago in Beverly Hills, and he drank enough to reach the point of zero inhibition. He told her he was a failed actor and that the closest he came to movies was dropping off Charles Stone at his office. He knew it was a good confession—the look of slight amusement as she listened, as if all she heard was false modesty. He asked about her own career, whether hanging out at studios had brought her any work. He thought he'd torn it with that last line, making her sound like a cult groupie or something, but she told him she frequented studios only for the good-looking men.

They married four months later.

It was a month posthoneymoon before he realized it wouldn't last—that fighting full-time didn't count as happiness.

With a split imminent, her death seemed like Bobby's fault: like God had leant an ear and heard the breakup pleas. Put the drugs in her system and sent her off the balcony. She was so high she was limp and silent the whole way, like she was already dead when she left the rail. He was never going to lose that image, and he'd never forget being there too late—nothing he could do but scream at the drop. Even watching felt like free fall.

He thought he'd never get over it. He'd had to buy a ground-floor condo. He'd find himself staring at the view from the edge, thinking this would be a good way to join her.

These days he worried he'd see her soon whether he jumped or not. He still had the six-figure pay, but he had the risk, too. For a long time it felt like there was nothing on the line. Maybe that was just a normal part of youth: that false certainty that your life wasn't on the risk ledger. But then he shot Frank Garcia's man, Lenny Burke, that day on the boat with Nina, and finally he could see the stakes. The jeopardy didn't stop at him. Payback could harm his mother. He wondered why knowledge so basic hadn't shown up sooner. Nothing that important should come crashing down on you, too late to make a difference.

A text message woke him: the flight was with Billion Air—a private outfit that flew out of Burbank. Charles had dirt on the CFO that had secured cut-price fares for a decade.

It was three A.M. He browsed the internet on his phone. News updates delayed him twenty minutes before he flicked to his Nina photos. The portrait shots had come up well. The reflections were minor, and the focus was perfect. He'd studied them last night on the drive home, every stoplight another look. She was locked in his head now, making false memories: he could see her in place of Connie, a face swap for all their big moments. That dinner at Spago, their wedding and the honeymoon. The Daydream Nina trying to phase out his dead wife.

That couldn't be all bad.

He was out of bed at three thirty, feeling rough with lack of sleep. He showered and dressed and put the TV on to try and reset his head. His thoughts were in a weird state. He jumped from Daydream Nina to the Grim Reaper. There had to be middle ground, no anxiety or fantasy. New York could fix it. The city that made dreams could solve his payback woes and bring him Nina. Anxiety gone, fantasy promoted to the real thing. He wouldn't even need the photos.

He put the TV on low and wandered to kill time. The condo was way bigger than he needed: four bedrooms, and a Jacuzzi tub in his bathroom. He used a bedroom as an office. It was full of framed Stone Studios crap that Charles had given him—posters from the *Bloodhunter* TV spinoff, obscure B-grade films that Bobby had never heard of. He would've tossed it all, but it helped with impressions. His mother thought they were the hallmarks of Hollywood success. He'd moved her in the day he saved Nina on the boat, told her there'd been a terrorist threat to the studio—possibly from ISIS. He told her he was following an FBI edict. She'd been easy to persuade. She'd lived in fear of Muslims for about twenty years.

He knocked on her bedroom door.

"Is that you?"

He said, "Yeah, it's me."

"Just give me a minute."

He went into the kitchen and turned on the coffee machine. He didn't see the point of it—a two-foot cube that served no function other than putting fluffy milk in your caffeine. But it was a gift from

Charles, and anything from Charles was a twofold burden: the thing itself, and the obligation to use it.

He was drinking a cappuccino when she joined him. She wore two gowns and a scarf even at this time of year, the garments trapped close by folded arms, and she swayed as she moved, as if she'd walked miles from her bedroom.

She said, "It's bad luck wearing hats indoors."

She told him that a lot, but it was easier not to query these rulings.

She said, "You tilt it back more, people can see your face. Much nicer."

He didn't answer, let her come over and fuss with his tie, brush nonexistent lint off his shoulder. It was a routine she couldn't break. He'd never worn a suit she couldn't improve.

He said, "I have to go to New York for a few days."

She touched his elbows as she leaned back to appraise him. "Okay. That sounds nice."

She took a mug from a cupboard and held it two-handed as it filled at the machine, standing slightly hunched as if she needed the warmth. He didn't know if it was feigned or genuine—this thing about always feeling frozen. Maybe she thought there was a role to play, the elderly mother growing delicate and needy, the child turned caregiver, life adhering to some mapped symmetry.

He said, "I don't want you to leave the building while I'm away—"

"Why, what's wrong?"

"I'll order the groceries online and have them sent to reception—"

"What's wrong?" The machine finished with a groan and a click.

He said, "You don't need to worry about it. It's bullshit, but I have to follow instructions."

Let her build the story: the best excuses were of others' making, tales he could nod to.

She said, "Is it this terrorist thing?" Then quieter: "With the Muslims?"

He nodded. "Yeah."

"Have they hurt someone?"

"They haven't told me details. They just said stay home, and you'll be fine. I don't think it's serious, but it's bad P.R. if someone's beheaded."

"They won't look here though?"

He shook his head. "Nobody knows this is mine."

She stood with a hip to the counter, looking pained, holding her mug close as if for comfort. He knew the drama of it appealed: she had peripheral contact with the stuff of headlines, the forces that shape eras. What a thrill. All she had to do was stay home and watch Kardashians.

He said, "I've got three days of meetings, so we'll reassess when I'm back. I'm supposed to get a briefing tomorrow."

That was good: like he was owed courtesy, made privy to hard data. He wondered how she'd frame it, what she'd tell herself about his trip. She'd seen him in the small print of movie posters that never bore his name—on that basis she could make his "meetings" with anyone. Maybe he was catching up with old presidents.

He finished his coffee, and she started on a long theory about how this was the revenge of ISIS, payback for the studio's depiction of women. They didn't like girls being uncovered and empowered. He zoned out fast. He rinsed his mug and went and fetched his bag from his room. He was sick of walking in circles. He might as well drive to kill time. He went back to the kitchen and his mother was still there, monologue complete, cradling her drink and looking at him with eyebrows raised.

She said, "You agree?"

"Yeah. Totally."

She hobbled to the living room and lowered herself to a sofa, lots of wince and caution. She and the leather sighed in unison. She changed the channel from news to faux reality: plastic-looking people trading gossip over coffee. She'd settled into house arrest already. The danger was abstract, negated.

He was living one excuse at a time, but he'd made it this far. Now he just had to draft the next mistruth, decide how he'd get her out of here.

He kissed her cheek and headed out.

He was up at Burbank by four thirty. He left the car in the Billion Air lot off Thornton, and a stretch limo took him around to the private gate on West Empire, and then out across the tarmac to the private terminal. A trio of bleach-white Gulfstream jets were being refueled, and there was a rank of four stretch limos lined up nearby. It looked billionaire-appropriate.

The driver let him out ten feet from the terminal door, and he went inside to the waiting area. The rich were trusted travelers: no security, just a smiling attendant at a check-in desk, and then nothing but leather furniture and free food. He gave the attendant his details, and she told him he was the first to arrive.

"I thought I had a plane to myself."

"No, sir. Mr. Stone booked two others in your party."

It made sense five minutes later: another limousine pulled up, and Charles's head of security got out, along with another guy Bobby recognized from last night. They'd swapped their ballistics gear for suits and ties.

Bobby said, "Chrissake," and headed outside to the tarmac with his bag, into the high whine of turbofans on idle, and a deeper rumble farther off as a 737 lifted off the runway. He climbed the shaking steps to their appointed Gulfstream, into a cocoon of leather and that metal taste of bottled air, like a taste of the future—the morning-breath of androids. A beaming pilot with a flawless tan welcomed him aboard. Bobby took out his phone and headed for the tail as he dialed Charles.

"Bobby, what do you want?"

"I didn't know you were sending minders. I thought the whole point was I'm tidying this up myself."

Charles gave him dead air. Bobby ducked for a porthole view and saw the two guys heading out to join him, carrying their own bags, two duffels apiece—probably guns galore.

Charles said, "So what's the fucking problem? You got backup, big deal."

"Who's watching your place?"

"I got other people."

Bobby said, "I don't like doing jobs with guys I don't know."

"Holy shit, grow a pair. It's my job, I get to use my people. I thought that'd be simple enough to wrap your head around."

He didn't answer.

Charles said, "Is it that you don't trust them, or you don't trust yourself to act like a normal human being?"

"It's a hierarchy thing. Is someone in charge, or are we all meant to run around doing what we like?"

"No, I think it's called cooperation. Look, don't call me up expecting I'm going to make you scout leader or something. I don't give a shit about who does what, so long as everything's fixed. So why don't you give me a call when you got something good to tell me."

He heard the tone go flat in his ear, and then the first guy was at the top of the stairs, smiling at Bobby like he'd guessed the nature of the call.

Bobby said, "I thought I was flying solo."

The guy took a seat midway down, facing aft. It was a plush setup: cream leather chairs in bays of two-by-two, with an aisle down the center. He nodded at Bobby's phone and said, "Thought you might change the old boy's mind?"

Bobby didn't answer. The guy had a heavy accent, Eastern European. He sat down opposite him, saw the second man appear at the top of the stairs.

The first guy said, "Charles said to tell you we're the best backup money can buy. So be grateful."

"Question is, does the backup do as it's told?"

The guy ignored him, looked idly out the porthole. He said mildly,

"Well, it's a pleasure to meet you properly. I'm Marko." He tilted his head at his companion as the second guy took a seat across the aisle. "This is Luka." He opened the drinks compartment in the panel next to them, lifted out a bottle of mineral water, and opened it with a muted crack. He said, "People always say you're the hat man, and now I get why it sticks." He nodded at Bobby. "It's not just the hat, it's the fucking stare that goes with it." He had some water and said, "Like a psychopath looking past a razor or something."

The pair of them spoke briefly in a foreign dialect and laughed. They both had a lean and weathered look that made it hard to guess their age. They could have been anywhere between thirty-five and fifty.

A steward came through and asked for drinks orders. Bobby kept his eyes on Marko and said that he was fine. The other two passed as well. The steward caught the vibe and backed off, ran through the safety check from the front of the plane. Luka hooked up earbuds and closed his eyes. Marko returned Bobby's stare while the steward told them crisis protocols.

The plane began to taxi.

Marko said, "Don't think we're just tagging along as extra baggage while you bring the trophy wife back. We know what we're doing."

"Sure."

Marko smiled. "All I know is the bitch has financial aspirations of her own. So if she's double-crossed Mr. Stone, I'm not going to be happy."

Financial aspirations. Maybe Frank Garcia had tipped him off . . .

Bobby said, "You mean Nina's going to be in trouble? Good luck."

Marko held the wall to brace himself on a corner. The plane straightened up and he said, "I don't know what you're getting out of this. But the prevailing opinion of Bobby Deen is that you hang around Charles Stone because you like his wife an awful lot."

Bobby didn't answer.

Marko said, "So you just be thankful we keep our observations to ourselves. Word got out, he might make you fly United."

"You can tell him what you like."

Marko shrugged. "All right. But are you coming along to bring her back, or are you coming along to get in her pants?"

Bobby didn't answer. They were both looking at him now, the second man's eyes fixed on him from across the aisle.

The plane roared as it accelerated.

The takeoff pinned him to his seat.

EIGHT

Miles Keller

Police had bland parlance for everything, killings included, so the event that had made his life come apart was simply an officer-involved shooting. A phone call set it in motion: a Sixty-seventh Precinct watch commander got in touch to say that a confidential informant was trying to reach him. The CI's name was Lucy Gates. Miles hadn't seen her in six years, but he called her anyway.

He said, "Thing about being a confidential informant, you're not meant to tell people you're a confidential informant."

"Yeah, nice to talk to you, too." She sounded out of breath, but he didn't know then what it meant. She said, "What they don't tell you, once you don't want to play the snitch game anymore, they don't want to hear from you. You call the number and ask for the transfer, nothing happens. You call the precinct direct though, they go on about how you're not meant to call them, and there's a special number. Maybe you could get them all to sit down together and figure that one out."

Miles said, "How can I help you?"

"There's a car outside my house that's been there for three days."

He said, "Call nine-one-one," and left it at that.

She called him back twenty minutes later.

She said, "Look. This isn't some bullshit tactic to win sympathy. I already called nine-one-one, each time they come past he's already gone."

"You think I'll have better luck?"

"Oh God." He let her have a moment. She said, "You remember I told you once, there was a guy used to come by the bar, sit there with a drink just staring all the time? Told you he looked like a pervert, you said he was probably a hit man?"

He did remember, but he didn't answer.

Lucy said, "I called the cops twice on him now, they don't seem to take me seriously. But read my lips"—it didn't make sense on the phone, but Miles got the point—"I'm dying of emphysema, and I got a killer outside my house in a white Buick."

He couldn't say no to that.

He'd been seconded to a BAND task force that month—Brooklyn Anti-Narcotics Drive—which meant he'd spent the last three weeks driving confiscated cars, looking for drugs. He logged out a gray Dodge Challenger and drove up to Lucy's place in Queens. She lived on a street of detached clapboard houses in Astoria, on a block that had been gentrified since his last visit. He saw a lot of fresh paint and swing sets. There were more windows with flower boxes than steel grilles now.

He could see Lucy's place coming up on the left. It was a former crack house she'd inherited from her old boss, a strip-joint owner called Manny Lyons. The house was looking okay now the addicts had moved on. Lucy had given it some paint, a shade of yellow that was vibrant but not quite to Miles's taste, and she'd taken the bars off the windows. There were cars parked almost solid on both sides, but the Buick stood out, bright white and brand-new, the latest Verano model.

The Dodge had smoked windows, and a stereo almost as bassy as its V-8. Miles turned on FM radio and cranked the volume up, figured he was doing a fine job of looking like a gangbanger on the prowl. He eased off the gas a touch, cruised past the Buick doing fifteen miles an hour, and saw that sure enough, there was an L.A. hit man named Jack Deen sitting in the driver's seat.

He didn't get a long look, but Jack had the kind of features you didn't need to see twice. Black hair in a short ponytail, so taut it seemed to yank his whole face back, the zit-pocked cheekbones pointing right at you. He had shades on, flashy silver Ray-Bans that only made him more conspicuous.

Miles kept going for a couple of blocks, pulled over where he could still watch the Buick in his side mirror. He took out his cell phone and called Lucy.

He said, "Yeah. You've got a guy watching your house."

"Are you going to shoot him?"

"He has to shoot first, is the problem."

"But you recognize him, right? He used to come by Manny's."

"Mmm."

"So who is he?"

Miles said, "I don't know," figuring a lie was safest. Better than saying a hit man had flown out from California and appeared to be lining her up.

She said, "So what are you going to do?"

"Sit and watch him watching you. Don't let anyone in, unless it's me."

"How will I know it's you?"

Miles said, "I'll whistle 'Yankee Doodle' in D major."

It was after four in the afternoon. He sat there another fifty minutes, watching Jack Deen watching the house, and when the Buick finally started up and moved off the curb, Miles followed.

They headed east out to Flushing, and Jack pulled in at a motel, a place called OTE by virtue of misfired neon. There was an auto repair place next door, and a diner opposite. Miles watched the Buick go around the building to the rear lot, and then he parked around the corner on the next block.

BAND undercover duty always meant nice equipment. In the trunk, he had a black duffel with about fifty pounds of ballistics gear: Glocks, an MP5K, two-hundred-odd rounds of nine-mil ammunition, a Kevlar vest, even combat boots in case things got dangerous underfoot.

He pulled the shoelace out of one of the boots and walked back around the corner toward the motel. He was almost at the parking lot when Jack Deen came out the front door by reception, the man only fifteen feet away but not clocking him. Miles let him cross the street and started down the little vehicle lane toward the rear lot, and when he glanced back Jack was stepping in the front door of the diner.

The lot was at two-thirds capacity, no one around except a guy by a Camry fussing with a suitcase, trying to collapse the telescopic handle. Miles tied a little slipknot in the middle of the shoelace as he walked to the Buick, held the cord at each end to keep it taut, and slid it carefully down behind the window frame of the driver's door. He eased the loop down over the lock button, tugged the slipknot closed, and then raised the string again to unlock the door. Twenty seconds, all up.

The horn chirped briefly, pissed off that he'd gained access without the key remote, but the noise shut off when he got in and locked the doors again. The guy with the suitcase glanced at him and then went back to his fiddling.

Miles checked the glove compartment. Jack had tourist brochures, a rental agreement for the car, and a folded sheaf of online booking printouts, all neatly clipped together. He'd been sloppy with precautions. Everything was on the same credit card in the name of Jackson Deen. He'd flown in four days ago. His flight back to L.A. was tomorrow night, a 12:00 A.M. red-eye. He'd been so lax with his papers, Miles thought he'd find a picture of Lucy, maybe a note saying, Clip her, Jack. There was nothing that damning, though. The last page was a Major League booking: Yankees vs. Orioles, 1:05 P.M. tomorrow.

The Toyota Camry started up and drove past. Miles saw the suitcase on the backseat, handle still extended. He got out and locked the Buick and walked out to the curb. The diner had windows full-width on the street-facing side, and he could see Jack Deen sitting over to the right, in the corner booth, working hard on something with his cutlery. Miles waited for a break in the traffic and then started across the street, made it to the other side before he changed his mind about how to handle things.

He would've enjoyed it actually, sitting down opposite the killer from L.A., maybe drink a coffee while the hit man finished his eggs, whatever he was having. They could run through old cases Miles knew—various people found dead by gunshot while Jack was in town, witnesses who fingered Deen for killings and then ended up deep-sixed themselves. So Miles could run that down for him, let the dead have their moment, and then tell Jack the game was up. He could see the whole thing: Jack's flat expression as he sat listening, no lights on behind his eyes, at least nothing on the human wavelength.

And that was partly why he walked away from it: remembering the fact that some of these guys represent a whole new species. But that Yankees booking had snagged in his head, so it was baseball, really, that clinched the ruling. There was no point talking sense with a guy who planned to see a ballgame once he'd killed a woman. He could picture Jack in the stands, in the sun with a hot dog, clean conscience and kissing sauce off his fingers, and he thought: Why the hell try to save him? Surely the quickest route to fairness was to let things unfold as Jack planned. At least up to a point.

It was after six in the evening when he showed up back at Lucy's. She answered the door holding an oxygen tank on a little two-wheeled trolley, and she had a transparent plastic mask dangling around her neck. She looked good though, despite the gear. She'd be late thirties now, Miles thought, but she still seemed trim and lithe. She had on tight blue jeans and a wool sweater, cuffs pushed back to show off lean forearms. She let the door go and put a hand on her hip, letting him see its curve, and the nice line all the way down her side. If it weren't for the air tank, he'd say time was treating her just fine.

She said, "I wondered if I'd see you again."

He spread his hands slightly, let them fall.

She said, "I'm trying to imitate that guy from *No Country for Old Men*. You know the one with the stun gun on the air tank?" She had brownish hair cut shoulder-length and combed behind her ears, a few loose strands hanging forward, giving it character.

Miles said, "You're better-looking."

"Yeah. I'm working on getting uglier."

He didn't know what to say to that.

She lifted the mask and had a hit of oxygen. "So you figured out I'm not talking bullshit?" Her voice sounded nasally through plastic.

He came inside and closed the door. "You've definitely got a watcher. He's at a motel out in Flushing."

Still with the mask on, she said, "Did you deal with him?"

"I haven't shot him and thrown him in a river yet."

It was a weird reunion—their only meeting in years, and the first talking point was a thug.

Miles said, "He's flying home tomorrow. He'll visit tonight, or you won't see him at all."

She kept her eyes on him, waiting to hear what he was going to do about it.

Miles said, "I'll hang around here, wait for him to show up."

He thought he sounded pretty mild, but she was still watching him, as if he might come clean, tell her things were dire. But he held his silence and stood there looking pleasant.

She said, "Maybe we should have coffee. You okay with instant?"

She wouldn't let him help her. She sat him down in the living room and talked to him from the kitchen, no issue with her volume. She said she got the diagnosis a year ago, the week after her thirty-seventh birthday. The doctor told her that was young even for a heavy smoker. She figured it must have been secondhand fumes that helped it along, working in the backroom for Manny, having to wave a hand to cut a path through the fog. Miles sat watching the street, waiting for Jack to show up again, and Lucy went on telling him about lungs, how the healthy types consist of dense tissue, but emphysema lungs get broken down, start looking fibrous and stringy, kind of like chewing gum if you stretched it apart. The thinner it gets, the less air you take in, and you obviously reach the point where you can't breathe at all, and in other words you're dead.

The exposition was getting louder as she made her way back down the hall, and she was in the room again on that last phrase, framed in the door tugging the air trolley and carrying a mug with the other hand as she said "dead."

Miles worried they were going morbid too early. He said, "You look like you're coping okay."

"Yeah, I guess. They don't know how fast or slow it'll progress. I might stay like this forever, or I might have no lungs left in ten years."

"How long have you had the tank?"

"Couple months. It's a prevention thing. I breathe all right, but it just takes the edge off if I'm on my feet all day. Apparently if you go around not getting enough air, it makes your arteries thicken up, gives you high blood pressure. So then you've got heart disease and stroke to worry about, too. Or that's the doctor's theory, anyway."

She grinned, like the information was more entertainment than prognosis, set the drink down for him on a coffee table.

She said, "Give me a sec, I'll grab the other one."

"I can get it."

"No, stay there." She was at the door before he was half out of his seat. At least she didn't seem inhibited at all.

Once she was back in the room, he said, "You know why you'd be targeted?"

"No, but I could guess." She smiled and said, "Old informants must get murdered all the time."

Miles said, "You got somewhere you can stay for a night?"

She sat down heavily and sighed into the mask, fogging the plastic. "What do you think?"

"I can put you in a hotel."

She shook her head. "No thanks." She held his gaze, making sure he knew she meant it. She said, "I used to get crackheads showing up, wondering if this place is still in business. Had a couple wanted to come inside, actually. First guy I had, he kicked the shit out of the door, actually broke the lock so it was just the chain keeping it shut. Didn't think I had time to reach the phone, but I had the vacuum cleaner right there in the hall, took the end piece off it, so it was just the steel tube, held it up like this." She mimed holding a shotgun, raising it to her shoulder. "Pushed the end of it out the gap in the door, guy backed up so fast he tripped on the step. I got a real one, now. Next guy tried coming in, I didn't have to say a word."

She adjusted a valve on the top of the tank, and Miles told her he had to make a call.

He used the phone in her kitchen and called Wynn Stanton in his office.

Miles said, "It's me. Can you send someone around to my place for the night, just to answer the phone? I need to show a call being put through. The apartment, I mean."

"What're you up to?"

"Hopefully nothing."

Stanton said, "Oh, God. Yeah, all right. You got Netflix there? I can send Kenny."

Back in the living room he found Lucy on her feet again waiting for him, the tank trolley beside her and the frame tethered gently by curled fingers, the way you might take a child by the hand.

She raised the mask. "You going to shoot him when he shows up?"

Miles said, "Hopefully not."

She said, "But you're making up alibis just in case."

"It's not an alibi. But it's better if it looks like I wasn't waiting for him all night. Premeditation's not a nice word."

"More heroic if people think you dashed here in your PJs, clocked him in the nick of time?"

Miles said, "Something like that."

They ordered takeout pizza for dinner and had it delivered. Lucy went upstairs around eight thirty, and Miles stayed in the living room and watched the street. He'd moved a chair to a far corner so he was well back from the window, and he left a reading lamp on so he could still make out the space.

Jack Deen's rented Buick Verano showed up a little before ten thirty, and reclaimed the space it had used earlier. Miles had brought the cordless phone through from the kitchen. Watching the street, he dialed his apartment landline. Kenny answered, TV noise in the background—the terse, formal cadence of an old film, that bygone era of black and white.

Miles said, "This is Miles."

Kenny said, "Ha. I'm watching your Netflix."

"Just stay on the line for me."

Miles counted to twenty-five in his head and then said, "Thanks, Kenny. You can go home now."

He hung up quietly and sat watching the road, Jack Deen invisible behind his windshield. It took him fifty minutes to finally emerge. No working streetlights on this stretch, and Miles could only see the shape of him as he climbed out of the car. Not a sound as he closed his door. There was a party farther up the street, a few guys hanging out in a garage with a boom box, and he watched Jack spend a minute checking them out, motionless beside his car with his head slightly cocked. The odd shout was audible, but no one sounded sober. Drunk was safe, as far as witness statements went. No one cares for plastered oaths.

He saw Jack cross the street, coming at him on a diagonal, an easy stride in silhouette, nothing in the shadow man's hand yet. Miles sat waiting, raised his gun when he heard Jack on the wooden step outside. A light tread, soft and measured. He wasn't hyped with adrenaline, but then neither was Miles. All afternoon, he'd seen this as the end point, some variation of guns-by-night. Now he couldn't change it: a convergence of Jack's doing. He just had to sit and wait for it to happen.

The hit man reached the door: fake church bells tolling as he pressed the button.

Miles sat waiting with his gun raised. Jack would've had an easy job if she'd just opened up for him. Give her two on the step and then be on his way, tomorrow's ballgame to enjoy. Miles heard him try the door: a click, a pause, and then a creak like some demented birdcall.

He heard the tongue tap gently on the catch and then Jack's feet on the hallway carpet. Silence, no motion. Maybe he was trying to seek out held breaths. He had the stairs ahead of him, but the light in the living room would be beckoning, too. He'd want to clear the ground floor first.

Miles watched him step into the living room, tracked him with the gun midway across the room, and said, "Hey, Jack."

He didn't jump or seem to get a fright. He just stopped and faced him square.

He said, "Huh. I remember you." Casual—like this wasn't life and death. He had a gray suit on over a white shirt, open at the neck, probably wanting to look like a killer with good taste.

Miles said, "People always leave their door open for you?"

Jack said, "Where's Lucy?" Which seemed like an odd note for a hit man to touch: too personal. Miles thought he'd be asking for the girl.

Miles said, "I kind of hoped you'd come in packing heat so I'd have an excuse to drill you. But here you are, walk in empty-handed."

Jack didn't answer.

Miles said, "So are you gonna go for it, or what?"

Jack said, "You got the wrong end of this."

There was a creak in the corridor outside, and they both looked over at the noise, Lucy standing there with no mask, no tank, but with a shotgun up at shoulder level.

They both shouted, "Wait," and Jack managed to raise a hand before Lucy pulled the trigger.

Shit, what a mess.

The guy was on his back, limbs spread and kinked, like a bad impression of a swastika. His coat had ridden up, but Miles couldn't see a weapon. There'd be something in his belt, at his spine. Shoulder rigs were too obvious.

Lucy moved in for a look as well, shotgun still raised and steady. She said, "Jesus, I killed him. I can't believe it."

She'd done a good job, too: Jack's chest was pulped. The bloodstain on the carpet was three feet across, and inching wider. Miles checked his pulse, but Jack was genuinely gone. The room smelled of gun smoke, and the hit man's freshly loosened bowel.

Lucy said, "Jeez, he stinks. I'll call nine-one-one—"

"No, wait a second."

He checked each ankle. No holster. Just keys in his pockets. He tried the coat. It was a two-button piece, wool by the feel of it, probably tailored. Maybe Jack had splashed out. Christ, no weapon though.

He slid a hand beneath the guy and found his belt.

No fucking gun.

The rush kicked in, that cold feeling of a drop into a crisis. His ringing ears made it worse, like his brain couldn't cope—every neuron humming at its limit.

He knew he had to rig the scene, and he knew he had no time. Castle doctrine wouldn't cut it: Jack didn't look like a burglar. He was in a thousand-dollar suit, no mask, no tools, no weapon, no forced-entry damage. It looked like he was welcomed in for murder.

So he has to have a gun—

"Miles, what's wrong?"

He said, "Call nine-one-one, say I shot him."

"What?" Her hair was bed-tousled and hanging forward, framing wide eyes.

"He's got no weapon. You were upstairs, and I shot him."

She couldn't be part of it. They'd be caught out if they both told lies. *I saw nothing* was simple enough. Then again, she'd have to say she touched the shotgun—if they cordite-swabbed her, she'd come up positive . . .

She was struggling though: "What? Why's he got no gun? What the fuck was he doing?" Like she was offended he'd come unprepared.

Miles didn't answer, put a hand on the shotgun as he stood up, but she wouldn't let it go. "Miles, what are you doing?"

He pried her hands gently off the gun, one then the other. "It's got to look right. And it won't look right if you're standing here with the murder weapon."

"So what do I do?"

"Call nine-one-one, and say I killed Jack."

He didn't wait around to argue. He left the shotgun on the ground by the body and ran for the front door, caught himself in the entry hall.

There must be a gun. He *must* have brought a gun. There'd be something in his car at least—

Lucy shouted from another room, a question garbled by his ringing ears. He didn't answer, just ran back for the body, head pounding.

Pat-check round two:

No ankle piece.

Nothing in his belt.

The coat again—

He pried the fabric off the sopping wound. Something crackled. A pocket held a bloodied envelope. He fumbled the flap—motor skills wrecked by stress—yanked out the page within.

A message in a careful, sloping hand. Classy stuff: a fountain pen on heavy paper stock. A pellet hole and blood had marred one corner.

Miles scanned it:

I don't really know how to say this, but I loved you since I first saw you . . .

Perfect. He'd come for love, not death, and she'd blitzed him with a shotgun. He stuffed the paper in his pocket and ran for the door again.

NINE

Miles Keller

Sunday morning, he was up at six thirty. He left the hotel and walked east in bleak, overcast light, heavy clouds trying for rain. The black SUVs were gone, and the traffic was mainly empty cabs, fatigued-looking drivers coming off the night shift. Predawn in New York City, down on Canal Street, was a glimpse of New York at the end of the world: doors shuttered and the foot traffic mainly ragtag folk in earnest conversation with themselves, like trying to reconcile the event that left them in an empty city.

At the Canal Street station, he was the only person who looked like a passenger. There were three other guys asleep by a supermarket cart stacked high with camping gear, and topped with a sign that read FUCK THE ONE PERCENT. He figured only one percent of people could get a cart through a subway turnstile.

He caught a Q train heading down toward Manhattan Beach, sat up by the forward door with the volume of his iPod cranked above the squeal of the track. He liked the subway on Sundays. Patronage was at its most diverse. This carriage had a dreadlocked surfer plus board; an old lady who looked church-bound, given her attire; a young guy rapping along to headphones; and a cop-cum-heist-man if you counted

Miles. All of them nodding with the train's motion and the rapper throwing in the odd hand gesture for good measure.

Miles got off at Avenue U in Sheepshead Bay, came down off the platform into light rain and found the city already facing the day: traffic solid even on the cross streets, trucks an earache of gnashed metal, and the sidewalks busy even with the stores still closed. He ate breakfast at the Three Star Restaurant, and then walked south through the residential streets, what used to be no-frills Brooklyn clapboard before it all got gentrified. Now there were picket fences and tidy little planter boxes everywhere, snazzy European cars parked along the curbs.

It was the same architecture down on Twenty-third Street, but not quite so refined. His house was in the middle of the block. The mailbox was beyond salvation, crooked on its post and choking on leaflets. The gate seemed to yelp as he opened it. He went up the driveway and knocked at the front door. A minute's silence, and then a black guy in his midthirties answered. He wore a sweatshirt with the hood up and had a cigarette behind each ear, one eyebrow raised as if the sight of Miles was vaguely novel: this coat-clad bearded stranger with sunglasses and no expression.

Miles said, "Is DeSean in?"

"Uh, yeah. You're the cop, right?"

Miles said, "Yeah. I'm the cop."

The guy leaned out to check the street, mouth ajar, like he was balancing a piece of raw meat on his tongue. It was a common expression among those considered badass. He stepped back and lifted his chin at Miles. "You can come in."

"Well thank you."

The house smelled like marijuana, and he could hear digitized warfare from a video game. He locked the door behind him as he entered and then followed the guy through to the living room. They had a PlayStation hooked up to his TV, some kind of army propaganda showing in high-definition, so precise it looked more horrific than reality.

There was another guy on the sofa with his back to the door, and he turned to Miles as he stepped in.

"Hey, Miles."

"Hey, DeSean."

The guy who'd answered the door picked up a controller and took a seat in Miles's La-Z-Boy, cranked the lever back to full recline. There was a Benelli pump-action shotgun on the floor beside him.

Miles said, "Do you have a name, too?"

"Ee-rack."

"Ee-rack?"

"Like the country, Iraq, but you say it with an 'E.'"

Miles said, "Cool. Where's Lucy?"

DeSean said, "Taking a bath. Probably knew you're coming over."

Miles didn't answer. They were Stanton's guys, but Stanton didn't know the full story. He thought they were just minding the place. There was no way he'd approve the real setup: Miles using this as a safe house for Lucy, with DeSean running protection.

It was overkill, anyway. No one could find him here. He'd made the purchase through a shell company, and used Chester Burrows of Stanton & Associates as his nominee on the LLC paperwork. Even NYPD didn't know about the place. His personnel file listed his address as a one-room apartment up in Bed-Stuy. It belonged to his brother, but he wouldn't be needing it any time soon. Nate was doing fifteen to twenty up at Attica for Robbery 1.

He walked along to the kitchen and saw that they'd already had breakfast, unless these were yesterday's dishes: possibly every utensil he owned spread across the counter and covered to varying degrees with what looked like pancake batter. There was a carton of premade stuff standing on the table. He looked around for the cat's bowl, saw a saucer of half-eaten meat on the floor by the refrigerator. He opened the kitchen door to the backyard and whistled lightly through his teeth. "Warren!"

He stood there a minute, and then a gray cat appeared from around the corner of the house. It trotted over on dainty paws, saggy under-gut gently pendulous, rubbed against his shin as it came inside. It was just a neighborhood stray, and he figured it had a long list of house calls, given its girth. But he still enjoyed the visits.

The cat mewed at him.

"Yeah, I know. It's the wrong food on the wrong plate."

It mewed again. Miles pulled his earbuds through his shirt and put his iPod on the counter. "Yeah, I got you covered."

The cat did figure eights around his ankles as he took its bowl down off the fridge and filled it with meat from a sachet of pet food.

"You need water as well?"

No answer.

"Yeah, probably."

He scraped the old food into the trash and then filled another bowl with water and set it on the floor. Then he walked along to the spare bed-room he used as an office, sat at the desk, and took a cell phone out of a drawer. The phone was a security weak point, but the risk was accept-able. The device had no GPS function, so it would have to be triangu-lated off tower pings, and that would require a warrant. It received one call a week, from his brother at the Attica Correctional Facility, up-state. He connected the phone to its charger, powered it on, and waited for it to ring.

Eight o'clock. Eight oh five.

He sat at the desk with the phone in front of him and listened to artillery noise from the living room. The phone didn't ring.

Eight ten.

He placed his hands on the desk and watched random fingers rise and fall, killing time.

The phone didn't ring.

Miles picked it up and dialed a number.

"Operations."

"This is Detective Miles Keller, NYPD. My brother—"

"This is an internal line, Keller."

"My brother's missed a call—"

"I'm sorry, you'll have to follow the procedure like everybody else. Don't call again."

He lost the line.

"Shit."

He put the phone down and leaned back in the chair and looked at the ceiling. He could hear the clank of tank tracks, a diesel rumble. Don't think about it now—

He got up and went through to the living room and said, "I thought two grand a week included keeping the place tidy, maybe clearing the mail every so often."

They were both perched on the edge of their seats, watching a head on the TV screen hover inside crosshairs. The head exploded. They both leaned back and sighed, seemingly relieved.

DeSean said, "Thought you were paying for my badass protection skills."

Miles said, "Some badass cleaning skills would be good, too. And Warren has beef. He doesn't like the venison stuff."

"Yeah, whatever. The cat's brutal, man. You don't give it what it wants, it's just on your case all day. Meow meow meow. Jesus."

"Who's been hitting the Mary Jane?"

"I don't know. Probably your pussycat, trying to chill the fuck out."

Miles waited.

DeSean said, "Man, not us. It's just Lucy on the weed."

"You realize she has emphysema, right?"

"Yeah, well, you tell her."

Miles didn't answer. He walked upstairs, marijuana scent growing stronger. He saw his bedroom door ajar, a narrow slice of empty bed, sheets in disarray. He listened at the bathroom door for a second and then knocked.

"Luce?"

No answer.

He said her name again and when she didn't reply, he tried the door. It was unlocked. He pushed it open and there she was on her back in the tub, just her head and knees above the foam. She had the air tank standing next to her, the plastic mask covering her mouth and nose. Her eyes had been closed but they opened as he stepped in.

He said, "Why didn't you say something?"

"So you'd come in and we wouldn't have to talk through the wall."

He stepped out again and began to close the door.

"Oh, come on. Don't be dumb." She fanned her arms through the water, waves going through the foam, the lumpy surface warping gently. He paused on the threshold and then stepped in again and closed the door, sat down on the corner of the tub.

She said, "It's like a freak show or something—pay a dollar and see the masked mermaid."

He said, "Marijuana meant to help your lungs?"

She shrugged. "It's helping something. I'm like Clinton, though: I don't inhale. I just light it up and sit it in an ashtray. You still get the smell of it, maybe a little high, I guess."

There was a cutthroat razor on the shelf beside her, blade open. He reached across the water and picked it up. "What're you doing with this?"

"Nothing. Backup plan."

He could see himself in the blade, a sliver of eye and nose and lip. He said, "Yeah? What does that mean?"

She closed her eyes again. A soft marijuana smile on her lips. "You know . . . Nice hot bath, light a joint, and then just disappear."

"Oh, Christ." He folded the blade. "Sure. You know how many people I've seen dead in bathtubs? You show up, everyone's crying, and there's a pale body in bright-red water."

She gave a long blink as if picturing it, and said, "There'd be variations though, right? Sometimes you'd show up, and no one would be crying."

He didn't like her tone: too conversational. Like she'd been thinking this through for a while.

"Luce, if you're going to cut your wrists, I'll have you committed."

She rolled her eyes. "Oh jeez, relax." She raised a dripping hand

and flicked the metal tank. It rang dully. "I'm not peering over the edge. Just thinking about my options."

He didn't answer.

Lucy said, "You're too easy to wind up." She built herself a mound of foam on her belly. "One day, people'll have a little pill in their medicine cabinet, and when they've had enough, you just swallow with a glass of water."

"Tidier than opening your wrist in the bathtub."

She rocked her head slightly as if settling on a pillow. "I'm not going to do it this week. Or this decade, hopefully. But it's nice knowing I've got a checkout option."

He rubbed his face with his hands. "There are better ways of doing it, believe me."

"Yeah. A better way would be to get rich—maybe five, ten million bucks—set myself up with a pad in Oregon, and then, you know." She ramped a hand upward, pointing heavenward. "Take off in comfort."

"Why Oregon?"

"It's on the coast, and euthanasia's kosher."

"You're a long way from needing to worry about it."

"Yeah, hopefully. But as I say: nice to have options though, right?"

He thought he'd just come to feed the cat and talk to his brother.

He watched the knife turn over in his hands a few times. He said, "Look. I don't mind helping you out. You can stay here as long as you want. But you're not doing me any favors if you clock out in my tub."

She didn't answer.

He listened to the water clapping lightly on the enamel. "I've got some money coming my way—"

"The tax-free kind?"

He said, "Enough that we can go somewhere and you can check out in comfort."

She said, " 'We'? I didn't know we were back to 'we.' Strange living arrangement so far, but it's a start, isn't it?"

She was smiling, but he didn't want to get into it. They'd had an affair, and it ended his marriage, and he thought he'd never forgive himself. He didn't know how to say that without it sounding way too heavy.

Caitlyn knew of Lucy for two months before the split. That's what she told him, anyway—a gut feel, based on his evasiveness. She'd made plans to leave him, rented an apartment in Williamsburg, and then moved possessions out by stealth. The day she left, he came home and found her suitcases in the entry hall, Caitlyn coming down the corridor with her arms folded—not so much angry as uncompromising. There was no way he could change her mind. She knew he was seeing someone else. She told him Lucy had called the house, wanting to speak to him.

His infidelity required no more proof. The call was enough. It brought her gut feeling to critical mass. She never came back to the house. He remembered the emptiness, and remembered hating it. He'd reach a point where he thought he was coping, and then he'd notice where items were missing—a vase or an album that she'd taken—and the feeling of her absence would reset to its most acute. It was the loss of small things he struggled to get over: hearing her in another room, walking past a doorway and seeing her with a book. He started reading more, listening to audiobooks, working through titles he knew she'd read, trying to guess what she'd have to say about them.

He wondered now what she'd say about this arrangement: protecting the woman who'd helped break up his marriage, and lying for her, too. The Jack Deen killing to his name for the sake of Lucy's freedom. What would Caitlyn say about all that? Probably that she was vindicated, right for claiming that Lucy was more than just a fling.

Whatever she was, she cut short his musing: "Funny how dead hit men don't bother you—like, happy to lie about it, make it look like something it wasn't, and then you probably slept like a baby, right? Then if someone wants to die by choice, you get all torn up about it."

He turned the knife over a couple more times. She hadn't seemed fazed about killing Jack Deen, but then why should she? Miles hadn't told her he had nothing but a love letter. He'd seen her all those years ago, and never forgot her. He'd flown up to make something happen, and she killed him. He couldn't tell her that. It'd wreck her life as well as Jack's.

He said, "It took you fourteen trillion years to get here—"

"Yeah, yeah, yeah—"

"And this is your one brief glimpse of everything that exists. So why leave any sooner than you absolutely have to?"

She didn't answer, just lay there with her eyes shut, seeming very tranquil. He guessed they were done with suicide.

He said, "What are your housemates like?"

"You need a happier subject?"

He didn't answer.

"They're good guys." A smile flickered. "Ee-rack or Eye-rack or whatever his name is, he told me he had this vacation planned, right? Going to take a week off, always wanted to see France. Then he found out the cost of flights, couldn't afford it, so he just did a virtual tour on Google Maps, spent a week going around the streets."

There was a knock at the door.

Miles said, "Yeah?"

DeSean said, "Thought there'd be more splashing and giggling."

"What is it?"

DeSean said, "Forgot to tell you Wynn Stanton's trying to get in touch. He called before you got here."

"What'd he want?"

"Just said call him."

"You got a clean phone?"

"Yeah, I got a bunch in the truck. You can grab one. We got an online tournament going, can't keep it on hold."

He found the keys in the kitchen. The truck was a Lincoln Navigator SUV that DeSean had parked across the street. Miles checked the glove compartment, found an operating manual, a Glock 17, a box of nine-mil shells, and a copy of *Need for Speed: Most Wanted* for PlayStation. He got out and looked in the trunk, found a box of prepaid cell phones, still in their packaging. He chose a T-Mobile flip-top and took it back inside, past more living-room gunfire and into the kitchen.

The cat was still there, done with its food but interested in seconds now. It hopped up on the table and stood watching him with its tail raised as he cut the phone from its packaging with a pair of scissors. It tipped its head and stared as he dialed Stanton.

Kenny picked up. Miles said, "It's me."

Kenny said, "Ah. It's you." Then offline, quieter: "It's him."

Stanton came on and said, "This phone clean, or are you calling from hotel reception on speaker?" He thought that was pretty funny.

Miles said, "The phone's clean."

"Your Covey job's got messy. Just giving you a heads-up in case you want to get some distance on it."

"What happened?"

Stanton said, "Sounds like they're all dead."

TEN

Miles Keller

Miles said, "Who told you?"

"It's public. I just turned on TV, local news has a story."

"What are they saying?"

"Home invasion, apparently. But yeah, what I was getting at—I mean, you know how clean the job was, whether you left anything in the house, so if you want to keep low a few days—"

Miles said, "Thanks for the heads-up."

"They're not saying how they died, just that there's three bodies."

He felt a little dip, like when you wake up falling and the mattress catches you. Three bodies: the lawyer and his wife and someone else.

Miles said, "Who's the third?"

"They haven't mentioned names. You know what's going on?"

"It's blowback from last night. Someone wants their money."

"Yeah I know, but—"

Miles said, "I need to think about it."

He clicked off with Stanton and stood looking at the cat for a moment. The cat looked back, tail still raised, hooked tip flicking one way and the other. He could hear a dull, rhythmic thumping that must have been Lucy's air tank on the stairs.

The cat won the staring contest. Miles closed his eyes and said, "Shit."

The Coveys were dead because they lost the money that he stole. The timing was too close for the killings to be unrelated. He'd always known about the possibility of harm—their deaths as payback for incompetence—and he'd told himself it was something he could live with. He even gave Marilyn that line about having thought it through, that he was happy to shoot the crooked wife of a crooked lawyer if he had to. There was a certain ring to it, and he'd been genuine, as well. So maybe if it was just two bodies in the house up in Kings Point, he wouldn't give the matter further thought. Who cared if someone else had pulled the trigger? They either deserved it or they didn't. But collateral was a different moral issue. Three victims skewed the balance. Innocent dead were harder to reconcile.

He picked up the burner phone again but didn't dial. He heard an explosion along the hall, Lucy's voice asking how many hours a week they clocked on their game. He didn't hear the reply.

At least there was another side to everything, the law-and-order aspect, and maybe that was the safer lens through which to view it: someone had killed three people, and he was in a position to stop a repeat. Yeah—that was the better way to look at it.

He dialed the detective bureau at the Sixty-third Precinct, but then thought better of it and clicked off before he got an answer. No point going through NYPD—they'd just want to know why he was chasing cases when he shouldn't be. He tried Stanton's number again. Kenny answered.

Miles said, "It's me."

"Ah. It's you."

"Can you get me the number for the local PD up in Kings Point."

"Where?"

"Kings Point." He spelled it.

"Okay. Let me Google it."

It took him a minute to find the number. Miles thanked him and then hung up and dialed again, asked the desk sergeant who answered for a transfer to Tom Miciak. The guy told him the detective chief was working a scene, but he put him through anyway. Miles hung on for a marathon twenty or thirty rings, and Miciak finally picked up sounding pissed off: "Yeah?"

"Tom, it's Miles Keller, NYPD. I talked to you a few weeks ago about Lane Covey."

"Yeah sure, I remember. You seen the news this morning?"

"I heard what happened."

"You calling to say who did it?"

He could have made a guess at least, turned him in the right direction. Miles said, "I was hoping to take a look."

Miciak sighed, the kind Miles heard when he told guys they're looking at twenty-five to life. Miciak said, "What's your angle on this, sorry?"

"We got a dead guy in Brooklyn who looks like a Russian mob hit. I think Covey set it up."

He waited through a drawn-out "okay" as Miciak got things straight.

Miciak said, "And now he's dead, it's looking real fucking messy."

"Yeah."

There was a pause, Miciak seeming to stop and then start, edging around something.

Miles said, "Who are the victims?"

"Covey and the wife, and another guy—Edward Rhys."

Rhys: the Coveys' security man from last night. Maybe not innocent, but he hadn't earned this.

Miciak said, "You know him?"

"Doesn't ring a bell."

"You sure you can't wait for our prelim?"

"I'd prefer to see it myself. I just need a walk-through."

Miciak did his sigh again, asked a question offline that Miles didn't catch. He came back on and said, "Shit, what a morning. State police does our weekend call-outs, trooper on first response phones in, tells me it's a B-and-E. I go, What's it look like? He says, Three DBs, GSW, but the house seems okay. I go, Pal, I bet you my dick and balls this is not B-and-E."

Miles let that image have its due pause and said, "If you let me take a look, I can probably back you up on that."

Miciak said, "All right, shit, what are we now . . . eight thirty. You get here in an hour, I'll take you through."

"Thanks. Appreciate it."

"Sure. I'll run a tally, see how many times I gotta play tour guide today."

He clicked off, but found himself still looking at the phone. He could try Caitlyn's number, tell her he'd seen the Covey deaths on the news, use it as a pretext to check she was okay.

He dialed her number, but it rang to voice mail: the gun lobbyist telling him to leave a message. Miles clicked off and put the phone on the counter with his iPod, and when he turned around, Lucy was leaning in the doorway watching him.

She said, "You leaving already?"

"I've got to go up to Kings Point. Triple homicide."

"I thought you're robbery police."

Miles said, "I dabble."

He moved to the door, but she was still in his way, smelling bath-fresh and looking good in jeans and a sweater with the sleeves rolled— the same outfit she wore three weeks ago, when he'd first knocked on her door.

She said, "You mind if I come along?" Offhand and innocent, like he couldn't possibly say no. "I haven't been out of the house for three days."

"It's better if you stay here."

She had a look in her eye like there wasn't going to be a compromise. She said, "I really appreciate the whole amateur witness-protection thing. But if I have to go another week with these guys"—she gestured down the hallway with a head tilt—"I might need a padded cell by the end of it."

Miles said, "I don't think visiting a crime scene is going to help."

"Yeah, but spending time with a normal human being might."

He didn't answer. He wasn't sure if he counted as normal. And he wasn't certain she was as stir-crazy as she claimed. He broke off their affair as penance for a broken marriage, and most of the time—*most of the time*—he managed not to think about her. But he wasn't sure if the reverse was true. Maybe he was on her mind. Maybe she thought that time together now could repair what they'd had . . .

She said, "Look. All I want to do is drive up there and drive back. And then I'll have enough energy to go another week with them."

He almost made excuses, but she could see a brush-off coming and cut in first: "I'll wait in the car so I don't cramp your style. And anyway, I'm sick. You have to give me what I want."

ELEVEN

Bobby Deen

Charles called two hours into the flight.

Bobby took it on the phone at his seat, picked up and caught Charles in a coughing fit. Bobby waited him out, heard a throat-dousing slosh of drink and then a big sigh to finish.

Bobby said, "You done?"

"Yeah, I think so. You got your attitude sorted? Not going to have a breakdown if you have to cooperate with someone?"

Bobby said, "We'll see."

"Yeah, sure. We'll see how bad you want to get paid. I've just emailed you some stuff—address and access codes and shit. The apartment's down in Chelsea, but the cameras are still offline, and she's not picking up, obviously."

The other two—Marko and Luka, whatever they were called—were both dozing, or at least making a good show of it: both of them blank as mannequins with their eyes shut. He'd prefer constant scrutiny, rather than wondering if they had ears on him. He looked out his porthole and saw a ragged quilt of white way below. They were up at forty thousand feet. Even the clouds looked distant.

Charles said, "I got two theories: Garcia could've come after her as payback for his fucking boat, or it could be something because of the buyout—you know, someone getting ballsy, trying to muscle in now Berkhov's dropping his share."

Berkhov was Peter Berkhov: Stone Studios' principal backer, and a guy whose wealth comprised mainly Russian mob profit.

Bobby said, "You mean someone could try and force you out now there's no mob to worry about."

Charles almost spat it down the phone: "Exactly! Fucking exactly. Buy up Berkhov's share, and then extort me into backing out for free."

Plausible, but Occam's razor said there was a simpler theory: Nina was running.

Charles said, "It's probably some ethnic thing—Chinese and Russians going at each other." Bobby heard another slosh-and-sigh. He was probably hitting whiskey to try and scorch himself out of bed. Charles said, "Asians are okay because they're so straightforward, always clear what they want: money, money, money. Slavs are a different ballgame, honestly—can't be trusted."

Bobby said, "So why did you give me two of them?"

Charles laughed. "They have their uses, put it that way."

The steward came through again, checking drinks. Bobby smiled and waved her off. He got a Nina flash as she turned, the headshot photo merging with that nice body in uniform. They had the same hair. It was undistilled Nina as she walked away.

Charles broke the spell: "Check out the apartment first—there might be something that says what's going on."

Bobby's ears popped. He said, "I know what I'm doing."

"Sure. But let's try subtlety this time: don't go drilling anyone on a boat. All you have to do is bring her back."

Subtlety. The approach had changed in less than eight hours. Last night he'd advocated bloodshed, now he wanted restraint. So what had changed? Maybe he slept on it and realized something didn't fit. Or maybe Frank Garcia called and said the wife was playing angles of her own. She'd tried it in L.A., now she was aiming for second time lucky.

The plane hit bad air. Bobby's guts went free-fall. He squeezed his armrest and rode it out. He said, "I need to be clear about what you want."

"Well, ask a clear question, then."

The steward popped the cockpit door and leaned down with a question. Bobby glimpsed dials, and remembered a childhood brush with fame: some dumb commercial he'd auditioned for, kids dressed up as pilots. Bobby Senior thought the kid would be a star . . .

Bobby said, "If something's happened, am I seeking compensation?"

He waited through internet crackle as Charles decoded: compensation meant violent payback. If she was hurt, he could seek fatal reparation.

Charles said, "No. I want low-key mitigation. Dead bodies mean lost commerce. All you have to do is find her."

Low-key mitigation. That hadn't been the case a few weeks back. When Nina went missing, he wanted L.A. leveled. Now reprisal was a no-go.

All you have to do is find her.

He didn't think payback was needed. Which meant he thought that Nina was playing him. So—

"Is this a rescue mission or a kidnap mission?"

Charles sloshed and sighed. Bobby waited through the crackle. Charles said, "Just bring her back."

Bobby didn't answer. He hung up the phone, and his brain reengaged with plane noise: muted engine drone, and the chime of ice rocking somewhere in its glass.

He looked across the aisle and saw Luka watching him, just a half-second before he closed his eyes again.

TWELVE

NEW YORK, NY

Miles Keller

He borrowed DeSean's SUV and drove east on the Belt Parkway, heading out around the lip of Jamaica Bay toward Kennedy Airport. It seemed more like Louisiana in these parts—the terrain flat and rural-looking, estuary systems breaking up the shoreline, as if the land had been dropped in place and broke on impact. There were hints of gray industry out in the hazy distance, a few houses on stilts along the water's edge.

Lucy spent the first fifteen minutes window gazing, and Miles worried she was brewing something dark and philosophical, get them back onto suicide while he couldn't escape. She took a long hit off the air tank, no doubt fueling up to talk.

She waited another minute and said, "Called my dad a few weeks ago, haven't seen him in fourteen, fifteen years. He moved out to Idaho in '08 I think. Anyway, I called his number, this lady answers, right? Turns out she's his wife—a new wife I hadn't met—and she tells me Dad died eighteen months ago."

She glanced over but caught him looking blank, homicide and Coveys on his mind, the slim chance that Edward Rhys was both dead and deserving. He mustered a grimace and said, "Shit. That sucks."

She nodded slowly, as if coming around to the idea. "Yeah, I guess.

Can't say I was devastated, just disappointed really. Wanted to tell him I was sick, see his reaction." She contemplated the traffic for a moment, had some oxygen. "My whole life, I never really knew where I stood with him, thought if I said I was ill, I'd get a read on what he actually thought. But he was gone already."

Miles knew he needed insight that leaned toward upbeat, but he couldn't think of anything that counted as a silver lining. He figured a parent story would be safe enough, on-theme and quid pro quo, more or less. And the upside of talking was it freed him from his own head.

He said, "My mom died twenty years ago. My dad's still around. He's had Alzheimer's about twelve years, so he's getting pretty loopy."

"He robbed banks, right?"

"Yeah. They both did. My mom was pretty good at it. I don't think my dad really had the spine to try it himself until she got him into it. Imagine she pitched it to him like the movies—you know how bank robbers, it can seem like there's something noble or principled about them?"

"Like they have the moral high ground, taking on institutions?"

He nodded. "Yeah. Or that it's kind of glamorous, maybe. I think he thought he was going to be like one of those gangster films—lots of slick tailoring and fast getaways—but it was just stress and poverty, looking over your shoulder all the time. People on drugs showing up at your house at ten o'clock at night to plot stuff."

"Is that why you're a cop? Because of them?"

He shrugged. "Maybe. Wasn't until I was older that I had an opinion on it. When I was a kid it was just what my parents did. I don't think I passed judgment."

"But you did eventually."

He didn't answer.

She studied him for a quarter-mile, like letting him know this was a question to get ready for. She said, "Would you really want to come away with me? Like, if I got rich and found a place in Oregon?"

Miles followed the curve of the road for a long moment, the broken dashes of the lane markers spitting past them. He said, "I can help you. But that's all I can promise."

"You mean pay me off, and then not have to think about it?"

He said, "It's complicated."

"All right." Light and abrupt, as if she'd dropped the topic, but she was still looking at him. She said, "Are you going to tell me where this money's coming from?"

He looked across at her and said, "You just have to worry about whether you're getting any."

"Sure. And where are you going to run to? If you're not running with me?"

He smiled. "I'll be all right."

They hit a lull. She turned the radio on and channel-hopped for a while, just killing time, not giving anything a chance. She settled on an FM station, opened the glove compartment and closed it again. He knew she'd seen the gun though, and he knew it was going to get them back onto suicide in a minute.

Sure enough, she said, "People with terminal illness, there's all these support groups you can go to. Cancer, MS, they've all got their own group. I've never gone, but you can look them up on YouTube. Play it in HD." She took a long hit off the tank. "People always talk about how it's a shock, that they never expected it, all that kind of thing. But it just seems like, I don't know. Death is guaranteed, and it's always looming there—how come people don't think about it more? You know."

Miles said, "You think it's going to stay in the corner of your eye, not jump out in front of you."

She nodded and turned the radio off. The sudden quiet felt obvious and solemn, like there was a mood to fix.

She said, "Can I ask you a question? Might seem kind of weird." Still sounding nonchalant about it, though.

Miles said, "All right."

Lucy said, "If you had to die, how would you want to do it?"

Miles said, "If I had to?"

"Yeah, like. You got some brutal illness and there's no way out."

"I like to think I'd carry on anyway."

"No, well." She waved a hand elaborately. "Just say you've decided. You don't want to carry on anymore."

He thought about it for a few hundred yards and said, "Probably gunshot."

"Why?"

He shrugged. "Follow the approved method, I guess they give you drugs and you fade out. But I wouldn't want to be dozing off and think, Maybe I should've waited longer."

"Whereas you pull the trigger and it's done?"

He saw Jack Deen dead by gunshot, Jack Deen bleeding on her living-room floor. He remembered going cold, thinking how hard this would be to fix . . .

He blinked out of it and nodded. "Less chance that 'oh shit' is your last thought, I guess."

Lucy said, "Leave that for someone else, right?"

THIRTEEN

KINGS POINT, NY

Miles Keller

The Covey place had a big turnout. Miles saw Kings Point PD cars, state and Nassau County police cruisers, a couple of unmarked detective vehicles, and news vans from three different networks.

Lucy said, "You get a showing like this at every murder?"

Miles said, "Depends who's killed. Good zip codes get better news coverage."

He pulled over a block from the Covey place. No rubberneckers at the crime-scene tape, but there were a few people watching from their front yards. Kings Point had a more refined class of voyeur. He noticed that Rhys's car was no longer out front.

Miles checked his pockets: cash and his hotel keycard, and another T-Mobile burner phone from DeSean's collection. He said, "You okay to wait here?"

She nodded. "Brought my own oxygen, don't even need the window down." She pointed up the street. "Used to do escort duty when I worked for Manny, few times I went out with these guys, they'd end up in some shithole in the Bronx or Harlem. Never knew what they did, always made me wait in the car. Used to sit there thinking they might not come back, get a free vehicle out of it."

Miles said, "I'm coming back, I promise."

He could see a cop heading over, Kings Point PD, the guy looking set for the recruitment brochure cover-shoot: clean cut and squared away, clenched jaw showing firmness and determination. Miles lowered his window and the officer stepped up and gave a stiff little nod.

"Sir. Ma'am. Can I help you?" Trying to move them on.

Miles said, "Miles Keller, NYPD. I'm meeting Tom Miciak."

The cop told him to wait in the car and headed back toward the house, brisk walk, exemplary posture. Lucy said, "Probably thinks you're talking shit—no way is this guy law: hasn't shaved in six weeks, driving some gangbanger SUV. Gas-mask lady riding shotgun."

Miles didn't answer. He could see Miciak in plain clothes standing by an unmarked car, the officer approaching him and then turning to point out Miles in the SUV. Miciak lit a cigarette as he started over. He was a fat man in his midforties, blond hair side-combed in wisps over a baby-pink skull, a blue polo shirt tucked into gray golf pants.

Lucy said, "You're more like a cop than this guy: looks like he's just played nine holes." Then: "Who was that Canadian mayor who liked cocaine?"

Miles said, "Rob Ford." He opened his door. "Back soon."

Miciak had a big stomach that gave him a big walk, arms at a slight angle from his body to prevent contact on the swing. He held out a hand for Miles and put the cigarette to his lips with the other, leaked smoke as he said, "Keller, how you doing?"

Miles said, "I'm all right. Who found them?"

They headed for the house, Miciak working hard on the cigarette, getting his money's worth before he was back on-scene. He said, "Lady across the street heard a gunshot about four A.M., went over and checked it out."

"She not heard of nine-one-one?"

"Yeah, exactly. I asked her that, said she thought it might've been a car or something. Nipped over in her slippers, saw a dead guy in the entry hall."

A news anchor with a cameraman in tow approached for comment, but Miciak kept walking, let the mike bump off his shoulder. A trooper lifted the crime-scene tape and they stepped under.

Miles said, "I better take a look before it's world news."

Miciak stopped then, put the back of a hand on Miles's arm to pull him up as well. He said, "I hope you appreciate I'm doing you a big fucking favor. State Police's got BCI people coming down, they don't want anyone going in other than their forensic guys."

Miles said, "But you want to piss them off just a little bit, right? Otherwise they start thinking they can tell you what to do."

Miciak deadpanned him. "Heavens, no. But I went to a conference last month, all about interagency communication, fostering strong links, so I guess this is a good opportunity to give it a go, build some mutual trust between me and NYPD." He paused and looked at the house, seemed pained as he said, "Shit, I was meant to be playing nine holes with my brother-in-law. We get out there early, right? No one around, fucking perfect, I'm literally standing to tee off, club-to-ball"—he acted it out so Miles got the picture—"and my phone goes."

"Nice." He followed Miciak to his unmarked, watched him stub out the cigarette on the roof, reach in the window to drop the butt in the center console.

Miciak said, "Anyway. That's why they pay me the big bucks."

Miles just nodded. The garage door was open, and he saw Rhys's Range Rover parked up beside Covey's sedan. He almost mentioned it—wondered aloud why it had been moved—and then went cold as he caught himself.

Act like you've never been here.

Miciak saw something in his face and smiled. "You okay? No one's making you go in. Fresh air's real nice, believe me."

"No, I'm fine. Let's just do it."

There was a forensics tent set up on the driveway, and he had to sign the attendance log to gain admission. He knew it was a risk, putting his name on the form. It was just more evidence of a visit he should not have made. But he had to know what happened, and he'd probably been broadcast on TV anyway. So he signed on the line, and hoped that piece of paper would pass its days in a never-opened file, and wouldn't constitute the eureka moment for someone out to get him.

He and Miciak donned disposable protective gear—gloves and overshoes and boiler suits—and then like a hostage parody they walked single-file with hands raised between the cars and into the house, Miciak leading.

He could hear the TV in the guest living room, and from the open door he saw CNN still playing. The furniture was unchanged, and for a second he saw their ghosts all sitting there, Miles in the armchair with his gun, telling them everything would be fine, provided he got his money.

A forensic tech was scouring the floor with a black light, and he stood and watched for a moment as Miciak moved on. It was impossible he'd left no trace: clothing fibers, microscopic flakes of skin, maybe even hair. It was already enough to cost him sleep, make him wonder what he'd missed, but one day science would reveal truth at the outset. He couldn't stand so close to something that had gone so wrong and pretend he hadn't been there. This kind of deceit had a finite life span.

Up ahead of him, Miciak said, "Here's your first one. Be my guest, but I don't need another close-up."

He stood against the wall and let Miles move past him to the entry hall. There was blood on the floor by the front door, and a body-shaped mound beneath a white sheet. A forensic tech in a boiler suit was dusting a side table for prints. It was like a dream vision, a glimpse of the cold and loveless future—horror covered up for the sake of sterile order.

Miles stood back, trying to grasp it all at once, wanting the context and the story. He saw the front door standing closed and the chain hanging from its sliding bracket on the frame. It had torn free of the door and left a spiky divot in the timber, clean of lacquer. He lifted the sheet by one corner and saw Edward Rhys on his side, eyes and mouth open and two bullet holes in his chest.

Miciak said, "This is the Rhys guy. Ran his details, he works for a place called Hayman Coates—private security. Called them up, they've never heard of anyone called Covey. So he's either moonlighting or doing favors."

Miles said, "What are these, forty-fives?"

"Yeah, through-and-through." He pointed at the wall opposite the door, a pair of tidy holes in the gypsum board. "Haven't found the rounds yet, but they must be hard-nose to be that clean." He kept moving along the hall and Miles heard him say, "Got the second one here. This is the lawyer. Same again, through-and-through. One in the guts, another one through the chest."

"You got any brass?"

"Nah, casings are gone."

Miles stepped into the hallway again and found Miciak crouched by a shape on the floor. "You want a look?"

Miles said, "No, I think I'm good."

"Yeah, fair enough. Jesus."

Miciak's knees clicked as he stood. He'd looked okay outside, but he'd lost some color, started to pop a sweat. He said, "Shit, I haven't worked a scene like this in years. BPD, I did fucking fraud, and then missing persons."

"Don't faint on me."

"No, no, it's just . . . you know. I'm cool. The wife's in the bedroom. We'll make it fast, I need some air."

There was artwork on the floor heading up the stairs—paintings in mangled frames, a photograph of Lane and Marilyn, obscured by cracked glass. He could sell it to the news crews. They'd love the symbolism.

He followed Miciak past more forensic staff—hunched and fastidious in their dusting—and then through the upstairs hallway to the master bedroom. Marilyn Covey was on the ground beneath a sheet on bloodied carpet, and beside her was the open door of the walk-in closet, in which stood an empty, three-foot-high safe.

Miciak stood over it, looking more judgmental than curious with his hands on his hips. He said, "That tells you a bit doesn't it?"

Miles didn't answer. He'd seen it before, via Marilyn's video call when she collected his money. That would be a good paradox for someone: the two-minute call between Marilyn and Edward Rhys, with their phones in the same location. Maybe they'd write it off as an accidental dial.

Miciak said, "She's got a close-range head shot, just beside the ear. Obviously fought him coming up the stairs—figure he was hanging on pretty tight, maybe shoved her away once the safe was open, kind of got her side-on as she was falling, you know?"

He mimed the shot to test his theory, and in his mind Miles saw the lead-up: Marilyn in a choke hold, tripping and falling in a half-turn as she was shoved away, and then the bang to finish it.

He stepped to the body and knelt and lifted the sheet, got the same look Edward Rhys had given him: open eyes and mouth, but Marilyn had a bullet wound below her temple. It had leaked a crimson rivulet across her cheek and nose, another down the line of her jaw.

Miciak was looking at the ceiling, breathing very carefully. He said, "They hadn't gone to bed—you notice that? Four A.M., no PJs, bed's still made? They must've known something was happening."

"Yeah. And why else would you have security."

"Well, exactly."

"Anyone see a getaway?"

Miciak shook his head, seemed to study the light fixtures, his face very glossy. "Not so far. But we're still canvassing."

Miles said, "Killer must've known where the safe was. Had to be a fast job with all the noise, five shots like that. And he knew it was high-risk, because he would've seen the lights on, but he thought it was worth it anyway."

Miciak stood at the window, a ladder of soft light bent across him from the closed blinds. He said, "Might've had a key—opens the front door, Rhys hears the chain, guy panics and kicks it open."

"Why would he have a key?"

"Because they know him."

Miles said, "If he knew them, he would've played it smoother, got them all in one room before he started firing."

"Or maybe he picked the lock, didn't realize they had the chain on. He knew what he was doing though—I mean, how often you see that: multiple homicide, and every shot's made contact?"

"Yeah. I know what you mean."

"And it's not flashy, either, you know? It's just competent. It's not like a statement killing where they leave them hog-tied in the woods or something."

Miles said, "Must've been silenced too, or he would've woken the whole street."

"Probably did wake them up, but only the lady was brave enough to come look."

Miles stepped back to the door, tried to get that glimpse again of how it unfolded. He wanted to know if Marilyn had closed the safe when he sent her upstairs, but he couldn't recall. He'd had to take his eyes off the video. Maybe it had stood open since he left.

Miciak said, "You still with me?"

He couldn't speculate about the safe being open: why would he even think that? It was too obscure and unlikely, unless you'd happened to be here—

Miles said, "I think there were two of them. She would've been fighting pretty hard, so why would he pull her over here to open the safe, and then take her all the way back there again for a headshot? I think someone held her, and someone else opened it."

Miciak had made a gap in the blinds, didn't seem too happy with the world as he saw it. He said, "What I want to know: was this what they were staying up for, and it all went wrong, or had it already happened, and this is something else?"

Miles didn't answer. He figured reticence was safest. He didn't want good theories looking like inside knowledge.

He said, "Thanks for the walk-through."

Miciak still had his fingers in the blinds. He said, "Here we go: BCI's showed up. You want to hang around for the shit fight?"

"Tempting."

He headed back downstairs, trying not to tread on broken glass.

Behind him he heard Miciak saying, "That guy you talked to when you showed up, he only started two weeks ago —did fifteen years in South Central L.A., thought he'd come up here for a change of pace, catches this shit straightaway. He's funny though, got this habit of looking in the distance, saying deep and meaningful things—he rolls up here, checks it out, comes outside and sorta squints at the horizon and goes, 'Well. Never let it be said that darkness isn't everywhere.' " He chuckled. "Reckon he said it in the mirror a few times before he got here."

Miles headed through to the garage and then outside to the tent, saw that more cars had shown up: three unmarked sedans that must be the State Police's BCI, the Bureau of Criminal Investigation, and an SUV marked HAYMAN COATES, parked over to his right. A silver Cadillac sedan had pulled up on the cross street opposite, facing the house, and he figured it must be more Hayman Coates royalty.

He was taking off the boiler suit as two guys climbed out of one of the BCI cars and started up the driveway toward him. They looked about right for murder police: midfifties with dull suits and ties, mustaches as square and careful as redaction marks, like their top lips were classified. Forensic staff, sexless in their crime-scene gear, parted to let them through, and the detective on the left called, "What do you think we mean by close the scene?"

Miles pulled his coat back on and ignored the guy, let Miciak launch a speech about this still being his jurisdiction, that BCI was welcome to make recommendations, but they had to recognize where the authority lay . . .

Miles stayed out of it.

He wasn't even meant to be here. There was no sense in being memorable, notwithstanding the fact he'd probably been caught on film. He saw, though, that two of the news vans had already moved on—gone in search of better bad things, presumably.

He walked down the driveway and heard someone crying as he reached the tape, looked over to see a woman in tears, totally distraught, beside the HAYMAN COATES SUV. He realized it must be Edward Rhys's wife. A state trooper was trying to comfort and restrain her simultaneously, an arm around her midriff, with the woman bent almost double trying to break free, sobbing that she just needed to see him, needed to see him. Two more state-police radio cars pulled up behind the SUV, lights flashing, and Miles guessed they must have followed her after giving her the news.

The TV crew had twigged that patience had been worth it, and the anchor was heading over at a jog, microphone thrust forth and the cameraman tugged along by cables, squinting at his viewfinder for the money shot.

Miles stood transfixed, seeing the wreckage of what he'd set in motion. He blinked and tried to block it out. He couldn't be part of it. Guilt would mean inaction, and that would just be added cost later: yet more guilt for failing to fix something when he had the chance. All he could do was try and find who did it. With a bit of luck, he had years ahead to agonize, grind through all the what-ifs and lists of who deserved it and who didn't.

He turned away and headed back for Lucy and the SUV, smiled as he saw her wave to him through the windshield, her simple act lifting the weight of the dead, if only for a second. He crossed the street, and in his periphery across the intersection, he saw a guy climb into the driver's seat of the silver Cadillac. He was fortyish and bald, but he'd changed his tracksuit—blue now, instead of the red one from last night, when he visited the Coveys.

Miles paused, and then felt a kick of adrenaline that got him moving again, tried to move naturally despite the guy's clear line of sight. He'd been masked last night, but his build hadn't changed, and maybe the guy was a savant at recognizing walks. He felt a hum along his spine that felt like close attention, glanced back and saw the shadow of the man behind his windshield, a hand raised by the look of it, maybe talking on a phone. Miles walked back to the SUV and climbed in. Lucy was scrolling through something on her phone.

She said, "Was it as bad as it's supposed to be?"

"Yeah. It was about right."

His breathing was steady, but he could feel his heartbeat in his ears. He leaned across and opened the glove compartment, removed the Glock and checked the load. The chamber was empty, but it had a full clip.

"What are you doing now?"

Miles said, "Can you drive?"

"I can do anything but run."

"Good. Keys are in the ignition."

He had his gloves in his back pocket, but barehanded would be best. He didn't want to tip the guy off. He slipped the gun in his belt and pulled the coat across to hide it.

"What the fuck are you doing?" It was the first time in a while he'd seen her looking surprised—it took a lot to shift her out of chill mode.

He kept his eyes on the road ahead as he took the burner phone from his pocket and passed it to her. "Send yourself a text. I need your number."

"You going to message me about what's going on?"

He didn't answer.

"Oh, we're being all grim now. Okay."

He waited as she typed, and when he heard her phone ding with a message he took the burner off her and pocketed it again.

He said, "I'll call you about what's happening next. But if I'm not back in thirty minutes, drive yourself home."

"Dude, what the hell is going on?"

He got out and closed the door on another question, walked back up the street to the Covey place and then around the corner of the intersection to the adjoining road. The Cadillac was still there, and the tracksuit man was still on his phone. Miles crossed the street and walked around the car's hood, and the guy only seemed to pay attention once Miles had opened the passenger door and climbed in beside him.

There was no look of recognition yet. The guy just seemed faintly perturbed. He would've seen Miles on the crime scene a moment ago, probably thought he was just a cop with excess arrogance, overstepping his entitlements.

Miles waited for him to wrap up his call, the guy turning to his window, voice dropping a touch as he said, "I'll call you back."

Miles let him put the phone down and then he looked him in the eye as he pulled the pistol, saw the man's gears click with a suddenness that made his face go blank. Miles rested the Glock on his thigh and said, "Remember me?"

FOURTEEN

KINGS POINT, NY

Miles Keller

The tracksuit man made a fast recovery, only spent a few seconds slack-jawed from the shock of seeing Miles for a second time. Once he got his face arranged, he didn't seem too bothered about being a captive in his own car, sat there with an eyebrow raised as if listening to the worldview of a madman.

Miles said, "Phone," and the guy allowed an insolent pause before offering up the Samsung he'd used a moment ago. Hanging out in murder-for-hire circles, he would've seen some fraught situations in his day, and Miles sometimes wondered how his own efforts ranked in the grand scheme of tense encounters. Sometimes guys were cool, and sometimes they were just good at putting it on. So how many times had he been the worst moment of someone's life?

He found the power button by touch and turned the phone off, dropped it in his coat pocket without moving his gaze from the man beside him. He said, "You see this on the news as well, or were you just in the neighborhood?"

The guy started on something, but then paused and seemed to change direction. He looked at the Glock in Miles's lap and said, "What are you—NYPD, or state police?" He looked up with a half-smile, kind of distant, like he was above all this. "Or does someone just owe you a favor?"

Miles said, "I guess I'm two out of three."

The guy nodded slowly. "Yeah, I thought so: definitely not a hundred percent."

Miles said, "Let's see some ID."

The guy kept his eyes on him as he reached in his pocket, came out with a fold of cash and a driver's license trapped together with a rubber band. He lobbed them into Miles's lap.

Miles flipped the bundle over and read the license details. He said, "You got to be joking. No way is your name Gary Peters." He tossed it back. "You know a good forger, or you got an inside man at DMV?"

The guy still had his smile. "Neither. Just an Eastern accent and a Western name."

"Yeah, sure."

Up the street he could see the BCI detectives arguing with Miciak on the Coveys' driveway, all of them fairly worked up by now. Miciak was in defense mode, bright red, elbows pulled in tight and his shoulders right up by his ears as he shouted something.

The guy said, "This is a good little scheme you got. How's it work: you go through all your databases, rip off whoever's got spare cash?" He let his head kind of loll over on his shoulder as he turned look at Miles, trying to seem bemused, like this wasn't the first time he'd been cornered by a lawman who dabbled in robbery.

Miles said, "Yeah, kind of. I'm old-school, though: tend to just go on word-of-mouth."

He paused, unsure for a moment about how to move things forward, whether to push the guy hard, or try to seem relaxed about the whole arrangement. He couldn't risk him getting out of the car though, which meant he needed full disclosure on his cop status—stop the guy viewing it as leverage.

Miles said, "I worked the Carl Tobin investigation. That was the credit-card scammer you guys whacked?"

"Never heard of him."

"Sure. Anyway. He worked for this printing outfit that had a contract with Chase Bank, doing their plastic. We found five and a half thousand of them hidden under his floorboards. Hacked his email, turned out he was running the scam with his brother-in-law. I tracked the guy down, he told me Carl had got cold feet on the deal, so he went to Lane Covey to have him killed. Even told me when the payment was going through. Shot himself in the head when I tried to cuff him."

The guy was doing a good job of seeming uninterested.

Miles said, "So. All you have to do is tell me who Covey hired for the job. There're three people dead in that house because you didn't make your pickup, and someone didn't get paid."

The guy was shaking his head, but Miles carried on: "So you can either tell me who did it, or I have to assume that this is your handiwork."

The head shaking stopped, but he still wasn't saying anything. Miles said, "Timing's not quite right though, is it? I saw you there at ten thirty, but the shooting didn't start until about four. So who'd you call in for the slaughter?"

"Why do you give a shit?"

Miles said, "Well, I don't really, far as the Coveys are concerned. But Mr. Rhys didn't deserve the end he got, so I'd like to tidy things up on his behalf. Even if he doesn't know about it."

The guy looked at the windshield and then back, trying to pick a way through. He shrugged and said, "Look. I'm just the fucking errands guy."

Miles nodded, like he was sympathetic. He said, "Nice car to be running errands in."

The guy didn't answer.

Miles said, "Nobody ever knows anything, right? Everyone who's been pulled over with a car full of contraband, always a big surprise when you ask them where they got it. You know what I mean?"

"Yeah. Life's hard."

"Definitely. You're a bit different though—gave me that little talk last night about how I could leave the money where it was, and you wouldn't take it any further? Shot me with your finger gun to make it seem real smooth. That's pretty dedicated for a courier. Unless you've actually got a decent stake in all of this."

"Yeah, sure. And this is like one of those weird things where the killer shows up at the crime scene, likes watching the cops try to put it all together."

Miles took off his shades one-handed. They were a gift from Stanton, chrome Randolph Aviators with PLAY TO WYNN etched inside one arm, and PURE STANTON etched inside the other. Stanton's pair was identical, except the text was on the outside.

Miles breathed on a lens and put them on again. He gave himself another moment and said, "You think because I'm law, this will all stay real civilized, and you'll be right as rain. But how does that marry up with the fact I stole a hundred sixty grand at gunpoint last night?"

The guy didn't answer. His finger was tapping fast and light on the windowsill, like doing its bit to find a way out of this.

Miles glanced around, more for show than a genuine appraisal. He said, "And this is pretty extreme in itself, don't you think? Sitting here in a car with you."

The guy said, "I could get out." He tipped his head toward his window but held on to Miles's gaze, needing to see how far he could push it. He was smiling, but his pulse was going strong under his jaw. He said, "What do you think they'll do when they find out you were there last night?"

There was a strong urge now to do some hard persuading, but Miles didn't rush it. He said, "How're you going to put that to them? Just gloss over the part about you being there too, hope the Keystone Kops don't notice?"

"I think you've got more to lose than I do." He opened his door. A digital tone began to chime.

Miles made himself wait a long beat and said, "I've got a badge and a thirty-eight throw-down. You can close the door now, or you can look like a police shooting. All I'll have to tell them is that you pulled first."

The guy looked up the street, dipped his head slightly as if gauging the distance to the corner. "You think you can rig the scene before they get here?"

It sent a jolt through his guts: "rig the scene" put him back at Lucy's house, Jack Deen dead on the floor, backup only minutes away and he knew he had a short window to get everything right. Blood spatter and ballistics and all the moral angles of it. How do you fix it up so you keep a clean slate and a clean conscience—

He said, "It's not rocket science. What I'll do, I'll shoot you maybe four times, put your hand on my backup piece. Then when they come running over, I'll wipe my brow and say, Gee that was a close one."

Neither of them moved.

Miles said, "Five. Four. Three."

He pulled the trigger.

The gun clicked.

The guy jumped like he'd been grabbed in the dark.

Miles racked the slide hard—a sharp clack—and said, "Pretty scary, right? Even worse if I actually shot you. And we're live now, so we can go that way if we want."

The guy swallowed. He had one foot on the road.

Miles said, "Don't make me start the count again. I was almost finished."

More staring, and then the guy pulled the door closed. Quiet in the car now without the chiming, and the tension seemed to have dipped with the volume. The guy took a moment to settle back into looking cool, ran a long breath out through his bottom teeth and then leaned against his door with an arm on the sill, half-turned to Miles like he had nothing to hide.

He said, "You figured you can risk talking to me now. But what's keeping you safe when we part ways?"

Miles said, "What, you think the facts are going to change? You only know I was there because you were there, too. It's not like that'll be different if you wait a week." He nodded up the street. "If you're going to blow my cover, might as well do it now, otherwise they'll give you a hard time for not coming forward earlier."

"Yeah, cute. I'm not talking about the law."

Miles raised his eyebrows, smiled at him. "Oh, right. You mean I have to watch my back, or bad things'll happen?"

The guy didn't answer.

Miles said, "Tell me what you're doing here."

"Same as you. Trying to find out what's happening."

Miles turned his lip out and nodded at the house, as if watching from here struck him as a good technique. He said, "Didn't think you'd get anything useful, watching from a car. I thought maybe you'd just sit here and keep an eye out for people having revelations, give someone a call if you thought they were getting close?"

"If I'm part of this, why am I not getting distance right now? Flying to Guatemala or something?" He had his confidence back: his pulse wasn't leaping out of his throat, and his finger tapping had settled down, too.

Miles shrugged. "I'm part of it, and I'm not in Guatemala."

"Great minds think alike."

"Yeah, sure." He reached across himself for the phone in his pocket, remembered Edward Rhys last night on the couch, making that same awkward move. He hoped this wasn't the start of something: Rhys flashbacks hitting him until his guilt glands were spent, everyone issued their comeuppance. He opened the messages and found the text from Lucy, twenty minutes old now: "Miles the Man." He could get that on a T-shirt maybe, once this was all squared away. He called her number, and she got it on the first ring.

"Hey."

Miles said, "It's me. Head back to the house. The guys are going to pack everything up and take you somewhere."

"What's happening?"

Miles said, "I'll tell you later."

He hung up on her, and the guy said, "I'd be intrigued too, getting messages like that." He leaned his head against the window as he pointed up the street at the house, a gesture with a limp hand, making sure he looked unbothered. He said, "What are you going to do if someone comes over for a chat? They might not approve of your conduct."

Miles looked up from the phone, gave the question genuine thought. He said, "Well, I couldn't shoot both of you, that'd be a real mess." He turned to the guy and said, "So I guess I'd have to drill you real fast, dress it up before anyone gets here." He looked down at the phone again as he dialed another number, said, "My advice though: keep an eye out for people coming over, back us up real quick if they look friendly."

He put the phone to his ear, kept his eyes on the man beside him, feeling a rejoinder coming and wanting to give something back if needed. But the guy just sat there quietly, and Miles waited through the ringtone until DeSean picked up and asked him, "Yeah, what's happening?"

Miles said, "It's me. We need to pack everything up."

"You think someone's coming by?"

"Yeah, there've been developments. Wait for our guest, and then go somewhere else."

"Like where?"

"I can't say it straight out, I got someone right here. Ask me questions."

"Okay. You want me to call Stanton?"

"Yeah. He'll fix you up with something."

"When's the girl getting here?"

"I don't know. Soon. But don't sit around playing PlayStation till the doorbell goes. You got to be ready to clear out."

"Yeah, yeah. 'Sall good. And what are you doing?"

Miles said, "Cleaning something up. I'll give you a call."

He clicked off and the guy had a smile ready, said to him, "I don't think it counts as cleaning up when you're wading into a ton of shit."

That had crossed his mind actually, but it wasn't like he could just turn around and walk out of it. He took the guy's phone from his jacket pocket and held it out to him across the console. "Power it up and unlock it for me."

The guy just sat there, Miles waiting for him, the phone cantilevered flat off two fingers like a giant business card.

Miles sighed, not breaking eye contact, like this was just tedious more than anything. He said, "Look. You seem to have grasped my situation pretty well. Which means you understand I don't really have anything to lose. I don't keep you in line, I'm probably looking at dying or going to prison. So you can unlock the phone, or I'm going to have to shoot you."

Maybe the guy had to weigh that one up carefully, because several more seconds passed before he finally took the thing and powered it on. He typed in an access code and then passed the phone back.

Miles juggled it on his palm to get it upright, and then opened the text-message app. The file was empty. He navigated to the call log. The last outgoing was to a New York City area code, a four-minute exchange cut short when Miles had shown up. He scrolled down and saw the same number several more times, once or twice per day, going back the last week. There it was at eight P.M. last night: two minutes' duration, a quick update before the visit to the Coveys, and then again at eleven P.M.—twenty-three minutes that time. Miles had left the house at ten thirty or thereabouts, which meant it took the guy about half an hour to call in and admit that the money was gone.

He memorized the number, and then typed it in as the recipient of a new message. In the text field he wrote, "A few developments. We should meet. Rockefeller Center in two hours?"

The tone seemed about right. Concision implied alarm without being panicky, but there was something between the lines as well. "Developments" was euphemistic. There was a hint of burgeoning crisis.

He read it through a couple more times, pressed send, and dropped the phone in his coat again. He said, "Change of plan. We're going for a drive."

FIFTEEN

Bobby Deen

He remembered his first visit to New York, and thinking he'd never make it big.

Charles had flown him up for film work. It was just a background role, but it was a thank-you gesture for all of Bobby's drug runs. The trip over felt like something he could get used to: flying across the country on someone else's dime to make a movie. Then he arrived, and got the true perspective on his status, saw the wealth and power and knew exactly where he ranked in the world. He knew first visits were meant to inspire—people seeing the scale of the place and doubling their ambitions—but driving through Midtown at night in the fog with the buildings turned to pillars of suspended lights, it all looked like a ceiling he'd never touch. Then he spent three hours in the rain, dressed as a cop and pretending to flush out terrorists from the ground floor of some south-of-SoHo shithole, and he worried that he was truly in his element.

He didn't visit again for a couple of years, but by that time he'd transitioned to an admin role, not just couriering for Charles, but chasing up his debts as well.

Cody Brink was a guy who'd borrowed a quarter-million dollars, and then decided not to pay it back. He was shacked up in New York with an ex-wife turned current girlfriend. Charles flew Bobby over first class. The ex-wife/current girlfriend had a place on the Upper West Side, and he could still picture the drive in: her tidy brownstone on a rich-looking street, both sidewalks lined with oaks, sunlight through the leaves making shadows like jagged camouflage. He parked out front and watched them from the car awhile, getting glimpses as they passed the street-facing window, worried he'd need some clever ploy to get in. In the end, though, he just risked it and rang the bell, figuring you can get a long way by dressing sharp and not being edgy, and Cody's woman let him straight in with a smile. Bobby told her he was here to collect two hundred fifty grand, and things turned frantic then: Cody went upstairs at a brisk walk that became a run when Bobby followed, chasing him at a sprint to the bedroom and catching him as Cody reached the bed. He had a Smith .38 under his pillow, lost his grip as Bobby shoved him out the bedroom window. The window overlooked the street, but there was a fire escape to catch him, and Cody lay there with his knees hooked on the glass-toothed sill and the rest of him draped on the iron platform.

He didn't even have the payment yet, but the view grabbed him: a frame of jagged glass and Cody limp and supine, trees along the mon-eyed street swaying, as if from the impact of the fall.

It looked like success, an image that said, This is Your Town. The elation hit with such purity, the first thing he did was pick up the bed-side phone, wanting to call home and tell someone he'd finally Made It. Then it was hard to know what happened next—whether the woman hitting him made him drop the handset, or if common sense got through in time to say you don't dial home from a crime scene.

He had that memory to go back to, and it improved with each visit, awkward edges disappearing and his words getting cleverer and more clipped. In his head, Cody didn't reach the gun. In his head, Cody never looked like a threat. In his head, Bobby wasn't shit-scared going into it. Now as he rode through Manhattan in the back of a rented car, Marko and Luka up front, he could go back and see himself standing at the broken window, flawless composure, smoothing his tie as he told Cody Brink he had three days to send the check.

The light through his lids softened, and he opened his eyes to the gloom of the Midtown Tunnel, Marko watching him in the mirror as he drove.

Bobby said, "I'm still here."

"Yeah, you don't look like it."

"You haven't seen someone with their eyes shut?"

He didn't get an answer. The car was a Mercedes sedan, an AMG model, V-8 engine that sounded like it ran on silk, black leather seats so smooth it was hard to stay upright. It had been waiting for them on the tarmac at Kennedy, courtesy of Billion Air.

They came out of the depths of the river and into the steel lockjaw of Midtown traffic. With careful German inflection, the GPS woman told them to take a left on Third Avenue. Marko obeyed and then found Bobby in the mirror again, eyebrows raised as he said, "So what's the going rate these days, if you save a lady's life?"

Bobby said, "Depends how good a job you do."

Marko turned his bottom lip out and nodded, and Luka said, "Say she's going to be murdered on a boat, and you tidy it all up, bring her back with all her limbs still attached?"

Bobby said, "I was well looked after, put it that way."

Very well looked after: a two-hundred-K involvement fee for his personal risk, fifty K on top of that for bringing Nina back unharmed, another fifty for impact and theater, making Lenny Burke and the boat disappear. Three hundred all up, but it wouldn't insure against death threats. Three hundred grand couldn't buy safety for long.

Luka turned in his seat, gave him a hooked smile. "Hope the lady paid for your efforts, too. Imagine she's got a bit to offer."

They both found that pretty funny.

Bobby ignored it. The Daydream Nina had made it worth his trouble: there was a parallel reality where they'd stayed on that boat a little longer, and she hadn't gone back to Charles. He'd run that through his head so often it was like bona fide memory. The problem now was that he didn't know what he was doing: he didn't know if he was here for Nina, or for Charles's collection fee. Either one could make him veer off course for the better.

He took out his phone and reopened the PDFs that Charles had sent him.

The first pages were a rundown on Peter Berkhov, Russian, based out in Malibu mostly, but he had real-estate interests countrywide. He ran hookers and made pornography, employed guys who'd done time for all kinds of aggressive action.

It was probably expensive intel. The photos were grainy covert shots: the guy crossing the street, squinting at the wind with his tie across his shoulder, through-the-window photos of him eating in a restaurant. There was background on a guy called Lee Feng as well, Chinese, operated out of New York—Chinatown, of course. He ran hard drugs, OxyContin, racketeering, protection . . .

Bobby said, "So who's this Feng guy? Does Charles think he's trying for a takeover?"

He thought they'd let the question pass, but then Marko said, "We're not paid to listen."

"You still hear things, whether you want to or not."

Marko would've made a great New Yorker: he rode a cab's rear fender for two blocks, forty miles an hour at a range of about ten inches, blasted his horn when the guy dared to slow down. Marko said, "You want to know what's going on, you're talking to the wrong people. We're just the pickup guys."

"You're not curious about the kind of circus you're signing on for?"

That amused him as well. Marko said, "We've done work in Ukraine—you think this is the circus, you never been shot at by a twelve-year-old with an RPG. Nothing in this town's a circus." He shrugged, ducked forward and looked at the cityscape, like assessing its potential for bad things. He said, "There's Russians involved, fine. I don't mind killing Russians. But I don't give a fuck what their business is."

Bobby said, "So all he told you was your bonus?"

Marko lifted his head, found his eyes in the mirror again. "We should've declined payment, really. Fly private, drive a brand-new Mercedes, might as well be a holiday."

"Better than standing around guarding the house though, right?"

He shrugged. "We cover all sorts of stuff. We've done maritime security, body guarding, asset retrieval."

"Which is what?"

Marko shrugged. "Normally child-related, international custody disputes. You take the pissed-off parent with you and go and bring the kid back."

"So is this asset retrieval or just an exercise in finding someone's wife?"

Marko shrugged. "One way or another, she's going back to L.A. It's easy when it's not international—fly private, no one checks your luggage. Put them in a duffel bag and then let them out at the other end." He smiled. "Easiest with women: they fold better."

They were trying to get a read on him, gauge his willingness to hurt her if it came to it. He thought of the payoff if he brought her back: a duffel full of currency courtesy of Charles, and a license to do anything. He held Marko's eyes in the mirror and said, "I'll take your word for it."

He hadn't seen the apartment before, and he'd been expecting something SoHo-esque—painted brick with the fire escape hanging off the front—but Charles's place was in a newish concrete high-rise off Eleventh Avenue, just south of the Hudson Street train yards. It looked very New Age and carbon-neutral. There was a coffee shop on the ground floor with a whole wall covered in some kind of creeper plant, benches along the windows lined with kids drinking green shit out of jars.

Marko said, "You think he'd mind if we brought him back a couple of kids instead of his wife?"

Luka said, "Yeah. Swap a forty for two twenties. I'd do it."

Marko had Charles's access card. They drove into the parking garage, into cold shadow, waited as the lights came on in sequence. He found an empty slot near the back of the structure, and a minute later the three of them were in an elevator, clinic white, a speaker playing the sound of trickling water, and a German voice that sounded like the GPS telling them that the building was carbon neutral and had a five-star energy rating.

He felt like a chaperone or something, standing there in black between them with his hands clasped as they checked their pistols. They had a Sig automatic each, and bags' worth of heavier backup in the car. He didn't know what he'd do if they found her—whether he'd let them take her at gunpoint, or intervene somehow. The moment would dictate it. There'd been no plan on the boat until they were on the water, and even then he stuck to this vague notion of zero bloodshed. Then Nina pulled his intentions out of shape, made shooting the fat man seem like the answer to everything.

Charles's place was on the eighteenth floor. They formed a little triangle at the apartment door, Bobby keeping back to watch the hallway, letting the other two go ahead of him. They stood with their guns held close and chest-high, Marko with the access card to the reader. The lock beeped, and it was frantic action as the pair of them rushed inside, guns snapping left and right for cover.

Bobby let them get a few feet ahead and then followed. He saw the cameras immediately, one in each corner above the main window, but the alarm panel in the entry was blank. He walked through to the living area, listening to them swap stage whispers: "Clear!" as they checked the place room by room.

There was a kitchen to his left, and a study and two more bedrooms over to his right. Nice place, but the view was the draw card: northwest across the train yard, the blue swath of the Hudson off to his left, and a dull gray rim of New Jersey out beyond the water, isolated high-rises like blips on a graph.

They were still calling "Clear" to each other, taking it all very seriously. He put his back to the window and waited. The décor was the Stone standard: posters for shit movies, a framed *Hollywood Reporter* article from Charles's pre-wheelchair days. The flagship piece was weirdo art: this quartet of Charles Stone headshots, each with wild colors and a different hairdo. It looked like some vain Warhol rip-off.

"Well, I'd say she's fucking split."

Bobby turned and saw Luka come out of a bedroom, tension gone, the gun hanging at his side. The guy paused and took in the room, the Stone Shrine in every shade of garish. He said, "Maybe she hasn't even been here. Why wouldn't she ditch his shitty pictures?"

More to the point: if someone grabbed her, why was there no damage?

Marko came out of another bedroom, running a hand through his hair. "Yeah, no sign of her."

Bobby didn't answer. A litany of what-ifs hit him:

What if she was running/what if she'd left at gunpoint/what if she was never here?

He cruised the apartment. Luka took an armchair in the living room and stared at the view, gun in his lap and hands behind his head.

Marko said, "You out of ideas already?"

"No. I think we should call the old man and tell him his wife's gone."

The kitchen was tidy. A couple of clean plates in the dishwasher, but they could've been there for months. The appliances were all cold. The coffee machine matched his one at home.

He checked the bathroom, wanting a sign. He was getting brain-swamped. Theories competed with Nina flashes. He could see her in here, and that eighteen-story view made him think of his wife—Connie looking back as she dropped, placid and at peace.

He didn't want that now.

He shut his eyes and brought back Nina. There she was steering the boat, hair straight out behind her and a faint smile that said, This is between you and me.

He knew he could find her and fix everything.

He checked the bedroom—nothing. Clean sheets, no perfume.

There was a TV in the corner, and a photo of Charles getting some award. Where were the photos of *her*? He had his trophy shot in L.A.—

that portrait Bobby saw—and that was all. Where were the photos of *them*?

He checked a closet but found weapons instead: four shotguns upright, and a shelf of Sig pistols in foam recesses. Boxes of ammo on the floor. It all stank of gun oil.

He walked back to the living room as Luka said, "We calling him or what?" He had his feet up on a stool, getting comfy. Marko seemed more alert, still with two hands on his gun. But they were both looking at Bobby, wanting his take on it.

He stood at a window looking down at the train yard, the feeder tracks spread out like frayed rope, long silver carriages waiting in staggered rows. There was a weld spark down there too, a white star that came and went.

Marko was pacing behind him. They'd geared up for a grab-and-go, and now they didn't know how to play it.

Bobby said, "Let's fill in Mr. Stone."

Marko didn't answer, but in the reflection on the glass, Bobby saw him put a phone to his ear and get back to his pacing. The room was so quiet he could hear the ringtone.

He closed his eyes and tried to see what happened. It was too clean. She must have just walked out. If it was kidnap there'd be camera footage, surely.

Behind him Marko said, "Yeah, we're in." Then: "No sign."

Bobby opened his eyes and saw his wife falling. He looked away from the drop and saw a sign in a window: APARTMENTS FROM $8 MILLION.

He put his back to the glass. There was a desk with a compact printer against the window by the kitchen. He wandered over.

Marko said, "Yeah, we don't know. I'm just filling you in."

He pushed the stool aside and rolled open a drawer. Nothing helpful: flyers for Broadway shows, catalogues with high-end homeware. Half a dozen restaurant menus. He thumbed through paper in the printer tray, saw blocks of red text, and a big header block screaming FUCKTHEPD.COM.

He scanned the pages. It was dialogue printed off a forum, some kind of cop-hate website. Maybe she was anti-law.

He riffled paper, saw Queens/shooting/homicide/Force Investigation/Miles Keller—

What?

He flipped back a page. Yeah, there it is. Miles fucking Keller.

He read it again in full.

@Fluke150: FID admin says robbery Det Miles Keller did the Jack Deen shooting.

Lower down:

@blueh8er: Keller has no priors but DA want him bad. The prick should burn.

Bobby dropped the paper.

It must be Nina's. She heard about Cousin Jack being clipped and ran some background.

Or was there some other connection?

He looked back at the other two, saw Marko listening to his phone—taking instructions, or waiting out a diatribe.

He scanned the pages again, wanting to know what she knew, and then his phone hummed in his pocket.

Incoming call.

He checked the screen, but didn't recognize the number. He answered anyway. Standing in the apartment, a Nina-rich environment, Miles Keller's name right there on paper, everything felt relevant, part of the mystery.

He put the phone to his ear, and Nina said, "Pretend it's your mother, and then go outside to the balcony."

He didn't move, but her voice changed gravity for a moment. The world dipped and leveled out. He didn't dare look back. He swallowed to stop his voice from catching, heard blood pound in his ears as he said, "Hey, sweetheart."

Then he opened the slider and stepped out onto the balcony, felt the breeze tug him and heard the traffic over on Eleventh Avenue, horn noise just a thin call for help.

She said, "Smooth. I didn't know if I could trust you to act natural, and then I remembered you're the King of Cool."

He liked that. Maybe she had a Daydream Bobby—a match for his Daydream Nina. Maybe she had her own parallel reality, where she hadn't gone back to Charles.

She said, "Face the view. Marko can lip-read."

"How do you know where I am?"

Nina said, "The cameras still work, the feed's just been rerouted. I'm looking at it right now."

He said, "What happened?"

She hesitated, and he knew he'd get something plain and unrevealing. She said, "I didn't want to stay there, so I left."

Making it sound that innocent and simple, you'd think she never put a foot wrong.

Bobby said, "What do you know about Keller?"

She took her time with that as well, and he could hear the blood in his ears. He watched the sidewalk and saw his wife falling. He closed his eyes and in the dark Nina said, "I'm sorry about Jack. I heard what happened."

He saw her tied up in the boat's forward cabin, asking him if she could drive, Lenny Burke facedown and sinking—

He folded his arms and leaned on the rail, repeated his question: "What do you know about Keller?"

She said, "I can't tell you just yet. Are you supposed to rescue me or just take me home?"

Bobby said, "I've been trying to work that out."

"Mmm. Well, I'm glad you're open to possibilities. I wondered who Charles would send, and I'm glad you drew the short straw."

"Why's that?"

"You helped me once, you'll help me again. Why make the first time a waste of effort? Plus I can make it worth your while."

Keller. She could get him to Keller—

He said, "What's going on?"

"I've decided to separate from my husband. Put it that way." Like it was just a routine parting of ways. She said, "Irreconcilable differences. But I'm trying to reconcile the difference in our net worth."

Bobby said, "Frank Garcia said you tried to rip him off in L.A."

"He tell you that himself?"

"He knew I saved you." He'd never put it that baldly to anyone, but why not? She'd be dead if it wasn't for him.

Nina said, "The rip-off shouldn't be news. Why do you think I almost ended up dead at sea?"

He said, "What are Luka and Marko doing?"

"They're not looking at you. But there's about a three-second delay on the feed, so if I see them heading over, it's probably too late."

"Tell me what happened."

"I left that place three days ago. What did my husband tell you?"

"He said he sent you for some time out."

"My husband lied to you. He didn't send me anywhere. I came up here on my own volition."

Bobby didn't answer.

She said, "We're forever entwined by what happened on that boat. Everything plays out by the light of history. It would feel wrong if you didn't save my life again."

"Are you running?"

Nina said, "My husband's a fiend and I should have left him years ago. But I don't want to be gone without inflicting damage."

Bobby didn't answer. He risked a look back and saw Luka watching him. Marko was still on his call, but he had eyes on him, too. Bobby said, "I need to wrap this up."

"Yes, I can see that."

"Where are you?"

She said, "I'm going to be interested to see how this goes, Bobby. I'm sure my husband pays well for a good result, but there's another side to it, as well. Saving me on the boat was one thing, but doing it twice would be quite a feat. So keep that in mind. Taking me back to Charles wouldn't do me a favor. But I'm going to have to trust you to decide what's best. Right now I need you to help me."

"Where are you?"

She said, "They're both watching you now."

He couldn't keep it up. He turned and made a V sign with his fingers below his eyes, and then pointed to a camera above the window. They both turned and looked straight at the lens.

Nina said, "Look at that. I thought these guys were pros. What happened to pretending you're talking to your mother?"

Bobby said, "I think they'd twigged."

"So how are you going to explain the 'hey sweetheart'? Or are we on sweetheart terms?"

Bobby said, "I'll say I got another call."

"Or you could just leave them in the apartment. There's a lot of space in that bathroom. Whatever you do, it'll have to be good-bye at some stage."

He glanced back and saw Luka watching him, Marko on the phone and pacing faster now.

Bobby said, "Where are you?"

"I'm at a hotel. There are people watching the building. I can't leave without your help."

"I can't help until I know where you are."

She said, "I'm at the Tribeca Gardens on Canal Street. Are you going to take me back to L.A., or do we ride off into the sunset?"

Bobby didn't answer.

Nina said, "There has to be a New York version of the last outing: blood in the water, making a clean break with the wind in your hair. I'm sure you'll think of something."

SIXTEEN

KINGS POINT, NY

Miles Keller

He'd been up to Kings Point a few times now, and he thought it would be a nice place to retire if he had a spare five million dollars and wasn't a fugitive. The streets were wide and quiet, plenty of trees along the verge, and people seemed to take their lawn care seriously. He mentioned that to his driver—the fact that people had nice grass—wanting to reinforce the sense that all was copacetic.

They came south down the western side of the point, and then had to join the main road again just south of the cemetery. The driver was extra cautious with his gap selection, and it paid off for him: waited a full two minutes to merge, and then slipped in ahead of two state police cruisers.

Miles got that feeling like hitting bad air in a plane, his stomach dropping out for a second or two. The cars had probably just come off the Covey scene. He didn't look back though, knew he wouldn't do himself any favors by seeming worried. He said, "Police can do first aid, but it's not quite like being in a hospital, you know what I mean?"

The driver didn't answer, seemed to think there was potential in this arrangement, having the law in pursuit. Miles saw him watching his side mirror as they rounded a bend on Middle Neck Road, a rural stretch south of town that was still wooded on both sides, trees tall and turning to gray wicker in the late autumn.

Miles said, "Should've told you I got X-ray vision. I can see your gears turning."

The guy looked over—slow enough to convey a challenge—but he kept quiet. Miles was quarter-profile to him, a shoulder against his door and the gun upright in his lap, frame propped across his thigh.

Miles said, "Have to admit, wouldn't be ideal shooting you while we're moving—I mean just in terms of my safety. But I'll do it if I have to. Take some explaining, but if it boils down to your word against mine, and I'm a cop, and you're dead, you know . . ."

He shrugged and let his voice trail off. This would be a long exercise in deadpan, but it was hard sticking to a cool tempo, his heart rate up and his breath coming short and a little fast. He wasn't sure how he'd actually handle things, given there were probably two cops in each car. There was no way he'd shoot them.

He said, "Take the next right and go around the block."

The guy's phone buzzed.

Miles felt it on his chest and brought it out of his coat, slightly awkward, left hand in his left inside pocket. He entered the passcode and saw a message from the mystery number, getting back to him about his Rockefeller request: "Somewhere closer?"

He held the phone high to keep the driver in his line of sight and typed "Where?"

His finger hovered by the send button, but didn't drop. He could see the driver watching him, eyes on the road's shoulder to keep Miles in the corner of his vision. If he was going to try something, now was the time, backup right there behind them if he went for the gun. Miles lowered the phone and waited for the guy's eyes to settle on their lane. There was a turnoff coming up and he didn't signal, went straight past with the needle holding steady on thirty-five.

Miles didn't move. Any sign of worry would be a huge concession.

He said, "I really can't afford to go more than two strikes here. So you can take the next turn, or I can shoot you."

That sounded okay, but the guy could probably hear his heart thumping.

He forced himself to look at the phone, hit backspace to erase his message. He didn't want to change location for the meeting. He needed crowds and multiple exits, and he wanted an area he knew well. Not that he was even sure yet what he'd do—whether he'd just see who showed up, and then revisit the matter at a later date, or if he'd draw a line under the whole thing today. He could see the latter scenario playing out, putting a bullet in someone and the crowd all ducking in unison. He could look shocked with the rest of them and then walk out in any direction he liked. Maybe straight west across Sixth Avenue, and he'd be on the subway in two minutes—

He saw movement that killed the thought, but it was just a car on a cross street, an SUV pulling out behind the cops. He let a long breath out quietly, trying to slow himself down, focus on what had to happen right now. He still had the phone in his hand, the cursor flashing patiently and two police cars not far off their rear fender, the whole of his world in the most fragile equilibrium.

He looked in his side mirror and said, "Don't go playing Morse code or something with your brake lights, that'd be real irritating."

He wondered if he sounded too laid-back, whether he'd come across as overcompensating. He gestured at the windshield with the phone and said, "There's another right just up here. Make sure you use your turn signal."

It was actually another quarter-mile, but the road looked no different, curving back and forth through woods. The turn finally emerged in his periphery, and his heart pounded even harder: the effort of feigned indifference, and the stress of getting through the next few seconds. If the guy didn't turn, Miles would have to make good on his threat, at least to some extent. He saw the driver's knuckles white on the wheel, eyes switching between the mirror and the road, and finally Miles's belt tugged him as the car slowed, and the turn signal went tick-tock with an idleness that didn't suit the tension of the moment.

Miles felt his pulse drop with the turn, and he had to stop himself from sighing. He leaned forward to see the cop cars in his side mirror going past on the main road. He said, "You going to tell me your real name, or will I have to think of you as just 'the guy'?" Trying to cover his relief by talking.

The driver shrugged, knuckles still white, a gloss along the top of the wheel. He said, "I'm thinking of you as just the guy, so you might as well do the same."

Miles nodded, like that seemed fair enough. There were houses set back among the trees, big stately looking manors that would have been perfect on a Georgia plantation two hundred years ago. He said, "I'll probably give you a made-up name when I write my memoirs. Maybe call you the tracksuit man."

He felt his adrenaline fading, making room for clearer thoughts. He looked back at the phone and typed, "Rockefeller is best. I have another meet-up beforehand."

He pressed send and dropped the phone in his pocket, checked his mirror again to see the SUV that had pulled out behind them a minute ago. It was only a hundred feet back now, and he could see that it was DeSean's Lincoln Navigator—Lucy was following them.

Miles breathed, "Oh shit."

The driver said, "You want me to find another block to go around?" Smiling a little, enjoying himself.

Miles said, "Take us back to the main road and go right again."

He dug his burner phone out of his trouser pocket and dialed Lucy's cell.

When she picked up she said, "I wondered how long you'd take to notice."

He said, "This isn't what I told you to do, is it?"

"You should've done a better job of acting normal. Disappear somewhere with a gun, I figured you'd need help."

"I'm doing fine, thanks."

"So where are you going?"

They were back at the main road, slowing for the turn. Miles watched his mirror as the SUV grew nearer, tree reflections sliding upward on its glass. He said, "I'm going to see someone, and then I'm getting out of town."

The tracksuit man made the turn—very sedate, like a hearse or a royal motorcade—and Miles tensed for something to happen. He wondered how long he could keep this up, his time span for total vigilance. He watched Lucy pull out behind them, and she said, "Does the getting out of town bit still include me?"

He wondered how he'd actually manage that: staying hidden and caring for an emphysema patient, too. She'd need tank refills obviously, and he guessed she had other medication as well. Maybe you just told Medicaid and that was it, but it defeated the point of staying off the grid. But he couldn't just leave her here and wait for retribution to show up. And he couldn't keep paying protection money, either. Two grand a week would hollow him out pretty fast.

Miles said, "You're not doing me any favors by following me."

"I'm your backup."

"Yeah? What have you got in mind if it gets rough?"

"I don't know. Run someone over. You going to tell me what the fuck you're doing?" She didn't sound wound up about it—like she was annoyed at being out of the loop, but not fearing for his safety.

Miles said, "I'm going for a ride, and then I'm going to meet someone."

She said, "You think you're being real clever not telling me anything, but all the bits you don't say, I fill them in with something bad."

He didn't answer. He wondered at what point people deserved an explanation, how long you had to know them for.

She said, "Look. I owe you—"

Miles said, "Yeah, I know. But tagging along now doesn't count as repaying me."

Lucy said, "You got that guy there at gunpoint or something?"

He was too slow coming back and she said, "I waited on a side street and saw you go past. I thought: Why are you sitting side-on like that, unless you got a real good-looking driver?"

Miles said, "I'm trying to solve some murders."

He'd had it in his head all morning, but it sounded like a long shot now, saying it aloud.

Lucy said, "Right, okay. And you're expecting a shoot-out along the way? The hell are you doing?"

They were midway down Great Neck now, passing through a little shopping district, brick stores done Tudor style. He felt the phone buzz in his jacket again.

Lucy said, "Whatever, you don't have to tell me. But you can get used to having me as a shadow. Never know, you might end up pleased I had your back."

He brought out the other phone and checked the message: "Who are you meeting?" He dropped it in his pocket again and put his back to the window a little more, wanting to be square to the driver if he tried something.

He said to Lucy, "Actually, there is something you can do."

"Uh-huh?"

"There's some stuff at my hotel that I need."

"Is this your technique for getting rid of me?"

Miles said, "No, it's a technique for not leaving any money behind."

That did the trick: silence for a whole three seconds. Then she said, "How much?"

Miles said, "Enough to be comfy for a little while. It's in a bag in the safe."

"Where's the hotel?"

"Canal Street. It's the Tribeca Gardens. I'll call the desk and have them leave a swipe card out."

"What's the safe code?"

"I'll text it to you."

She said, "We're not splitting up. I'll follow you there."

He wasn't sure what he'd do after that. He couldn't have her following him up to Rockefeller Center, but he could handle that as it happened. He said, "Okay, fine."

Lucy said, "We'll take the Long Island Expressway to the BQE to the Manhattan Bridge."

He didn't hear a question mark at the end, but he said, "Yeah, that's right."

Lucy said, "This time tomorrow, we'll be rich and in the wind."

SEVENTEEN

NEW YORK, NY

Bobby Deen

Heading downtown on Seventh, they caught a string of green lights and sailed through three blocks without stopping, pedestrians at crosswalks standing in the lane as if the traffic was some great spectacle, people close enough you could run them down with just a flick of the wheel. It was funny really, how people put it all on the line: death at touching distance for the sake of a head start across a street.

Marko had Charles on the phone as he drove, giving the old man the latest, telling him that Nina was at a Tribeca hotel on Canal Street and that they were heading there now. He shut up awhile as he listened to instructions, Charles talking loud enough Bobby could almost catch the words, even with New York at midday volume in the background. Eventually Marko said, "Yeah, here you go," and passed the phone back to Bobby without looking.

Bobby came in midsentence: ". . . the cost of keeping a jet on standby at Kennedy. So do it fast—I don't have the blackmail power to hold a plane there overnight. I'm running light on leverage as it is."

Bobby said, "We're looking for her," wanting something active but nonspecific. He still didn't know what he was going to do. He was hung up on opposing stories: Nina told him she was here on her own volition, but Charles had said the trip was his bidding. Maybe it didn't matter. Charles could have lied to save face, make Bobby think he kept his wife on a tight leash. And if Nina lied, it was benign—somehow. It had to be. The thing on the boat entwined them, or however she'd put it. She knew he'd saved her life.

Right now though, it felt like he'd just done cocaine:

Sensory overload with the street blurring past; Nina in his head telling him he could save her again; that image of blood in the water that he thought he'd never shake; Charles still talking at him; Bobby thinking he should have killed the pair of them in the apartment, that this would be easier to handle on his own.

Charles was shouting at him now: "Who's watching?"

"What?"

"She said people are watching the hotel—who's watching the hotel?"

"She didn't say."

"You mean like she didn't know, or she just didn't want to tell you? There's a big fucking difference."

Bobby said, "Could be Garcia's people up from L.A., I don't know. She was cagey."

Charles said, "She thinks she can still play some kind of angle. She'll tell you just enough to get her out of it, and then take off on me."

There: he was being upfront now. He knew she was running.

Charles still in his ear: "She thinks because you saved her once, you'll do it again." Crackle on the line, probably spit hitting the mouth-piece.

Bobby said, "That's the intention."

"Yeah, but it's all about what happens afterward: she wants to be in the wind, and I want her on my plane. Only one of those outcomes gets you paid. You understand what I mean?"

Bobby didn't answer. They reached Greenwich Avenue and slowed, traffic bottlenecked to get past a barricaded steam vent: this white-and-orange tube standing ten feet high in the middle of the road.

Charles said, "You with me, Bobby? You thinking about your hopes and dreams, how you're going to make them happen?"

Bobby said, "All the time," and ended the call.

Marko was holding out his hand for the phone, watching him in the mirror as he drove.

"What'd he tell you?"

Bobby said, "Wait a minute," and brought up an internet app. He Googled, and found the number for the Tribeca Gardens on Canal Street. Bobby called the front desk and asked for room 1503. There was a long pause and then a slow ring as the call transferred. Nina answered with a "yes" that sounded faintly interested, not at all concerned.

Bobby said, "It's me."

She said, "So you don't trust me."

He didn't answer, and she said, "You went through the front desk to see if I'd lied about my room number."

He faltered. His brain whirred. He said, "If I got you on the cell there's no way of knowing if you're being coerced."

Nina said, "I can be coerced all sorts of places. Maybe I'm being held at gunpoint now."

"At least I know you're in your room."

He could see her, too: standing at the window, holding the phone with her shoulder. She'd be there when he came in the front door, and she'd walk over to him holding his gaze, stand close and say something that would make him smile.

Bobby said, "Who's watching you?"

"There are two SUVs on rotation. Black Chevys with smoked glass. You'll see them."

"Who are they?"

"I don't know. I just know that they're there."

"Are there people on the street as well?"

Nina said, "Have you decided yet who you're with?"

Bobby didn't answer. Luka was twisted around in his seat, watching, listening.

Bobby said, "Two of us will come and bring you down. We'll wait in the lobby for a pickup."

Nina said, "You didn't answer my question. What happens when I'm in the car?"

"You've got nothing to worry about."

Nina said, "I realize you're being listened to, so let's put it in straight yes-or-no terms. This is important, Bobby. Are you with me or not?"

There was a ringing in his ears that almost drowned the question.

EIGHTEEN

NEW YORK, NY

Miles Keller

On the freeway, the tracksuit man seemed to forget he was a hostage, settled into his driving with a nice low posture, holding the wheel with one hand like they were off for a weekend together. Miles was still propped against his door half-facing him, and the Glock hadn't moved either. Every now and then he checked his mirror to see Lucy sitting two cars back. He thought he'd have to do a round of tough-guy talk back and forth, the driver asking who the girl in the SUV was, whether he was prepared to watch her back for the rest of his life. But there was none of that: they just rode in silence until about a mile before the BQE, when the driver looked across and said, "Would you really have shot me?" Trying to sound like it didn't bother him one way or the other.

Miles said, "I'm still holding you at gunpoint. Why would I tell you anything except yes?"

The guy didn't answer.

Miles said, "You trying to figure out if you died and gone someplace else? That'd be strange, wouldn't it? Heaven and hell no different to where you were a moment ago."

The guy took a minute and said, "Thought if you're solving murders you wouldn't want to make another one along the way." Looking across with a smile starting in his eyes, like he'd figured all this out and Miles hadn't.

Miles said, "I wouldn't need to solve yours though, would I? Know it was me who shot you."

The guy looked at the road and then looked back at him again, still with that look in his eye, but the smile not quite taking hold. He said, "How'd you get into all of this?"

Miles grinned. "You've got awful chatty, haven't you?"

The guy didn't answer.

Miles said, "You say that like I'm stuck in something that's out of my control. But we're doing okay, aren't we?"

The guy said, "Yeah. We'll see."

The road was more congested now, southbound traffic out of La-Guardia slowing the flow. Miles said, "People end up on the wrong side of the law for all sorts of reasons—debts, extortion, I don't know—maybe they take a risk somewhere and get in deeper than they wanted." He shrugged. "I didn't do any of that. I'm where I am because I made conscious decisions, and I knew what I was getting into. But you're here because you went for a drive this morning and didn't see me coming. I don't know if that's bad luck or if it's like a common feature of your life. So you tell me: how did you get into all of this?"

The guy didn't answer, and Miles felt the confiscated phone buzz again in his pocket. He said, "This guy doesn't give it a rest, does he?"

He entered the passcode to view the text message: "Call in. I'm concerned."

Miles thought about it. He could put the driver on speaker, but it would be hard to keep him on-message. He couldn't really use force while they were doing seventy miles an hour. Safest way would be to pull over somewhere while the guy made the call, but that had risks, too: no way of knowing what might be a coded tip-off. But by not calling he was potentially inviting trouble later. Show up at Rockefeller Center and find a hit squad waiting. Or maybe he'd just see the flash, and that would be it.

There was a call incoming now, but Miles silenced it and brought up the internet app. He Googled the number for the Tribeca Gardens on Canal Street and called the front desk with his burner phone. He told the lady on reception his room number, and asked for an access key to be ready for pickup.

"Yes, sir. Of course."

"Great. There's a lady with an air tank coming by to get it in about thirty minutes."

Traffic thinned out again coming along I-278, the straight east-west section where it parallels Flushing Avenue. On their right was a view of standard Brooklyn: boxy low-rise apartments in mismatched shades and sizes, and on their left a stretch of Housing Authority stock: brick high-rise apartments in sooty brown, one after the other after the other, like some dystopia being trialed, a new kind of bleak living right there by the freeway.

The damn phone was ringing again. Miles let it quit and then sent a text: "Can't talk. See you in 30."

He said, "Stay right. We want the Manhattan Bridge exit. We're going via Canal Street first to pick up a bag of money. After that, we're going to the LEGO store."

NINETEEN

NEW YORK, NY

Bobby Deen

It didn't seem like a Nina kind of neighborhood. He pictured her on a street with little trees and high-priced stores—Gucci and the stuff they had in *Vogue*—but this part of Canal was cheap goods: electronic gear and tourist shit crammed in behind neon storefronts.

They were coming in from the eastern end of Canal, the hotel on their left just past the post-office building, a tired brick monstrosity that looked like an army facility.

Luka said, "I don't see any black SUVs." He was playing with his gun to burn off tension, dropping the magazine an inch and then clicking it home. They'd brought a pistol for Bobby, too—a little Colt .38— no doubt trying to tell him he was second-class, and not worth a Sig. Compact was better though, in New York City: unlicensed carry would get you three years in lockup.

Marko looked at Bobby in the mirror. "Call her back and see what's happening."

Bobby called the hotel on his cell and gave the deskman Nina's room number. She picked up and said, "I'm still here."

Bobby said, "I don't see any SUVs."

"Then you timed it just right. They come and go."

Bobby said, "Stay in the room. We'll come up and get you and then wait in the lobby for the car."

"What are you driving?"

"Black Mercedes."

"Matches your suit, I bet. See you soon."

Gone—just the tone in Bobby's ear.

Marko caught him in the mirror, eyebrows raised: "And?"

Bobby said, "She says they come and go, so we lucked out."

Luka said, "Hopefully they show up. There's an AR-15 in the trunk."

He didn't look eager for a gunfight, though. He looked nervous, kept touching his cuffs, smoothing his tie as he glanced around to check adjacent cars. No one looked back. Manhattan drivers don't have time for that shit.

Marko said, "All right. I'll drop you and do a loop. I don't know how long it'll take. Fuck this traffic—why do people want to live here anyway?"

He shifted to the left-hand lane and cut a U-turn just before West Broadway, changed lanes again to get them over by the curb, pulled up outside the Tribeca Gardens.

"Make it fast. I don't want to have to keep doing laps."

A concierge stepped up and opened Bobby's door, leaned down with a smile and swept an upturned hand as he moved aside. Bobby got out into the city noise and tried to act natural, buttoned his jacket as he crossed the sidewalk to the hotel entrance, his back prickling with the thought of gunsights on his spine. He glanced back and saw Luka following, Marko already taking off with a chirp of the tires.

The foyer was air-conditioned, and seemed bright with all its shiny stone veneer, but it was just a normal hotel scene: reception crew looking pleasant and attentive in their ties and blazers, a few guests milling around, an even split of corporate types and tourists. He saw three guys in red polo shirts standing by a sign that read INSTITUTE OF WIRE ROPE FABRICATORS—CONFERENCE ROOM 2. They weren't talking, just standing there hand-on-wrist and looking at the distance, and as Bobby came past they all turned to him, as if he might be the one to save them from the silence.

He turned and checked the sidewalk as he waited for Luka to catch up, but all he saw were pedestrians in motion, no one stopping for a cigarette or looking at him across a newspaper.

"We going up or what?"

Bobby smoothed his coat, making sure it covered the gun. He said, "Stay here and watch the lobby."

Luka made a little O shape with his mouth, like blowing out a candle. He cocked his head and said, "They got small elevators or something?"

He wasn't so tense now, though Bobby wasn't sure why. Maybe being in a hotel put him at ease: all those happy tourists, in the business of happy memories.

Bobby said, "Someone could follow us, or be waiting when we come back down. I just don't want any surprises."

Luka looked away as he nodded and touched his tie knot. Then he stepped in close and used a thumb to tilt Bobby's hat back so he could look him in the face. Bobby stood there and let it happen. He knew he could even things out eventually.

Luka said, "Yeah, I don't want any surprises, either. So I think I'll come up with you. Unless you want to stay down here?"

He was close enough Bobby could see the flecks in his irises, the tiny motions as his focus shifted. Bobby shrugged without breaking eye contact. He noticed they'd got the polo-shirt guys out of trouble: something to talk about now he and Luka were facing off.

He said, "All right, then. After you."

Luka stepped away, and as he did so he flicked the underside of Bobby's brim, a hard flat click like the first raindrop, a storm on the way. Bobby followed him to the elevators and pushed the up arrow, and they stood there in silence as if part of some strange ceremony, hands clasped and looking up at the floor counter as they waited for the doors to open.

TWENTY

Miles Keller

He made his driver take a left onto Broadway from Canal, wanting to approach the hotel from the west, keep it on the near side of the street. He called Lucy again on the burner and told her what was happening.

He said, "You can pull up right outside and go straight in the front door."

She said, "It's probably no stopping, or cabs only or something."

"I wouldn't worry about it. We'll wait farther up and you can bring the bag over."

"Am I going to be able to carry it with one arm?"

Miles said, "Yeah, probably."

"Otherwise I'll be throwing out money till it's light enough."

He said, "There's a photo on the desk, too. Just put it in the bag."

"All right. If I have to drop something, do you want the money or the photo?"

He covered the phone with his shoulder and told the tracksuit man to go right again onto Walker Street. He put the phone back to his ear and caught Lucy midsentence.

"Say that again?"

She said, "I've done pickups before, but no one ever told me what I was actually carrying. You're the first guy to be straight up with me, and you're a cop. I don't know if that counts as irony, or if it's just a funny way things work sometimes. You know?"

Miles didn't answer. They reached Sixth Avenue, and he watched his mirror as Lucy rode the Cadillac's fender through the right-hand turn.

He said, "I'm going to get off the phone. Just call me back if you need anything."

"Yeah, sure. So if I call back and ask, you'll tell me what's going on?"

He didn't answer.

She said, "And Miles? After this is sorted—whatever it is—we're even, okay?"

She clicked off, and he had the dial tone in his ear as they turned right onto Canal Street off Sixth.

Miles said to his driver, "Are you being all well-behaved because you've accepted what's happening, or are you planning a getaway?"

The guy craned his neck to see himself in the rearview mirror, gave a long sigh through his nose. He said, "Oh, you know." He did that lazy turn of his head again, like it took some effort to look across the console. "Guess I'm just coming to terms with it."

Miles said, "Well, that's great: I can relax then."

He saw the hotel coming up on his right, cabs at the curb with their trunk lids up and a group of people loading them with luggage.

Miles said, "Pull up just past these guys."

The tracksuit man found a gap and swung the Cadillac to the curb.

Miles said, "Leave the engine running."

He saw Lucy pull up just behind the cabs. There wasn't enough room to get the SUV in against the curb, and she had the rear fender sticking out in the lane.

Miles said, "We're going to sit here for a few minutes. Take your hands off the wheel. We're not moving till I say."

TWENTY-ONE

NEW YORK, NY

Bobby Deen

Afterward, he realized how easy it would've been to take him out. As soon as he got in the elevator, his focus was Nina Nina Nina. Someone could've walked up and shot him and he wouldn't have noticed.

They went along the hallway reading door numbers and found her room, and Luka hung back to let Bobby knock.

"She'll like that, won't she? Bobby Deen framed in the doorway."

Bobby ignored him. He felt light as his knuckles touched the wood, the same feeling as when the elevator reached their floor, that slight lift in his stomach.

Nina opened the door with half a smile, like she knew for sure it was going to be him. She stood there briefly looking him up and down, only her eyes moving, and Bobby thought back to that image he had of her at the window, Nina facing the view and then walking over to him, making some remark. This was close: she didn't move back as he came into the entry hall, held her ground and touched his jacket and then his tie, like making small adjustments. She looked up at him but didn't say anything, and Bobby decided this was better than being face-to-face with Luka.

She let her finger trail off his lapel as she turned and moved into the room, glanced back at Luka in the hallway and said, "You too?"

"Yeah. You don't have to sound so thrilled."

Nina's smile grew. "Oh, I'm definitely not."

In Bobby's head she'd been Audrey Hepburn—wearing a little dress and a big hat, big shades to go with it, even indoors—but she looked just as good in jeans and a sweater. She hooked her hair back with a finger as she bent to pick up a bag, no different from anyone he'd been past in the lobby, except she was the kind of woman you couldn't look away from.

Bobby held the door for her as she came out into the corridor, and Nina said, "You could've brought some luggage with you, make yourselves look less like bodyguards."

He hadn't thought of that, but she made it seem more endearing than an oversight, saying it lightly and looking him in the eye. He heard the metallic hum-tick of an electronic lock, and he glanced over to see a woman with an air tank on a little wheeled trolley go into a room along the corridor. He saw Nina watching too, eyes on the door even after it was closed.

Bobby said, "All good?"

She nodded. "Yeah. Just interesting." She gave his tie a tug, holding it high and letting her knuckles touch his chest. "Let's get out of here."

Going down, they had an elevator to themselves again. Nina stood next to him with her back to the door, looking at him in the glass as she said, "You never told me about your hat."

Funny how it was all about who asked the question: if Luka had given him that line he would've ignored it, brushed it off as the guy trying to make a dig. But Nina made it different, and he could hear her wanting to *know* him. He wished it had more of a story, that it showed some strength of character. Maybe like a cowboy arrangement, where he'd killed a guy and took his hat. That might be overdoing it. He could tone it back though, think up a scenario where someone gave him attitude, acted smart, so Bobby sought penance—

Luka said, "He just wears it so you can't see him going bald."

Which was a good way to dodge an answer actually. Bobby looked at him and smiled briefly, like there was a lot more to it, but he wouldn't deign to lay it out in the presence of an asshole.

They got out at the lobby and headed for the street, Luka and then Nina with her bag, Bobby bringing up the rear. Being in the lobby crowd put his brain back in threat mode, let him see past Nina to the other people in the room—pastel-clad tourists with their brochures, businessmen who looked up from their phones to track Nina walking past. He couldn't see the Mercedes at the curb. There was a Lincoln Navigator parked at an angle in behind a taxi, a few people still fussing with luggage. The polo-shirt guys had moved on, but they'd left their sign behind. Wire rope fabricators, conference room two.

He touched Nina's elbow and said, "Just hang back here a moment."

He saw Luka moving ahead to where the doormen stood and the view of the road was better, felt his heart skip as a black SUV went past, slow at first and then punching the gas hard as it moved out of sight. He watched Luka track it up the street and then turn away, checking the oncoming cars again. The woman they'd seen in the hallway came out of an elevator behind them, walked past towing her air tank on its trolley, carrying a duffel bag with her other hand. Guys turned and watched—she got as much attention as Nina had—this beautiful woman maybe forty years old, making the air tank a sought-after accessory, not diminishing her cool.

Bobby watched her to the door and said, "We'll wait here until the car shows up."

Nina turned and faced him, looking up and making him feel exposed, no protection from his hat brim. She said quietly, "And then what happens?"

Miles Keller

It happened too fast.

In his side mirror he saw Lucy come out of the hotel and turn toward them, ignoring her skew-parked SUV and not hurrying in the slightest, the bag in one hand and her trolley in the other. For a moment, watching her come toward him with her easy walk, he seemed to float out of the stress of the moment, and it was just the image of a woman in a mirror. He had maybe two quiet seconds before he landed again: all the pressures of a safe getaway thumping back, amplified by absence.

He told the driver to open the trunk, and as the guy hit the button, Miles saw Lucy turn and head back for the hotel, as if his order had been the cue for cold feet. He watched her walk around the hood of the Navigator and unlock the driver's door, and then heave the tank up onto the seat.

What the hell are you doing?

He dug in his pocket for the burner, thinking he could call her back. But in reaching for the phone he took his eyes off the mirror, and on the street ahead, one block up, he saw a black SUV idling curbside, and a guy with a gun standing next to it. No, two guys: the car's rear door was open, and a second man jumped out, a copy of the first: head-to-toe black from mask to Doc Martens, and carrying the same weapon. They had a submachine gun each—MP5s, Miles thought. The second man slammed the door as the SUV took off, rear end sitting low and its tires squealing as it angled back into traffic. The first guy had his weapon up, swinging it to clear the sidewalk, passersby tripping backward with palms raised, like recoiling from brutal heat.

He felt the drop—the plunge into horror—and his first thought was:

They're for me.

It was karma wrought perfect, the sort of thing that happened when you made a man your prisoner.

But they were moving now, and not in his direction—he watched them run through traffic toward the deadlocked westbound lanes—and Miles saw his driver wasn't in on it. He was panicked, breathing "shit" as he glanced around, as if looking for the button that said EASY EXIT.

Miles said, "Don't move."

It was a weird sight on this kitschy stretch: cloned dark gunmen on the run, slightly hunched with weapons raised—cramped two-hand grips on their little MP5s. They stopped at a black Mercedes, guns aimed broadside from three feet, one man each at the front and rear windows. Miles's driver threw an arm up in pointless reflex, and the noise as the guns fired was a jackhammer rattle, the Merc's windows copping a full-auto blast, the shooters' aim swinging for cabin-wide damage.

Miles knew that parts of him ran colder than in other people, and it was those parts telling him right now that he could just sit and wait this out. He'd be coming in late anyway, now the shooting had started. But then there'd be afterward, and afterward needed thought as well: how the moral value of every moment of his life could be summed, and the bottom line would be black or red when he ran the numbers late at night in the dark.

The tracksuit man was hunched forward, hands on his head, putting faith in plane-crash protocol. The mayhem was only seconds old, but the Merc was pockmarked and windowless, hunkered down on blown tires as Miles opened his door and brought the Glock up two-handed.

The noise on the street was a nightmare carnival, shouts and screams, and car horns to back them up. The gunfire had stopped, but the echo was still fading, rat-a-tat rolling down Canal Street. Miles laid the Glock across the Cadillac's roof for balance, lined up the nearer shooter, and squeezed off two rounds. The guy was moving again as Miles fired, and both shots went wide, the Merc's rear quarter panel notching two more holes. He corrected with a leftward jerk, but held his fire as the gunmen ran through stopped traffic, a slalom between bystanders as people ditched their cars to get away. Miles swung his aim, and then ducked as he saw the lead man break cover and line him up with the MP5.

He heard the gun's chatter first and then the crash of breaking glass, the car's windows falling in a curtain of white pebbles and the chassis listing suddenly as a tire went out with a boom.

A second's pause, and the world was quieter post-gunfire, noises softened by the ringing in his ears. He risked a glance above the door, looked past jagged windows to see both shooters still running, the lead guy swapping out his magazine.

They were headed for the hotel.

Miles stood and felt glass slide off his back. He couldn't fire again—the street was packed, and all he saw was collateral. And shit—he couldn't see Lucy. The Lincoln was still there at the curb, and the driver's door was half-open.

No air tank on the seat—she must have gone back into the lobby.

He saw a doorman sprinting in a crouch with a hand on his hat, pedestrians dodging stopped cars to get away. It was like a human mimic of a blast wave, crowds fleeing radially from the terror.

He was too far back.

He watched from fifty feet away as the shooters reached the hotel, and went in with guns raised.

Bobby Deen

He heard shots outside—machine-gun fire—and saw the whole lobby tense. The crowd ducked as one, like one of those dumb flash-mob dances, everyone losing two inches and then coming back to full height.

Nina said, "That'll be for us."

Bobby didn't answer. People wasted time looking around, wanting a consensus on next moves, and then it was a race for the elevators.

He saw they didn't have a chance.

There was already a rush behind them, and there wasn't time to fight through. All very well keeping back from the door, but it had put them in no-man's-land. He saw the air-tank lady again, hurrying with a group of people who'd come in off the street, and she wasn't quite so cool this time, looking back across her shoulder toward the noise, unsure about where to go.

He heard more shots—a pistol followed by machine-gun fire—and he pushed Nina back behind a column as he drew his gun. The .38 felt like a fucking toy.

She said, "Don't miss, whatever you do."

He looked for Luka and saw him on the sidewalk, arm raised as he tried to shove his way inside. He must have got brave when he heard the noise, and then had second thoughts.

Bobby waited with his shoulder to the column, frantic people running past. The vibe was full panic, and he knew the shooters must be close. People were tripping and then crawling to get away. It looked like world news, footage from the Middle East, somewhere under UN sanction.

He saw Luka with his gun raised over by the check-in desk, check on his shoulder as he found his aim, and then the machine gun started up again, deafening in the stone-clad lobby, metal chatter and the dings of lead on concrete, veneer chips going everywhere.

People screamed.

He saw Luka go down, a red stitch line up his front, the guy still firing as he fell backward, glass in the street-front windows crazed with spiderwebs. Bobby's view cleared, people hunkered fetal and letting him see the shooters: masked guys all in black, submachine guns held tight and high.

Nina was still there with him, close enough she could tell him things with just a look:

Kill them.

Save my life.

This was what she'd meant, the New York equivalent of blood in the water.

The fact that she was standing told him he could take them on. She wasn't prone, making last-ditch prayers. She knew he could do it. He was right there with her.

At this range, she'd be safe forever.

He targeted the nearer guy and fired, hit torso but didn't put him down. He heard a shot from the street and saw the second guy drop, and the nearer man was turning as well, bringing his gun around and moving sideways for cover, and Bobby saw that goddamn robbery cop, Miles Keller, coming in the front door with a Glock.

TWENTY-TWO

NEW YORK, NY

Miles Keller

He could see it in his mind before he got there, the lobby packed with victims and Lucy lying maimed. She came to him in nightmare glimpses, dazed and supine, mouthing things he couldn't hear.

He dodged and shoved pedestrians, heard more gunfire from twenty feet away—a pistol crack this time, and then a machine gun in response.

Reaching the hotel entrance, he felt like the center of everything, like this was madness with him in mind. He saw bystanders watching from a block away, people hands-to-mouth in disbelief and others with their phones raised to get the footage. He could die now but have an e-life forever: searchable on YouTube until the end of the internet.

He had the Glock up as he went through the door, saw the lobby above gunsights, and with adrenal clarity: smashed glass on the ground and brass casings mixed through, a crowd of people by the elevators, most of them crouched or prone. He saw a guy lying bloodied at the check-in desk, someone else beside a column with a pistol raised, the two black-clad shooters closing in, wreaking bedlam.

Even midcrisis, everything breakneck and elapsing in split time, there was still part of him worried there'd be a bit to explain—why he hadn't given them a blood-free option, whether it was a good idea to open fire with a crowd right there in front of him.

But what-ifs were a dead end even at the best of times, and right now he could see the nearer guy only ten feet away, an easy shot even with a borrowed Glock, and Miles lined up the guy's collar and put a bullet through the back of his neck, just below his balaclava.

The bang and the red cloud came at once, and then the body was pitching forward, the guy's arms slack and his open hands welcoming the floor. Miles kept the gun level and twitched left to aim at the second man, saw the guy was fast, turning at the sound of the shot, and the MP5 swinging with him. Miles waited a half-second—a long stretch of heart-in-mouth crisis time—delaying for a squarer target, and then went for it as the guy came quarter-profile.

His first shot hit the man's chest, and Miles let the muzzle climb slightly with the recoil, put the next round through the guy's nose and finally dropped him.

The dead trigger finger must have twitched on its way to heaven, because the corpse was firing as it fell, the MP5 in one hand shooting on full auto, tracing out a half-circle low to high, chips of tiled floor and concrete dancing.

People screamed with the last zombie volley, and Miles switched his aim to the man by the column, yelled at him to drop his gun. The guy seemed unperturbed with a weapon pointed at him, and he didn't rush anything: put a hand on his tie and knelt carefully as he laid his pistol on the floor. He looked sharp in his suit, and he had a little hat that came low across his eyes. The clothes were spotless somehow, and with his calm demeanor and no trace of blood or dust he was an odd addition to the scene: like some emissary from another world, dispatched to study conflict.

People were still screaming, others on the ground or in shock, someone giving chest compressions to the bloodied man at the check-in desk. Maybe Miles was in shock too, the way he was hung up on this man in the hat. But it was hard to see how he fit the picture, whether he was a target or just happened to be there with a gun. He wasn't a cop:

a cop wouldn't just stand there taking Miles's measure with this backdrop of calamity, but then Nina Stone stepped out from behind the
column, and things made sense.

The catastrophe was hers.

The killers wanted Nina. Who else was worthy of broad-daylight
murder?

She saw him and waved, lifting a hand to him as she bent to collect a duffel bag. Shell casings and chips of concrete on the floor, three
dead people, maybe more, and she took it all in her stride. Miles's gun
was still raised, aiming at the man in the hat, and the guy nodded
slightly and touched the brim with one finger so it hid his eyes, and
Nina's look said: Isn't it funny how this is all for me?

She took the hat man's arm and they turned together—a gentleman and his lady, a bizarre sight amid the carnage—and Miles watched
them cross the lobby until someone shouted, "Miles!"

He turned and there was Lucy, looking terrified behind her air
mask. Her expression alone was a metric of how bad this was. How
many times had he seen her looking anything but calm?

"Miles, what the fuck is going on?"

The mask was fogged, like she'd been hyperventilating. He pushed
her hand away as she touched his wrist, trying to make him lower the
gun. He saw she had his bag of money, and he realized he hadn't
thought about it since the shooting started. He'd come in wanting to
save her. He didn't care about his cash. That was one thing he could
cling to at least: whatever they said about his actions, he hadn't done
this for the profit.

She was pointing now, but still looked ashen: "Jesus, you killed
them. Look, they're both dead."

That was a new tone from her. She was normally the woman who'd
seen everything.

She said, "How did you do that?"

He didn't answer. He knew they had to leave, but instincts were
at odds. Police training said secure the scene, ensure the dead were
dead, help with first aid. But his inner heist man said he had to split.

The heist man won.

The heist man knew the cost of waiting. He put the gun in his coat and picked up the bag, grabbed Lucy's wrist with his other hand.

"What happened? What's going on—"

"We've got to go."

"Look, they're taking the car."

He'd noticed already: Nina and her backup man in Lucy's Lincoln Navigator, Nina at the wheel. But there was nothing he could do, and he watched the car take off eastbound, straddling the centerline to make it through the gridlock.

They came out onto the sidewalk, passed a concierge heading back inside, the guy walking with his hands on his head, face blank, moving so slow he seemed hypnotized.

There was a crowd of onlookers lining the far side of Canal, half of them with phones raised, like the stopped traffic was a grand parade that would start again soon. He saw the busted Mercedes with a crowd of people at the driver's door, the shot-up Cadillac—

Shit, the Cadillac.

He glanced left and right, only a second's indecision, but Lucy caught it anyway.

"Are you okay? Miles?"

On their left were more onlookers, flashing lights farther off and sirens sounding thinly. There was a subway entrance a block away, right there on West Broadway. Thirty seconds, and they'd be gone.

Miles said, "Shit. Dammit."

"What—"

He said, "Take the money and get out of here."

"What?"

He dug the burner phone from his coat and dialed Stanton. He passed her the phone. "If he doesn't pick up, call him again. His name's Wynn Stanton. He'll help you out until I'm done here."

"What are you doing—"

He cut in with a yell: "Take a train uptown—wherever—just go. And call Stanton."

She said something else, but he couldn't hear her through the mask.

He ran to the Cadillac.

The car looked like it had been dropped fifteen stories: glass everywhere, three tires blown. He opened the driver's door, and the tracksuit man slumped and sagged against his belt. He was shot in his chest and stomach, eyes closed, drooling as his head hung forward.

Miles said, "You can't die on me now. Jesus, don't die."

He leaned into the cabin, the blood smell thick and coppery, unclicked the guy's belt. He sagged into Miles's arms, head lolling like a sleeping child's. Miles lowered him to the road, kicking aside glass, trying to make clear space.

The guy was mouthing something, focus distant as his lips moved. Miles stripped his coat off and bunched it on the guy's chest wound.

The guy breathed, "Bent cop," and went still.

"Shit. Don't die. Don't die."

He checked for a pulse but didn't get anything. He started chest compressions. Police showed up and had to pull him away. He watched from the sidewalk as tactical medics put the guy on a stretcher and loaded him in an ambulance. A minute later the detectives were there, asking for his weapon, and he knew he'd be going nowhere for a while.

TWENTY-THREE

NEW YORK, NY

Bobby Deen

Seeing Keller's name in the apartment earlier lessened the shock of see-ing him in person. The guy was in Nina's orbit somehow, but the mo-ment still had a dreamlike quality: Keller in the hotel lobby with what looked like a Glock, the man who'd killed Jack Deen now coming to Bobby's aid. It was perfect irony that he'd probably never click to.

The guy looked like he was undercover as a hobo: long hair and a beard, aviator sunglasses, knee-length gray coat. Bobby watched him put the guys down in less than three seconds—one round for the first man and then two fast shots on the second, not quite a double tap.

It occurred to him obviously, that right now was the perfect chance to nail the guy. He was only fifteen feet away. He could just drill him and say it was an accident, claim he lost focus in the melee, aimed for a balaclava and hit Keller by mistake. Tragic. But the guy was so fast, sighting on Bobby before the second corpse had hit the floor, the Glock snapping up and ready for a headshot.

Bobby could've made it work.

Maybe.

He could've moved behind the column for cover and let Keller have it, but even brief hesitation was delaying way too long. The time to do it was when he came in the door, but now the other two were down, it'd be harder to claim a dead Keller as collateral. He'd bc on camera, too—hotel security, and about fifty different cell phones. He'd end up on Twitter as the guy who shot the hero cop. And dead Keller was not worth the risk of internet fame, or the birth of a stupid Bobby Deen hashtag.

So he just put the gun down and got out of there. He didn't know what was going on, but he made out as if nothing rattled him, touching his hat brim at Keller on the way past, feeling the cop's gun following as he and Nina walked away.

She had him by the arm, and he almost said something about taking the subway, but where were they going to go?

Nina said, "This has worked out well, hasn't it?"

He thought she meant getting out alive. But as they stepped out of the shattered lobby doors onto the street, she walked around the rear of the SUV idling at the curb, and Bobby saw through the window as she climbed into the driver's seat.

A moment later, eastbound along the middle of Canal Street with stopped cars to either side, he said, "You have any idea what's going on?"

Nina said, "More or less." Sounding breezy about it.

He gave her a few seconds, and then said, "So are you going to let me in on the details?"

She wasn't looking at him, and he wondered how carefully she was prepping her reply. She said, "Let's get lunch first."

He wasn't sure about the etiquette—what you're actually meant to do post-shooting. Whether you take a few moments out, let everyone think about what they could have lost. But there certainly wasn't any deep reflection or deep breathing. Nina just drove up Sixth Avenue to Times Square, turned in at a parking garage on West Forty-third and pulled up in the drop-off lane.

She swapped the keys for a ticket, and they went out onto the street into the theater-district crowd, people with I Heart New York bags walking four across, uniformed guys pushing brochures, harried business types trying to dodge the bullshit. Nina led the way with her luggage, over to a place called the Brooklyn Diner, on the corner of Forty-third and Broadway. It was a perfect fit with the hyperlit Times Square vibe, loopy bright-red neon spelling out its name above the Forty-third Street windows.

The lunch rush was over, and they got a booth straightaway. Bobby sat down and stretched out, and it felt absolutely fucking perfect. Warm and safe surrounds, and being in close range to Her.

He should have been worried about what was coming next, whether there were others chasing them, and how Keller—Miles Keller of all people—had showed up when he did. Maybe under different circumstances, he'd pause and think about death, how close he came to wearing a bullet. But even the Reaper came second to Nina. She'd been in his head for weeks, and now here she was right in front of him, and that fact deserved his undivided focus.

She said, "Charles brought me here one time—our first date, actually. I was in a Broadway show of *Breakfast at Tiffany's*—you know Cort Theatre? Up on Forty-eighth, I think?"

He didn't, but he nodded anyway. She was sitting with one elbow on the backrest and her hand hanging next to her, fingers clicking idly as she talked. He could have watched her all day.

She said, "I hadn't actually read any Capote, but I saw the movie, and the script had that same feel, somehow. Charles was in the audience one night, and they brought him backstage after." She looked away and smiled, going back to the memory, seeing him come over. She said, "He wasn't in a wheelchair yet, so he sort of ambled up to me in his suit, swaying his drink a bit like he's Mr. Carefree, you know? And he goes: You were way better than Audrey." She looked back at Bobby, raised an eyebrow. "You know how Audrey Hepburn was in the film version?"

He nodded. That had to mean something. The image in his head had been a Nina/Audrey mash-up. Nina at the window with a big hat on, à la Ms. Hepburn.

Nina said, "Anyway." She pulled her menu toward her and opened it and then let it fall closed. "We got a cab. I said to him, Don't think you're going to impress me with a two-hundred-dollar entrée or something. So we came here." She shrugged. "That was the start of something, I guess."

He waited for her to finish the line, tell him that this could be the start of something, too. But she just left it hanging there, unsaid.

A waiter came over, and Nina ordered a cheeseburger, medium, and water on the side. Bobby asked for the same. The waiter moved away, and Nina put her head on an angle and said, "Do we just have the same taste, or do you not trust me yet?"

He liked the way her hair stayed neatly on the vertical, even with her head tilted. He shrugged. "Why do you say that?"

"You're so busy wondering what I'm doing, you didn't read the menu."

She was overthinking it. He didn't need food. Safe surrounds and Nina right in front of him, he wouldn't need anything, ever.

Nina said, "But here's what I want to know." She leaned forward, seeming to enjoy herself, like she got a kick out of Q-and-A, and the implications didn't bother her.

Bobby waited.

Nina said, "Are you actually helping me, or is that just a good poker face"—she nodded at him—"and I'm going to end up drugged and on a plane back to L.A.?"

The way she said it, it was like she didn't care, or she didn't think it was actually going to happen.

Bobby said, "I told you on the phone I'd help you."

She nodded. "Yeah, you did. Thing is . . ." She glanced around, like the diner crowd could encapsulate her reservations. "My husband surrounds himself with pretenders. I don't know if it's a conscious move, or just the way things go when you're in his line of work."

Bobby didn't answer.

She said, "You know what I mean? It's like, everyone's there for some other reason. Half his security guys started out as extras on his projects. They hang around the house with guns thinking it's just one long audition. You know, do it long enough, they'll end up as the next Schwarzenegger. Have a great story to tell when they're interviewed by Ellen DeGeneres: working as security, and someone from the studio thought they looked good with a gun, cast them in a movie. People would love it."

The waiter came back with their waters and Nina took a sip. She said, "But whatever. I guess that's just a long way of asking if you're committed to helping me."

How would she ever tell if he was honest? Although she was probably better than most when it came to reading minds. Bobby said, "I must get some credit for saving you again."

Nina said, "Mmm, twice in a row. You had help, though."

She had enough gravity and allure, she'd kept Keller out of his mind, but now the killer cop was back center stage.

Bobby managed not to rush it. He said, "When are you going to tell me about Keller?" Like there was no hurry, like he'd get around to dealing with the man sooner or later.

Nina had some more water and said, "I have to tell you this first: You didn't actually save me. And neither did he."

He didn't answer, waited for the big reveal.

She said, "I set the whole thing up."

She paused, waiting for a reaction maybe, but Bobby didn't answer. It was hard just sitting there, like he didn't care either way. She studied him a moment and said, "The only thing that went wrong is they weren't supposed to shoot at you." She shrugged, one shoulder only. "But it all turned out fine, didn't it?"

Any revelation could be made to sound banal. It was just something about her. He looked away and saw their waiter coming back, a plate in each hand. He said, "And presumably Keller wasn't meant to kill anyone."

Nina said, "He wasn't part of the plan. A nice twist though, there at the end."

Bobby waited for their cheeseburgers to touch down and the waiter to move away again. He said, "So what's going on?"

She did her one-shoulder shrug as she picked up the burger, like it should all be fairly transparent. "You know Charles's partner is selling his share of the studio?" She waggled her pinkies to make inverted commas: "Getting out of the 'movie' business."

Bobby nodded. "The Berkhov guy, right?"

"Yeah. The Berkhov guy. Long story short: Charles wanted to buy him out. I found someone up here in New York, willing to pay more. So I set it up with Berkhov, came up here to facilitate."

"And you thought you needed a shoot-out to go with it?"

"Well." She turned the burger this way and that before taking a bite. She said, "I knew Charles would send someone. So I needed to address that. And I'd say he'll get the message. I don't think he'll send anyone else. Repossessing me isn't exactly a discreet exercise."

Bobby said, "Could've just done it at the apartment, leave a mess for next time he visits."

Nina smiled. "Don't you think the hotel was so much better?"

Bobby didn't answer.

She said, "It's more of a statement, isn't it? Shooting someone in public. It'll be all over Facebook, Twitter, TV news will run it. Put it on-screen, it's like communicating in his terms. He'll be more responsive to it. And the brand recognition probably helps too—they'll give it more coverage if they think people know the hotel." She smiled and looked away, thinking of something else, amusement growing as the theory formed. She said, "He'll be personally offended out of capitalist solidarity. I've tarnished a premium hotel brand."

Bobby didn't answer.

Nina worked on her burger for a moment and said, "And the nice thing as well, he won't quite know what's happening. He'll suspect I set it up, but maybe he'll trust what you told him. I presume you said I'm being followed."

Bobby didn't answer. He hadn't touched his food yet, or his water.

Nina put her elbow on the backrest again. She said, "So. You're going to get a phone call soon, and it'll be Charles, wanting to know what happened." She took her time getting to the crux of it: sitting there unmoving, looking him in the eye as the diner patrons carried on with their meals, and outside the Times Square TV screens refreshed, and a new range of ultrabright commercials went out to the masses.

She said, "What are you going to tell him?" Lifting her chin slightly, letting him see that nice line of her throat.

Bobby said, "How's Keller part of this?"

Nina said, "Someone's got to answer first, and my story's going to take a while." She smiled. "So why don't you have the first turn?"

Bobby said, "I don't know what I'm going to tell Charles. All I know at the moment is I'm not taking you back to him."

Nina had to mull on that, chewing slowly to an even rhythm, like her thoughts were jaw-powered. She said, "What's he offered you?"

Bobby said, "Two-eighty."

She chewed some more, and then raised her wrist to cover her mouth. She said, "I can do better than that."

"You don't have to pay me off. I already said I won't bring you home."

She smiled. "Think of this as a guarantee, then. I can help you find Keller."

Bobby didn't answer.

Nina said, "I've got a commission fee for setting up Berkhov's sale. Plus Keller has money. He's getting ready to run, so he must have something up his sleeve." She had a drink and said, "So whether you're interested or not, I can offer you way more than Charles can."

Bobby smiled. "I knew that already."

She lifted her eyebrows, seeming to know what he meant. "Is that right?"

They sat looking at each other, Nina amused, and he realized he didn't know where to take it next—how to keep a flirty tone without crossing the line too early.

He ended up just playing it safe and said, "Why are you doing this?"

"Why do you look so concerned?"

Bobby put his elbow on the seat back, mirroring her. He said, "Charles is not a nice man." Talking quiet and pronouncing each word, clear he was understating the matter.

Nina said, "I can't disagree with you. But there's nothing to tell you. He doesn't chain me up or beat me. I'm not mistreated. I just wanted out."

Bobby sat watching her, wanting her to unpack it a little more.

She said, "I'm thirty-six years old, and I live in Los Angeles. And every day, how many gorgeous twenty-year-olds show up wanting to make it big?"

He didn't see where she was going with it yet.

Nina said, "Charles's gears turn in a pretty straightforward way. He's a consumer. When a better car comes along, he gets it. When a better stereo comes along, he gets it." She shrugged. "When a better wife comes along, he'll get it." She smiled. "So I'm just preempting what's inevitable."

Bobby said, "He needs his head checked if he's getting tired of you."

It set his heart thudding as he said it, but Nina just nodded, like he'd told her some bland fact. She said, "Anyway. It's not like there's some great backstory to all this that'll give you the moral high ground if you help me. I'd just had enough."

Bobby said, "I think I'll cope."

Her mention of backstory put him in the hotel elevator—Nina asking about his hat. He touched the brim and said, "I was trying to think of a good story for this, but there isn't one. The main guy on *Breaking Bad* had one, so I bought one, too."

"You suit it better than he did." Saying it flat, but narrowing one eye a little, giving the line something extra.

He smiled and speared his burger near the edge and sliced off a chunk, the filling exposed in neat layers, like something geological. He said, "How do I get to Keller?"

Nina said, "Through the girl in the gas mask. Remember her? We saw her in the corridor, heading into Keller's room."

He should have just gone with it, but he couldn't help himself: "He's staying on your floor?"

"Well. More like I'm staying on his. He checked in first. I think he had money in the room and sent the girl to get it."

"How do you know he's got money?"

She started to say something and then dropped it, came in on a different angle. She said, "That's why he played hero in the lobby when the shooting started. He didn't want his courier being murdered." She shrugged. "But it's not rocket science. Clip Keller, and you get sweet revenge, and whatever cash he's got with him. Find the girl, and he won't be far away."

"And how do we find the girl?"

Nina shrugged, and then smiled at him. "We've got her car. So why don't we start there?"

She settled the check with clean twenties and they went outside again into the Times Square hustle, Nina walking ahead and looking back across her shoulder to speak to him. She said, "You're going to have to tell him something eventually."

Meaning Charles Stone. And he'd have to be convincing, too. Charles didn't want to lose his trophy wife. He'd take it out on Bobby's mother, or take her hostage until Nina was back in his possession. Wheelchair or not, he was still a threat.

Bobby said, "I'll tell him I've almost got you."

She said, "And what are you going to do when he finds out we left together?"

"That'll take him a while."

"Yeah, but he'll know eventually. He knows everything eventually."

He didn't answer, but he was banking on "eventually" being a long time—long enough for Bobby to lock in a happy ending that couldn't be undone.

They went along Forty-third and into the parking structure. Nina gave the attendant her ticket and paid the fee with more creaseless twenties. Her timing was always so good, even with the little things—no delay searching in a bag for the stub or the money, no pocket patting like a regular mortal. Bobby wondered if this was a symptom of something—fixation going up a level—the fact that he was wowed by every detail.

They waited by the booth while the guy collected the car, Nina looking like a moody promo shot for some band: shoulder to the wall and one leg crossed and tiptoe, gray concrete underfoot and rows of cold cars down the neon-lit rows.

There were two guys on duty, but the second man was just sitting in the booth, feet up on the desk and nodding to pop on FM radio. He had his eyes closed and mouth ajar, as if the song conveyed otherworldly data, catered to his ear. A photo on the wall behind him showed a Times Square subway sign.

Nina said, "You know what I never figured out? How come it's twenty-five years in prison if you assault a cabdriver, but it's only seven if you hit a subway employee? You ever noticed that? It's like they don't care about the undergrounders."

The SUV had been over in a far corner, and now it was inbound at high speed and high revs, the attendant hunched with his chin to the wheel, keeping the gas on through the final corner and stopping with a howl. Bobby figured there'd always be that need to beat your best time, set a new record for the back corner to the pickup lane. There was a line of cars waiting to pull out onto the street, and each vehicle when its turn came took off with a catapult start, busy Manhattan people with places to be.

He said, "Maybe this is Keller's ride. It's banged up enough."

And it was full of shit as well: boxes in the trunk, paper and fast food containers in the backseat, stuffing coming out of the upholstery.

Nina walked around the rear of the car and had the guy's tip waiting in two fingers when he got out. He took it wordlessly and headed for a Ferrari that was nosing in off Forty-third with a growl. She said to Bobby, "No, I don't think so . . ." She stepped back from the open driver's door and took it all in. "This isn't his style. The mess, I mean."

She looked at Bobby and said, "I can see him in something classic—like an old Gran Torino maybe. Kind of beat-up, but still running okay."

She moved to the rear passenger door and did the same move, held the door handle and stood back to make her appraisal. She said, "This is a young guy's car. Keller wouldn't drive around in a pigsty."

Bobby opened the back door, dug through one of the boxes in the load space, but it was burner phones all the way down.

Nina said, "You always been a hat wearer, or did you only take it up when you started watching *Breaking Bad*?"

Bobby said, "I've always been a hat guy, I guess."

He closed the door and stepped around the back of the truck again, saw Nina standing in the same position, bag in one hand, but with a piece of cardboard in the other. She must have just conjured it—he hadn't seen her move.

She said, "Someone's got mail." She looked at him. "DeSean Copeland. He ring a bell?"

She held up the box—hardback-book-size, maybe an inch deep—so he could see the address label. DeSean Copeland, down in Sheepshead Bay. The sender was ARC Gaming, up in Queens.

Bobby said, "Maybe he's worth a visit."

Nina consulted the label again. She said, "Sheepshead Bay. It sounds like the kind of place where things could go wrong."

Bobby said, "Yeah, hopefully. Maybe Keller calls himself DeSean Copeland when he buys his video games, keep himself off the radar."

Nina tossed the box on the seat. "I've got a picture forming now. Keller playing video games, driving around in a Gran Torino."

Bobby said, "Probably drives a rust bucket, pretends it's just as good as the one on his PlayStation."

Nina said, "Or maybe he plays those shooting games, and it's the other way around: pretends his PlayStation skills are just as good as his real skills."

He saw the hotel lobby again, Keller's smooth moves as he took down those two guys. Seeing it in his head, seeing Keller and his speed, he couldn't ignore the fact that getting rid of the guy might actually be a lot of work.

He moved around to where Nina was standing, and said, "Let's make a house call."

She said, "All in good time." She was fanning the driver's door gently but looking somewhere else, off where her thoughts were. She looked at him and said, "Right now, it's only number three on the list."

Bobby said, "So what's one?"

"I've got people coming by the apartment with my commission fee. And we don't want them leaving it at the door."

We.

So they were in it together. His stomach did something funny—a dip and a swoop.

He said, "And what's two?"

The Ferrari went past, squealed its tires through a turn. Nina waited for quiet and said, "I'm not sure. I'm leaving room for something good to come up."

TWENTY-FOUR

NEW YORK, NY

Miles Keller

They were keeping witnesses in separate hotel rooms, waiting for the
detectives to come through, but Miles got special treatment: a patrol
supervisor bagged his gun, and then two investigators from the PD's
Force Investigation Division drove him over to the First Precinct building at Varick and Ericsson.

Being in the moment, as they say, when he'd actually shot those
two guys, he'd seen it all as morally pristine. But the black-letter-law
part of him knew the DA's office would never see it in the same terms.
Even if they didn't put the shooting to a grand jury there'd still be
grief about the Glock—why he even had a weapon, given he'd turned
in his badge for the time being. Then it'd be suit-and-tie in front of the
FDAB—the Firearms Discharge Advisory Board—trying to make his
actions marry up with Department Procedure, tell them all about why
it had been a good idea to shoot into a crowd.

He'd thought as well that they might send him the same people—the
guys who'd covered the Jack Deen fiasco. But these two FID detectives
were new to him: a female captain of about forty-five called Medina,
and a guy of about fifty named McKenzie. They looked like they'd been
paired by someone with a yen for contrasts. McKenzie was six-four

and fat, and Medina was about five-five and had a sharp, sinewy look, like she did that boiling-hot kind of yoga every day.

The precinct house on Ericsson was an old three-story building in white stone that was going gray with age. Miles was normally out in Brooklyn, but he'd been here a few times. Medina parked in one of the reserved slots on Varick, and McKenzie got out and opened Miles's door. He kept wondering what had happened up at Rockefeller Center—if people were still hanging around, waiting for the man in the track-suit to show up, or if word had got out that their guy was in an ICU somewhere, hopefully still alive.

He followed Medina over to a blue steel door, McKenzie bringing up the rear, and they stood waiting while Medina found her key. Two kids on bikes rode past and called out:

"Busted."

Funny how the feeling of trouble seemed to come down harder and harder. Right after the shooting he was just pleased to be out the other side with his life. Then in the car, obviously, there was no ignoring the fact he was going to face some hard questions. Then in the precinct building, Medina leading him through the detective squad room, people looking at him, knowing he was a cop with a shooting history, a loud voice told him he'd better get this right.

He saw McKenzie go over to a glass cubicle at the end of the detective bureau and talk to the squad supervisor, and then Medina led him down a corridor to an interview room. There were only two chairs, one each side of the table.

Miles sat down on the far side. He said, "You going to get another chair, or does someone sit on the desk and stare at me so I get nervous?"

Medina ignored it. She left him alone for a minute and then came back with a copy of the PD's Firearms Discharge Investigation Manual, and a handheld Breathalyzer.

Miles blew zero-zero-zero.

She noted it in the report template and said, "You need anything? Coffee, water?"

"Coffee would be good. And a phone."

Her own phone was ringing, and she stepped out to take the call. She was back five minutes later with a pitch-black brew in a polystyrene cup, set it on the table in front of him. She said, "There's a spare phone in the squad room you can use if you like."

He was mid-sip, so nodded his thanks.

She folded her arms and leaned in the doorway. She said, "You know how to shoot. On-scene guys called me about the lobby footage, said it was three shots in three seconds."

Why would she tell him that? Other than to catch him off-guard, make him say something clumsy or incriminating—like he'd enjoyed it. But he just nodded and said, "That sounds about right."

The coffee was unimpressive, but he took his time with it, thinking about where to go next. He said, "My parents used to rob banks. Does it say that in my file?"

No need to bring it up, but he wanted to see how she handled it, how hard they were looking at him. She raised her eyebrows and shook her head, kept her gaze on him.

Miles said, "My dad didn't really have the fortitude for it, always used to throw up afterwards, apparently. Stress used to get to him."

"What a hero."

"Yeah. But I think because he was antsy, he used to do a lot of prep. Had me doing shooting drills when I was about seven, eight years old."

"Thought you were going to follow in his footsteps."

"Yeah, maybe. They used to do road trips now and then, hit a few banks in Texas."

She glanced out at the corridor again, looking for McKenzie, and then said, "Imagine that'd get the adrenaline going."

"Mmm, I think it probably would."

"But the prep paid off for you, right? Just like robbing a bank."

She was looking at him closely, wanting a slipup, trying to read him on a level that he wasn't conscious of. Miles didn't answer. He drank coffee and heard feet in the corridor: a long, heavy stride, and then McKenzie was in the room, and Medina looked away, and the moment was gone.

McKenzie said, "Still waiting to hear from the ADA whether they want an interview, so we'll get you started on the eff-dar in the meantime."

The eff-dar: firearms discharge/assault report. Miles was getting good at them.

He could keep his story narrow, but if they wanted to talk, there'd be a lot of ground to cover. Nina and the hotel, and the guy in the hat who was with her. He'd probably have to tell them all about his trip up to Kings Point too, what he'd been doing at the Covey crime scene. So many story points to address, tick off to their satisfaction. Maybe they'd relitigate all the Jack Deen stuff too, make him explain how an L.A. gangster ended up dead on Lucy's floor that night.

He looked at Medina and said, "I think I better use that phone first."

The two FID cops shared a look, and McKenzie shrugged, and Medina stepped out and gestured for Miles to follow. He brought his coffee with him and trailed her out to the squad room. She led him to an unused desk and gestured at the phone. "All yours."

"Thanks."

He saw detectives at other desks checking him out, taking their sweet time before looking away.

He put the cup on the desk and stayed on his feet so he could see the room. He picked up the phone and dialed Wynn Stanton. Kenny answered.

Miles said, "It's me."

"Ah, it's you."

"Is he there?"

Kenny put Stanton on the line. Stanton said, "Man, what a day."

"Has Lucy called?"

"Yeah, she did. Whyn't you tell me you've got her as a houseguest?"

"Is she with you?"

"Yeah, I got her. Picked her up at Sixty-eighth and Lexington. Shit, that was a sight: show up, there she is by the subway entrance in a gas mask, carrying four hundred grand of your money. Had to kind of look twice, you know?"

"Because you can't believe she didn't just run off with the loot."

"Yeah, I did sort of wonder. Where you calling from?"

"First Precinct. Force Investigation brought me over."

"They talked to you yet?"

"No."

"You want me to come down?"

"No, it's fine. They're talking to the DA, but they'll probably just want the report."

"What happened?"

"Ask Lucy."

"She seemed to be in the dark on a lot of it, so let's hear your version."

He wondered how much Lucy had told him, whether Stanton knew about his trip up to Kings Point, and his trip back with a hostage.

He said, "I went into the hotel and a shoot-out started, so I finished it."

Stanton said, "I guess because you're in a police precinct, you're kind of erring on the side of parsimony?"

"Yeah."

The biggest unknown was Nina. What was she into, and what had he got her out of? But he couldn't chew on that aloud on the phone.

Across the squad room he saw a door open, and two more detectives enter: quiet middle-aged guys in well-worn suits, jackets open to show gun and badge nestled under paunch.

Miles said, "You know how you see some cops, they've just got the look absolutely spot-on."

"You got some now, do you?"

"Yeah, these two guys, you'd love them."

Stanton said, "How long you going to be?"

"I'm not sure yet."

He saw the two new detectives go over to the squad supervisor's cubicle, trade handshakes, and then start talking grimly. It must have been hard information they were dealing with. They all had a good, wide stance, hands on hips, lots of frowning at the floor.

Stanton said, "And I'm supposed to babysit in the meantime?"

"She doesn't need babysitting, that's for sure."

"And what's going to happen when you're done playing with the cops?"

Assuming they let him go, but he wasn't going to say that aloud, give fate bad ideas.

Miles said, "Me and Lucy are getting out of town."

Stanton said, "You haven't thought this through, have you? Or are those air tanks real easy to get hold of?"

"I've got to go."

He saw the supervisor pick up his desk phone and speak briefly. Then the office blinds went down.

Stanton said, "I'm going to come in."

Miles said, "No, don't. I'll be fine."

He dabbed the cradle to disconnect the call, but kept the handset to his ear, saw Medina go into the supervisor's office and close the door.

Miles stood watching, saying "Mm" every so often, saw the clock above the office window notch two, three, four minutes.

The office door opened.

Medina stepped out and headed over to him, arms folded. Miles said, "I'll call you later," to the dead phone, and put the handset down.

Medina said, "DA's office has okayed an interview, so we can get things started if you like."

He smiled. It sounded like bullshit. They could undermine the grand jury process, interviewing cops on a fatal OIS. The DA's office almost never recommended it.

So something else was happening.

He looked at the supervisor's office as the blinds went up again, and the two new detectives stepped out the door.

He thought, What do you want, fellers?

But he looked at Medina and said, "Yeah. All right."

She led him back down the hallway, and the two new guys fell in behind. McKenzie stood looking at him as Miles came into the room. There was a camera and a tripod already set up.

Miles walked around the table and took his seat again, sat with his forearms resting parallel and his gaze on the square of table between them, as if contemplating a meal that had been laid before him. He looked up at the sound of the door closing, and saw that he was the focal point of undivided attention. McKenzie, Medina, the new boys, and no one looking pleased. He leaned back slowly so he was sitting straight and said, "Okay then."

TWENTY-FIVE

NEW YORK, NY

Bobby Deen

They took the Lincoln back downtown to the apartment overlooking the rail yard. He liked watching her drive. Or maybe he just liked watching her do everything. She parked in the basement and they rode an elevator up, FM radio playing something poppy, Nina humming along as she watched the floor numbers ticking over. He wondered if she was like that at home, but couldn't quite see it—Charles fuming and hitting whiskey all day, Nina breezing through the house with Kanye on the stereo.

She let them in with her swipe key and walked straight across the living room to the window. "Not a bad view, right?"

It was better keeping back slightly, putting Nina in the picture, too. He could still see sparks down among the trains. He found himself wanting to tell her things—how the sparks reminded him of his father, all his weird projects. Garage-based ventures that never went anywhere. But it was hard going back there. Revisit those times and there were other things to face as well. Look at me, boy. He could still hear it, clear as a voice in his ear.

She turned around and clicked him out of it, saw him looking but seemed to play up to the attention, putting more swing in her hips as she walked to the kitchen. She laid her bag on the counter and brought out an Apple laptop, lifted the screen and typed something while Bobby stood looking at the view. He could see her reflection in profile at the kitchen counter, Nina's image hanging palely over the river, her weight on one leg and the other on its toe as she read something on the computer.

She said, "Well, we're not famous yet. Unless we're still being uploaded to Twitter."

He heard tinny speaker noise, hysterical interviews by the sound of it, maybe a news clip she'd found online. The noise died and then a calmer tone started, probably studio commentary, analysis from behind the desk.

She said, "They've got a terrorism guy on, wondering if it's ISIS."

She read some more and said, "No mention of the man in the hat, or the dazzling woman he was with."

She made herself smile saying that, looked up as she closed the laptop's screen and ran a hand through her hair. He kept seeing her on that boat, little moments now that were a perfect match to what he'd seen already, as if time could fold back on itself. There she is in the kitchen, hand in her hair. And there she is on the launch, hand in her hair. He wondered what else he could summon. Maybe he could relive his whole life and makes things perfect.

She picked up a cordless phone from a charger on the counter and came and joined him at the window, the mirror-Nina walking through air to stand just on the other side of the glass.

She dialed, and Bobby heard the ringtone. He turned and faced her, a shoulder on the window. She looked him up and down and he thought she'd touch his tie again. He willed it to happen, knowing every action is a door to something else. What he'd do, he'd take the hand gently and run his thumb over the back of it, feel the tendons one at a time, leave the other arm free to pull her close . . .

The ringtone finished, and Nina stepped away and said, "Yeah, it's me."

She listened for a moment, pacing slowly as she looked out toward New Jersey, and said, "He wasn't part of the plan. He just happened to be there."

Meaning Keller presumably, and his save-the-day spectacle.

Nina said, "No, I think the less shooting the better. I thought you'd come in and take them off with bags on their heads or something. Gunfights work but they're a mess, aren't they?" She'd seemed happy enough at lunch, but maybe displeasure was a stronger look. Everyone would want to impress her.

He tried to fill in blanks: maybe Marko and Luka were meant to be kidnapped at gunpoint, and someone upped the ante. Maybe they thought a shoot-out would be easiest.

Nina was still pacing, turned neatly on her heel as she said, "Cash is fine."

She listened again and said, "I'm at the apartment," and then clicked off.

She came over to Bobby and handed him the phone. "Your turn."

Meaning call Charles Stone, and spin a story.

Nina said, "You're going to have to tell him something good."

Bobby said, "The truth should do it, then."

She was back in the kitchen, opening the freezer, taking out a bottle of vodka—Grey Goose by the look of it. She said, "You can tell him the part about the gunfire, but I'd keep the rest of it to yourself." The stopper made a *thock* as it came out of the bottle. "Maybe don't mention the part about not taking me back to California."

Bobby said, "Maybe I will, just not on his time frame."

"Yeah. That could work." She looked at the ceiling, like she saw a plan already: "Maybe you could find where we left that boat. A month or two at sea wouldn't be bad."

The boat, the boat: maybe it was a sign. He'd had his little flashback, and now it was on her mind, too.

She raised the bottle at him. "You want one?"

Why not? He liked where this was going, even though he knew the clocks were running, counting down to various dilemmas. They would've lifted his prints off the gun in the hotel, maybe even got a hit off his LAPD file. And his luggage was in that shot Mercedes. Which meant there could be a notice out on him already. But then the scene in front of him had a lot of punch to it: Nina right there, offering a drink. That one-woman tableau seemed to say:

This will all be fine.

So Bobby nodded and said, "On ice, if you've got any."

He looked at the phone again, and knew that this was high-pedigree deceit, standing in another man's apartment, preparing to tell him lies, meanwhile said man's wife pours drinks for two.

He dialed Charles, the landline number for the house in the Bird Streets, and watched Nina drizzle vodka over ice as he waited for an answer.

She raised the glasses to check the levels, and said, "Make sure you tell him why you took so long to call. No good saying you're obsessed with his wife and can't think straight."

He went free-fall for a second, but then Charles was on the line and pulled him out of the drop: "Yeah?"

Bobby kept his eyes on Nina. "It's me."

"You're back at the apartment?" Recognizing the number. "What happened?"

He'd expected more volume, but Charles sounded measured.

Bobby felt his pulse in his ears. That didn't usually happen—he was meant to be the Ice Man. He said, "Put the news on."

"Or you could just tell me what's happening."

He watched Nina coming over with their drinks, tumblers gripped overhand, wrists swaying gently to make the ice tinkle.

Bobby said, "We met her in the hotel but got intercepted on the way out—"

"Shit—" There was ice tinkling at Charles's end, too.

Bobby said, "Two guys came in and shot up the lobby. Marko and Luka are dead."

"Oh Jesus . . ." Getting breathy now—borderline panic.

Bobby said, "I went with Luka to ICU, but they couldn't keep him going. Nina's meant to meet me back here." He watched her nodding as she drank, approving the story, looking out at the river.

"But she's okay?"

"Yeah, she's fine."

"Isn't it bodyguard rule one: keep the principal real close. Especially after a fucking shoot-out?"

That was a point. Nina's eyes shifted to him, like maybe she'd heard. It was that same pose he'd seen earlier in the diner, eyes slightly narrowed and her chin up a touch, looking strong.

Bobby said, "It's hard telling her what to do," and Nina smiled, liking that just fine.

Charles said, "You should have held on to her—"

"There were cops around. I didn't want to end up in the cells."

"Jesus . . ." He subvocalized awhile, awful stuff, like some rosary to the devil. Bobby waited for him to come right, and eventually Charles said, "So where is she?"

Bobby said, "She took a train uptown. I was doing first aid, but the cops were rounding up witnesses, and she didn't want to hang around. There was an exhibition at the Met that she wanted to see." Now that was inspired—fucking *perfect,* and Nina thought so, as well: nodding along to a rhythm, like the lies had flow.

Charles said, "Great—she going to do some shopping too, maybe catch a movie? Shit."

Bobby said, "She's got time. I'm back sooner than I planned. I thought Luka would hang on longer. They gave him three pints of blood but he kept flatlining." That was a nice touch, as well.

Charles said, "Shit. All right. Goddammit." Sounding weaker, like the shooting news was only just getting through. He said, "So who was it?"

"Not sure. They had masks."

"And what happened? You killed them?"

Bobby said, "They came in shooting, but there was a cop in the lobby who sorted them out." That was a funny way to put it—sidestepping Keller's proficiency, the fact he'd dropped them clean and easy.

Charles said, "So they're dead?"

"Far as I know."

"All right. Okay. Okay." Grinding through it all, working out a narrative. "It must be Garcia's people."

Bobby ran with it: "Yeah, probably pissed off I didn't bring his boat back."

He heard squeaks at Charles's end, wheelchair tires on polished concrete, the old man doing tense laps of the living room.

Charles said, "Why did you let her go off to a fucking gallery?"

"No one's looking for her in a crowd of tourists."

"Yeah, but . . ." It took him a while to get there, trying to wrap his booze-smashed head around the different angles. After a moment he hit the obvious question: "You realize, I sent her up there because she's running on me. So how do you know she's coming back?"

This was getting too hard. Bobby said, "Trust me."

"Or, just fucking tell me. There's enough gone wrong, I want to hear how everything's going to work."

Bobby's heart went *slam, slam, slam,* and he said, "I saved her on that boat, so she trusts me." He didn't dare look, but she was there as a shape in his periphery. He said, "She thinks I'm helping her."

He knew it was a high-stakes claim—she was right there, and how could it not put ideas in her head? But she was still nodding along to his story, as if the words had gone straight past her.

He heard Charles's breath on the line, rhythmic crackle with a bit of wheeze, and the old boy said, "All right." Then in a lower tone, like he was being overheard: "You put her on the plane, bring her back, we'll double your fee." Then as an afterthought: "I didn't know it was going to get this messy."

Bullshit—Bobby knew the mess didn't bother him. He was scared of being lied to.

She thinks I'm helping her.

The line had got Charles's gears turning. Maybe the lies didn't stop at Nina. The old man wanted insurance.

And that was fine. Bobby might as well capitalize. He said, "How about six hundred even," and looked at Nina to see her eyebrows going up.

Charles wheezed fast as he thought it over. He said, "You're a greedy prick, Bobby, but fine. Call me when you've got her on the plane. And remember: no wife, no money, either."

Bobby said, "I think I can live with that. You might want to book a return trip, too. New York cops'll want to ask you about Marko and Luka."

The old boy scoffed. "I'm Charles Stone. They can come to me."

The tone went *beep* in his ear.

Nina passed him his drink and said, "He's giving you more money?"

Bobby took a sip as he walked the phone to the counter. "He's worried I've swapped sides."

Nina smiled. "Which you have."

She was totally at ease, leaning back against the window with her legs crossed, looking him in the eye. But did that mean she trusted him, or just that she could handle whatever came her way?

Bobby said, "Charles has a plane on standby to take us back to L.A."

"Of course he does."

"So how does this sound: we collect your commission fee, then we go and find Keller and take his money too, and then we fly back to California and take a bit more off Charles."

"How much is a bit more?"

Bobby said, "He's promised me six hundred grand."

Nina swirled her glass. "Every little bit counts, doesn't it?"

Bobby wondered what her spending was like, how long she'd take to get through six hundred grand. He said, "We can sell the boat when we're done with it, make another million."

He kept saying "we," but he didn't have a clear idea of what that actually meant. But Nina seemed to be going along with it happily enough. She said, "Getting to Keller might take a while. It's more than an afternoon's work."

Bobby said, "I'll make up a new story for Charles, buy us some more time."

"He's not renowned for his patience."

Bobby said, "The less he trusts me, the more he pays me, so maybe it'll all work out."

He thought he'd get a smile out of that, but she just sipped her vodka, not dropping eye contact. She said, "What exhibition was I seeing?"

Bobby shrugged. "I don't know. Probably some kind of Renaissance shit."

There it was: she smiled.

He said, "Should've told him it was promo posters for B-grade nineties movies, he'd have loved it."

She laughed, and he found himself wanting a follow-up line, something perfect that she'd find even funnier, throw her head back and let him see that white arch of upper teeth. Time it well, and he could be right there when she opened her eyes again. He was coming up blank though, knew he shouldn't move closer until he had something to say—it'd only seem natural if he walked up delivering a line. Close the gap in silence, he figured there was a high risk of making it awkward.

He moved in anyway, trusting that a cool one-liner would show up at the right moment, and maybe by accident Nina actually helped him: took a drink and watched with one eye as he came over, and he figured that vodka was a good enough topic.

He said, "You always hit the spirits in the afternoon, or is it a special treat because I'm here?"

Kind of lacking in the humor department, but it wasn't bad. It set a playful tone, at least, and now she had to give him something back. They were close enough their glasses could touch—not to mention the rest of them—and Nina clinked her tumbler against his as she said, "You know in movies, when they want to make someone look in-control, they give them something to eat? Not so they're stuffing their face, but just so they have a snack on the go?"

Bobby thought about that one and said, "Like Brad Pitt in *Ocean's Eleven*?"

"Yeah, exactly. Let you know he's Mr. Cool, eating nachos while he plots a casino takedown."

She was leaning back with her head on the glass, and Bobby knew if this was going anywhere she'd step forward. He'd done the hard work closing the big gap, but that last little push had to be hers.

He said, "So you're giving me a drink to find out if I'm as cool as Brad?"

Nina shook her head. "No, I knew that already." Not saying, though, whether he measured up.

She said, "Way I see it, if someone comes to your apartment to drop off a bag of money, you want to make people think you've done this all before, and none of it's a big deal. That way no one tries to play you, or renegotiate, or just shoot you and keep the cash." She raised the glass and looked up at the base of it, smiling a little, like seeing the whole situation in fresh terms. She looked at him and said, "Maybe I'm wrong, but I think I'm giving the impression that I'm fine with everything."

She drank to that, and Bobby did as well. He wondered if she could see the pulse in his neck. He wanted to just get it over with, grab and kiss, but he figured he could give it another minute.

He said, "Have you done this before?"

She shook her head. "Not really. I was in this movie—seven, eight years ago. Final scene was a meeting between these two crime families, going over this deal or something. And of course the whole thing gets a bit unpleasant, everyone starts shouting and then it's a full shoot-out. Remember I took a bullet in the leg, had to go down shouting, 'dahlia,' I think it was. The scene got cut."

Bobby said, "So it didn't work out okay."

She smiled and shook her head. "But that's what I've got you for this time."

Bobby said, "I think a gun would be better than a glass."

She looked him up and down, just her eyes, and said, "You've been standing right in front of me for a while."

Bobby said, "Yeah, I was waiting for the right line so I could seem real smooth."

It sounded kind of cryptic, but Nina seemed to know what he meant, and maybe she even looked hopeful about where this was heading, so he reached around her with his free arm, and their glasses clinked a second time as he pulled her in, and she was cold and tasted like vodka as he kissed her. They came up for air, and their heads swapped angles and then went for it again, and he heard her glass drop and roll across the floor.

She broke away and stepped back from him with her hands on his shoulders. With the window behind her and the view of the city, it was like the whole world was watching.

She said, "We could have got here weeks ago, but you took me back to Charles."

Only a whisper, and he wasn't sure if she was sad or curious. With her so close and looking her in the eye, he could see her deeply, and he knew they were the same. There was a world in her head where they'd been together, and right now was that perfect moment: reality coaxed to match the form of shared imagining.

He said, "We made it eventually."

She was kissing him again, and he felt her hands on his back, under his coat, sliding it off, and then the doorbell chimed.

Nina's hand trailed off him as she stepped past him, and she said, "We'll pick this up in a minute."

TWENTY-SIX

NEW YORK, NY

Miles Keller

The two new guys were called Dodd and O'Shea. He'd never seen them before, and they hadn't told him what division they were with. Whatever they did though, they'd been at it awhile. They had that patient-but-skeptical look police detectives get after twenty-five years on the job.

O'Shea had brought in a chair from along the hall, and he got himself comfy across the table from Miles, slightly off to his right, legs crossed and a clipboard propped on one knee. To Miles's left, Medina was fussing with the video camera, and McKenzie and Dodd were leaning against the wall to either side of the door. On the table was Medina's yellow legal pad, and some forms on NYPD letterhead he'd no doubt have to autograph.

Something on the camera beeped, and he turned to see a red light glowing above the lens. He should have known better than to look. If this went to court, they'd probably cut the first half-second of footage, have him looking straight down the barrel in the opening frame, wondering what he was in for.

Medina took her seat beside O'Shea and ran through the preamble: time and date and everyone's names, and what the interview related to. He said he was happy talking to them without a lawyer, and she made him sign all the forms. His signature was the only sound in the room, a hard swish in triplicate.

Medina lifted a page on her pad and spent a moment scanning over something. She said, "All right," drawing it out slowly, the way a doctor might, not sure how to break bad news.

Miles waited.

Medina let the page down softly and said, "Walk us through it to start with. Where were you were when you heard the first shot?"

The pen had a cap, and he took a moment clicking it into place, laying it on the topmost page, sliding everything back across the table. Four pairs of eyes and the red light held him steady.

The first shot.

Or the first volley, really, when they'd blasted that Mercedes. He'd been sitting in the Cadillac, and if he told them that, it'd lay out another thread for them to tug on. But he couldn't lie about it, because he was on film up at Kings Point, looking through the Covey crime scene.

Medina prompted him: "Mr. Keller?"

So they weren't calling him "Detective" anymore, which was fair enough, he supposed. The thing that bothered him most was that he didn't know what the other two wanted. A four-strong inquisition was getting pretty busy, which reinforced his feeling that Dodd and O'Shea were here for something else.

He said, "I was on Canal Street, just east of the Tribeca Gardens Hotel. I saw two men with MP5 submachine guns get out of an SUV on the sidewalk ahead of me. They crossed the street and opened fire at a Mercedes sedan stopped in traffic in the westbound lane. I opened fire in return, but didn't put them down." He closed his eyes briefly, saw the men in black and their MP5s, heard that blitz of noise like the world tearing on a hidden seam. Miles's Glock leaping as he squeezed off his shots.

He said, "I fired twice, but didn't hit them. They were moving across me so I didn't have a great line."

Medina said, "And they were heading for the hotel?"

He nodded. "They entered the lobby and opened fire again."

"So you followed them?"

He nodded, tried to keep his tone level, as if to say the next move was obvious, ethically immaculate, the type of action any decent and concerned citizen would take. He said, "Yeah. I went in behind them and shot them both."

"You weren't concerned about bystanders?"

"I was mostly concerned about them being injured by an MP5 on full auto. But people were keeping low, and I was shooting high, so I think it turned out all right."

Medina said, "You had a Glock pistol, is that correct?"

He nodded. "Glock 17."

She said, "Given you're on leave, turned in your badge, why were you carrying a firearm?"

She'd changed direction. He'd handled her bystanders question with a pretty light touch, and given collateral damage was a life-or-death issue, he thought she'd want to give it a bit longer before they moved on to gun ownership matters. And he wasn't sure how much they already knew. Did they have a print on the Glock that tied it back to DeSean, which in turn could link the weapon back to Miles? It was a small question in the scheme of things, but he felt very aware of his need to pretest every claim, see how much bullshit it could hold.

He said, "I was in a car outside the hotel with someone who happened to have a gun."

Now they were into the good stuff.

Medina said, "Who were you with?"

Miles said, "He told me his name was Gary Peters, but I don't think he was telling the truth."

O'Shea said, "You're right: he wasn't."

Miles looked at him, knowing that this was where things would pivot, and the guy said, "He was an undercover cop called Vincent Petrov."

Well, that changed things slightly. Petrov. As far as Russian names went, it was way more convincing than Gary Peters. And for some reason that thought took precedence, getting through before the important stuff: the fact that he'd taken a police officer hostage, the fact that an undercover cop knew that Miles had robbed the Coveys, the fact that if said cop was alive, then that information was still out there for discovery. And what about his Rockefeller Center meeting? Who had actually been waiting for him? Maybe all that phone messaging had just been setting up his own arrest.

O'Shea said, "You still with us?" He had a perfect voice for these little interview rooms: quiet and a little bored, but with a gravelly, cigarette undercurrent.

Miles didn't answer. If this Petrov guy was dead, then things were okay for now. But if the guy was recuperating in an ICU, Miles's freedom was on a short timer.

He said, "I gave him first aid on the sidewalk. He was shot when the suspects were heading for the hotel."

O'Shea said, "But you forgot about that part earlier?"

He thought back to how it had played: firing at the guy but hitting the Mercedes, ducking for cover when he saw the MP5 taking aim, glass from the car's windows raining on him and the noise of it drowned out by the rat-a-tat. He should've known it right then, that a wrecked car probably meant an injured driver, but he was too busy planning how to save Lucy.

He said, "I didn't leave it out, it just wasn't my recollection. It wasn't until I'd come outside again that I saw the guy was shot."

O'Shea said, "When you fired at the suspects you drew their aim, and that's when Petrov was injured."

So he was hanging in there.

Miles said, "If you're just talking about the order of events, then I agree. If you're trying to imply culpability, then I think that's a pretty stupid way to look at it."

Nobody answered.

Miles said, "In any case, I hope he's all right."

O'Shea said, "What were you doing in Petrov's car?"

Miles looked at Medina, saw that she was happy to let O'Shea pur-

sue his little side road. They would have settled the agenda earlier, during their office powwow. The way she was sitting back, not worried
about her notes anymore, she seemed genuinely interested to hear the
story.

Miles said, "I met him up on a crime scene earlier today."

O'Shea waited, and then he shrugged and spread his hands. "You
going to tell us the story, or do I have to ask for it line by line?"

Miles said, "I turned on the news this morning, saw an attorney
had been murdered up in Kings Point. Guy called Lane Covey."

O'Shea said, "So you thought you'd cruise up there and check it
out?"

Miles looked at him, gave it a couple of seconds. "You want me to
tell the story or not?"

O'Shea didn't answer.

Miles said, "I had a case that Covey was connected to." He paused
and looked away, thinking how to summarize his dealings without
wading in any deeper than necessary. He said, "We had a robbery victim who we suspected was running a credit-card scam. We got a tip-
off that Covey was a facilitator."

O'Shea said, "Facilitating in what sense?"

"I don't know. There was a Russian mafia angle apparently, so it
got moved to Organized Crime. You'd have to ask them about it."

He had a feeling they knew the answer already. If they knew
Petrov was undercover, then they were most likely from an OC unit.
Which meant they were trying to catch him out, rather than gather
information.

Miles said, "What's the prognosis? Is he going to pull through?"

O'Shea said, "We really hope so." He lifted a page on his notes and
set it down gently, not seeming to read anything, buying time while
he formed a question.

He said, "All right. So you saw the Covey guy had been killed. But
why was it your problem? You're on leave, the case had been reassigned
anyway."

He thought about going with a kind of liberal cliché—how this was a free country, and he could go and stand at a crime-scene tape should he so wish. But he said, "I know the local cops up in Kings Point, and I figured they'd want to know what I had to say about it."

"How do you know the Kings Point guys?"

Miles said, "I talked to their detective chief a couple times about Covey, before OC took it off me."

"So then why were you up there today? If the case had been moved to OC and you didn't really know the details?"

Miles said, "Well. I knew to tell them who to ask about it. I'm just lowly robbery police, but I understand in these murder cases, time is of the essence."

He left it there a moment, but no one cut in.

He said, "They had State BCI up there throwing their weight around, wanting to do things exactly their way, and Kings Point PD was putting a lot of effort into holding their ground, so I thought it might've been a day or two before anyone thought to call Organized Crime at NYPD."

Yeah, that was good. But O'Shea only held back for a second or two. He said, "So how did you end up pals with Vince Petrov? You go around chatting up the rubberneckers until you hit someone friendly?"

He felt like he needed to come in close to the truth here. O'Shea definitely knew more than he was letting on.

Miles said, "I'd seen him before—"

"Oh yeah? Where?"

Miles shrugged. "Not sure. I spend a lot of time following shady characters. I recognized him."

He thought O'Shea was going to keep working him on that point, but he said, "So where was he?"

Miles said, "Standing by his car, not far from the house. Hard to miss him in that tracksuit."

O'Shea said, "And so you had a nice little chat? Obviously went okay if he gave you a ride." He turned and looked at McKenzie and said, "Pretty friendly, right?"

Miles said, "I didn't get that impression."

O'Shea looked back at him, eyebrows up.

Miles said, "Like I told you, I'd seen him before. So I just walked up to him and asked what he was doing, if this was like one of those strange psycho traits—you know how murderers sometimes show up at the victim's funeral?"

O'Shea deadpanned him: "Yeah. I've heard about that."

Miles said, "Yeah, anyway. He got in the car as I was heading over, so I got in as well and gave him the line, just to see how he handled it."

"And how did he handle it?"

Miles said, "He started driving."

No one answered.

Miles said, "He told me that what he was doing was none of my business. Which in a legal sense was all well and good, but it didn't stop me being curious. But he said I could either fuck off, or be stuck in the car with him."

He waited, but O'Shea was keeping quiet.

Miles said, "So I called his bluff, and sure enough I was stuck in the car with him. Said he had a meeting in Manhattan, and he wasn't going to be held up."

"And you just went with it?"

Miles shrugged, like this kind of thing had happened before— unwanted rides from dubious characters. He said, "He loosened up, we got talking."

He left it at that for now, not quite sure what they would've chatted about, but imagined he could iron out those details when he had to.

For a moment he thought O'Shea was going to make him do exactly that, but he said, "Lane Covey was robbed last night."

He was sitting with his hands linked on his clipboard, not interested in his notes anymore, just waiting—as Miles had said—to see how he handled it.

Miles said, "How do you know that?"

O'Shea said, "Because Vincent Petrov saw it. A masked man with a gun showed up at Covey's house and stole two hundred thousand dollars."

Miles said, "That must've taken balls."

O'Shea said, "Yeah. But my theory's this: you ripped off the Coveys last night, and then dropped by the crime scene this morning. Like one of those weird psycho traits, where the killer shows up at the victim's funeral."

TWENTY-SEVEN

NEW YORK, NY

Bobby Deen

Nina pressed a button on the intercom by the door, and a polite male voice told her she had a visitor. Nina said, "Send them up," and then fetched her glass from the floor by the window and poured herself another vodka and soda. She made it a dance for him, dipping her knees as she moved between fridge and countertop, swaying her hips. There was a fine balance in it that she managed to get just right: putting on a show, but pretending not to notice his attention.

She raised the glass in Bobby's direction. "What do you think? Probably looks best half-full, right? Like I just happened to be drinking it."

It was funny hearing her say it, or make the admission, really—that she was getting into character, playing someone who did this all the time. He thought of her as an expert in everything, no pretense required.

He said, "You need special rounded ice cubes, so they look melted."

"Yeah, there's an idea. And I should spray dew on the glass, so it looks like it's worked up a sweat." She smiled at him. "Might be too much admin."

She came around the counter again, heading for the door, still holding on to the smile. Something caught her halfway, and she turned back to him and said, "I remember Charles saying whenever people visited for business, he always had the door open, ready. That way you see them come in, and you've got time to do something if there's an issue."

Bobby said, "Shoot them one at a time as they come in."

"Yeah. Otherwise you open up, and they have you by the throat before you know what's happening. So I said to him, why don't you just get a camera, and then if they look like they want to break bones, you just never let them in? Think he decided I was onto something."

There was a knock at the door, brisk but deferential. She was still looking at him.

Bobby perched sidesaddle on an armchair. He said, "So are you going to check the camera?"

Nina said, "No, I've got you for backup," and went and opened the door.

She wouldn't have needed help anyway. She stepped aside, and Bobby saw a small Asian woman in her forties, a duffel in one hand and a big wheeled suitcase in the other. Maybe it was just the luggage, but she looked like a flight attendant, trim and polished, hair pulled back in a bun, wearing a dark suit that looked tailored.

She said, "Good afternoon. Delivery for you, ma'am."

Nina told her to put it on the table. The woman did as asked, a consummate professional, faint smile and indifferent eyes. She stood to one side as she raised the lid on the case, like making a little ceremony of it. Cash was stacked to the zipper—hundred-dollar bills in bands of ten thousand, Bobby guessed.

"I have a cash counter if you'd like to verify the total."

Nina said, "No, it's fine." She was standing ten feet back, arms folded, working on her drink. She looked at Bobby and said, "Maybe it's rigged anyway."

"I can assure you nothing has been tampered with."

Nina said, "It's okay, I'm only shitting you." She took a band and fanned the corner, checking for fakes. She said, "Looks okay."

She dropped it back with the others, and that was that. She stepped away and drained her glass as she headed back over to the counter.

"The bag is complimentary, ma'am. Samsonite. And it meets standard carry-on dimensions, too."

"Excellent, thank you."

The money scent was starting to work through the room. Bobby knew at certain concentrations it could dissolve any problem.

The woman bid Nina a good afternoon, and the door clicked, and then she was standing in front of him, blocking his view of the case.

She said, "Well that was easy. I was worried I might need your expertise. Hotel lobby, round two."

"I might not shoot straight after the vodka."

She tilted her head as she looked at him. "I actually thought it'd be more low-key—pictured maybe three or four guys looking like trouble, and you just sitting there telling them how it is."

He said, "How much is in the case?"

She looked over at it, as if running the numbers. "Eight hundred grand, in theory. Million-dollar commission fee, less two hundred thousand for the performance at the hotel."

"You didn't want to count it?"

She pursed her lips slightly, as if being diplomatic, and said, "My mind was elsewhere."

Bobby said, "What's going on?"

Nina came closer and said, "You want to hear the story, or shall we get back to other business?"

He opted for other business.

He followed as she walked backward to the bedroom, the pair of them lock-lipped and Nina effortless in reverse, steady-footed and with Royal Ballet poise. She freed his shirt buttons top-down, one then the next with no fumble, and he knew that right now was a rare and perfect moment: so often the thing you want is forever out of reach, and yet here she was, leaving fantasy for dead.

He said he wanted her forever. Before now he didn't know how to say it—how to stop it sounding trite or adolescent, like a wish from heady daydreams. But in between the sheets the tone was different, and it sounded right. It wasn't naive or out of reach.

She wanted the same.

He'd been on her mind since he saved her life. She knew that day had gravity, enough to make them re-collide. Here was proof: he'd been pulled across the country, and now he was hers. He felt a kind of inner lurch, his life being pulled back on course. She saw it in his eyes and held his face.

He knew then that he was safe and he could tell her everything.

It poured out:

He'd been scared for thirty years, scared that the good life would never find him. He'd had a vision of picket-fence suburbia—forget that blood-money condo, full of Charles Stone's trinkets. He wanted two boys. They'd have everything he hadn't, and a boyhood worth remembering. He knew where his youth had gone awry, and how to fix it. He'd be different from his father.

She asked him what he'd done, and Bobby heard that voice: What are you looking at, boy?

He couldn't stop now, and she kept holding him. Bobby knew she could fix everything. He laid out the old man, the sad précis of Bobby Senior.

He'd had grand plans for his boy. He was meant to be a child film star. Kids' movies made megabucks—the parents' profit must be huge.

He told Bobby he had the looks and natural flair. He rented movies and transcribed dialogue by night. They read lines at the kitchen table, working through a stack of bootleg scripts, eighties blockbusters written out by hand. Bobby learned *E.T.* off by heart.

They went to auditions, but he couldn't make the cut. His career high point was a McGee's Cheese commercial—Bobby as a cowboy kid in the starring role. He got callbacks for films, but he never got the Big One.

Senior kept him at it.

They upped rehearsals, but Bobby couldn't crack it. Senior put it down to lack of dedication. Bobby got the belt if he missed a line. He got the belt if he didn't get a callback. The equation was straightforward: you work hard, you make progress.

Bobby did work hard. He was eight years old and wanted to please. He auditioned, and the phone didn't ring.

Senior started drinking, and getting real violent. Missed lines meant a belt and a fist. He heard about Macaulay Culkin, and lost his shit—that could've been you, kid. He took out his frustration on *Home Alone*—the VHS cartridge turned to broken plastic and black ribbon.

His mother copped beatings too, punishment for not helping with the boy, not keeping him on The Path.

Then he'd sober up and feel guilty, confess all in church. The priest was a pedophile and had a soft spot for the wicked. He'd absolve anything. Senior would come home sobbing and swear he'd changed.

He did change.

He ditched the Bobby-as-child-star dream, and took up drinking full time. He swapped violence for resentment. He looked at Bobby like a shit stain he had to live around. All he said was, What are you looking at, boy?

The trick was to stay away completely, and he started wearing hats so he'd never catch his eye. It worked too, and now he hadn't seen him for sixteen years. Senior lived alone with liver cancer in Modesto, California.

Nina listened and didn't let him go. She read his mind too, and told him they were different people. He was nothing like his father.

But she'd tapped a lifetime of buried angst, and there was way more to come.

He didn't know if life was slow to fix itself, or if he was just trapped in Charles Stone's orbit. He was a fraud: his mother thought he was a big-shot producer. He was just a no-mercy enforcer. He'd justified his lies as the cost of admission—it wasn't easy gaining access to the good life.

Nina said he was wrong. She had him right here, and she could see the real Bobby. He wasn't a fraud.

But comfort was nothing without full disclosure. He went all in:

He feared Connie's death was his fault. He had these dreams where he pushed her, but they couldn't be the truth. He'd been there at the edge, but he couldn't have hurt her. Reality clashed with the fact of his nature. He loved her too much. The fury was from trying to save her. There was no way he pushed her. The cops grilled him, and he ran it down a dozen times. The mantra became the facts.

He'd buried it so deep: pain and his parallel life he couldn't dare to conjure. She was pregnant, and he didn't know it when she fell. Maybe if he had, he could have changed things, tried harder for a different end. It made him sick to think how big a swerve he took: one mistake—family gone. Brief moments had wild power, but why did that lesson come too late?

They were all secrets until now, but Nina just held him and told him that she understood. She read his mind again. Now they were together, they could fix everything.

He stayed in the bed, spread-eagled beneath the sheet, and listened to her in the shower. He felt so blank it was like being reborn. The white room and the white bed, and the water on the tile telling him *shhhh*.

He heard the door open, and Nina's feet on the carpet. The mattress dipped as she kneeled, and she leaned into his view, a towel around her body and another in a turban.

She said, "That's the sight of a happy man."

He smiled, and that little motion got his thoughts in order. He said, "Who sent the money?"

She looked away briefly, and he knew she was toying with a lie. It was her default setting.

But things were different now. She looked back at him and said, "A Chinese crime boss called Lee Feng. He's a gentleman. I think you'd get on well."

Feng. He remembered the workups Charles had sent him.

Nina said, "It was an easy setup. The Chinese are very interested in movies, apparently. I told Lee I thought films were dying, maybe he was better buying in somewhere with a TV focus. And he leans in and goes: I have a feeling we're going to be all right. Gave me a wink, as well. I think I was almost charmed."

She was trying to make him jealous already.

He said, "So they're not interested in cinema."

She lay down next to him. Her elbow nudged his ear as she put her hands behind her head. "Maybe they'll give it a try. All those shitty *Bloodhunter* movies that Charles did—they were just cleaning up mob profits. You put in seventy or eighty million bucks of drug money, you cast Dick McShithead in the lead role, it's a box-office smash, all your heroin money gets paid back squeaky clean."

Bobby said, "No wonder there were six sequels."

She rolled over to face him, her breath on his cheek.

She said, "McGee's Cheese, huh?"

"Yeah . . ." He closed his eyes, laughed through his nose. "It was like a Wild West bar or something. All these cowboys sitting around, the doors swing open—bang—and the villain cowboy comes in looking mean. Everyone glances around scared, like he's going to shoot the place up. But the guy goes up to the bar, brings out this plate of nachos, whatever it was, and says, 'Cheese,' or something like that. You know, wanting cheese for his meal. And everyone looks terrified because they don't have any . . ."

Nina smiled, seeing it already. "But then cut to Bobby Deen . . ."

"Yeah. Cut to me as this cowboy kid—still don't know why they needed a kid for it, but anyway. I bring out this can of McGee's, and sort the guy out. Then there was a shot of the guy stuffing his face, and this voice-over going, There's no cheese like McGee's."

Her breath on his cheek again: "Mm. I bet you were perfect."

He didn't want to be distracted just yet. He said, "Tell me about Keller."

He felt her lips on his ear. She said, "I checked into that hotel and there he was."

As if that gave him the whole story.

Bobby rolled over and faced her. He smiled, trying to match her vibe, like none of this was too serious. He said, "I just poured my heart out. You can tell me the Keller story."

He could see her thinking about it. Flecks and different colors in her eyes—twin galaxies of Nina he was finally being let in to.

She said, "It looked like film noir. I was in a cab at night, eleven o'clock on Canal Street. Shiny dark from the rain."

Her lips on his. She said, "Are you picturing it? Can you see it?"

"I think I'm with you."

She said, "We pulled up outside the hotel and the lights from inside caught the water on the glass and made it look like drops of gold. How's that?"

She was amused, playing up to the fact she had his full attention, or maybe just enjoying the embellishment. He went along with it though, knowing he had her, that she couldn't duck the truth forever. He said, "I like it so far."

She glanced away, building the picture for herself, and then her eyes clicked back to him, narrowing as she said, "He came out of the lobby, and I could've missed him in the dark. He was just another guy on the street. But there was a crowd on the sidewalk that he had to go around, so he came right past the car window. I almost got out and stopped him."

He brushed a rogue hair off her face. "Why do you sound like you're just telling me a story?"

"I don't know. Because I'm trying to paint the picture. So you feel the strange weight of the strange moment. If that doesn't sound too weird."

"So how do you know him?"

She cupped his jaw in her palms, seemed to study him. "I got accused of robbery up here, and he investigated it." Saying it lightly, like a throwaway line—no biggie. "Which was why it was funny, showing up in New York again, and there he was."

He wanted to stay with the robbery, but she had something else on her mind, looking off as she chewed on it. She said, "You know how when you leave a place, there's this sense almost that you've left a life behind? Friends, places you go—everything sort of waiting in limbo? And you could just pick it up any time."

He'd only ever lived in one place, but he knew what she meant.

She said, "Anyway, running into Keller, it was like someone had flipped the switch on my New York life: on pause for five years, and then suddenly it's all go."

He said, "What did you steal?"

She smiled. "I always maintained my innocence. Apparently I robbed a banker. Went to a dinner party, took some money out of a safe behind a Monet. Well, a print, actually."

"That sounds like your type of job."

She gave him nothing, though—not a twitch.

She said, "And do you know who else was there? At the dinner?"

Bobby shook his head, waited for it.

She said, "Lee Feng, the guy buying into Stone Studios. So it felt almost perfect, really—I mean in the cab the other night, showing up for this Feng-related deal, and then Keller happens to be there, too, walking past. You know: five years later, the three of us in the same sphere, like the unholy trinity. And then it turned out he'd shot your Jack, and I just thought, Well, maybe it's like a cosmic sign or something."

He didn't answer, but she was still running with that same thought.

She said, "You know how sometimes you just get that feeling, like everything's been set up in your favor?"

It had been on his mind since he saved her, and now he had no doubt.

She said, "It felt right already, but then I knew Charles would send you after me, and I thought that would be a nice reward to have waiting: Miles Keller just hanging around, none the wiser."

Nina was a pretty good reward in herself. But maybe she'd thought he'd need more convincing—she might have had Keller there as payment for letting her go free.

Bobby said, "And what if Charles hadn't sent me? What would have happened then?"

She had an answer ready, but she took her time with it, propped herself up on an elbow and looked down at him. She said, "I'd get Keller to save me. Seems like he knows how to handle himself."

Just like that.

Bobby said, "You don't think he'd take much convincing."

"Well. I'd say please." She pulled the towel off her head and shook her hair out, looking like someone in a shampoo commercial, face up-turned and eyes shut. Bobby felt moisture hit his face.

Nina said, "I offered him half a million dollars if he wanted to work for me. I didn't tell him what I needed, but I figured if Bobby Deen didn't come to my rescue, it'd be nice to have Keller rip off Feng, or maybe rip off Keller myself."

Like she could put this all together without too much bother. She said, "Soon as I saw him in the hotel, I knew there were a few different ways I could push things. Obviously this is best."

She laid her head on his chest, and with the contact he could feel his heartbeat.

Thud, thud—

Bobby said, "What makes you think he'd be up for anything at all?"

Nina said, "Call it female intuition."

No, it was more than that—she knew something, but her head was turned, and he couldn't see her face.

Thud, thud—

Bobby said, "Did you rob that banker, or was Keller going down a dead end?"

Thud, thud, thud, thud—

Nina said, "That'd be telling, wouldn't it?"

TWENTY-EIGHT

NEW YORK, NY

Miles Keller

"Are you going to read me my rights?"

O'Shea said, "We can if you want." Acting surprised, like he hadn't been serious with his accusation.

Miles looked under the table as he crossed his ankles. He said, "Well, if you think I'm going around ripping off crooked lawyers, maybe we'd better make this official."

A glance went around the four of them, and then O'Shea got back to looking at Miles. He seemed to prefer eye contact whenever possible. Miles just sat there and played the game, trying to seem calm while his head churned.

O'Shea took a card from his wallet and started running through the right-to-silence routine, and Miles tuned him out and thought about next moves.

If they had hard evidence, he'd be locked up already. And if they thought they could build a case, they wouldn't be making accusations now, tipping him off early while they were still putting things together. Unless they thought they could shake him with tough questions, get him scared and then follow him to the money. Maybe put a tail on him, catch him with the Covey loot.

God, he wouldn't be that stupid. And modesty aside, he thought they probably knew that. Which meant their surest bet was to use Petrov's testimony: that Miles had committed abduction and armed robbery. But clearly they didn't have that yet. And if they were taking the risk of talking to him now, maybe Petrov's prognosis was less than cheerful. They figured this might be the one chance—apply some pressure and see what shakes loose.

So what to do?

It was pretty dark luck he was dealing with. All would be fine, as long as Petrov didn't make it. What a thing to wish for. But he couldn't think about that now, freedom being contingent on fatality.

He zoned back in, and the room's volume seemed to rise, and O'Shea was asking him if he understood everything.

Miles said, "Yes, I do," and saw the card go back in the wallet and the wallet go back in the coat, O'Shea watching him the whole time, like the pressure of sheer attention would break him eventually.

"Are you happy for us to continue with the questioning?"

That was a big question in itself. He could just exercise his right to silence, sit there until they arrested him or let him go. But arrest wasn't on the cards, or it would've happened already. And when he walked out of here, it'd be nice to know what they had on him.

Miles said, "Yeah, go on then."

O'Shea said, "All right. I haven't heard you deny it yet."

Meaning the robbery.

Miles said, "I haven't robbed anyone."

Being conscious of his tone, trying to give a smooth delivery, made his voice sound very different. He sounded like he was lying.

"So where were you yesterday night? Say nine P.M. to two A.M."

Miles said, "Home alone, listening to an audiobook. About midnight, I got a cab to Union Square, met a friend for coffee."

"Thought were you living in hotels."

"I like to go home and get my mail. Embarrassing for a robbery detective, getting cleaned out because someone sees a stuffed mailbox."

O'Shea nodded, like taking it seriously. He glanced around and said, "This is probably a bit embarrassing, too."

Miles shrugged. "Only if you make it stick. Otherwise you get the red face."

There was a pause, but O'Shea didn't have another one in him, had to bring it back to serious business. He said, "Who'd you meet for coffee?"

Miles said, "The staff will remember us."

"You didn't see anyone on your mail run?"

"Not unless a neighbor saw me."

"That's unfortunate then, isn't it?"

Miles shrugged. "It's normal life for millions of people on any given night."

O'Shea let that have a moment's quiet, and then changed direction. He said, "Petrov was on a call to me when you ran into him."

Miles didn't answer.

O'Shea said, "And he didn't mention anything about needing a meeting. Fifteen minutes later, he sends a text message, asking to see me at Rockefeller Center."

Miles said, "So I guess he changed his mind."

O'Shea said, "There's a protocol for meetings, and he didn't follow it."

"You'd have to ask him about that."

Miles managed to hold on to the guy's stare.

O'Shea said, "I want to know what happened in that car to make Petrov suddenly want a meeting. Up at Rockefeller Center of all places."

Miles said, "You're asking the wrong person."

"Ditching protocol, wanting meetings in strange places, I got the impression he was under duress."

"If so, then it was self-imposed. He seemed kind of agitated."

"So can you tell me why his phone was found in your coat?"

That's right: he'd taken the coat off to sponge the blood. With the confiscated phone still in the pocket.

Miles said, "He'd been texting on and off while he drove, so the phone was right there in his lap. I opened his door and I think it fell on the road. I was going to call for backup, but everyone on the street seemed to be way ahead of me, figured there was no point loading up the switchboard."

"But you kept the phone?"

"You going to charge me with theft?"

"I'm just very interested in how you ended up with it."

"He seemed to be bleeding to death, and that took up a lot of my attention. I must have pocketed the phone without thinking. I don't intend to keep it."

There was a knock at the door.

The sound took his focus off O'Shea, and he saw the whole room again: Medina still there across the table, Dodd and McKenzie leaning against the wall, as if waiting to step in with even tougher questions.

McKenzie opened the door, and a plainclothes guy in his twenties leaned in past the frame. He said, "Phone for Keller."

Miles said, "I think we're done anyway."

O'Shea didn't turn around. "Give us a minute. They can hold."

The door closed.

O'Shea took a moment looking at his pad, wanting a hard question to close things out with. Maybe he realized he wasn't gaining any traction. He looked up and said, "Well, you know the script." He started rocking his head, like he was tired of saying it: "Do it the easy way now, or the hard way later."

McKenzie's phone started ringing, and he stepped out into the corridor to take the call, walking stooped like he was ducking out of a funeral.

Miles waited for the door to close and said, "What's going to happen later that's going to make things so hard for me?"

"Where's Covey's money?"

"Don't be ridiculous."

"When they run forensics on his house, are they going to find your prints, or your clothing fibers, or your DNA?"

"They won't find my prints. But fibers, DNA—maybe. Kings Point PD was nice enough to show me around the crime scene, so you never know, there might be trace evidence."

O'Shea didn't answer.

Miles said, "Whatever's there, it'll be easy enough to explain."

O'Shea said, "Yeah, fuck you."

Miles stood up. "Unless there's something else . . ."

He came out from behind the table and moved past the camera as Medina was saying, "Interview paused at five thirty-eight P.M."

O'Shea said, "Keller."

Miles stopped but didn't turn around. He could see McKenzie on the other side of the wire-mesh window, back to the door and his phone to his ear.

O'Shea said, "When Petrov wakes up, you're fucking cooked."

He knew that already. He didn't answer.

O'Shea said, "Bit of luck we'll be two-for-two as well. I heard you rigged the Jack Deen shooting, tried to make it look clean. So we can talk about that, if you've got anything to say."

"No, I think I'm good."

O'Shea said, "Oh, I was hoping you'd tell us about the paper you took out of his coat. Figured he was blackmailing the girl, right? Just have to make sure next time, don't shoot through the guy's pocket. Bit of a giveaway when you have paper all through the wound."

He knew it was an oversight, but he'd had so little time. That sprint in the dark to his car, hunting in the trunk for his throw-down piece. He'd never felt so frantic. The PD had sonic gear that triangulated gunshot noise. They could hit a shooting scene in less than three minutes . . .

He wanted to turn and give O'Shea a parting sentiment, but his head was full of Jack Deen worries, and he couldn't think of a line. He saw McKenzie wrapping up his call, and stayed back to let him through the door. McKenzie did his best to occupy maximum space, taking care to brush shoulders as he came past.

Medina said, "I need you back here in five."

Miles didn't answer. He stepped out into the corridor, and heard McKenzie in a low voice say that Kings Point PD couldn't find the wife's car. Miles paused, knowing it meant something but not quite feeling it click. He waited for O'Shea's answer, but then the door closed and the young plainclothes guy was beckoning.

In the squad room, everyone seemed to be on a phone. He saw people turn and look away, as if all the talk was about *him*. The plainclothes guy pointed out a phone lying off the cradle, and Miles thanked him and headed over.

He heard his name, and turned to see Pam Blake coming for him, threading between desks. She had a ball cap on, and a raincoat over faded street clothes, walking with a hand on her hip to show the badge and gun on her belt.

"Miles, what happened? I heard you shot someone."

"You didn't have to come all the way down here."

"Yeah, I know—should've just stayed home, watched it on TV, right? The hell happened?"

He said, "I basically walked into a shit storm."

"Yeah, sounds like it. You shot up a hotel or something?" She had a hand on her head, pulling her hat back, like she was trying to get a better view of him. He could see the lines around her eyes and mouth, pinch marks from stress, and sitting in a car doing night surveillance, chaining smoke after smoke.

Miles said, "Give me five minutes. You got a car?"

"Yeah, I'm out front. Is FID done with you?"

"I'm done with them. I'll meet you outside."

He turned away, but she caught his arm.

"Are you okay?"

"I will be if you just walk out like nothing's the matter."

"Dude, what the hell—"

"Sorry. I'm just tired. I'll see you downstairs in five minutes."

He turned away, and this time she didn't stop him. He picked up the phone and said, "Keller."

Stanton said, "I was worried they wouldn't let you out."

Miles said, "Where are you?"

"Driving. I got a call for you—"

"Where's Lucy?"

"With me. We're heading down to your place. Said she needs meds or something—look, I got a call for you, she's on hold."

"Who is?"

"The Stone woman. The Nina lady. You want to talk to her?"

Nina. He saw her leaning on his hotel room door, making luck lean as well: life veering for the worse. So why was he still holding the phone?

Stanton said, "I don't know what she wants—"

Miles said, "Put her through."

There was a pause, and then a beep, and then Nina said, "Hello, Miles."

As measured and knowing as a robot. Like some rogue AI talking to the last man on earth.

He said, "What's going on?"

She said, "I'm sorry things didn't work out quite like I said. We can still make some money, though."

"What did I just walk into?"

"Business, essentially. We don't have much time. My husband sent a man to take me back to L.A. He was with me in the lobby earlier. You might've seen him."

"The hat man."

"Yeah, you got him. I think I've . . . what's the word? Forestalled his recovery efforts for now. He seems to be deeply in love with me."

"And I presume he's not eavesdropping."

"No, I took him to bed, and now he's taking a shower."

Miles said, "What are you tied up in? I just killed two people."

"And saved my life, most importantly. I'm not about to forget that in a hurry."

He had to resist the urge to keep looking around. He'd seem paranoid if he did. But he kept expecting a shoulder tap, a summons back to the room with O'Shea.

He said, "So tell me what's going on, and we'll call it even."

Nina tutted. "You shouldn't write off your credit so easily. What's going on is I've had a deal turn adversarial."

"Yeah. It looked kind of tense."

He knew he should get out of there: the longer he waited, the longer Petrov had to wake up and give him an abduction charge. But there was another Miles at work, one who wanted to hear out Nina Stone.

She said, "I was selling my husband's business on his behalf and without his knowledge. The nature of the business made that a very dangerous undertaking. I hope that gives you the general picture, but really that's not important. What I'm trying to tell you is that my offer still stands."

Big, easy money—and morally spotless if you take it off a thug. But that was the other Miles talking, and things had changed since last night. He wouldn't survive another crisis.

He said, "Sorry, I'm not interested."

"You're still talking to me though. These people in the blood trade seem to be very well looked after. So if you want to help me roll a man named Bobby who wears a little hat, you'd stand to make some money."

Miles shut his eyes.

Nina said, "Let's not take too long, he's not going to shower forever."

Miles said, "Last night you told me half a million."

"I needed your attention, and five hundred grand's a clean and compelling figure, isn't it?"

Yes it was. Not now, though. He couldn't take the risk.

She said, "It might not be half a million, but if you go up against Bobby and win, you stand to make a bit."

She had a knack for dodging specifics: was this straight murder-robbery, or something with more finesse?

But who cares. Get out of there—

He said, "You want my advice: ditch Bobby while he's still in the bathroom. Or even better, get the cops onto him. I'm sure they'd like his take on what happened at the hotel."

Nina said, "Mmm. I'm all about subtlety and profit, though. I'm sure that there's a better way of handling all of this. And the offer stands. If we see each other up the road, just keep in mind that I'm in your corner. You're a nifty character, Miles, which means we're two of a kind. I want to make something happen."

"Bye, Nina."

That was nice: a perfect conjugate to her "Hello, Miles," even the same volume and tone.

He put the phone down and got out of there.

He went out the same blue door through which he'd entered, and saw Pam Blake sitting on the hood of an unmarked Chevy, smoking a cigarette. He opened the passenger door and climbed in, the eavesdropped line from McKenzie still caught in his head.

Kings Point PD can't find the wife's car.

Pam took her sweet time.

He couldn't hurry her though, lest it look like a getaway. She made him wait a full minute and then dropped the butt down a drain and got in next to him, making a good show of being pissed off.

She started up and turned east on Walker, and Miles said, "Sorry. What I should've said is, Thanks for coming down to check I'm okay."

Funny how it was so much easier saying that now they were both looking out the windshield. She didn't answer, though. The car radio was keyed in to local dispatch, and he kept expecting to hear his name on a BOLO. How would he even play it? Try and explain it to her, or just run for the nearest subway? He dropped his window, and that helped things a little, city noise covering the operator.

Pam said, "Even when I was in Baltimore, working CID, detectives hardly ever shot people. Patrol, yeah, they notched a few, but CID, sometimes you'd get down to the car, realize you left the gun behind—where you want to go, anyway?"

Miles thought about that, half his mind still up in Kings Point at the Covey crime scene. He looked out his window at the street, this man-made chasm with the old buildings hemming in the one-way traffic, CHINATOWN BUILDING SUPPLIES going past in bright-red letters, a thicket of scaffolding and then the Chinese Baptist Church with its signage at a lower volume. He said, "Brooklyn, please."

"Which bridge you want? B, M, or W?"

A dispatcher read a BOLO notice: white male, early forties—

Miles shut it off. He said, "I should just take the subway."

"Yeah, and then I won't find out what your deal is."

Miles didn't answer.

She let him sit there for a block before she looked over. "Dude? Are you going to say something?"

"Take the Williamsburg."

She kept looking at him.

He said, "I thought you were going to come back to your Baltimore CID story, work it into a question."

That got a smile out of her. She said, "Yeah, how come some people go a whole career without killing anyone, and you managed three in a month?"

He said, "It's been a strange few weeks."

"Yeah, I gathered that. So why not just start by running through today?"

She made the turn onto Kenmare—brick apartment buildings with a sooty tint, a wall of graffiti in pink balloon letters. It was like a less polished SoHo. Miles rubbed his eyes and saw it all in acid-trip colors. He said, "There was a girl at the hotel—"

"Yeah, see, that's a bad start already."

"I looked at her for robbery five years back. Some banking guy said she stole some money from him at a dinner party. I let her go."

"Because she didn't do it, or because she seemed nice?"

Miles shrugged. "She was okay. She was a character, though. Man. I hadn't seen her in years. Then last night she just showed up at my hotel—came back and there she was waiting outside the door." He could see her too, and that was the thing about Nina: she always showed up vivid when you said her name.

"How'd she even know you were there?"

"Saw me on the street I think, figured I was a guest."

Pam said, "Must be a common thing, though, right? Strike up a bond with a cop who's gone after you, only natural that you try and catch up every so often. Should roll that policy out to homicide—"

"Yeah, yeah, yeah. Hilarious."

He went back to his window watching. They were on Delancey Street now, queued taillights jeweling the way to the bridge in the middle distance.

She said, "So what? Did you think that was pretty fucking weird, or did you just say come in, and then give her a cup of tea?"

"I just gave her water."

"Oh yup."

Miles said, "She had some deal going. Offered me half a million dollars if I wanted in on it."

"Oh man." The traffic stopped, and she shut her eyes. She let out a long breath and said, "That all sounds pretty legal, doesn't it?"

He didn't know whether to keep talking, but he said, "I was up at Kings Point this morning, got back to the hotel this afternoon, and that's when it all happened. Didn't know what it was at first—I mean, why people were shooting—and then I saw Nina standing there, and it started making sense."

He noticed she was gripping the wheel a lot harder than usual.

She said, "You pass this all along to FID?"

He said, "Bits and pieces."

"Right. Sure." She had her elbow up on the sill, fingers on the bridge of her nose, eyes closed again.

He said, "Watch the road."

She opened her eyes but didn't move her hand. "So how come she knew it was safe to talk to you at all?" She looked across at him. "Obviously wasn't worried she'd end up under investigation again, making you a six-figure offer."

Miles was quiet a long time. Then he said, "She robbed a very bad guy. So I let her get away with it, basically."

The car seemed to be quiet for a long time. Then she said, "God-dammit." Letting it out on a sigh.

He hated the quiet, but he needed to hear her take on it.

She said, "Maybe you better keep this to yourself."

"Or I can keep talking, and you can record it if you want."

"Oh, Jesus." She shook her head some more. "I don't know what to say. I honestly don't."

He waited and watched the traffic.

She said, "What are you going to tell me?"

"Look. I don't know what to do. I don't know if you think ignorance is bliss, or whether coming clean is the thing to do."

Her head was still shaking, as if working off the disbelief, and then finally it stopped. She said, "Depends how clean you gotta come."

He risked a glance and saw she'd tightened up even more: tendons standing out in her wrists, hands white on the wheel.

He said, "If I lay it out, don't have a hernia."

She didn't move.

Miles said, "I've been ripping people off."

Silence.

He said, "Dealers, and organized-crime guys."

He checked her hands again, and thought she'd actually relaxed slightly. Like she'd been bracing for the impact and now it was over. Traffic came to a stop, and everyone gave a horn blast to try and get it moving again. Pam's head tipped back on the rest. "Fuck. Man, I thought you were straight up."

Miles said, "You could've just said don't say it."

She still wasn't looking at him. She said, "I thought you were good. Now I don't know what to do."

"I am good."

"Yeah? How do you figure that?"

She went to run a hand through her hair, but seemed to forget she had the hat on, pushed it off the back of her head.

He said, "Look. I'm not trying to justify anything—"

"But?"

"But the divorce screwed me up. I didn't think I'd ever lose her, but I did. And then I met Nina six months later—this woman who took a million bucks off a guy who fucking deserved it." He looked across at her. "And I thought: yeah, I could do that."

"You been doing this for *five* years?"

He didn't answer straightaway. Then he said, "I'm not proud of anything. But ethics come in shades, you know?"

"Oh, don't give me that shit."

Miles stayed with his point, though: "Which means that me ripping off a dealer is a slightly better outcome than said dealer keeping all the money to himself."

"Not as good as everyone being arrested, though, is it?"

"Well, if you want to go down that road, I guess now's your chance."

She said, "Why can't you just be a normal, low-maintenance asshole? Instead of dropping me in this. Jesus Christ, fucking dilemma."

He said, "Look. I'm telling you because I'm worried maybe I'll never see you again. And I figure that's a pretty shitty way to take off, me leaving with things I should've told you."

"Why, where you going?"

"I haven't figured that out yet."

"Or you haven't quite figured out whether you should tell me?"

He let his breath out through his teeth, mimicking her by accident. "There was an old CI I used to run. She's got emphysema—"

"Oh shit, here we go."

He didn't answer.

She said, "What—you going to take off to Florida or something, hope no one recognizes you with a tan?"

Miles said, "I always knew I had to get out eventually. Every time you rip someone off, it's just another chance that something'll come back at you. And then eventually the stakes get pretty high."

"Which is what you're looking at now."

"Yeah. I don't have a lot of time."

"Oh, God." She pulled the hat back down, the brim low over her eyes. "Part of me wants to just turn around and take you back to the fucking precinct." Her voice was going wobbly. She gave herself a minute and then said, "You know, sometimes, you go out on calls, roll up at some piece-of-shit crack house, or a shooting or something, where everyone's seen it but no one's talking. And it's like: you know on kind of a formal level that there's laws, but then when you're actually on the street and see it through their eyes, you realize it's just dog-eat-dog, same as everything else. So that part of me doesn't really blame you."

Miles said, "Is it a big part or a little part?"

She shook her head, like she didn't actually know the answer. She said, "Is it just FID after you, or does Internal Affairs have a hard-on, too?"

"I don't know." He chose his words carefully and then said, "They think I visited a bent lawyer last night, walked away with some money. The Covey guy we looked at, up in Kings Point."

He was too delicate with his words, and she didn't even ask him if he'd done it. She just sat there shaking her head, as if gripped by some kind of vision, the whole city falling down beyond the wind-shield.

She said, "What's in Brooklyn?"

He toyed with telling her the truth—how the Coveys were dead, and he knew who killed them. But he didn't know how to thread the needle finely enough, how to convince her that he had nothing to do with it. So he just said, "Maybe you better let me out across the bridge."

TWENTY-NINE

NEW YORK, NY

Bobby Deen

She was in the bathroom again, doing some kind of beautification, he figured. He heard water running, the click of scissors now and again. Bobby figured she'd spend thirty minutes in there and come out looking no different—still ten out of ten. That was how it worked with women.

He wrapped one of her discarded towels around his waist and went through to the kitchen. The case of cash was still open on the table, and her bag was open on the counter by the laptop. He lifted its screen. The cursor blinked slowly, wanting a password. Her profile photo had been shot on Charles's balcony, L.A. hills in the background. He typed "Bobby" and hit Enter. No luck. The text field shook in disapproval. He listened for a moment, and when he heard water running, he checked her bag. A sweater, a cell phone, a charger for the computer, a slim leather wallet. All standard stuff, but it was a view of the real Nina. They were part of her in a way, except she couldn't influence impressions. He popped the button on the wallet. Plastic galore: credit cards, and fake ID. She had a New York driver's license in the name Joan Ryder, a California DL as Sally Lake, both with the same photo. He checked the pockets in turn, and found more licenses: Wisconsin, another California, Washington, Maryland. The credit cards were all Joan Ryder and Sally Lake. She had nothing as Nina. Maybe her life was just Pick a Card.

He made another drink—soda only this time—and turned on the TV while he waited for her. It felt like the life: nothing on but a towel, windows with a river view, channel hopping, drink-in-hand, and Nina getting pretty.

He flicked back and forth through news stations, half-expecting to see his own mug shot looking back. No Bobby, though. Middle East, Middle East, some kind of book-burning festival in Kansas. He brought up the TV's YouTube app and searched "Tribeca Gardens." There were about twenty clips of the hotel mayhem, but everything had been filmed from outside. He chose a clip at random, and watched twelve seconds' worth of people running through stopped traffic. He sampled another, and waited through an eighteen-second-long shot of the hotel entrance, the sound of gunfire cutting off the satisfied hum of a pretzel cart. He searched "Tribeca Gardens lobby," but the clips on offer all looked like shaky sidewalk junk. He exited YouTube and went back to channel hopping, heard "Canal Str—," a blip of broken speech, as he surfed past CNN. He flipped back to catch the story, and shit—there's the cop, Miles Keller. Security footage from the hotel lobby. Keller in action, with his gun up.

He called, "Check this out," and then turned in time to see her come out of the bedroom naked, walking past full-length windows and the bag of money on the table to stand next to him in front of the TV. He wondered if she'd show up online eventually, a nude parade caught by accident on camera. She'd have a million views in no time.

". . . want to speak with Keller in relation to a robbery-homicide last night in Kings Point. Three people are dead, and police say a large sum of cash was also taken . . ."

Bobby said, "Funny they don't say he's NYPD."

Wanting to sound cool about it, but he knew murder and extortion got a whole lot easier when you're dealing with a bent cop.

Nina waited until the picture was in Kansas again—a bonfire close-up of books in flames—and then she kissed him on the cheek and headed back to the bedroom.

THIRTY

NEW YORK, NY

Miles Keller

He caught a J train east into Brooklyn and got off at Gates Avenue. The tracks were on a bridge above Broadway, stilted on columns painted lizard green. He took the stairs down to street level and waited at the light to cross. The train started off again, wind and squeal gathering to match the speed, and dog-eared posters on the ironwork ticked and flapped like some hysterical greeting all up and down the road.

The shops were lighting up in the evening gloom. He stopped at a deli over on Ralph Avenue and bought coffee and a pastrami sub. He hadn't eaten since that morning. He finished the sub on the sidewalk and drank the coffee as he walked west along Gates.

Walter Stokes—his driver from last night, his would-be Covey accomplice—had a place just off Malcolm X Boulevard. The real estate was mainly brick apartments, but Stokes's address was one of two clapboard places side by side on weedy lots—these skinny, two-story houses holding out against the four-story walk-ups.

The neighbor's place was white on the upper level and pink on the ground floor. A shirtless guy in his seventies wearing pink-daubed jeans was sitting on the porch, sipping from a takeout cup, and he raised it at Miles as he came past, as if pleased to see another man who drank his coffee out of Styrofoam.

Stokes had a waist-high fence along the sidewalk with a gap where there should have been a gate. Miles walked into the yard and knocked at the front door, not actually sure yet what he'd do if Stokes opened up. Maybe talk his way inside if the man still seemed chummy. Or maybe let it open an inch, wait until he saw an eye above the chain, and then kick it open.

But no one answered, and the curtains were all drawn. He saw the old boy watching from his front step, so Miles stepped across the little chain-link divide and walked over to him, trying to seem genial, just another guy enjoying his beverage.

Miles said, "You seen Walter around?"

The guy nodded past him at the little fence. "It's not soundproof, you know. Could've asked from over there."

"Thought it'd seem more polite if I came over."

"No. Makes you seem more like police."

Miles looked down at his attire, like trying to spot the giveaway, and the guy shook his head and said, "I been stopped by those narc guys. They don't look like police either. But you can still tell."

Miles said, "I'm one of those rare examples of someone who doesn't look like a cop, and is also definitely not a cop."

The guy seemed skeptical about that.

Miles said, "Have you seen him or not?"

The guy shook his head. "Went to ask if I could use his ladder, but he didn't answer."

"You find the ladder?"

The guy nodded. "Had to leave it, though. Can't take a man's ladder without his okay." Keeping eye contact as he said it, like checking Miles was on board with that philosophy.

Miles said, "What makes me look like police?"

"I don't know." The guy looked him up and down. "Everything."

Miles nodded. "Okay. I'm going in the house. Don't call nine-one-one."

He left the guy thinking that over and walked back to Stokes's place and around to the backyard. There were a couple of bleached and tattered lawn chairs, and the toppled metal skeleton of what had once been a shade umbrella. By the back door was a coal barbecue on a tripod standing on a patch of bare dirt, like a cutting-edge drone that had touched down by rocket power. He set his empty cup on the hot plate and stood at the back door, listening. No point knocking: if someone was going to let him in they would have done so already.

He stepped back and took his gloves from his back pocket and pulled them on, and for a moment saw a house in Venice Beach, thirty years ago: Miles walking in to ask if they were going yet, and there were his parents and half a dozen others high on marijuana, lying around on sofas and studying the ceiling fan, the thing spinning so slow it might've been stoned as well. He remembered the soft ring of the wind chime on the porch, even though there was no wind, and then the door crashing open, Miles fleeing through an unfamiliar house as people chased him.

Maybe if he'd stayed longer with that image it would've kept him in the yard: the thought of being the horror moment for some other little kid could've made him take a different course. But the more you have on the line, the more you're trapped in a certain mind-set. Everything's okay, and you just have to keep moving forward.

His kick landed just below the handle, and he stepped into the house as the door flew open before him. Through unadjusted eyes, the kitchen gloom was full dark for a second. He paused, and then the twilight showed at the edges of the curtains—gray light—like the sun coming up on a dead planet, the first day postapocalypse. There was a doorway ahead of him, a hallway beyond, and a figure standing there—

Miles ducked left, and the shotgun blast made a truck-wheel hole in the kitchen wall, a cloud of gypsum dust like talc, and wood chips flying everywhere. He turned to run, but a better instinct held him back: don't get framed in that doorway. He ducked low beneath the damage, and then leapt upright as the figure and its shotgun rounded the corner, two muzzles right there, double zero, this welded infinity symbol right in his face.

He swatted backhand as he rose and caught warm steel, yanked sideways and down as he grabbed for the stock, felt his glove slip on lacquered wood. He kept the muzzle pointed down, tried to yank the gun free with one hand, and the second blast was quieter under the ringing in his ears.

The pellets blitzed the floor, and he felt wood chips hit his shins. He yanked the gun again, but the shooter was falling, screaming, and the gun was his.

He stepped back and felt dizzy, veering so close to good-bye and then coming back again. He hit a light switch and saw debris every-where: shredded wallpaper like the aftermath of some weird ceremony, a brutal union replete with confetti.

The woman on the ground was fortyish and tall, six-two maybe, although it was hard to tell with her lying fetal, holding a bloodied shoe. She was talking as well, but he had to kneel to hear her, his head full of high-pitched buzzing.

She was loaded on something—not meth or she wouldn't feel the pain—but her features were slack and her focus was miles away. He stayed out of the blood and tried to hear what she was saying, but she was forming sounds that made no sense, like her brain was running backward.

He still had the shotgun, but he dropped it on the floor now both barrels were empty. He cupped the woman's face. "Where's Walter?"

No answer—or nothing useful at least. She just rambled on seam-lessly, like some kind of sleep talk that made perfect sense, deep inside her head.

He didn't have much time.

He left her and moved to the front of the house. There were stairs by the entry leading to the first floor, and he had to breathe through his sleeve as he got halfway up.

Stokes was on his back on the mattress in the master bedroom, sheets in a twist, and a syringe still spiked in the crook of his arm.

Miles checked his pulse and got nothing. Stokes was dead cold. He'd been gone for maybe six hours. Miles hit the lights and saw the full squalor. Used needles, spare tourniquets, blackened spoons, cotton wool, plastic dime bags of heroin by the bed.

Miles wondered how much he'd blown on the drugs. He could've set himself up for a while. He had the twenty thousand Miles gave him, plus whatever he got from the Covey place when he went back the second time. He'd probably pawned Mrs. Covey's car this morning, and decided to treat himself.

His ears were still ringing, but he could hear sirens now, thin and distant. He started down the stairs at a trot, but a thought caught him halfway down.

He needed the gun: the pistol Stokes used in the Covey house.

If the police found it, they could link Miles to the Covey robbery. It was circumstantial, but it put him in range of the crime. The pink-house neighbor could put him at the Stokes scene, and the Stokes scene contained the murder weapon.

He took the stairs two at a time on the way back up, went into the bedroom, into the reek of piss and body odor. You couldn't accuse Stokes of being fastidious, so wherever the gun was, it'd be somewhere stupid. He wouldn't have been clever and ditched it.

The foul air made him gag, and he used his sleeve as a mask, neared the bed with his arm bent across his mouth, like some vampire parody. The corpse was spread-eagled, the head tipped backward off the pillow and the mouth wide. Stokes seemed to be loving every moment.

Miles ran a hand under the pillow and felt something metal, came out with a Colt 1911—the same one Stokes had pulled on him last night. It was cocked and locked. Stokes liked protection while he got a load on.

He slipped the pistol in the back of his belt as he ran down the stairs, hand gliding the rail and his footwork a scurry. He swung a one-arm pivot around the end post and sprinted hard back along the hallway to the kitchen, seeing red and blue—maybe in his mind's eye or his real eye.

The woman was still on her side on the floor, but she'd let go of her ruined foot, and he could see her fussing with the shotgun. He heard it snap closed as he ran past her, and the shot took a bite out of the kitchen doorframe as he went out into the yard.

The sirens were screaming, and when the second shot came, it was followed by a tinkle of falling glass, and he looked back to see a smashed kitchen window, and a ragged scrap of blind clawing for fresh air. Miles grabbed his cup off the barbecue and hopped the fence into the alley behind the walk-ups, and he didn't stop running.

THIRTY-ONE

NEW YORK, NY

Bobby Deen

Nina said, "Could be a song, don't you think? Raided the gun closet, headed down to Sheepshead Bay."

She tried it under her breath, a low note from the back of her throat. "Maybe 'gun safe' is better—raided the gun safe, going down to Sheepshead Bay. Yeah, there you go."

It was a gun closet in real life, of course. They'd taken a Sig each from Charles's bedroom stash, and now they were heading south on Ocean Parkway in the stolen SUV. They were somewhere in Brooklyn, three lanes of traffic each way and low-rise commercial buildings on either side. It felt more like L.A. than New York—maybe Venice Boulevard, but with more trees and fewer gangbangers.

Nina was driving with her phone in her lap, Google Maps showing her the route. She said, "So how does Charles pay? He write you a check, or is it just money in a bag?"

Bobby said, "You wondering if you can afford to double-cross me?"

Nina said, "Yeah. Whether I'd have to hollow out your head and wear it to the bank to get the money."

Bobby laughed. But it raised the issue of how he was getting back to California. He couldn't catch a flight until he talked to the cops about the clusterfuck at the hotel. They'd have his prints on that gun he left behind, and they would've found a few in the Mercedes, too—whatever was left of it. So he either needed fake ID, or he was in for a sit-down with NYPD. He rubbed his face, ran his hands through his hair.

"You still with me?"

He looked over at her, and managed to push the thought aside.

He said, "He pays the old-fashioned way: money in a bag."

"Unmarked, and nonsequential, and all that kind of thing?"

Bobby smiled. "Just good, honest Stone Studios profit."

She said, "So it's just a matter of collecting everyone's bag of money." She changed lanes and said, "Kill Keller and take his, fly back to L.A. and take a little more off Charles."

"I don't think I'll be flying anywhere."

Nina said, "Cold hard cash is the great enabler. You know how much an Idaho driver's license costs?"

Bobby shook his head.

Nina said, "Neither do I. But I bet it's way less than what we've got in that suitcase."

He made himself watch the road. There was a temptation to fixate on Nina, revel in the fact that she could shape the whole world.

She said, "I guess what we have to do is iron out the rules of collateral."

She looked across at him, but he waited for her to take it further. The car in front braked and Nina slowed without looking, keeping the trailing distance perfect.

She said, "Are you going to lose any sleep if we have to kill the gas-mask girl too?"

Well, he probably would lose sleep, actually. He had a kind of No Innocents rule. Guys he got sent after were in The Life: you signed up for it knowing things didn't always go your way. And normally it was straightforward, more or less. People skipped payments, or they had something big owing, or they made a move on someone they should have left alone. So you gave them what was coming. But he wasn't sure he could put his hand on a stack of Bibles and say the girl was covered by the rules.

So he said, "I'll defer to your judgment."

Nina smiled and said, "That's nice to hear."

Bobby said, "You not used to being in charge?"

She shook her head. "No, I'm always in charge." She looked at him, head dipped toward her shoulder, like telling him a secret. "I'm just not used to people figuring it out."

THIRTY-TWO

NEW YORK, NY

Wynn Stanton

He toured the downstairs while the girl got ready. He'd asked about her medication, and all she told him was, "steroids and oxygen." He could hear her in the bathroom upstairs, taking things out of the medicine cabinet. She'd only been in a couple of weeks, but it sounded like she'd taken over the place.

He called, "Not that it's my business or anything, but, you know . . . Are you going to get sicker . . . ?"

He let it trail off at the end, hoping she'd come in with an answer straightaway, but she didn't. And then with the pause, it made it seem like a real shitty thing to ask.

He said, "Sorry, just trying to, you know . . . But you don't have to talk about it, obviously."

He heard the cabinet door scrape closed, very slow, like she was coming up with something to tell him. She said, "I have stage-one emphysema, which is the mild kind. It might stay as stage one for years, or it might get worse. You never know what the actual prognosis is."

He liked what Keller had done to the place. The kitchen had been extended out the back, and he'd put some folding doors in on one side with a little deck that wrapped around the back of the house. You could see him living a different life, really: all the photos he had up in the corridor, he was like some thwarted family man. Miles and his brother from years ago, the wife who'd actually left him. There'd be another Miles out there somewhere—a parallel Miles in a parallel reality—where everything had turned out fine. A house full of kids, and a nice legal cop pension, full of retirement loot.

He called, "So what about the oxygen tank and stuff? Is that easy to get hold of?"

She said, "I don't know. Probably not. But people get scripts on the quiet for all kinds of things."

Jesus—glad it wasn't him going off the grid with the girl in tow. You'd spend your time trying to chase down medication. He really needed to take a shit as well. There was a bathroom along the hallway, and he opened the door and worked the angles for a moment, seeing if he could get everything done and keep talking to the girl at the same time.

But her voice was louder now, closer to the stairs, and he didn't want her coming down and catching him halfway through a big job.

She said, "The oxygen's actually optional. I just have it for the fashion value."

He wasn't sure whether to laugh or not.

Lucy said, "They've done studies, it doesn't really affect mortality, but it affects quality of life. Obviously you have to tow a tank around, but you don't get as tired."

Stanton said, "Yeah, I had an aunt had emphysema, she lived for ages, didn't seem to bother her." That wasn't true—he never had any aunts—but there was nothing wrong with a lie in the name of reassurance.

She said, "Yeah, lot of people know somebody. They all tell me they managed okay with it, but you end up dead eventually."

Stanton said, "Not my aunt—she got hit by a bus." What the fuck? He could do better than that . . .

Lucy said, "Probably because she was towing an air tank, couldn't move fast enough."

He felt he had a duty to get the story right for this fake aunt, make it Stantonesque, worthy of Stanton honor. He said, "No, she was just standing there, not looking, and it clipped her as it went around a bend. Think she stayed conscious for a minute too, gave the driver a piece of her mind." Yeah, she fucking would have, too—vintage Stanton.

He heard the squeak-bounce of the air-tank trolley coming down the stairs, and he leaned in the hallway, looking suave, waiting for her.

She said, "You been a dodgy lawyer your whole career, or is it just something that happens a little bit at a time?"

"Dodgy" grated, but then there she was smiling at him, making it a joke, a box of pills on her hip under one arm, the trolley tugged along by the other.

He said, "I'm not a lawyer, I'm a talent agent."

That made her stop. "What, like they have in Hollywood?"

Stanton said, "Yeah, that's how I got the idea. This producer flew me to Atlanta one time, wanting me to be like an expert consultant on this heist movie. And that was fine, put me up in a hotel, but I thought, you know, fuck being just the consultant, I want to be the guy who puts everything together—you know, finds the writer, finds the lead, pairs them up with a producer, helps pitch it to a studio." He rubbed his thumb on his first finger. "Get some dollars in the frame."

She liked this story—he could tell from her expression, kind of bemused, not saying anything.

Stanton said, "I stayed in L.A. awhile, but it didn't quite work out." He shrugged—*c'est la vie*, who gives a shit. "So I came up here, and now I do the same thing really, just for other kinds of work. You know: see the opportunity, find the right talent, put a team together, take my ten percent."

He'd told the story enough times he could lay it out pretty smooth, make it sound like this was the way he'd wanted it all along. Problem was, no matter how well you spin it, there's no fooling yourself, no changing the fact that this was plan B, and that he hadn't had enough— what? Verve or panache probably, or enough pure Stanton to go legit, and make everything work.

Lucy was still watching him, wanting more backstory, but he

didn't know where to take it next. He could tell her about the cover bands he'd had in L.A.—Six Ton Stanton, Pure Stanton when he was solo, and then a stint with Full Metal Stanton. But nothing had worked out, and he didn't want to imply that failure was a life theme. He turned away while he thought about where to steer things, and he found himself looking out at a man in a suit: the guy standing on the other side of the folding glass doors, wearing a hat and pointing a gun at him.

Bobby Deen

The guy was about sixty, and heading fast down the wrong side of the hill—round in the middle, and sort of twiggy in the limbs. Bobby said, "Open the door."

The guy probably couldn't hear through the glass, but how could he not get the picture? He spent a moment thinking about it, looking left and right, realizing distance and geometry weren't in his favor, and then he came over and crouched to free the catch at the bottom of the frame.

The glass sections all concertinaed with a whisper on a metal track, and Bobby stepped in with Nina following. The guy hadn't seemed too shocked at the sight of Bobby, but now with Nina, he lost some composure. He said, "Holy shit, what is this?"

Like a lone man with a gun was okay, but a lady packing heat was too much to reconcile. Bobby took a step left into the kitchen, keeping the pistol raised, and said, "We're looking for Keller."

The guy wasn't sure how to play it, and then he said, "I don't know any Kellers."

Nina strolled past him, one hand on her hip and the other hanging at her side with the gun. She said, "I recognize your voice. We spoke on the phone. You're Stanton."

Stanton said, "Oh, yeah. And you're the *New York Post* reporter."

Nina was off behind the guy, not looking at him. Bobby watched her checking out the photographs on the wall, getting up close to study each in turn.

She tapped one with her fingernail, a hard click on the glass. "This is his place. He had a photo of the woman in his hotel room."

Stanton said, "Also he's got some pictures of himself, which is a real good clue."

Bobby saw Nina holding back a smile. She turned to the Stanton guy and said, "You tell us where he is, we can be out of your hair. He's wanted for robbery-homicide, or so I understand. Doesn't sound like the kind of guy you want to associate with."

Stanton didn't answer.

Nina got right up close to him—close enough the guy could have gone for her gun if he was quick enough. But she had a strong don't-fuck-with-me vibe, and it kept the man in his place. She said, "You seen any bags of money lying around?"

Stanton did a good act of thinking hard. He said, "No, I don't think so."

"Who were you talking to just now?"

"No one. Myself."

Nina's eyebrows went up, indulging his bullshit. Stanton kept at it, held eye contact and deadpanned her: "Sometimes when I'm alone, I just say my name over and over, like: Wynn Stanton, yeah, Wynn fucking Stanton, he's the man. Then I come in a bit higher, like: Wynn, Wynn, Wynn, he's the fucking Stanton. Sorta barbershop, I guess."

He turned, still holding it together well, not a glimmer of a smile, and said to Bobby, "Imagine that's what you heard."

Nina seemed to find the guy quite entertaining. She looked at him a long moment, smiling faintly, the hand with the gun doing an idle pendulum so the frame slapped against her thigh. She said, "I'll go and get the girl, you stay here with Ricky Gervais."

Lucy Gates

She recognized the woman's voice from the hotel earlier—they'd been stepping out into the hallway as she went into Miles's room. She figured they must have guns, or Stanton wouldn't be so helpful.

So much for the air tank helping quality of life: she couldn't hide with it, and if she put it down, it'd be clear she was nearby.

The bedroom doors were all open. She went into the guest room she'd been using and stood the tank in the corner, left the box of pills on the floor beside it, out of view from the door. Then she slipped along the upstairs hallway to Miles's room.

She lay down on the floor on the far side of the bed and crawled in under the frame, chin on the carpet and watching for feet in the doorway. She heard the woman on the stairs, a steady rhythm, no different from her pace downstairs.

Lucy held her breath, and everything seemed to stop with it:

Silence in the house. No footsteps. She waited until the breath burned and then let it out her nose, terrified she'd cough.

The woman said, "Let's just take the comedian. He'll be better entertainment, anyway." Her feet going down the stairs, and then her voice again, quieter, saying, "She's probably hiding up there with a gun. I don't want to stick my head above the landing and end up wearing a bullet."

Quiet for a while, and Lucy strained to hear. She elbow-crawled forward and stuck her head out from under the mattress.

She heard the woman say, "This will all be easy. You just sit in the car, and we'll go for a drive, and you'll be on your best behavior. You can keep telling jokes—that's fine—but you can imagine what'll happen if you try and make a scene."

Something she didn't catch, and then the woman said, "Okay, great. After you. Just a nice, steady walk, no bullshit."

She heard the folding door close with a slam, and then the house was silent. She listened for footsteps or a car door, but the blood in her head was pounding too hard. She commando-crawled out from beneath the bed, pushed herself up onto all fours and then fully upright, dizzy with stress, her pulse slamming madly.

She ran to the stairs and started down them at a trot, out of breath already, only a few minutes off the tank.

The woman was standing at the bottom by the front door, a pistol in one hand at her side, and the shock of seeing her stopped Lucy with a jolt, like she'd been pulled up by a leash.

The woman shook her head and said, "What an amateur."

Bobby Deen

Man, he hadn't even seen Nina raise her gun yet. The woman he'd seen in the hotel—the lady with the gas mask, but with no gas mask this time—came along the hallway with Nina following, the pistol still hanging at her side.

Nina said, "We could keep them here and wait for Keller to show up."

Stanton said, "He isn't showing up. He's a fucking fugitive."

Nina said, "Yeah, we noticed. Nice picture of him on the news."

There was a cell phone on the counter in the kitchen. Bobby picked it up and brought it back over to the little gathering, ready for the requisite call for help. Ideally they'd get the girl a bit teary and desperate, have her phone up Keller and give him the hard news. Then Bobby could just wait for him to arrive. Sit down with Keller in the living room and run through why things were playing out as they were. Grant him some decorum. Nina would approve. Then just shoot the guy in the head, walk out of there with a bag of cash and a level score.

Stanton said, "I'm glad we're hanging around here, though. Like, when someone's a fugitive, the cops never actually go and check out the guy's house, do they?"

Nina said, "Must be safe enough, otherwise why are you hanging out here?"

Stanton said, "I'm not a fugitive. Neither's she."

"You must have heard of aiding and abetting though?"

Stanton turned his bottom lip out. "Nah, haven't heard of that."

The backlight on the phone timed out, and the numbers went dark. Bobby hit the power button and lit the screen up again. He saw Stanton watching him, and he wondered what they'd been doing in the house.

The guy wasn't thick, and somehow he guessed the thought. He smiled and said, "What on earth were we up to? Were we calling someone? Were we waiting for someone to show up?" He looked around with mock interest and said, "Is this the kind of house where you can shoot someone, and nobody hears? So many goddamned unknowns, right?"

Nina wasn't enjoying the show so much anymore. She didn't have her gun up yet, but Bobby thought she'd have an answer, something to kill the guy's hot air.

Bobby looked at the phone, the buttons lit up in orange. He pressed redial, and a phone number appeared on the little screen.

He put the phone to his ear.

It rang and rang, but he hung on, keeping eye contact with Stanton, trying to read his play—trying to see if he had something going, or if it was all just bravado.

The ringing ended.

Bobby waited, and then a woman's voice said, "Miles, you've got to stop calling me."

The line went dead in his ear.

He looked at Nina and saw her already watching him, a click as something went between them, a synapse flash, shared futures aligning, pulling them on the same perfect curve.

Bobby said, "I've got an idea."

THIRTY-THREE

NEW YORK, NY

Bobby Deen

Sitting in the back of the car with a captive girl beside him, he felt as if things were coming full circle. It was like the Nina rescue all over again, except this time Nina was up front, in the driver's seat, running that phone number through Google.

She said, "It must be the ex-wife. He's obviously got a thing for her, still." She looked up from her cell phone and found the girl in the mirror. "So don't get your hopes up—he's got his mind on other matters."

The woman—Lucy, her name was—didn't answer, probably trying to conserve energy now she'd lost the air tank.

Nina said, "Kings Point exchange." She looked at Bobby in the mirror. "Where have I heard Kings Point?"

It caught the girl's attention, too—Bobby saw her chin come up a touch. He said, "It was on that news bulletin. His murder-robbery was up there."

Nina said, "Yeah, that's it." She had her head down, typing something. "Bear with me, I'm Googling."

Bobby let her Google.

Eventually she said, "Kings Point. Okay. I think I'm sufficiently intrigued."

She tapped her phone screen to dial, and a ringing tone played at high volume through the speaker. She looked at the girl again and said, "This is a test of your good behavior. If you can sit quietly, you'll be fine."

The ringing quit.

A woman answered—the same voice Bobby had heard a moment ago: "Caitlyn speaking."

Nina said, "Good afternoon, ma'am. It's Maddie Rogan from the Kings Point Police Department. How are you?"

"Oh, fine, yeah—are you calling about my ex-husband?"

Nina said, "Have you been in contact with a complaint, ma'am?"

"Well, no, I haven't. I mean—I just got a call a few minutes ago, so I assumed that's what this is about. My husband laid a complaint previously about Miles—"

"Of course, ma'am. Yes, that's exactly what I'm checking up on. Your phone provider has a flag for incoming traffic off Mr. Keller's number, so we received an alert."

"Right, sure. He didn't say anything, he just hung up."

Nina said, "Has this been a common occurrence, ma'am?"

"No, not really. I mean, every couple of months maybe. It's not threatening, but it's just, you know . . ."

"Yes, I understand. Ma'am, we're making a real effort toward domestic safety, and if you've got some time available this evening it would be great for me to just drop in for a moment—"

"Oh, it's okay, I don't want to trouble you on a weekend."

Nina said, "No, ma'am, not at all. In fact under our faces-to-names department policy, I do need to drop by at some stage. Especially with our VIP residents, we want to make sure you know we're here all day, every day."

The VIP mention did it. The lady said, "Well, sure, great. Yeah, my husband's overseas with work at the moment, so it's nice having that comfort of security."

"Of course. That's exactly what we're here for. What does your husband do?"

"Oh, he's in corporate banking."

Banking: that chimed with something. He remembered from that afternoon, Nina telling him her Keller connection—how she'd robbed that banker at a dinner party, and Keller checked her out. So maybe that's why the cop had let her go: his wife had ditched him for a banker prick, and Nina's theft felt like payback, somehow. Her victim as a proxy for the wife's new man. Train-wrecked logic, but love did funny things. Bobby guessed he knew that better than most people.

He listened to Nina tell the lady to keep the phone off the hook once they hung up, send a strong message to Mr. Keller if he tried to call again.

"Sure, okay. It's not that it's threatening, it's just . . . You know. He can't really move on, I guess."

They small-talked for a minute longer, and then the woman told Nina her address, and Nina said she'd be dropping by in an hour or so.

She ended the call and turned the key, looked at Bobby in the mirror as she said, "Everything just got so much clearer."

THIRTY-FOUR

NEW YORK, NY

Miles Keller

The subway felt dangerous. His carriage was ultrabright and near-empty. It felt like an exhibit on wheels. He stayed on his feet so he could turn his back to the platforms. He could see people reflected in the windows—just a glimpse of them as the train flashed by—and they were all staring in at him.

But he made it out of the station at Sheepshead Bay, and no one stopped him. No one pointed, or had a second look. He walked south into quiet residential streets, and his heart stopped slamming.

Stanton's car was at the curb across the road. Miles went in the front gate and saw the cat coming out to meet him, bright-eyed and alert and moving in a dainty trot, collar bell tingling.

"You're always pleased to see me, aren't you?"

He picked it up under one arm and felt it purr. The front door was locked, so he knocked and called, "Luce, it's me."

No answer, but he heard a dull, rhythmic knocking, like a phone book being picked up and dropped, over and over. He put a hand under his shirt and felt the stolen Colt, checking the draw, and walked around the side of the house to the kitchen.

The folding glass door was unlocked. He stepped in and pulled it closed behind him. One of the chairs from the kitchen table was missing.

He took the Colt out of his belt and said, "Luce?"

More thumping, and he could hear humming as well. He walked down the corridor with the cat in one hand and the gun in the other and found Stanton in the living room, duct-taped to a chair. There was tape across his mouth too, and his eyes were bulging as he rocked from side to side in an effort to create noise.

"This wasn't the plan, Wynn."

Miles ripped the tape off his mouth. Stanton sucked air. His whole head was scarlet, and it fell forward and hit his chest.

"What happened?"

Stanton's shoulders were heaving. He wiped his mouth on his shoulder. "A dude in a hat, and a fucking *New York Post* journalist."

Nina.

Miles put the gun in his belt and sat down in an armchair. The cat poured out of his grip and slipped away. "What happened?"

"Can you untie me? I really need to drop a stack."

Miles didn't answer.

Stanton said, "Come on, I've been here an hour. I really need a shit."

Miles fetched a knife from the kitchen and cut him free.

"Oh, man. Finally. Thank you."

He was unbuckling his belt as he headed down the hallway. Miles stayed in the living room, and Stanton called, "Lucy was getting her stuff together, I look out the window, there's a guy standing there aiming a fucking Sig at my face. I let them in—he's got the lady there with him, whatshername, Nina—and then they take off with Lucy."

He put his face in his hands, trying to think, but even basic questions had trouble getting through. He took a breath and said, "Where are they taking her?"

Stanton said, "No idea. Hey, where's your toilet paper? You got some spare?"

Miles didn't answer. He opened his eyes and noticed that DeSean's gaming console was gone, but there were still chip packets and used plates on the floor. He turned the TV to CNN and killed the volume.

Stanton said, "Actually don't worry, I got some."

Street riots somewhere. Kansas. He watched a harried reporter being jostled by a crowd.

He called, "Is Lucy okay?"

"Yeah, far as I know."

A bird's-eye view of Canal Street, flashing lights along a two-block stretch.

"So what did they say? They didn't just come in and keep quiet the whole time."

"What?"

Miles heard the toilet flush. He closed his eyes and rubbed his face. He opened his eyes and saw his own photograph on TV. His driver's-license photo, and then an image from the hotel lobby: Miles with his gun up. He snatched the remote and hit the volume.

"—in Kings Point last night. Three people are dead, and police say tens of thousands of dollars were taken."

He was sitting down, but he felt himself dropping, like he was bleeding out the bottom of the chair. He said, "Shit. I'm wanted."

He'd known it at some level, but now it was official. Petrov must have woken up and fingered him for the robbery. Not to mention abduction.

Stanton said, "What?"

"Come and see this."

The photo disappeared, but it was back again by the time Stanton entered the room.

He said, "Oh. That's you."

"Yeah. I believe it is."

"Oh, God." Stanton sat down in the kitchen chair, curls of duct tape still hanging off it. "This is getting too heavy, man."

Miles said, "Don't faint on me."

"Look, I'm just the agent—I'm just the facilitator. I don't want to be this close to everything, you know?"

Miles stood up. He said, "They know I did the Covey job."

"Who does?"

"Nina Stone. And her friend in the hat."

Stanton stood up, fingers raking the last of his hair, forehead creaseless with the tension. "Look, if you're wanted, I can't be part of this. I gotta have distance. If I'm too close, I'm compromised, and then I'm no good to anyone."

Miles didn't move. "Sit down. Stop acting like this is your first rodeo."

"It is my first fucking rodeo."

He couldn't afford a walkout. He needed backup.

Miles said, "Wynn, you owe me. That Stokes guy—"

"Yeah, yeah, you told me: he tried to roll you, but shit happens."

Miles shook his head. "No, it's more than that: He went back for extras, and killed three people in the process. And now I'm neck-high in shit for it."

It wasn't quite true. He was in trouble because he abducted the undercover cop who witnessed the job, but at least Stanton was quiet now, and keeping still. Miles brought the Colt out of his belt again.

"Hey, whoa—"

"Relax. This is Stokes's gun. He went back to the Covey place this morning and killed them for a bigger take."

"What? How do you know?"

"Kings Point PD said the wife's car was missing. I said to him last night we could have taken the cars, made another three hundred grand. I figured he went back for it, and then fenced it for extra profit."

"What, he told you all this?"

Miles shook his head. "He loaded up on heroin to celebrate, over-did it slightly. So it's either a real sad loss, or a just outcome." He held the gun up. "Ballistics will tell us one way or the other."

Stanton closed his eyes and sat up straight in the chair, let his breath out his nose. He looked serene, as if with focused wishing he could erase all setbacks. He opened his eyes and there was Miles still in his chair, still looking at him.

Stanton said, "Shit."

Miles said, "So what I'm getting at is I need help, and you owe me."

Stanton didn't answer.

Miles said, "Eventually, the phone's going to ring, and they're going to tell me we're swapping Lucy for the Covey money."

"And what do I have to do?"

"I'm still thinking about it. At the very least you can answer the phone."

"Why, what are you doing?"

Miles said, "I'm going to take a shower and decide what to do."

THIRTY-FIVE

Bobby Deen

He said, "How did you come up with Officer Maddie Rogan?"

It didn't sound like a Bobby question, but being around Nina had turned him into a talker. He was coming out with idle stuff he wouldn't normally say, or even think of. Maybe her attitude was rubbing off on him, making him more pleasant.

Nina said, "I was at elementary school with her. Good name for a cop, don't you think? The Maddie part's friendly and feminine, and then the Rogan toughens it up, makes you sound like competent law enforcement."

He got the impression her whole life was well thought out—ask her about anything, and there'd be some astute basis for it. He thought what he'd like to do, he'd like to just sit there for a day looking at her and asking questions.

He had the Sig in his right hand propped in his lap, aiming at the woman. She didn't look worried, but she was sitting there without saying a word, kind of prim and with no expression, like some lawbreaking celebrity being driven to court. He preferred it when they wouldn't shut up. Folks who sit quietly are the toughest to read. Hard to know if they're just resigned to what's happening, or if they're thinking about how to turn things around.

They were in the realms of crazy wealth now, though: massive houses that looked like European castles—even a few with those fancy brick parapets. The hedges were impressive, too: rich people loved a good, dense hedge. And those driveways made out of white shells seemed to be in vogue as well.

Nina said, "You want a made-up police name, too? Or do you want to be Detective Bobby Deen?"

Bobby said, "Maybe Detective Robert Deen. That sounds pretty official."

Nina clicked her tongue. "Beautiful. It just screams trustworthy, doesn't it? This is us up here."

There was no gate, which meant the front door would be the only hurdle. Nina turned in at a polite and responsible speed, and they went popping and crunching along the stone driveway. At the end of it was a Greek-looking statue—maybe Cupid—standing on a plinth in a pool at the center of a turnaround. The house was just beyond it: a horrible two-story place done in white plaster, and separated into three wings, each of them with a pointy terra-cotta roof. It looked like a witch's house that had been bleached.

Nina said, "Funny how some of them are discreet, some of them don't even bother having trees—want you to drive past and have no doubt that they're dripping money."

Bobby said, "We're going to have to make some hard decisions. Are we going to be discreet rich, or flashy rich?"

Nina said, "I think we should be ostentatious for a while, just so we know what it's like."

The entrance had full-height glass around the door, and he could see a kind of atrium area with a chandelier and a staircase at the rear curving to the upper level. Nina stopped the car and picked her gun up from the footwell and slipped it in a little holster on her hip.

She said, "I'll give you a wave in a minute. And I'll borrow your wallet if you've got one."

Bobby passed it across the seat, watched her get out and walk to the door holding the wallet up and open, like a plainclothes cop with an ID holder. She rang the bell and stepped across so she was visible through the window, smiling patiently and holding the wallet open against the glass.

The door opened.

Nina stepped in, and moved out of sight.

Ten seconds later she appeared at the window, the gun hanging by her side in one hand, and the other beckoning to Bobby.

The girl wasn't even watching—still just looking out her window. Bobby pulled her across the seat and out of the car by the arm, over to Nina as she opened the door for him.

He wondered if she was resigned to the fact that something like this would happen eventually. Married to a cop, and then married to a banker, it must have crossed her mind that she could get caught up in revenge or robbery at some stage. She was very pale, but pretty composed really, sitting there thin-lipped and rigid on the living-room sofa with her hands clasped white-knuckled in her lap.

He'd done a circuit of the house, but it was obvious she was home alone. He found one wineglass, one dinner plate, one set of cutlery. The guest bedrooms—all five of them—were as spotless as a hotel commercial. There was a study in the ground floor of the bedroom wing, looking out at the fountain, but everything was squared away, and when he lifted the laptop on the desk the wood beneath was cool.

So now the four of them were in the main living room: the cop's ex-wife, Caitlyn, sitting stiff and speechless; Lucy next to her, more relaxed but still silent; and Nina and Bobby opposite them on another sofa. The TV was paused on Netflix—a close-up of Kevin Spacey as the president.

Finally the woman said, "What do you want?"

Bobby didn't answer, waited for Nina to fill her in while he sat thinking that this looked exactly like a house for rich folks. Splotchy artwork on the walls that looked like one of those psychiatric exams—a Rorschach test—little busts of naked people in the corner, even this dumb gold statue of a bag of golf clubs standing by the door. Charles Stone would love it.

Nina said, "Well, rest assured, it's nothing to do with you."

"And yet here we all are."

"We'll be gone before you know it. All I ask is one favor: you're going to call Mr. Keller, tell him that you have some guests, and that they'll be peacefully on their way once he's arrived here with the Covey money."

"The what?"

Nina said, "The Covey money. He'll know what you mean."

The ex-wife was shaking her head, gaze on Nina. "I've got no idea what you're talking about."

"That's all right, you don't need to."

The ex-wife tried a derisive sniff, but it came out too high. She said, "And you think Miles will just show up here as he's told, and won't bother calling nine-one-one?"

Nina said, "You haven't been watching the news, have you?"

The ex-wife didn't answer.

Nina said, "The police want to talk to him about a robbery-homicide up here—"

"Up *here*? What, in Kings Point?"

Nina said, "Yeah, apparently he robbed some lawyer and then killed him."

Murdered lawyers must have rung a bell: the ex-wife was shaking her head, eyes closed. "No, there's no way. That's ridiculous. . . ."

But she sounded more incredulous than certain.

Nina gave her a moment to wrap her head around the information, and said, "If they've caught him or he's turned himself in, then I guess we're out of luck. But he's a resourceful sort of guy, so I imagine we're still in play." She nodded at the TV. "We can check the news if you like."

The woman didn't answer. Her gaze was on the floor now, like Nina and the new reality were too much to take in. Her eyes were moving, though, trying to find a safe way out.

Nina said, "Okay. We'll assume we're good to go."

The ex-wife's gaze roved a moment longer, and then she hit on something, looking up at Nina again and sounding confident. She said, "If he's smart, he'll just call the police, never even come here."

Nina shook her head. "He's not going to do that. He's not going to trust both your lives to other people."

"But you think he's going to trust you with his?"

Smart lady: even pressure like this hadn't turned her brain off.

But Nina just smiled. She said, "I'm not an idiot. I've thought about what happens if the wrong people show up. And rest assured it doesn't offer you a great outcome."

The ex-wife didn't answer. She was a clever lady. But there were clever ladies, and then there was Nina. She'd always have a comeback you could take to the bank.

She said to the ex-wife, "So the sooner you call, the sooner everyone goes back to their happy lives."

The ex-wife was looking at Lucy though, like she'd just discovered she wasn't alone on the couch. She said, "Jesus, I know you. What, he stopped sleeping with you, so now you're getting even?"

Nina said, "Don't burn your bridges. She's on your side. The clue is, she doesn't have a gun."

No answer.

Nina said to Caitlyn, "Let me guess: Miles cheated on you with her, so you ran off with a banker?"

No answer. The ex-wife just sat there, waiting for it to end.

Nina said, "Well, it worked out well for me. I robbed a banker once, and Miles let me get away with it. Probably his way of getting even with your new man."

No reaction, but Nina pushed on. She said, "Explains why he's been up to no good in Kings Point, too." She shrugged. "Kill a lawyer, take some money, probably feels like revenge on your zip code." She looked around: the art, the stupid golf-club statue, the boardroom-table-size TV. "Anyway. If you'd stayed together, things would've been better. I'd be in prison, and none of this would be happening."

THIRTY-SIX

Miles Keller

He found an old beard trimmer in a drawer in the bathroom, plugged it in to charge. There was a high chance the thing was on the fritz, which meant he had a correspondingly high chance of a breakdown midtask. He didn't want to be stuck flaunting some eccentric portion of his current facial hair, but he needed to change his appearance, so the gauntlet would have to be run.

His suits were still all in his closet. They were the police standard: fine, but definitely off-the-rack. The only tailored suit he ever owned was his wedding tux, but he'd tossed it when Caitlyn left—part of a monthlong purge he'd undertaken, before he realized what she meant to him.

He showered and then put the trimmer to the test, cut his beard back to an even stubble without the motor giving out. He dug around in the cabinet drawer again and found a plastic attachment for trimming hair. He'd be quite the sight if it died on him now. He pulled his hair back with his free hand and leaned in to the mirror, as if building up to self-surgery, and then started in with the trimmer again.

He came downstairs a new man: gray suit, no beard, and his hair cut down to a half-inch. He could smell bacon cooking. He went into the kitchen and found Stanton sitting at the table, eating an omelet and a precooked sausage, a glass beside him holding a couple inches of Coke.

He saw Miles and said, "Oh my, don't come any closer. You're making my heart go all fluttery."

The stove element was still heating up an empty pan. Miles turned it off. Stanton said, "You want food?"

"No thanks."

His iPod was on the bench where he'd left it that morning. He picked it up and wrapped the earphone cord around the case and slipped it in his pocket.

Stanton said, "You look like a suicide bomber."

"Yeah? Why's that?"

Stanton tapped his jaw. "They always shave their beard off before they do it. Go into it pale-chinned. Clean face, clean conscience."

Miles took a glass from a cupboard and poured himself some Coke and sat down at the table facing Stanton.

Stanton ate his egg and sausage. He said, "You didn't tell me how it went with the Force Investigation dipshits."

"Well, I got out of there. But I think I'll be in trouble if I go back."

He didn't want to run through it all, but Stanton was still looking at him, wanting more of a story.

Miles said, "They thought my shooting was pretty slick. I was telling them how Dad used to make us do drills, hit targets and stuff. Thirty years ago, probably, but I had to give them something." He ran his hands through his hair, the new do feeling strange and bristly. "Imagine their faces if I said I robbed a bank when I was seventeen, perfect training for that hotel lobby."

Stanton gulped egg. "Shit, you actually did one?"

Miles nodded. "My brother took me on a road trip. We robbed this place down in Kansas. That was my one and only time."

Stanton smiled. "And then you went straight."

"Yeah. Mostly."

Stanton sat looking at him.

"Don't think you can act quizzical and I'll tell you more. 'Cause I won't."

Stanton shrugged, chased an egg gob with his fork. "I'm not. Just thinking most people are lucky they don't have to do something that hard to know what road they're meant to be on."

Miles said, "Well, I'm on it now."

Stanton's phone was ringing—a chirpy jingle that went from annoying to deeply irritating when he brought it out of his pocket. He answered and said, "Stanton." Pause. "Yeah, he's here."

He passed the phone to Miles, a tinny voice coming through the speaker before he even had it to his ear. Miles came in midsentence and heard Caitlyn say, "—have to do exactly as they say. You have to bring the Covey money, and then they'll let us go. We're at my house, and they have Lucy, too. If you bring the Covey money, they'll let everybody go. You have to bring that phone with you, and call when you're at the house."

He shut his eyes and felt himself panting. How the hell had they found her—

She said, "What's going on? What the fuck is going on—"

He said, "Caitlyn?" Just the one word to test his voice, check it was steady.

"Yeah?" It was amazing to talk with her, hear something more than "don't call." But he couldn't dwell on it.

He said, "Everything will be okay, but you have to listen."

"Okay."

He heard a man's voice in the background, telling her hurry up.

Miles said, "You're not on speaker?"

"No."

Maybe this was like dying, having your life flash before your eyes. His memory whirred, looking for ways out. He saw Caitlyn, he saw the Kings Point house, he saw himself on the driveway, and the new man with his gun coming out to meet him—

He said, "Okay. Listen carefully, and just answer yes or no."

Bobby Deen

The Caitlyn woman was struggling with the pressure. Bobby saw her tearing up, lip going wobbly as she talked to her old flame on the phone. She said, "Okay. No. Okay. No. Yes. No. Yes. No."

Bobby said, "That's enough of a reunion."

The ex-wife put the mouthpiece to her shoulder—probably long-ingrained habit from years of phone gossip. She said, "He wants to talk to Lucy. He needs to know she's okay."

Nina said, "Give her the phone."

Caitlyn did so. Lucy put it to her ear and said, "Hey. I'm okay." She listened for a while and said, "Yes." Then: "No."

Nina said, "No one's told him the instructions yet."

Lucy said, "What're the instructions?"

Nina said, "Just the standard: come alone, and bring the money, or else."

Lucy said, "Come alone, and bring the money, or else."

Nina said, "And remind him what I last told him: I always get my way."

Lucy passed it on, and then Bobby took the phone off her and killed the call.

Nina said, "There's no point sitting here tense. You can put the TV back on if you like, but keep the volume low."

THIRTY-SEVEN

NEW YORK, NY

Miles Keller

Stanton was leaning across the table, trying to hear the other side of the conversation. When the call ended, he leaned way back in his seat and said, "Ouuuuuu, God," as he rubbed his temples.

Miles said, "How the hell did they find her?"

Stanton had his eyes shut, brow furrowed. He gestured with one hand as he talked. "Look, yeah, I forgot: the guy in the hat checked the phone. They must've found her number."

Shit, the burner. He'd left it right there. They'd just have to hit redial . . .

Stanton said, "What was with all the questions? Are they going to try something themselves?"

"Hopefully not. But it's good to have a plan B."

Stanton said, "But there's no need to go up there—just call nine-one-one, but don't give your name."

"No, I can't do that."

"Yeah you can. Fucking easy, and your hands stay clean."

Miles shook his head. "I know what she'd do."

"Who?"

Miles just shook his head again. "Where's the money?"

"Out front in the car."

Miles rubbed his face. "You could have just given it to them."

"Yeah, well, I didn't know if you were prepared to pay."

Miles shut his eyes, counted to five, opened them again. All he'd been told was bring the money—they hadn't named a figure. Although frugality probably wouldn't end well.

He said, "Call DeSean and tell him to meet us up in Kings Point."

"He's on another job—"

"Well Kenny, then. Anyone. Anyone who can meet us up there and bring me a gun."

Stanton made calls while he drove.

For a third-party listener, the most irritating side of any phone call was the Wynn Stanton side: thick with bullshit, self-reference, self-reverence, and Stantonese. He tried DeSean first:

"Yeah, D-Man. It's The Stanton. How you doing? Yeah, good. Listen . . ."

Miles tried not to. He knew Stanton was panicked, out of his comfort zone, trying to compensate with attitude, but he still didn't want to hear it. They riffed back and forth for a minute, gutter talk and code words, Stanton looking across every now and then to see if Miles was impressed. DeSean was tied up, as suspected, so Stanton tried Kenny.

"Yeah, hey, it's me."

Kenny's answer came as tinny speaker noise, and a part of Miles—a small part not preoccupied by ransom and abduction—begged for a normal conversation.

But Stanton said, "No, it's The Stanton."

He asked if K-man could run a pronto ten fifty-six with metal accessories up at Kings Point. Kenny had no clue what he meant.

Stanton said, "Can you meet us up at Kings Point right now? I got Keller with me, and he needs a piece."

Speaker noise. Miles checked the glove compartment for something to do, found the photo from his hotel room: him and Caitlyn on their honeymoon. Lucy had grabbed it, as asked.

Stanton said, "What type of piece do you want? Oh man, don't look in there, you'll go all misty-eyed."

He was probably right. Save the poignant throwbacks for later. Miles shut the glove compartment and said, "Something small, but I'll work with whatever. If he's got a snub thirty-eight, that's perfect."

Stanton passed it on. He said, "Where are we meeting?"

Miles said, "Parking lot of the golf club. Tell him to Google it."

Speaker noise.

Stanton said, "He wants to know what you're paying."

Miles rubbed his face. "I'll go five hundred for the courier fee, plus the gun cost."

Stanton passed it on and then said, "And what are you paying me?"

Miles shook his head. "Just drive."

Kenny lived in Queens, up near Astoria, so he beat them to the club. He was in a mud-brown Chevy people mover with a broken taillight.

Stanton put his window down and cut his lights as he pulled alongside. Kenny was sitting with his elbow on the sill, looking across at them, seeming unbothered about their nighttime rendezvous. He had K-pop on the stereo and he was nodding to the beat, dyed red hair teased and gelled and looking like a well-stoked bonfire.

Stanton said, "What were you going to do if you got pulled over for your taillight, cops found you packing heat?"

Kenny said, "Didn't happen, so I don't worry about it."

"Yeah, because you been working for me, got a bit of Stanton in your blood."

"Right: make me like a no-threat has-been . . ."

Miles tuned them out. The parking lot was almost empty, but it was high pedigree. Black bitumen that looked freshly hosed, little shrubs with brass name plaques carefully spaced along the curbing. The lane markers were probably freshened up every week. The street was out of sight, hidden by trees, but he could see the portico for what must have been the clubhouse, over to their right. There was a second building as well—a restaurant, maybe. He could see the yellow glow of windows through the trees: this perfect frame hanging there in the dark, like a portal to a new dimension—or a new tax bracket, perhaps.

He said, "So that's the clubhouse over there—and is that a restaurant?"

Stanton was sweating, breathing through his mouth. He mopped his brow with a forearm. Miles caught a line in English from Kenny's stereo: "love me all night." Stanton said, "That's the restaurant I told you about—real good. One of those celebrity chefs set it up. They got a section that's just normal American, and then this other bit that's full-on Japanese. Sushi and stuff." He was overdoing the chat, trying to forget he was scared.

Miles said, "Do you have to be a member to get in?"

Stanton said, "No, it's cheaper, but they still let you eat. We should go back sometime, Ken. Shit it was nice."

Miles sat for a moment trying to think.

Stanton panted and wiped his brow. He said, "You know what I think: I think you should just call the cops and get the hell out. You got the money, you can just be gone, say *sayonara* to the whole thing."

Miles ignored him, looked across at Kenny. "What did you bring me?"

Kenny said, "Smith thirty-eight. I'll come over."

"No, stay there a minute."

He got out of the car and walked across the lot toward the restaurant. Twin lines of solar lights marked a path to it through the trees. He wandered halfway down for a better view, and then stood with his hands in his pockets, as if weighing up his dinner prospects. Straight ahead was a lobby area, and on either side were banks of windows looking into the restaurant. He saw chopsticks in action on the left—obviously the Japanese section. There were tables with people eating in twos and fours, and a horseshoe bar with plates moving on a sushi train.

He could hear cutlery chiming faintly, and a breeze making a low moan in the trees. There was a waiter in the lobby behind a maître d' station, but he couldn't see Miles standing out there in the dark. He turned around and walked back across the lot and got into Stanton's car.

Stanton said, "They got a table for three?"

Miles said, "Kenny, if you want to hang around, I'll pay you twenty grand."

Stanton said, "Oh Jesus, here we go."

Kenny patted his door panel—two dull booms. He said, "Depends what I gotta do."

Miles said, "Are you in or not?"

"You have to tell me what I'm doing."

"I need a yes right now. How bad do you want twenty grand?"

Kenny puffed his cheeks, let the air out slow. "Thirty. And the courier fee and gun charge on top."

Miles looked at Stanton and said, "I need to borrow your car."

Bobby Deen

Having the TV back on made the ex-wife even more uncomfortable. She must have felt a certain obligation to sit looking at it, because she did, watching the picture vacantly as Nina in turn watched her.

He figured she was a college lecturer. There was a legal pad at her feet, with a page of notes headed, "Popular culture and reflections of politics—is reality worse than fiction?" Bobby had no idea, and he had no idea why people devoted brainpower to those kinds of questions. His mother followed politics, and Connie had a little bit, when she was sober. She'd liked Clinton, because he had a kind voice and looked responsible.

He didn't like the atmosphere, and he suddenly realized why: watching TV in your own home is like the peak of relaxation—self-awareness disappears. So being *watched* while you watch TV is to give up something private. And doing it at gunpoint would be a whole new level of intrusion. They were wrecking one of the great urban pleasures.

He walked out without saying anything—getting this funny feeling that talking was prohibited. He still had the cordless phone with him. He went into the study and stood looking out at the fountain while he dialed Charles Stone in California.

Charles took a long time. Eventually he picked up and said, "Yeah?"

Bobby said, "I've got her. If you keep the plane on standby, I'll have her back tomorrow morning."

For a brief, weird moment he wasn't actually sure what he believed. He gave the line, and felt empty as he said it. And maybe that meant he was vulnerable as well, like all kinds of convictions could take root and change what he was going to do.

Charles said, "The plane's gone. I didn't have the pull to hold it overnight."

That threw him for a second.

Charles said, "People came by the house—fucking New York guys who're moving out West. Said they have a controlling share in the business now."

Normally there was background noise—drinks, or things being thrown—but not now. It was like he was locked in the bedroom, coming to terms with it.

Charles said, "And I mean . . . I'm screwed, basically. Nina went behind me and let this East Coast outfit buy in."

Strange to hear the old man just telling it straight, not raising his voice. He must've been devastated. He said, "So if you're part of it—"

"I'm not—"

"If you're part of it, Bobby, I suggest you watch your back."

Here we go: here's the threat coming. But Charles surprised him. He said, "I only ever gave her what she wanted. House on the hill, pool to swim in, car, whatever. And she still turned on me. And it'll happen to you too if you don't keep looking behind you."

Bobby didn't answer.

Charles said, "But I guess you're no different, really. I set you up, gave you the job, turned you into somebody. And now you believe you've got better options. So don't come by the house. You probably think you can take my wife and take your fee as well. I'm not that fucking stupid, Bobby. You're lucky I don't send someone past the condo, check in on your mother."

That should have made him say something, but he didn't bother. It was just empty musing. He actually felt sorry for the old boy, everything coming apart around him. And it was the Nina effect, too: when you had her, you needed nothing else.

Charles said, "Maybe if I'm lucky, one day she'll knife you in the back. Or you her. Something like that anyway." He laughed emptily. "You can take her to bed, Bobby, but you can't trust her, believe me."

Charles hung up, and Bobby stood there looking out through his own reflection to the Cupid statue in the driveway.

THIRTY-EIGHT

KINGS POINT, NY

Miles Keller

He stopped on the shoulder just past the golf club and turned on his iPod. Someone—probably DeSean—had swapped audiobooks. Hawking's *A Brief History of Time* had replaced *The Luminaries*. It didn't matter. He wasn't listening for entertainment. He just needed something to reset his head, so he could go into it calm.

He drove with one earbud in and the other dangling. The narrator talked about black holes, and time running backward. Reversed time didn't bother him. There were things he'd like to revisit. He wondered, though, if mysteries were infinite, or if science had so much traction that eventually people could discover anything. There'd come a time when they could plug you into a computer and see your whole life as information. Dots on a graph, seventy or eighty years long. They'd point to a dip and say, That was the worst thing he ever did. Or, That was the moment he could have pulled out of it. They'd do summaries for you: best and worse, read it out on your deathbed, so you knew your finest moments. Or whether your gut feeling was right about your low points.

He could see the house coming up on his right: the long driveway with the statue in the turnaround. The white walls and the terra-cotta roof. DeSean's SUV was parked down the end. He remembered they'd stolen it from outside the hotel. He turned in and let the car coast gently, used Stanton's cell to dial the house.

A male voice answered—probably the hat man he'd seen in the hotel lobby: "Yes?"

Miles said, "It's Miles. I'm in the driveway."

The hat man said, "There's a garage to your right. I'll open the door, and you can pull in. What you're going to do, you're going to put your window down and have one arm hanging out, and the other on the wheel so I can see your hands."

"Okay."

"Easy, right?" And he was gone.

Miles pressed pause on the audiobook and pulled the earbud out. He didn't want it mistaken for a phone accessory, make them think he had the cops in his ear. But he'd pushed pause without thinking, as opposed to just letting it run. So maybe he'd be coming back to it. Maybe his subconscious had made a ruling on the matter, and figured he'd be okay.

He used the button and buzzed his window down and hung his left arm out over the sill. The night was cold and smelled of cut grass and dew. He saw a rim of yellow light along the bottom of the garage, a thin band that grew wider as the door went up for him. He crunched across the gravel at walk speed and nosed into the vacant space beside a Porsche SUV.

In a doorway to his left, the hat man stood backlit by warm house lights, one hand on the garage-door switch and the other holding a gun.

Miles waited, his arm still hanging out the window, the hand feeling fat and tingly from the pressure of the sill against his biceps. The motor was still running, but he didn't want to touch the key unless he was told. The headlights were blazing off the wall in front of him, putting stretched nightmare shadows through the cabin.

The electric door motor groaned and the door came down behind him.

The hat man said, "Turn the engine off."

Miles put the car in park and killed the engine, put his hand back on top of the wheel.

"Open the door using the outside handle and step out."

The guy knew what he was doing. He didn't want to be shot with a gun hidden below window level. Miles patted blindly for a second before he found the handle, and then flicked his wrist to make the door swing open a few degrees. Then he sat there facing forward with both hands raised.

"All right. Push the door open with your knee, swivel on your ass, and step out. Keep your hands up."

Miles did so.

"Kick the door closed."

Miles nudged the door shut with his heel.

"Lean against the car and put your hands flat on the roof."

Miles did as he was told, and let the hat man pat him down for weapons.

The hat man said, "So now I can open that trunk and take out a bag of money, right?"

Miles swallowed, felt his heart slam against the car window, and said, "It's back up the road."

There was a long silence, and then the gun touched the back of his neck—a quick tap, not so long that he could spin and take it.

The hat man said, "That should be a bullet for you right now."

"And then there's no way you'll get the money."

"Why'd you leave it? Did you wonder what it feels like to take a bullet?"

Miles said, "They had a homicide up here last night. Anyone who hears a gunshot is going to call it in. No one's going to take the risk it was just a car backfiring."

No answer.

Miles said, "Shall we see what Ms. Stone has to say about it?"

The hat man seemed to think it over. The pause stretched. Then he said, "Walk backward. Slowly. We're heading for the TV noise."

He managed all that as well, and didn't try anything. He thought later that it must have appeared quite surreal: the three women sitting in the living room, Kevin Spacey on the TV yelling at someone, and then the gun-toting hat man walking in backward and his captive doing likewise.

Lucy had the first line. She said, "I wondered if I'd see you again."

It struck him as a strange opener. But then he got the reference, and he knew he'd have to play this differently.

He turned around and lowered his hands slowly and saw the four of them watching him. The hat man standing with his gun, and the three ladies on couches: Lucy and Caitlyn on one, and Nina on another, facing them. She had a gun of her own and one leg pulled up under her, as if settled in for a cozy night.

The hat man said, "He doesn't have the money."

Miles said, "I thought you'd probably kill us once you had it."

Nina said, "Now we can just shoot everyone except you."

Miles said, "You fire a gun, you need to be on the road thirty seconds later. Won't have time for a treasure hunt."

Nina was enjoying the repartee, hitting lines back and forth. She looked over at Kevin Spacey—poor Kev still quite worked up about something—and said to Caitlyn, "Would you mind?"

Caitlyn used the remote and killed the sound. Kev ranted on mutely.

Nina turned to Miles and said, "What do you have in mind?"

Miles said, "I'll take the hat man to the money. It's about thirty minutes up the road. He can call you when he has it, and you can be on your way."

"You need to be more specific than that. Where's the money?"

Miles said, "The golf club."

"How civilized. Where at the golf club?"

"If I tell you where it is, you'll just kill us all and collect it yourself."

Nina didn't answer. She watched Kevin on the TV. He'd finally chilled out a bit. Nina looked at the hat man and said, "All right. Off you go, then."

Bobby Deen

The guy had dressed up sharp, wearing a gray suit that actually looked quite good on him. He'd cut his hair, too, and Bobby almost asked was he going to a funeral. He kept that to himself, though—too easy for the guy to put it back on him: Bobby all in black was way more funereal than gray Keller. Nina would've had a comeback. Something ice cold, too slick to turn around.

He let the guy walk ahead of him out to the stolen SUV and made him get in the driver's seat. Bobby kept the gun on him and walked around the hood, only tossed him the keys once he was in the passenger seat with his belt on.

But the cop had been right about a couple of things: people would be edgy after last night's killing, so once he'd drilled Keller, he couldn't hang around. He'd have to get the money, go back for Nina, and then pop Keller on the way to the freeway. Yeah, that's the way: walk him out into the trees somewhere and put one through the back of his head. He saw himself on that boat again, giving Lenny Burke his farewell Magnum. Giving one to Keller would be even better. And what would Nina say? Maybe just the same as last time: "You mind if I drive?"

The two of them, the open road, and a car full of money.

He wondered if he could ever tell her no.

Miles Keller

It took a second to catch what Lucy was telling him. But she'd given the line enough weight to set his memory working:

"I wondered if I'd see you again."

It took him back three weeks, and put him on the front step of her house in Queens: the first time he'd seen her in years, and those were her first words. It was repetition, and it wasn't idle. The phrase implied a link. He'd gone to her house because Jack Deen was watching her. So was this something Deen-related? If so, then this was payback. He doubted he'd get a thank-you for setting the boy straight. He almost smiled at that. Far more likely, he figured, that the hat man planned to kill him.

How had Nina set it up, or found the center of it all? It didn't really matter. It was happening.

God, he felt the whole thing coming full-circle on all these different levels, karma having its way with him: up in Kings Point, captive in a car, the Jack Deen fiasco rearing its ugly head.

He kept to thirty-five and followed his headlights through the dark streets. Every now and then they passed another car: a white diamond up ahead, then it split in two, and then a stream of light came rushing past, chased by shadow.

How would it happen? The hat man wouldn't shoot him before he had the money. So maybe he planned to get the cash and then do it somewhere quiet. Maybe pick up Nina and kill him on the way out of town.

Miles looked across at the guy, but couldn't see his face under the shadow of the hat. The headlights had killed his night vision.

The guy said, "What?"

Miles turned back to the road, the centerline paint going dash-dash-dash, counting him down to something.

Bobby Deen

The guy gave him a long, blank look for maybe five seconds, finally turned back to the road when Bobby said, "What?"

He wondered how many close scrapes the guy had been through. There was the shoot-out earlier, now he was hostage in a car, and he'd obviously seen some action in Kings Point yesterday. So was it a bad patch, or was the Reaper always peering in his window?

The golf club was coming up on their left, and Keller signaled for the turn. There was a low sign with writing you could barely read—fancy script, like a grandma's diary. They went down a short driveway and emerged into a parking lot, very tidy with no one around. That suited Bobby fine.

He said, "Don't tell me you buried it in a sand trap?"

Keller let the SUV coast. There were a few cars over by the clubhouse, picked out by the headlights. He said, "It's in the bathroom of the restaurant," and nodded over at a building Bobby hadn't noticed—just its lit windows showing through the trees.

Bobby said, "Oh, that's nice. So you go in, come back out with a gun, shoot me while I'm sitting in the car?"

Keller took a long time to answer, and Bobby knew he was on to something. The cop didn't quite know how to play it.

Bobby said, "All right." A softer tone, going easier on the guy. "I tell you now. If we get in there and find there's no money, I'm going to put your head down the toilet, pull the trigger, and then pull the chain." That was great, and it really hit the spot. The cop still hadn't said anything, and Bobby actually saw him swallow—subtle, like Bobby mightn't notice.

Bobby said, "So let's play this absolutely straight, no bullshit: is there money waiting, or do we need to drive somewhere else?"

The car had stopped now, alone in the middle of the empty parking lot.

The cop said, "No, it's in there."

"You're pretty sure about that?"

No answer.

Bobby gave him some time and said, "I'm just a guy in a suit in a restaurant. No one's going to know what I look like if I put a bullet in you and then walk out again. They'll see a guy in a hat. That's it. They don't see past the accessories."

Keller looked at him square and then looked out the windshield again. There was a little portico thing attached to one of the buildings up ahead, an SUV parked under it and two guys standing nearby, checking out a set of golf clubs.

Bobby said, "So what's it going to be? Is the cash here or not?"

The cop said, "It's here."

Bobby gestured with an upturned hand. "Choose a slot, then."

The cop chose a slot, and killed the lights and engine. Now it felt more private, just the two of them in the dark.

Bobby said, "Don't think I'm new at this. You stay six feet ahead. You speed up, slow down, change direction, say anything that sounds off—I'll put a bullet in you."

Keller said, "I think I get it."

The cabin light came on as Bobby opened his door. It cast the guy jaundice-yellow, sitting with his hands in his lap, looking out at the Bible black of the woods ahead of them. Bobby backed out and shut his door, holstered the gun on his hip, and walked around the back of the SUV.

Keller got out without being asked and stood waiting, expression-less and motionless and his suit coat hanging open.

Bobby said, "Remember the rules: Six feet. We go in, get the cash, and then we're on the road again."

The cop didn't answer. He started walking, and Bobby fell in behind. He followed the guy across the parking lot toward the build-ing he'd pointed out earlier. There was a little path leading through the trees to reception, and either side of it a long row of windows showed off the dining areas.

Keller paused outside to button his jacket. A harried-looking Asian guy with dyed red hair asked if they were sixty-eight on the club raf-fle. Keller said no without even looking, and stepped up to the maître d' station, even managing to smile.

The maître d' said, "Hello, sir. Do you have a reservation?"

Classic: empty parking lot, but they had to imply high demand.

Keller seemed uncertain, glanced back at Bobby. He said to the maître d', "We're meeting some friends—maybe we could just have a drink at the bar until they get here?"

Nice.

The maître d' said, "Of course, sir. Would you like pearl, or plains?"

Bobby didn't know what he meant, but Keller gestured to their left, at twin glass doors with PEARL in frosted text.

The maître d' said, "Of course, sir, excellent." Faultlessly obliging.

The glass doors slid back as Keller approached, and he walked in looking like any other diner: glancing around as if lining up a good table. The long bank of windows was on their left, and on their right a big horseshoe bar protruded from the wall beside the door. Keller didn't hurry, fixed a cuff button while he stood checking out the other guests, and then he walked up to the bar and claimed a stool. Bobby followed, took a seat two down on Keller's left, perching side-saddle with his gun-side leg toeing the ground and his elbow on the bar.

He said, "I thought we were going to the bathroom."

Keller looked at him. He was leaning forward, forearms on the edge of the bar, fingers knitted, plates of food going past on one of those food-conveyor things—a sushi train. It was quiet in here, but he didn't like Keller's attitude. Something had changed between the car and the restaurant. Bobby told himself if anyone walked up looking funny, he'd pull the gun.

He gave Keller the bloody version, let him know he was serious: "If anyone walks up looking funny, I'll give you the first round."

Keller didn't answer. The prick just sat there looking at him.

Bobby said, "Count of three, you're taking me to the money."

Keller didn't answer.

Bobby said, "You won't hear 'four.' There'll just be a great big bang. One."

And Keller, still looking straight at him, said, "Can I ask you a personal question?"

Bobby almost said "Two," but held it, caught wrong-footed by the line.

Keller said, "When was the last time you took a shower?"

THIRTY-NINE

KINGS POINT, NY

Lucy Gates

The Nina woman wasn't so relaxed without her backup man. The TV stayed muted, and she did a lot more glancing around.

Lucy said, "What do you want us to do if you have to check out a noise? Do we wait here, or shall we follow you?"

Nina didn't answer. Thirty minutes ago, it might've got a smile out of her, but she wasn't seeing the funny side now.

Lucy said, "You had an exit plan while Bobby was here, right? Like, if the cops showed up, you could have shot everyone, said he'd taken us hostage and you saved the day. But what're you going to do if the police arrive while he's gone?"

She could sense Caitlyn getting more and more anxious, willing her not to push it. Too much strain, and the poor woman might crack in half. Her knuckles were so white, Lucy worried she was almost at breaking point. But she was getting under Nina's skin, no question. And Nina wouldn't just sit there and not answer. She'd have to say something to maintain her vibe—that air of easy control. Finally she said, "I guess I could shoot you both now and lock myself in the bathroom." Head on a tilt as she said it, like she was really thinking it over.

And it was half-plausible, actually. She could tell them Bobby had two guns, left one behind when he went off with Miles . . .

She looked back at Nina and saw her smiling, like she'd read her mind.

Lucy smiled right back, feeling sick but knowing she had to match it. Bobby Deen.

She still wasn't sure if it meant something—the man being a Deen. It was a common enough name, so there was every chance he had no link to Dead Jack. In fact, he was probably a Dean, not a Deen. And they didn't seem to realize that Lucy was part of it.

But it was Miles who got the credit for the killing—if that was the right way to put it—so maybe they just wanted him. And however the hell you spelled it, two Deens in three weeks seemed like too big a fluke. She hoped her tip-off hadn't been too cryptic. Maybe she should've just said straight out that Bobby was going to kill him, but that might have been a fast way to a room full of dead people. Same as if she'd told him on the phone. She almost did, but she was scared what would happen: cut off midsentence by the bang . . .

The more she thought about it, the more this seemed like a two-for-one opportunity: they wanted to make a bit of money, and seek penance for Dead Jack. Take Miles's money, and then get rid of him.

All very well knowing their plan, but she didn't know how she was getting out of it.

She could sit and wait for the phone to ring, and Nina to leave. But the risk with that was it might never happen—or not happen until she and Caitlyn were dead.

So option two was to try what Miles had told her. . . .

Bobby Deen

He said, "Did you lose your mind on the drive over?"

Keller was still sitting with his fingers linked, thumbs bouncing lightly off each other. He shook his head. "No, I don't think so."

Bobby knew he should shoot him, but the cop seemed too calm and self-assured, and Bobby thought maybe this shower issue—weird as it seemed—was worth staying with for a moment.

He said, "What the fuck are you talking about?"

The man from the foyer—the raffle guy with the red hair—took a seat at the bar on the far side of the horseshoe, almost opposite them. There was a woman drinking alone over to their left, right on the tip of the curve. Between her and the raffle guy were a couple eating sushi.

Keller scanned the lineup and then looked at the shelved liquor over on their right. He said, "You took a shower about five thirty, right?"

Bobby didn't answer, but something ran along his spine, and the cop must have sensed it: he was getting somewhere.

Keller said, "So the question is, How do I know that?"

The barman came over and asked if they wanted to order. Keller seemed to actually think it over. He said, "Can we order food here, too?"

Holy shit—that alone was worth a bullet.

The waiter said, "Yes, sir. I can serve you drinks immediately. Food orders will come out on the train."

He gestured at the conveyor.

Bobby, still looking at Keller, said, "Maybe just give us a minute."

"Certainly, sir."

He withdrew with a little bow, went to tend to the raffle guy.

Keller said, "She's playing both sides. She's loyal to you while you have the upper hand. But if I get out of this, she wants to make me think she had my back all along."

The cop was desperate to get out with his life and his money, and Bobby knew he should shoot him. But how did he know about the shower?

Keller was still bouncing his thumbs, as if pacing out his story. He said, "What did you think was going to happen if the police showed up at the house?"

Bobby didn't answer. The background noise was quiet chatter, and a low hum from the conveyor. Sushi and a silver food dome tracked past.

Keller said, "First she'd shoot you, and then she'd shoot the women. Tell the cops it was all your idea, but she nailed you at the last moment, saved the day."

Bobby said, "We can ask her about that."

Keller shook his head. "You don't have to go back. You're out of it now. And why would you want to go back anyway? She was prepared to sell you out."

Bullshit: she was probably just getting in Keller's head. But why hadn't she told him?

Keller said, "You remember what she said just now, when Lucy had me on the phone? Something about how I should remember what she last told me—that she always gets her way."

Yeah, that rang a bell—

Keller said, "She never told me that. I remember her saying she'd be in my corner—that might've been the parting sentiment. But she couldn't repeat it with you listening, could she?"

He must have made that up—schemed it in the car on the drive over. And now a voice was saying, Kill him. The money wasn't here.

Keller said, "You've got to pull out of this, Bobby. The stakes are too high. You're in a restaurant, at a bar, with five witnesses right there."

Bobby shook his head. "Time's up. Good story, but you didn't sell it to me."

He knew he could kill him. He had Nina Stone, and bags full of money. No cop could touch him. There was nothing to worry about. The bang would have twofold meaning: Keller's end, and the start of the good life.

Bobby said, "I'll do you a favor, start the count again. One."

Keller wasn't chilled anymore: he had his hands off the bar, bouncing them slightly palms-down, like trying to soothe a pissed-off audience. He said, "Let's not do this."

"Get off the stool."

Keller swung square to him, moving slow, palms up in a be-cool gesture. He said, "She's played you. Let's not wrap it up like this."

Bobby thought, Fuck him, and said, "Two."

Keller hadn't moved, but he was looking down at the bar, the sushi train with the plates coming around. Bobby followed his gaze, and finally saw the play—three things lining up right in front of him, and the shock was like a fall into cold water:

He saw that plate with its silver dome coming past on its third or fourth circuit; the Asian raffle guy staring at them panicked, as if Bobby and the cop had some massive bearing on his life; and he saw, too, that the silver food dome had a ticket trapped under it, the order number printed bold:

68.

It chimed with something from a minute ago: the fucking raffle man, asking if they had ticket sixty-eight.

The number was a signal for Keller—

Bobby had his jacket pushed back and a hand on his gun by the time Keller lifted the dome, and he saw a snub-nosed revolver lying on the plate. Keller grabbed it clean and found his aim, and the bangs were so close he didn't know who shot first.

Miles Keller

Maybe the audiobook inspired him—all that Stephen Hawking physics—but he'd had a speech in his head about electrons, how they needed quantum energy to go up a valence. Then with that explained, he could've told the guy he needed to jump a level as well: that he and Miles were in different orbits. But it was kind of long-winded and un-friendly, and in any case he'd got the message across.

The room wasn't packed, so people cleared out fast. Chairs top-pled. A yanked tablecloth made a racket of broken dinnerware: a rich acoustic, everything from tinkle to smash. He rolled on his side and got up on his hands and knees, saw people running hunched for the door. It was just the two of them left: Miles and his thwarted killer. Even Kenny had split. He saw the hat man's hat upside down, its owner nearby but much worse off, splay-limbed and faceup, covered in blood. He'd taken two in the chest.

An alarm sounded: soprano pitch, ear-bleeding wattage.

Speaking of blood:

His shirt was scarlet—the whole left side. Nothing he could do now, though.

Get out and fix it later.

He found Kenny's revolver and pressed the frame and the grips against the guy's limp hand. He needed to confuse the prints. He doubted people saw his gunplay, and the cleanest story said the hat man had two weapons—Miles was just lucky to overpower him.

He got to his feet and limped for the door. His chest ached with each breath, keeping him on sips of air.

Broken ribs?

Internal bleed—

Don't think about it.

The doors parted, and the alarm grew even louder as he stepped out. He could see people ahead, running up the path toward the parking lot.

Parking lot—

He needed the car keys.

The doors were closing again, almost tripping him as he went back into the restaurant. The hat man was in a pool of blood, creeping wider. Miles knelt and pat-checked him, tugged the SUV keys from his trouser pocket, and then got the hell out of there.

In the parking lot two cars tore past him for the road, and he saw half a dozen people at the clubhouse portico, ducked down by an SUV.

He limped across the lot, saw Stanton and Kenny by Kenny's van. Stanton was sweat-drenched, shaking, standing with his hands on his head.

"Oh, God, you're okay. Man, look, he's okay."

Miles tossed the keys to Kenny. "Open the back for me."

The words came out as a wheeze. He limped to the van and slid the passenger door open, torso blowtorched with the effort. The Coveys' money and Stokes's murder weapon were in the duffel on the rear bench. He'd made the swap from Stanton's car earlier.

Stanton said, "Whaddya want me to do? Whaddo I do?"

Miles said, "Get in the car."

The bag seemed twice as heavy since he last moved it, and he had to drag it two-handed for the SUV. He saw Stanton wipe his palms down his shirtfront, and then jump in the Chevy's passenger seat. He was talking to himself, strange mutterings of comfort: "It's all good, we're fine, it's all Stanton . . ."

Miles hauled the bag up over the rear fender and into the load space of the SUV. He slammed the door and felt a burn down his abdomen.

The van revved.

Miles jumped in, and Kenny had it rolling before Miles's door was closed. He wrenched it shut with his good arm and fell back in his seat panting.

Kenny hit the end of the driveway and braked hard. Stanton braced himself off the dash. "Ken, gentle, gentle."

Kenny said, "Where to?"

Miles said, "Right."

"Freeway's left—"

"Turn right." He tried to shout, but didn't have the wind.

Kenny got the message though, spun the wheel and floored it, leaving the club with a howl. He said, "When am I getting my thirty grand?"

Miles took shallow breaths, fueling up to talk. He said, "How do golf clubs hold a legal raffle? They give it all to charity or something?"

Kenny said, "Yeah, dunno. Probably. He didn't know though, did he?"

Stanton said, "You okay back there? You sound real wheezy."

"I'm bleeding a little."

"Oh shit, really?"

The van rocked as Stanton heaved himself around in his seat and stretched for the dome light. He clicked it on and said, "Oh man, it's all coming through your coat. We need to turn around."

"No, keep going. I'll tell you where to go."

Kenny swiveled his mirror for a better view, and the van swerved in the lane when he took his eyes off the road. Stanton grabbed the wheel and straightened them up. "Shit, Ken."

"Wynn, he's bleeding bad—look at him."

Miles said, "If you turn around, your money's forfeit."

Both of them shut up.

Money. It was in their source code, way down at base-instinct level. Profit was everything.

Kenny put his foot down and leaned over the wheel.

FORTY

Lucy Gates

She wondered if Nina was getting agitated. They hadn't been gone long, Miles and the Bobby guy, but being sole-charge on a hostage job was probably bad for the imagination. She'd be seeing all kinds of grim endings, wondering what she'd do if Bobby didn't come back, what she'd do if she saw blue and red lights through the window. Whether she'd have the guts to shoot the hostages and then clear out.

By the look of her, maybe she did have the courage. She was still sitting on the couch, relaxed and comfy, like this was the tail end of a pleasant evening. Mostly she watched her captives, and every now and then she checked what Kevin Spacey was doing on the mute TV.

Lucy said, "Is this one of those hostage setups where you let us go at the end?"

It sounded casual, but she didn't feel relaxed. One of those hostage setups. Like she'd done this before.

Nina said, "As opposed to what? The kind where I shoot everyone at the end?"

Lucy said, "Well, you know . . ."

And Nina inclined her head, half-smiling, like she was interested in hearing an opinion, like it might change how things went.

Lucy said, "I guess you could shoot us both and lock yourself in the bathroom, like you said. But that'll only work if Miles is dead. Same as if you shoot us and leave: he'll come looking for you, unless your Bobby's shot him."

Nina said, "Why are you giving me all these options where you end up dead?"

Yeah, good point. She turned her head so she could see more of Caitlyn, but she wasn't holding up well: eyes shut, clenched hands white at the knuckles.

Lucy said, "Because they've been gone long enough, it seems like something's wrong. So when you get picked up as well, probably best you don't leave two dead bodies behind."

Nina smiled. "I don't worry about any of that."

Lucy said, "Well can I make you an offer anyway?"

Nina sat up a little straighter, like preparing to be open-minded. "Please do."

Lucy said, "Be nice if I made some money out of this, too. So how about I help you get away, and you cut me in on the profit?"

She saw Caitlyn's head move—a stiff-neck turn through a few degrees—but Nina stayed still. She said, "And what do you have in mind?"

Lucy said, "We can keep it simple. How about I drive, and you sit in back, counting money? Ten percent of whatever's in the bag, and I'll take you wherever you want to go."

She wasn't exactly jumping at the idea.

Lucy said, "I used to be a police informant, but they let me go because I was holding things back. There's more money in keeping quiet and doing as you're told."

Nina didn't answer, but the pitch was well timed: a three-second pause, and then sirens were audible. Nina sat there for a few howls. They weren't getting nearer, but they were out there for someone.

You had to hand it to her, though: Nina's composure was immaculate. She stood up—no rush, leaving in her own time—and said, "Where are the keys for that Porsche in the garage?"

They both looked at Caitlyn.

"I hope we haven't lost her." Nina clicked her fingers. "Earth to Caitlyn. Where are the keys?"

For the first time she had the gun horizontal, aimed at Caitlyn's face as she came toward her. She grabbed a fistful of hair and yanked her head back, pressed the gun to her throat—smooth and blue by TV light.

"There we are. We're awake now."

Lucy saw tears on her cheeks, and with stretched vocal cords, Caitlyn's voice came out breathy and cartoonish: "In the study. In the desk drawer. Or maybe in the kitchen, in that bowl on the counter."

"Where's the study?"

Under pressure, she really had to think about it. "Right of the entry. First door."

Nina, dangerously sweet, said, "Lucy, would you please fetch the keys? We'll be right here. If you take off, Caitlyn's getting a bullet. Or if you feel like a drive, you can have your ten percent."

FORTY-ONE

Lucy Gates

They had to walk around Stanton's car to get to the Porsche—Lucy, and then Nina with her bag of money and the ever-ready gun. They'd left Caitlyn in a downstairs bathroom with a chair under the door handle.

"Porsche" had made her think sports car, but this was one of those seven-seat SUVs, built like some chrome-and-polish tank. She clicked the remote, and the garage went orange as the turn signals flashed. She opened the driver's door, climbed up into full leather and new-car smell. Maybe there were built-in reservoirs that leaked the scent, made every journey like the first drive off the lot.

A door thunked behind her, and Nina slid across the rear seat, towing her bag.

Lucy started up and hit the lights, pressed the button on the remote unit clipped to the sun visor. The door behind them began to rise.

Nina propped the gun on the passenger seat and leaned forward. "Just because I'm paying you doesn't mean I'm trusting you. Keep to thirty, or it's lights out."

The door was halfway up. Lucy dropped the car in reverse. The atmosphere was very male: gun oil and new car. There must've been six cows' worth of leather on the seats. But there was a pink air freshener clipped to an AC vent, so surely this was Caitlyn's ride. No male human with an SUV-size ego would ever buy pink plastic.

Lucy said, "Should've used Caitlyn as your chauffeur, that way nothing looks suspicious if you're pulled over."

Nina sat back, gun upright on her thigh. "Yeah. Except me sitting here, with a pistol and a bag of cash."

The door motor quit. Lucy turned around, laid an arm along the passenger seat as she steered in reverse. They dipped down off the slab onto gravel. She could see taillights fading off up the road, but no flashing blues or reds.

Lucy said, "We can stop at the golf club—drop me off with my cut, pick up Bobby."

It was a nice thought, but between the black muzzle and the look in Nina's eye, payment seemed unlikely. They were still crunching backward across gravel, heading for the Roman fountain, Cupid lit bloodred.

Nina said, "A minute ago you thought Miles would kill him. So what's made you reassess?" She was more relaxed—absence of police soothing her anxiety.

Lucy dabbed the brake and brought them to a stop. "He's too nice. He'll avoid it if he can."

"He didn't mind about Jack Deen."

Lucy touched the gas again and got them rolling. She said, "Yeah, because he was only covering for me. He didn't kill Jack—I did."

She floored the pedal and heard gravel pinging off the undercarriage. Nina twisted in her seat to see the back window, the statue looming crimson.

They hit the fountain wall doing thirty miles an hour.

FORTY-TWO

KINGS POINT, NY

Miles Keller

He said, "It's just on the right."

"You want me to turn in?"

"No, stop here. Let me out."

Stanton said, "Man, you sound like you're a ghost already."

"Stop the car."

Kenny slowed, and leaned in over the dash. The driveway was a hundred yards away, blue solar lights picking out its edges, the house with its glowing windows standing just beyond the statue—more like a gargoyle in its night shadows.

Kenny took it all in, checked his mirror to see his bloodstained passenger pale and clench-jawed, an arm across his midriff and a red right hand to his wound. Finally some other instinct—something attuned to human well-being—fought past the dollar signs, and he said, "Miles, this is fucking stupid."

"Just let him out." Stanton was ready to call it a night. He was checking his mirror as well, less worried about Miles than who could be behind them.

Kenny said, "Fuck it," closed his eyes as if putting better judgment on hold, braked, and then skidded the last few inches. Stanton braced himself off the dash. "Ken, gentle, gentle."

Miles already had his door open.

Kenny said, "We're not waiting. This shit's too hot."

He didn't answer. He was running—or trying to, at least. The van took off with its door still open, Stanton looking back across his shoulder and Kenny watching in his mirror, both of them probably wondering if this was good-bye or Good-bye.

He ran in the grass alongside the driveway, not wanting to make a noise on the gravel. His breath came wet and desperate. He could see the garage door rising, red light within. Not Stanton's car. It must be that Porsche—

You don't have a plan, and you're bleeding. You should've stayed in the van.

He was only halfway there. The Porsche rolled out in reverse and stopped, white smoke in eddies at its heels.

Miles sprinted, panic hitting some last-ditch lever in his mind, numbing him for his final dash.

The car's taillights dimmed, and the vehicle surged backward, nose sitting low, all four wheels spraying gravel.

He tried to shout but couldn't.

The SUV cut a straight line to the fountain and smashed it hard. He heard the whump of the airbags, and the concrete wall cracked and gushed water. The car alarm wailed, like it knew the damage bill.

He heard a bang, and the Porsche's windows flashed yellow. He closed the last few yards tasting blood, shouting, "Lucy," in a hoarse whisper.

The driver's door opened and he rounded the hood, a hand on the grille for balance, and there she was carrying a smoking gun. "Oh man, you're bleeding."

That gun, that smoking gun: he'd seen it when he visited before, the pistol in the new husband's hand. Now it had been put to good use—

He staggered to her buckle-kneed, but didn't quite make it. A hand on the car broke his fall.

"Oh, God." She cupped his face cool-handed. "It's okay, it's okay. Hold on."

He closed his eyes, and when he opened them she was running, chasing her long shadow to the house, the car's headlights white on her back. He was soaking wet. Another door opened, and he heard feet on gravel, a scuff motion that sounded geriatric. He turned his head and saw Nina, back against the car and sliding slowly to earth.

It went dark for a moment, but he came back with Lucy's shaking. She was crouched over him, pressing on his wound, and Caitlyn was there as well: hand in her hair, pale and bleary-eyed as she stammered at a phone. He couldn't quite hear her, and she talked so fast it was like she knew this would happen—like this was vindication of years of midnight worry. He turned his head and saw that Nina was still there with him, wide-eyed and openmouthed, like she'd finally been taken by surprise.

Her lips were bright red.

She said, "Well. Almost."

He said, "Everything will be okay, but you have to listen."

Caitlyn said, "Okay."

He heard a man's voice in the background, telling her hurry up.

Miles said, "You're not on speaker?"

"No."

"Okay. Listen carefully, and just answer yes or no."

"Okay."

"Is there a gun in your bedroom?"

"No."

"Is there a gun in the study?"

"Yes."

"Is it in a safe?"

"No."

"Is it in a desk drawer?"

She said, "Yes."

"Is the drawer locked?"

Pause. "No."

Miles said, "Okay. Put Lucy on."

The man's voice cut in: "That's enough of a reunion."

Caitlyn again, muffled, like she had the phone to her shoulder: "He wants to talk to Lucy. He needs to know she's okay."

Words he couldn't catch, and then crackle, and then Lucy said, "Hey. I'm okay."

Miles said, "Only answer yes or no. I'm going to get you out. But there's a gun in an unlocked drawer in the study. Do you know where the study is?"

"Yes."

"Your best option is just to run. Don't go for the gun unless you absolutely have to."

He woke up in the ambulance, and knew he'd be all right. No one leaned over him with the paddles. There were two paramedics looking like bored churchgoers, sitting side by side and hunched, smartphones instead of Bibles. A machine was beeping. He wasn't going to die. He felt something in the crook of his elbow. He raised his arm to look at it, but his wrist was tethered to the gurney by a handcuff.

The handcuff rattled.

The paramedics looked at him. No, wait: the second guy was a state trooper. The gun was the giveaway.

Miles said, "Where's Lucy?"

No one answered.

She was with him soon enough. He woke up and she was sitting by his bed, holding his hand.

He said, "That's a nice sight to wake up to."

His throat was dry, and he only heard the last three words. But she seemed to get the message. She smiled and handed him a cup of water, pressed a button on the bed frame that brought him upright. His sense of balance couldn't keep up, and he lost half the water.

She said, "You want the good news, or the bad news?"

Miles said, "Good then bad."

Lucy said, "They cleared you on the Jack Deen shooting. I heard them talking outside."

He wanted to feel a weight come off him, but he didn't. Too much had gone wrong. He opened his mouth for something cheery, but came up empty. He said, "Those reports are meant to take ninety days."

Lucy said, "Maybe they wanted to do it the Keller way, break all the rules."

He smiled faintly. "What's the bad news?"

She said, "Well, now they've got you for something else."

He was holding the cup, so that was one hand accounted for. He tried the other one. A cuff rattled. He closed his eyes. "Shit."

Maybe she thought that summed everything up, because she didn't answer for a while. Eventually she said, "Normally when it's a flesh wound, the hero keeps going."

He opened his eyes. "I am still going."

"I mean, they don't end up in the hospital. He nails a few more bad guys, and then he sits with his shirt off while the female lead bandages his cuts."

Miles said, "Was mine a flesh wound?"

She shook her head. "There were ribs involved. They had to pick the splinters out of your side."

He could see people in the hallway outside his room. White-coated medical folks, someone in a suit, someone in police uniform.

Lucy said, "They let me come in first, so you didn't wake up to those guys."

Miles didn't answer.

She said, "Don't worry. Whatever's happening, we'll figure it out."

He had to keep his eyes closed. He said, "I didn't do . . ." But found he couldn't say it. There was a barrier in his mind he couldn't cross. He couldn't lie to her about this.

And maybe it was just the anesthetic—drugs trialing new pathways in his brain—but he felt for a moment that he could tell her everything, and with spotless clarity. But like those fleeting mental glides along the edge of sleep, where space and time reveal all their mysteries, the feeling was born and then gone. So for now, he'd manage to be grateful she was here. Then one day he'd tell her that all this was for her—everything he'd done. And maybe he'd tell her how hard it was to love her: the need to be with her, and the need to be apart as a kind of atonement. Penance for breaking up his marriage.

She let him have some time with his thoughts, and said, "I'll let you talk to the fuzz. I'll be outside. I'm not going anywhere."

She leaned in and kissed him on the cheek, and then she got up and walked out. Miles drained his cup and watched her go, and he still had a mouthful of water when the man in the suit walked in. It was O'Shea, the Force Investigation guy he'd talked with yesterday.

Miles swallowed with little sips, not wanting to gulp as an opener. He said, "I've been keeping you guys busy."

O'Shea sat down in Lucy's chair.

Miles said, "If you don't mind, there's a button down there that tilts the bed up."

O'Shea looked like he might just sit there, but he couldn't say no to an invalid. He leaned forward and found the button and gave Miles another ten degrees.

"Thanks."

O'Shea sat back, laid an ankle across his knee. He said, "Is there anything you want to tell me about the last two days? Clear up some misconceptions? Clear a guilty conscience?"

Miles said, "Nothing I say will be admissible. I'm full of medicine."

O'Shea said nothing. He'd got his man, but he didn't look happy about it.

Miles rattled his cuff. He said, "What are the charges?"

O'Shea seemed to think about how to answer. He said, "Petrov's dead. But he was awake long enough to tell us what happened."

Miles waited.

O'Shea said, "He told me you robbed the Coveys at gunpoint two nights ago."

Miles didn't answer at first. Then he said, "If he's dead now, it's just hearsay."

O'Shea shook his head. "We deposed him on his deathbed."

"Wasn't much of a deposition, if you only got one line."

O'Shea didn't answer.

Miles said, "What about this alleged abduction you said I carried out? Making him send text messages, under duress? Did he forget about all of that?"

O'Shea said, "I guess he wanted the big stuff cleared up early."

Miles said, "How'd you even know it was a deathbed deposition? Did he not want to pull through?"

O'Shea took an envelope from his suit coat, wagged it gently in two fingers, gaze still with Miles. "I don't care about semantics. The judge seemed to think we'd satisfied the evidence code."

Miles didn't answer.

O'Shea said, "Maybe they'll let you share a cell with your brother."

Miles shook his head. "We're not there yet. This has to be dragged through court first."

O'Shea's eyebrows rose. "Oh yeah? And what are you going to tell them?"

Miles said, "Probably start out pretty standard, say it wasn't me. Then get on to the part about Nina Stone and her friend who wears a hat. They were running a kidnap-for-ransom up at Kings Point last night, I don't think it's a stretch to say they did the Coveys the night before. Especially with the murder weapon and the money in the back of their car."

O'Shea leaned in, elbows-to-knees. "Who says it's the murder weapon? Who says it's their money?"

Miles said, "Well, maybe they pulled off a murder-robbery some-where else. But it seems most likely they did the one just down the road the night before, don't you think?"

O'Shea shook his head. "Petrov says it was you."

"And I say he was mistaken. I say it was Nina's friend. Or both of them, and Petrov was talking nonsense, because he'd just been shot, and didn't know which way was up."

O'Shea sat quietly for a moment. Then he said, "That man you killed last night—Bobby Deen—he's Jack's cousin. Your shooting from three weeks ago. So there'll be some other FID people coming to chat about coincidences."

Miles said, "And what are you here for, exactly? Just to rub my nose in it?"

O'Shea actually managed to come forward a little more, craning his face out off his neck. Miles saw veins standing out, the strain from the cantilevered head, smelled his aftershave.

O'Shea said, "You sacrificed the Covey money to try and set up Stone and Deen. It's not going to fucking work. I'll have twenty guys checking their backstory. Something'll come unstuck for you, Keller."

Maybe he was right, but Miles figured he had an outside chance. And O'Shea's choice of words had been odd. Something'll come unstuck for you, Keller.

Hadn't it come unstuck already?

O'Shea said, "Well, much as it pains me, I'm done. Unless there's anything you want to share." He smiled. "You know, just the two of us, make you rest a little easier."

Miles didn't answer.

O'Shea stood up. He dropped the envelope on the bed. He said, "I'm going to get you. And whoever else you rope in to lie on your behalf."

Miles didn't answer. He looked at the envelope as O'Shea came around the bed and unlocked his cuff. He didn't even take it with him. He left it dangling as he walked out.

Miles was shaking so much he tore the corner of the paper inside. There was one sheet only.

It was titled "General Affidavit."

He saw Pam Blake's name and signature at the bottom, along with a notary's details. He didn't need to read the full text. He glimpsed the first line of the statement of facts and saw *Detective Miles Keller accompanied me on surveillance the night of—*

It was all lies.

She'd given him an alibi for the Covey job. It negated Petrov's deposition.

A monitor somewhere was beeping.

O'Shea's visit had been a Hail Mary—a last try for confession before he unlocked the cuff.

He lay back as a nurse rushed in, trying to soothe the electronics.

FORTY-THREE

MANHASSET, NY

Miles Keller

He checked himself out three days later. Thursday morning in the rain. All his life, he'd felt this strange elation, walking out of hospitals, like his DNA was telling him to make the most of it. There'll come a time when you can't leave on your own steam. Then again, that's the case for everything: all things in life have a number on them, and every day you're running down the count.

The ground floor had public phones. Ten minutes to nine in the morning, he called Attica and asked for his brother.

"This is an internal line, Keller."

"You told me that last time. It's an emergency."

"What's the emergency?"

Miles said, "I'm calling from a hospital. Use your imagination."

He got put on hold for fifteen minutes. His weight went foot to foot, and the phone went ear to ear. Then Nate came on the line.

Miles said, "It's me."

"Oh, hey. How you doing?"

Faint surprise, but nothing extra. He hadn't heard what happened.

Miles said, "I'm okay. I just got out of the hospital. Got shot the other day."

"What—"

"I'm okay though. Just a scrape, with a bit of rib."

"Oh shit. What happened?"

Miles said, "I was up at Kings Point, shot a guy, he shot me back. He's dead and I'm all right."

"Okay . . ."

"It's still with FID, so I won't run it down on the phone."

"Sure, yeah."

Miles said, "See if you can catch some news. I was on TV a couple of days."

"You only just had that thing a few weeks back."

"Yeah, I know."

"Everything all good?"

"Yeah. I think I'm going to be okay."

"You sound wrecked."

"I . . . yeah. Shit." He was wrecked, and hearing his brother say it almost made it too much. He ran a hand through his hair, closed his eyes. "You know the Tribeca Gardens Hotel? Down on Canal Street?"

"Yeah, vaguely."

"I had a gunfight in the lobby."

His brother didn't answer.

Miles took a breath, said, "FID brought me in, wanted to know how I shot so well. Told them about Dad and his targets . . . You remember he had us doing those drills, draw and fire?"

"God, that was years ago."

"Yeah. Made for a good story though. Listen, I . . ."

His brother waited.

"Ah. Forget it."

"You all right?"

"Yeah, I just. It's been a shitty few days. Wanted to talk to you. Sorry I haven't called sooner. I'll come visit."

Nate laughed. "Yeah. I'll take you out for breakfast. They really love cops in the cafeteria."

They hung up, and he took a breath, and tried Caitlyn's number. The phone just rang and rang.

Lucy was waiting for him by Stanton's car, and she got in the driver's seat when she saw him coming over. He got in beside her. She had the air tank in the rear footwell, the mask hanging over the seat.

She said, "New wardrobe?"

The hospital had a data center with public computers, and he'd ordered himself new clothes on Amazon. He had on jeans, and a gray sweater that almost fit him. It needed another inch in the cuff.

She said, "I could've just brought you something."

"Figured you had enough on your plate."

"Who were you talking to?"

He looked at her.

She nodded across the lot. "Saw you on the phone."

Miles said, "You remember my brother's in prison?"

"Yeah. You did tell me that."

He looked out the window, over at the hospital foyer, as if reliving the call. He said, "We went on a road trip once. I was seventeen, he was nineteen, I think. We robbed this bank down in Kansas. Only time I ever did it." He looked over at her, but she was just waiting for him to finish the story. He said, "After that I went straight. Kind of. But being in that hotel lobby the other day, it put me right back there. I wanted to tell him about it, but I couldn't. They monitor the calls." He shrugged, smiled. "So I gotta tell you instead. I don't know why I have to tell anyone, really. But it just felt like I had to."

Lucy put a hand on the key but didn't start the engine. She said, "Well, I'm not going to tell you it's all right. And I'm not going to tell you don't worry about it, either. So shall we just carry on?"

Miles didn't answer. He opened the glove compartment. His honeymoon photo was still there. Lucy gave him a few seconds with it and then said, "I don't think this is going to work, if you're going to spend lots of time looking at photos of your ex-wife."

Miles closed the door again. He said, "Maybe I could keep the photo, but not look at it too often."

She had a hit of oxygen and said, "I'm sorry I wrecked your marriage. But I never knew there was a marriage to wreck. And looking back and wishing you'd done things different isn't exactly the path to happiness. Yours or mine."

Miles didn't answer.

She said, "Hey." He felt her hand on his leg. "You all right?"

He smiled. "Yeah, I'm all right."

She said, "You probably don't even know where you are."

"The sign says North Shore University Hospital. So I imagine I'm in Manhasset, New York."

"And where do you want to go now?"

Miles said, "We'll go see Pam first."

She had a place in Pomonok, Queens, on Seventieth Road. It was only thirty minutes away, even in morning traffic. Her block was tree-lined, and her house was a single-level brick place with a porch, the railing loaded up with potted herbs, and flowers that drooped down past the balusters.

There was a car in the driveway, and a car out front at the curb.

Miles said, "She skipped work," and his heart skipped a beat as he said it, knowing she'd be there.

Lucy said, "You want me to come in?"

"No, it's okay. Just give me a minute."

She coasted to a stop at the bottom of the driveway, and he got out and stood alone at the mailbox, watching her drive away.

The bell by the front door didn't seem to work. He knocked and waited. The house was silent, and he thought maybe she'd just wait for him to leave. But then the door opened, and Pam's husband Richard was standing there on crutches.

"Hey—"

"She doesn't want to see you, man."

"I just . . ." He faltered and turned, gestured at the cars. "I know she's home. Can I maybe—"

"No, you can't maybe anything. She doesn't want to see you."

Miles took a step forward, and the guy jerked taller slightly, arching his back, jutting his chin. "Don't you fucking dare."

"All right." He raised his hands. "We're good." He wasn't going to shove past a cripple.

"No, we're not. I told you don't come in. I say it again, I'm calling the police. Get out of here, Miles. You're done."

When Lucy came past with the car again, he was standing at the curb where she'd dropped him. She stopped and he got in.

"Not home?"

He sighed out his nose, looking for life in his side mirror. "Yeah. No one home."

"You could slip a note under the door or something . . ."

He hadn't told her about the affidavit. He wasn't sure he'd ever tell anyone.

She said, "You want to try Caitlyn?"

Yeah, he really did. Even just to say that he was sorry. And he wanted to see the wife of the Coveys' security man, tell her the same thing, but he couldn't even remember his name. And there was Petrov's family as well . . .

He said, "No, not today." He looked at her. "I don't like my chances."

She said, "You look like the world's ending. But you got us out of a crazy situation. And you saved my life."

Maybe she thought it was that straightforward, that he'd got them out of a squeeze, and the true facts of it had no gray area. He wondered if that would be the cost of coexistence, that he'd never tell her the full story.

He said, "Let's just get out of here."

EPILOGUE

Miles Keller

KEY LARGO, FL

He found a guest room to rent for seventy-five dollars a night. The owner was an eighty-year-old woman, currently in Dallas receiving treatment for melanoma. Her son had put the place on Airbnb—at Ma's request, or so he claimed.

They flew to Miami and took a rental car south through the Glades, U.S. 1 curving thin and gray in this vast expanse of green, like Texas desert swapped for mangroves.

The house was a block back from the beach, on the Gulf of Mexico side. They arrived midday on Sunday, and he spent the afternoon sitting on the sand, looking at the water. He got double takes from people walking past, and they must've wondered what his story was. Lucy said he looked fresh out of prison: short haircut, IV marks on both arms, a bandage down one side, ten pounds lighter after his hospital stay. He undertook to fix appearances, figured a few days of sunshine and overeating would be sound rejuvenation.

They took a cruise Monday evening on a forty-foot catamaran, run by a company called Sunset Cruises. It was really just a one-man band—a deaf guy in his sixties called Ernie, using private boat charters for retirement money. Miles thought he was on to a winner. He took you out with a chiller full of alcohol and cruised south, let you sit there drinking and watching the sun get doused in the Gulf of Mexico.

The colors were acid-trip, and the ocean was flat enough it looked oiled. It was deep blue at the boat and red where it touched the sun, and the thin cloud layer was all tints of orange-yellow.

He lay on the foredeck with an empty bottle, and thought this might be coming close to perfection. The boat's engine cut, and they drifted gently.

Lucy sat down beside him, legs outstretched and crossed, a full-length tan and a light sun-block glazing. She said, "You think maybe I could start a trend—bikini plus air tank?"

She always acted like it didn't bother her, but then why mention it?

Miles said, "Looking like that, you could pull off a bikini plus anything."

"Maybe you could pull it off for me."

Miles said, "Yeah, I could do that." He heard bottles clink as Ernie helped himself to a cold one.

They were quiet awhile, watching the sun disappear, and then Lucy said, "I told Nina what happened."

Miles looked at her, not following just yet.

She said, "Sorry to wreck the atmosphere." She glanced back at Ernie and said, "Right before I shot her, I said I'd killed Jack, and you'd just covered for me. Set it up to make it seem legit." She picked her beer label, scored her thumbnail down the side. "I don't know why I told her. All just part of the rush, I guess."

It should've worried him, but the beer in him dulled his fear glands.

She said, "I thought I'd kill her. But if she makes it, she'll be in on the secret."

Add it to the list of things hanging over him. He didn't want Nina Stone as the keeper of the truth. Secrets meant leverage.

He said, "We'll be okay."

He hoped he was right. He hoped he had some credit when it came to Nina. She owed him—a five-year debt and counting.

She'd been caught on film doping up a banker, and then walking off with a million dollars cash. He'd corrupted the footage with a kill-disk program, and blitzed the case against her.

She could have gone to prison, but fate gave her leverage off his life's bad turn. Divorce: the end of love sent his moral compass haywire. Past the spinning dial, Nina's theft resembled justice served. He'd take the shame to his grave.

He felt Lucy's hand cover his. The boat turned slowly in a current, dipping and rising with the softest motion, water clacking on the hull. Maybe this was a bad habit, lying on your back, seeing the whole cloudscape turn. It was a false perspective of the world: Miles as the center of everything. He'd start thinking good luck was forever.

ACKNOWLEDGMENTS

Thanks are due again to the wonderful people at Thomas Dunne Books and Minotaur for their support of my novels and their hard work in publishing *The Stakes*. I'm especially grateful to Stephen Power and Janine Barlow for their careful and intelligent editorial guidance.

As always, my agent Dan Myers was an invaluable sounding board, and instrumental in helping to straighten up my first draft.

I'd also like to acknowledge the great team at Allen & Unwin, in particular Jane Palfreyman, Melanie Laville-Moore, and Angela Radford, for promoting me so well in my home market and in Australia.